DON'T KILL
THE
MESSENGER

EILEEN RENDAHL

ACE BOOKS, NEW YORK

THE BERKLEY PUBLISHING GROUP
Published by the Penguin Group
Penguin Group (USA) Inc.
375 Hudson Street, New York, New York 10014, USA

Penguin Group (Canada), 90 Eglinton Avenue East, Suite 700, Toronto, Ontario M4P 2Y3, Canada
(a division of Pearson Penguin Canada Inc.)
Penguin Books Ltd., 80 Strand, London WC2R 0RL, England
Penguin Group Ireland, 25 St. Stephen's Green, Dublin 2, Ireland (a division of Penguin Books Ltd.)
Penguin Group (Australia), 250 Camberwell Road, Camberwell, Victoria 3124, Australia
(a division of Pearson Australia Group Pty. Ltd.)
Penguin Books India Pvt. Ltd., 11 Community Centre, Panchsheel Park, New Delhi—110 017, India
Penguin Group (NZ), 67 Apollo Drive, Rosedale, Auckland 0632, New Zealand
(a division of Pearson New Zealand Ltd.)
Penguin Books (South Africa) (Pty.) Ltd., 24 Sturdee Avenue, Rosebank, Johannesburg 2196,
South Africa

Penguin Books Ltd., Registered Offices: 80 Strand, London WC2R 0RL, England

This is a work of fiction. Names, characters, places, and incidents either are the product of the author's imagination or are used fictitiously, and any resemblance to actual persons, living or dead, business establishments, events, or locales is entirely coincidental. The publisher does not have any control over and does not assume any responsibility for author or third-party websites or their content.

DON'T KILL THE MESSENGER

An Ace Book / published by arrangement with the author

PUBLISHING HISTORY
Berkley Sensation trade paperback edition / March 2010
Ace mass-market edition / March 2012

Copyright © 2010 by Eileen Rendahl.
Excerpt from *Dead on Delivery* by Eileen Rendahl copyright © 2011 by Eileen Rendahl.
Cover art by Tony Mauro.
Cover design by Diana Kolsky.

ISBN: 978-1-937007-34-8

ACE
Ace Books are published by The Berkley Publishing Group,
a division of Penguin Group (USA) Inc.,
375 Hudson Street, New York, New York 10014.
ACE and the "A" design are trademarks of Penguin Group (USA) Inc.

PRINTED IN THE UNITED STATES OF AMERICA

10 9 8 7 6 5 4 3 2 1

To my real life heroes:
Alex, Andy and Ted

ACKNOWLEDGMENTS

So many people contribute to the creation of a book in different ways. There are many people to thank for many different reasons. I'm sure I'm only scratching the surface here. Many thanks to my agent, Pam Ahearn, who no longer turns a single well-coiffed hair when I tell her I've got an idea for something new. Thanks to Leis Pederson for giving this book a chance. Very special thanks to Alesia Holliday, who has lent her helping hands in more ways than I can count. A truer friend cannot be found. Thanks to the Were-armadillos and the Tiny Killer Bees for emotional sustenance in good times and bad. Thanks to Carol for spinning backstories for characters and to Spring for always being willing to hammer out plot points. Thanks to Adam for giving me the idea for the start of the book and helping me find places for the end of the book and for creeping me out ever so slightly with how quickly he came up with a place to hide a body in downtown Sacramento. Thanks to Stacy Desideri for helping me choreograph fight scenes. Thanks to the real Alex, Ted, Ben, Sophie, Melina and Norah for lending their names (and, I swear, nothing else) to characters. Thanks to my darling Andy for always being willing to suspend disbelief to help me figure out how best to play with my imaginary friends.

1

I STOOD IN THE EARLY MORNING SUNSHINE OUTSIDE
Sacramento City Hospital, where I work my second job as a
night filing clerk every Sunday through Thursday of the
whole blessed year (including holidays because I get paid
double for those). I stretched my arms, breathed in deep
through my nose and then nearly coughed my lungs out my
mouth as the fumes from the ambulance bay mixed with the
scent of freshly poured blacktop and damn near choked me.

"Gotta watch that breathing thing," a voice said behind
me. "It'll kill you."

If only it were that easy. I turned. His voice hadn't surprised me. I'd known he was there within a few seconds of
walking out of the hospital and onto the sidewalk. I can't
quite describe what it's like. It's not like a smell or a sound.
It's more like a vibration, like a buzzing that I feel in my
flesh, a lifting of the hair on the back of my neck. A bit of
a tingle.

To be fair, that wasn't the only thing that tingled and
buzzed when he was around. Knowing he was there had a

way of sending electric shocks up my nerve endings and down to places that a lady doesn't mention in public.

I wasn't sure exactly why he wanted to risk being out here after dawn had broken on the horizon, but that was most decidedly his business and not mine. As long as I stayed in the sun's path, it was bound to stay that way, too. I inched a little farther from the shadows.

The he in question was Dr. Alexander Bledsoe. Dr. Bledsoe was six foot two inches of broad shoulders and thick chest and long legs. He had thick black hair with a touch of gray here and there that he wore swept back from his face and a little tousled. I'd never gotten close enough to touch it and see if he had product in it or if it was just naturally hella sexy. I certainly didn't plan to get that close now. Getting close to Alex could be dangerous, even for me.

His eyes were the rich brown of the dark chocolate roux my grandmother uses as the base for her jambalaya, and he invariably had a touch of stubble no matter what the time of day. Basically, every time he walked through the corridors of the hospital, he left groups of nurses, techs, support staff and a few patients swooning behind him, female and male. Not me, though. I'm not the swooning type. Plus, as I mentioned, I keep my distance from the not-so-good doctor. That doesn't meant I didn't notice, however. Dr. Bledsoe was very hard not to notice.

He was also a vampire.

On the face of things, being a vampire and an emergency room doctor might seem incompatible. Not so. Dr. Bledsoe had easy access to blood pretty much whenever he wanted it with no questions asked. No one even had to die. People showed up at his doorstep and spurted blood all over him. If you were an accountant, that wouldn't happen. At least, not literally. Generally, it didn't happen in lawyers' offices either. Not in schools or most offices. Dentists may get a little blood but not in nearly the quantity that it sprays around even the tamest emergency room, and how many dentists do you know who only work nights? Nobody at Sacramento City questioned Alex's strange hours, weird sleeping habits, pale skin or generally antisocial behavior. He was an attending, after all. Honestly, given the perks, I don't understand why all vampires don't become emergency room doctors.

Oh, yeah, there's that pesky caring-about-people thing. Most vampires fall pretty short in that category in my personal experience. Of all the things that go bump in the night that I have to consort with in my "day" job, vampires are among my least favorite. They give me the heebie-jeebies, even Dr. Hottie McHottster with the ever so chilly skin standing over in the shadows right now. I'll take a troll over a vampire any day, and you have no idea how bad the average troll's breath is. They are totally not into good oral hygiene.

Granted, my experience isn't terribly vast at this point. I'm twenty-six. I wasn't sure how old Dr. Bledsoe was. It's really hard to tell with vampires. I'd guess in the three- to five-hundred-year range. Practically a baby, when it comes to bloodsuckers.

He dropped a manila envelope to the ground and kicked it toward me. It slid out of the shadows where he stood and into the sunlight a few feet from me. It looked innocuous enough. I've learned over my short but eventful years, however, that looks can be deceiving.

"What is it?" I asked, without making a move to pick it up. "And where is it supposed to go?"

"It's nothing. Just something that came through the ER that I thought Aldo should see." He looked from the envelope to me with one eyebrow raised, but he didn't move from where he leaned against the textured concrete wall. His sliver of shadow had narrowed a bit, but if he noticed, he wasn't showing it. Then again, what did I expect? It wasn't like a vampire was going to sweat.

"Aldo?" I kicked the envelope back to him and felt a

minute tingle in my foot. Aldo de la Tarantarina was the nominal head of the loose association that governed the local vampires. He was not my favorite person. He wasn't even my favorite vampire. He's officious, slimy and a little bit poncey to boot. Vampires give me the heebie-jeebies. Aldo gives my heebie-jeebies goose bumps. Besides, I don't usually do vampire-to-vampire hand offs. No one needs me to do them. One of the main reasons anybody needs a Messenger is to take things between different groups that don't get along.

Northern California is a melting pot. Or a tossed salad. Or whatever they're calling it these days. Everybody on earth came here, especially in the 1800s with that whole Gold Rush thing. With them, they brought their own gods and their own demons and everything in between. The place started to get crowded. Then, when you put a lot of prey in one place, the predators—like vampires and werewolves— come along, too. A lot of these groups don't get along. That's where I come in, generally. If a werewolf, who typically won't be able to stand the smell of a vampire, needs a message sent to a vampire, I'm the go-between. With the emphasis on *between*. Since that's where I seem to exist: between everything but not really fully in anything. "But he's another vampire."

Alex made a hissing sound. "Take an ad out, why don't you?"

Oops. That was, at best, indiscreet. At worst, slips of the lip like that could wind up with Alex sporting the latest in stakes in his heart or me possibly locked up in a padded room, most likely the latter. Nobody really believes in vampires anymore, not even the idiots who pretend to be vampires on the Internet. It was a stupid mistake. "Sorry," I said.

He kicked the envelope back toward me with a sigh. "Take the envelope and zip it, okay?"

Fine. I deserved that. Still, I was curious. "Why can't you take it yourself?"

Alex sighed. "We've had . . . a bit of a falling-out, Aldo and I. I think that he would prefer not to see me face-to-face for a while."

I turned back into the sunshine, in part because I was cold. The hospital is way over-air-conditioned and the air outside still held an early morning chill. The sun felt good. I also turned so Alex couldn't see me smile. His frequent fallings-out with Aldo and the others of his kind were some of the things I liked best about Alex. I'm a sucker for bad boys. Just ask my mother. Trust me, you'll get an earful on the topic. Plus, Alex is not quite like the other vampires. For one thing, he washes his hair a lot more. He has a much more human idea of appropriate personal hygiene than most of his fellow bloodsuckers. Maybe it goes with the medical training. "What was this little tiff about?"

"Nothing you need worry your pretty little head about, Melina. All you need to do is do your job and deliver the package to Aldo."

It sounded like Dr. Bledsoe was getting a bit irritated. I glanced back over my shoulder. No wonder. His protective shadow was getting narrower by the second. In a matter of minutes, he'd be cut off from the entrance to the hospital by a rather large swath of sunshine. I sighed. He was right. He was just asking me to do my job. It wasn't his fault that it wasn't one I'd chosen myself and had a lot more pitfalls to it than my night job. When I file, I run only the risk of a nasty paper cut. Nobody is generally supposed to mess with me during my day job either, but not all the things I deal with have great reasoning capacities nor are they the best rule-followers on the planet. Case in point: vampires. They're as bad as those creeps that try to cut around traffic jams by driving down the shoulder.

"Can it be a daytime drop?" I asked. Aldo's place was creepy enough in the daytime. I much preferred to avoid it completely at night.

"It can be straight-up noon and you can deliver it in your

teeth while you walk on your hands, for all I care." He looked down at the envelope and up at me again. Then he smiled. "Although I might pay to see that."

Damn his already eternally damned soul, he'd broken out the big artillery, that damn grin of his. It transformed his whole nearly wolfish face with a boyish charm so potent there should be an amulet to ward it off. I took a step toward him in the shadows, my heart beating like Travis Barker on speed, and only managed to pull myself back with a giant dose of willpower. I wondered what quotient of my daily willpower allotment I'd used up with that move. I'd probably end up eating three hot fudge sundaes tonight. Damn him anyway.

"Come on, Melina, do it for me. I'm not that bad, am I?" His voice was low and rough and sweet, like a piece of aural sandpaper that scratched in all the right places.

It was true. He wasn't bad. He was, however, evil, but it's not like it was his fault. Vampires are just built that way. I didn't hold it against him. I knew all about not getting to choose how you were built.

I reached out with my foot, carefully keeping it in sunlight, and slid the envelope toward myself. "Fine, then. I'll take it." I picked it up. The vibration I felt in my foot when I'd come in contact with the envelope was stronger now. Whatever was inside the plain manila wrapping had some kind of mojo on it. I wanted it in my hands as little as possible. That stuff can be like cooties, infectious and hard to wash off.

Alex was already slipping his way along the wall back toward the hospital entrance. I didn't blame him. I'd seen what even a few seconds of sunlight could do to vampire flesh. I'd want to make sure I was back into the artificially lighted, windowless hospital interior before the sun exposed the rest of that wall, too, if I were he. "That's my girl," he said as the automatic doors slid open and he darted through them.

Good thing he'd saved that one until I'd already agreed to take his stupid envelope. I started to snarl, but he was already gone, which left me with nothing better to do than fume as I went to my car. I may well be his Messenger, but I damn sure wasn't his girl.

I SETTLED BEHIND THE BIG STEERING WHEEL OF MY CAR. It's a Buick LeSabre. I inherited it from Grandma Rosie when she went into the assisted living facility. It is a classic old lady's car, which could be mortifying, but that is mitigated by the fact that the front seat is more comfortable than my living room couch. In fact, driving the Buick is a lot like driving a big couch around Sacramento. Plus, I've tricked out the inside with a zebra-striped steering wheel cover, a dancing hula girl on the dashboard and some fuzzy dice hanging from the rearview. My father says that all these items are distractions and will cause an accident some day. He still hasn't figured out how much better my reflexes are than his and everybody else's. One of the perks of the job. The Messenger one, not the hospital one. The hospital one comes with health insurance and paid vacation, which kick ass in their own way, but no enhanced physical abilities. Those all come from the Messenger gig.

Dad doesn't know about my Messenger job at all. Dad's a sweetheart, quick with a hug and fast to open his wallet, but not the most clued in man I've ever met. He is one hundred percent 'Dane, as those of us in arcane circles say. It's short for *mundane* and is not particularly flattering according to some. Alex won't use the shortened version. He shakes his head and mutters about kids these days. Me? Well, I'd give just about anything to be one hundred percent 'Dane or mundane or whatever you want to call it. I can't even remember when I was.

I need the superfast reflexes for the Messenger job. My job description generally doesn't put me in harm's way. Or, at least, it's not supposed to. I'm a delivery girl, a glorified gopher to the things that go bump in the night. I'm one of the little cogs in the big machine of the unseen undercurrents that keep all our everyday lives moving smoothly. I may not be the most well-oiled of those cogs, but I generally get the messages and packages where they need to be by the time they need to be there. Occasionally, however, things don't go according to plan and I need to defend myself or hightail it out of a situation like Usain Bolt in the last leg of a relay.

It's not a job I asked for. It just kind of happened. I blame it on my mother being a clean freak.

If she hadn't been so determined to keep germs and dirt at bay, she wouldn't have been scrubbing the tiles of our backyard pool with a wire brush while I took my nap twenty-three years ago. If she hadn't been so focused and intent on removing every last bit of scuzz on the tiles, I wouldn't have been able to sneak past her and slip into the water behind her.

If I hadn't done that and she hadn't been so absorbed, I wouldn't have drowned and I'd probably be doing something normal and harmless like going to graduate school like my brother plans to do or perhaps going to a management training job from nine to five every day like my cousin Marsha. But no, my mother had to have the cleanest pool in our subdivision and I ended up dead for a couple of minutes.

It still amazes me when I think about the split-second moments that change lives forever. A person looks away from the road for a moment and suddenly they've plowed into the back of the car in front of them. Another makes a careless step on a muddy hillside and ends up in the hospital with a mangled foot. Three-year-old me decides to take a quick dip in the cool, refreshing pool without telling my mama and I end up with a crappy job toting and carrying for werewolves, vampires, skinwalkers and the occasional chupacabra. Whatever.

See, after the whole drowning-at-three thing, life changed. I started seeing things that no one else seemed to see and talking to people that no one else seemed to hear. I didn't understand it at the time. I was only three, after all. That near-death experience, however, apparently opened up something inside me. I hesitate to call it a portal. It's not an external thing at all. It's totally inside me. It's like it opened up pathways in my brain that connected me with all those things people suspect are out there but can't seem to prove for sure. It made me into a 'Cane, which is short for *arcane* when one is talking with the hipster contingent of the unseen.

I pulled up to the tollbooth and flashed my employee badge. I scratched my head while I tried to decide my day's agenda. My hair felt greasy. I had plenty of time to go back to my apartment and shower before delivering the envelope to Aldo and then heading off to the Little Dragons karate class at the dojo where I teach part-time. It's my second day job. Or maybe it's my second night job. Whatever. I show up, do stuff and someone gives me a paycheck. Luckily, along with quick reflexes, one of the perks of being a Messenger is that I don't need much sleep. A few hours here or there in the course of the day and I'm as fresh as a daisy. Although daisies seem somewhat earnest and straightforward for me. I need a more ironic flower to symbolize my freshness. Is there some kind of lily that grows out of dead stuff? If there is, it would be me.

Regardless, it's good I don't need a lot of sleep because the whole Messenger gig? It doesn't pay. I'm not speaking in a metaphorical crime-doesn't-pay kind of way either. It literally doesn't pay shit. Hence, my filing job at Sacramento City that pays enough for me to make my half of the rent on an apartment in Mansion Flats and cover my food bill.

Sometimes, when I look at my life and feel like crying, I try to see how it all works out for the best. It's tricky, though. The whole Pollyanna thing suits me about as well as daisies.

I got on H Street, made the dogleg turn on Alhambra to G and headed home, miraculously finding parking on Eighth, by my apartment. A black Lincoln Navigator whooshed past me, damn near taking my door off. Stupid SUV drivers. Think they own the damn road. I live in an old Victorian that's been subdivided into four apartments. Norah and I share the second-floor north unit. I grabbed the newspaper off the doormat and let myself into the apartment, trying to be quiet so as not to wake up Norah. Turns out it didn't matter. She was already up and in her yoga gear, saluting the sun while twinkly, chimey music played. She'd also lit a buttload of candles. I sighed. I did not feel like cleansing my chakras or realigning my vibrations and knew I was about to be exhorted to do so. Worse yet, Norah'd be all pleasant and sweet about it so I wouldn't even be able to snap at her without feeling like a total turd.

I've known Norah since eighth grade. I love the stuffing out of her and not because she's one of the only people who can put up with my schedule and my "moods" as my mother calls them. I also love her because she accepts everything before her at face value, never questions my lame explanations for my crazy life and is generally about the sweetest pea in the world's funky pod. I, therefore, put up with her exhortations to open myself to the unseen forces that she's convinced are all around us, pushing and pulling us in millions of directions with our cognizant awareness.

If she only knew. Which she doesn't, and I try my damnedest to keep it that way. Norah would be mortified if she knew what was around her most of the time. The magical world ain't all rainbows and unicorns, you know.

I slipped as unobtrusively as possible into the kitchen and started some coffee. I saw Norah's sidelong glance from the living room and knew I'd probably earned myself a lecture on the evils of caffeine and its addictive qualities, but figured that it would actually be brewed before she was finished with her downward dogs. It's much easier to listen to lectures on the evils of coffee with a hot steaming mug of my dark mistress in hand.

I hit the brew button and headed into the shower. I figured all the cleansing I needed was available right there.

When I came out, my hair done up in a towel and me done up in my big fuzzy terry cloth robe, Norah was standing in the kitchen, slicing an apple into quarters. "You know," she said, not looking up at me, "studies have shown that eating an apple first thing in the morning made people feel as alert and awake as a cup of coffee. It's the glucose."

"Really," I said, pouring myself a cup. "They also showed that hormone replacement was good for women, and then all those nice old ladies had heart attacks."

Norah's head shot up and she looked stricken. "No," she said. "Really?"

I felt like a shit. "Yeah, really." I took one of her apple quarters and bit into it. She smiled a little, but I could tell it was fainthearted. I wished I could keep myself from doing stuff like that. Seriously. It's like kicking puppies. It always makes me feel worse about myself and, honestly, I don't need much help in that department.

Norah headed to the shower, and I opened up the newspaper. The Kings were not getting in the playoffs, and the narcotics squad was reporting a new kind of marijuana showing up on the streets, something similar to BC Bud, the superstrong variety of marijuana grown hydroponically in Canada. The two items weren't related. Or, at least, I didn't think they were. There'd also been two more deaths in Elk Grove. Police thought both were gang related. Things had been tense lately in Sacramento and were only getting tenser. I couldn't wait until summer hit full force with its triple-degree heat that made short tempers into rages and put people in the mood to stab, shoot and throw punches at their loved ones and strangers alike. I sighed and grabbed another apple quarter—they were actually tasty—and went to my room to get dressed.

I looked into my closet and sighed again. I'm not entirely certain how someone who lives in a climate as hot as I do has so much black in her closet. Norah's laundry looks like a freaking rainbow, all pinks and blues and greens and patterns. Mine looks like an advertisement for cold-water Cheer. I pulled out a pair of jeans and a black tank top and threw them on.

I blew my hair dry even though I knew the heat would make it frizz within seconds of walking back outside. At least I'd know I'd made an effort even if no one else did. Or would notice. I loved teaching the Little Dragons karate class and they loved me. It had nothing, however, to do with my hair and everything to do with the fact that I can break a stack of eight two-by-fours with the side of my hand.

No wonder I can't get a date.

Norah was out of the shower by the time I came out of my room. "You working today?" she asked.

"Same old same old." I helped myself to another piece of her apple. "I've got some errands to run, then the dojo."

"I might meet Tanya over at McClannigan's in Old Sacramento tonight. Wanna join us?"

"Maybe." It sounded fun. It sounded normal. It sounded like something I wouldn't be able to do. One of the many, many problems with living life with feet in two different worlds is that I really don't get to enjoy either one.

"I'll call you and let you know the details." She stuffed her lunch—another apple, some nuts and what looked suspiciously like a hunk of tofu with spices on it—into her bag. "Or are you just going to blow us off like you usually do?"

That stung a little. Unfortunately, it was also kind of deserved. I did back out of a lot of social engagements at the last minute. It's not like I wanted to blow Norah off, but when a gremlin stops by with a package that has to make it to an elf before midnight, a girl simply has to do what a girl has to do. Or, more accurately, a Messenger has to do what a Messenger has to do, whether she wants to do it or not. "I'll try not to."

"That's all I can ask, I guess." Norah blew me an air kiss and left.

I slumped at the counter over my coffee, which had gone cold and bitter. There was no point hanging around the apartment. I mean, I liked it well enough, but I already felt restless. What was I going to do? Watch *Law & Order* reruns? I'm only twenty-six. Surely, it's not time for that yet. Besides, if I got my errand for Alex done soon enough, I might get to the dojo in time to have lunch with Mae. That wouldn't be all bad. At least I wouldn't be alone.

I headed back to the Buick. It was all of ten thirty and I could already feel the promise of the heat that was to come for the day. Maybe it wouldn't be so bad to be a vampire. At least your skin stayed cool all day. Or so I've heard. I tried not to get close enough for them to touch me. Have I mentioned that they give me the heebie-jeebies?

My downstairs neighbor's kid was sitting on the front stoop already. Ben was fifteen—at least that was what he was in people years. In how-to-get-into-trouble years, he might already be thirty. According to his mother, Valerie, he'd been turning his scene around. That's how she put it, too. I occasionally wondered how old Valerie was in get-into-trouble years, but that seriously was none of my business.

I suppose Ben wasn't my business either, but he was a charming kid in his own trouble-on-the-hoof way and I sort of related to him. In case you haven't guessed, I don't have a lot of friends. People find it hard to get close to me. Hell, I find it hard to get close to me. Anyway, I wasn't the easiest teenager in the world back in the day. I knew a little about how he felt.

He was going above and beyond today. Despite the fact that the temperature would easily get into the high nineties, he had on black jeans, a black T-shirt, a black hoodie with the hood pulled up and big, thick black skate shoes. I'd be sweating like a pig in that outfit. He looked as cool as a cucumber, however. I suppose some people are specially suited to their own personal styles.

"'Sup?" Ben asked as I stepped around him. Our stoop is not exactly spacious. In fact, even calling it a stoop is probably being generous. It's two concrete steps, a landing and two wrought iron railings. There are a couple pots of geraniums, courtesy of Valerie, and a window box arrangement of herbs because, as she told me while she was planting them this spring, adding a little natural beauty to her scene gave her some serenity. I suspect that Valerie may be a tiny bit more of a stoner than her kid, if only a less angsty one.

"Not much." I sat down next to him. "You?"

"Nada."

"Where's your mom?"

"Work."

"You got plans?"

He shook his head. "I'm gonna chill for a while, then who knows?"

"Wanna come to the dojo with me this afternoon? Help out with the little kids?"

He snorted and shook his head. "And be a role model? All that perseverance and indomitable spirit stuff kind of gives me a headache."

"Suit yourself. The offer's always open." Like I said, I liked the kid, and I was still in that dress-in-black-and-be-a-loner stage myself. Plus, Valerie could use a break. The single-mom thing isn't as glamorous as it looks on TV.

"Cool," he said and leaned back on his elbows.

We both made fists and touched knuckles, and then I was on my way to Aldo's.

THE FIRST TIME I WENT TO ALDO'S, I WAS SHOCKED. HIS place so didn't look how I expected a vampire's house to look. I expected something, you know, gothic and creepy. A castle kind of thing surrounded by overgrown thickets. With bats. Possibly even some kind of vestigial moat.

But no, once again, another one of my bubbles had to be burst by painful reality. The head of the Sacramento Valley Seethe and representative to the Council lived in a ranch house on a quiet street with a well-tended lawn in front. It was an okay neighborhood tucked in between several not-so-nice ones. Once I thought about it, I could see how it was perfect. As long as Aldo kept his yard up, the neighbors didn't care if they never saw him. In fact, they probably preferred to never see him. Aldo is not a pretty vampire. Plus, he had easy proximity to what passes as projects in Sacto, with lots of young men and women likely to disappear without anyone commenting. It was like a vampire buffet practically. And so convenient!

Aldo's place was unremarkable. In a way, that made it creepier than any Gothic monstrosity or spooky Victorian. Evil is right there living cheek by jowl with the rest of us. Most of the time it looks normal as hell. Although, be forewarned. A predator—and make no mistake, a vampire is a predator—is often at its most dangerous when it looks harmless. It's the best disguise, and Aldo liked to keep it that way. I knew, from learning the hard way as always, that he didn't like me to park in front of his place. The street was lined with minivans and SUVs in neutral grays, blacks and tans. Neighbors noticed young women in old turquoise Buicks who stopped by too often. Aldo preferred that I park a few blocks away and saunter past, dropping whatever it was I needed to deliver as inconspicuously as possible.

I was occasionally tempted to tell him to ram it, but I'd

also decided it was wiser to choose which battles I wanted to fight at any given moment. Aldo had at least nominal control of all the vampires in the Sacramento Valley area. They were under strict orders not to suck my blood. I appreciated that. I mean, you're not supposed to kill the Messenger, no matter what. That didn't mean that no one had ever lost control and done it anyway. Mae told me about a very nice young man who had wound up sucked down into a sinkhole when some dwarves up in Gold Country had had enough of him. They got in a buttload of trouble for it, but that didn't bring the kid back to life. It was nice to know there'd be some kind of retribution if someone came after me, but I'd just as soon only get in fights that I think I can win.

Plus, if I die, I'd like to know someone will suffer after I'm gone. I'm just that kind of little ray of sunshine.

So in order to avoid antagonizing Aldo, I parked Grandma's Buick a few blocks over, near a 7-Eleven. The only reason it would be noticeable was that it was slightly cleaner than some of the other junk heaps parked nearby. Not as noticeable as the shiny black SUV parked in the one shade spot, though. I grabbed Alex's envelope off the front seat and started the stroll over to Aldo's, humming "Love Shack" to myself for reasons even I can't quite explain.

The sun shone down on me, but it wasn't too hot yet. Bees buzzed around the jasmine that had taken off like a weed through some of the yards. All in all, it didn't suck. Certainly it wasn't the worst assignment anyone had ever given me. I wondered if Alex would be grateful to me for making the delivery and began to speculate on ways I would want him to show that gratitude if only he weren't a vampire. He is pretty hunkalicious. I'm not blind. I just don't fish off the company pier, if you get my drift. It doesn't seem wise. If Alex weren't a vampire, though, and I weren't a Messenger . . . well, that might be a completely different story. My mother would be ecstatic if I started dating a doctor. She'd be more ecstatic if I became a doctor, but she'd still be pretty freaking happy with a doctor-boyfriend.

I floated deep in that thought, tripping along the street on a lovely day.

That's when the ninjas jumped me.

2

OKAY. MAYBE *NINJAS* IS OVERSTATING. THERE WERE NO throwing stars or nunchakus. There was, however, a group of guys in black pajamas with their heads swathed in black scarves so their faces weren't visible, who seemed to materialize out of nowhere and proceeded to kick the crap out of me.

That may not seem like a great feat. I am merely one not terribly large girl. Five foot seven in my stocking feet and my weight is none of your damned business. I am also, however, a lot stronger, faster and more skilled than I look. It's one of my charms. Fine. It may well be my only charm. That and very strong, white, even teeth. My mother insisted on excellent oral hygiene. Even trolls wouldn't have stood a chance against her militant stand on flossing. Still, I can take out a goodly group of people without breaking too much of a sweat. These guys, however, had my number.

I totally did not have theirs.

I'd also had almost no warning. No strange buzzing feeling. No hairs standing up on my arms. There was maybe the tiniest moment of unease before the seven guys dropped out of the trees—yes, that's what I said, dropped out of the trees—and started wailing on me.

One of them slammed me on the point of my chin with his open palm while making these fast shoving motions with his hands, and I literally saw stars.

I looked around for a weapon. Something. Anything I could use to smack somebody or to shield myself with. There was nothing, not even a stick.

Another one spun around and kicked me in the kidneys, which I so did not appreciate. I use those things, you know?

I considered trying to kick one of them where it counts, but the truth is that most guys will protect that area fast and they know how to do it, too. They've been doing it since about third grade when the little girls realized that that was a weak point on all the little boys.

I backed away, trying to control the distance between them and me, but it's hard to back away when there's someone at your back.

It was at about that moment, however, that I dropped Alex's manila envelope. One of the guys behind me swooped in and scooped it up. He held it aloft and then, just as quickly and as silently as they had seemingly dropped out of the sky and attacked me, the ninja dudes took off and I was left, empty-handed, staring after them with blood dripping from my bottom lip.

I hate it when that happens.

I WALKED SLOWLY BACK TO THE 7-ELEVEN AND THE BUICK. I could already feel the bruises forming. The ninja dudes had really done a job on me. I couldn't figure out what kind of martial arts they were using either. I'm pretty good. I've been studying at Mae's dojo since I was seven and managed to talk my mother into letting me try it.

Mae's an awesome teacher, and I am now proficient in

tae kwon do, jiujitsu, aikido and capoeira. I'm fairly good at judo, and don't even try to take me in Chinese checkers. I'll kick your ass from here to next Tuesday.

These guys, however, had me snowed. Well, not totally. I got in a few licks of my own. It just happened that they were getting in way more of their own licks and there were more of them. I have to admit. It scared me a little.

Their movements were familiar but not quite familiar enough. They were especially not familiar enough to let me anticipate what was coming next and therefore avoid it. Plus, did I mention the seven-against-one thing?

I went into the store and grabbed a Popsicle and a bag of frozen peas from the freezer section. I plopped them down on the counter in front of the clerk. He looked up from his sudoku and took in my face. "¿Qué pasa, *mamacita*?"

"I'm not entirely sure," I told him, slapping a ten down on the counter next to my selections.

"You okay? You want me to call the cops?" he asked, ringing me up. His tone was nonchalant. His appraising look was not.

"I'm peachy," I said. "No cops."

Seriously, no cops. I avoided cops at all costs. If vampires gave me the heebie-jeebies, cops gave me *shpilkes*, and there's nothing worse than a bad case of *shpilkes* when you're sitting in a cell. Cells happen to be exactly where you end up when you deal with cops. Believe it or not, I have it on good authority that if you tell a cop that you were trying to deliver an envelope to one of the lamest vampires on the planet when a bunch of ninjas dropped out of the freaking trees and kicked the crap out of you, they don't buy it. They think you're nuts and not in a good way.

What had Alex gotten me into? What had been in that envelope that was worth lying in wait and attacking me? Who had even known I had whatever the hell it was? Whatever it had been had a hell of a lot more mojo than I thought it had based on the low-level buzz it generated.

The dude behind the counter gave me an incredibly small amount of change considering what I was purchasing. I dropped it in my wallet and went to the Buick. At least I would be able to lick my wounds in comfort. I peeled the wrapper off the Popsicle and ran it across my split lip.

Who could possibly care if Aldo got whatever was in the envelope? He was not a power player. His place on the Council wasn't an honorary one. He actually worked at it, but the Council reminds me a little of the school board. Anyone who actually wants to be on it probably shouldn't be. Think about it. What self-respecting denizen of the night would live in a place that gets this much sunshine? There were no power vamps here. Everyone knows that the seriously cool California vampires live in San Francisco and the ones with any power at all live in L.A. Aldo was nothing but a meaningless title with a penchant for dressing like Elton John.

Why the hell didn't I have any warning before those guys dropped out of the trees? I couldn't think of a single thing other than humans, which didn't set off a little warning buzz in my flesh. To be honest, there were a few humans who set me off, too. I'm not always sure why. Sometimes they turned out to have a little witch blood or a jigger or two of shaman in their personal genetic cocktail.

Sometimes they were just nasty-ass examples of the species and needed to be avoided.

The other question that nagged me was what were the repercussions of this little misadventure likely to be? I hadn't left a job uncompleted since I was fourteen and decided that no one could really expect me to bike some stupid box all the way down to Twelfth and J when I had cramps.

I had shoved the box deep enough under my bed that I was sure Joy, my mother's housekeeper, wouldn't find it—nobody's that good with a vacuum, not even Joy—and let it sit for a day or two. Fine. Three days.

When I developed a huge zit on the end of my nose, I figured it was nothing. Shit happens. Then the zipper on my jeans stopped working between third- and fourth-period classes and I had to spend the entire day trying to tug my T-shirt down low enough that not everyone I walked past in the halls yelled out "XYZ, Melina." That made me a little bit nervous. But then a pipe burst in the girls' locker room and flooded only my locker, forcing me to wear the dreaded borrowed PE clothes and earning me the nickname Wedgie Girl for the rest of the year.

I got on my damn bike, delivered the stupid box and never pulled that crap again. Give me something, tell me where it's supposed to go and I will whine, complain and insult your forebears, but I will definitely deliver it. I'm a Messenger. It's what I do. Mainly, because if I don't, I know bad shit will rain from the skies until I do.

I didn't say it was a great work ethic, but it seems to work for everyone. I often wish it didn't. In case you haven't guessed, I'm not exactly crazy about my job.

I flipped down the vanity mirror on the Buick. My lip was still pretty puffy, even with the Popsicle ice pack. I wondered how noticeable it would be tonight. Another one of the perks of my job is that I heal fast. Not freaky fast like a werewolf or a vampire, but faster than your average Josephina. With any luck, the worst of it would have passed by the time I was downing margaritas with Norah in Old Sacramento.

I started the Buick, slipped the frozen peas between me and the seat back, strategically positioning them by my kidney, and headed for the dojo. Mae might not have answers, but she'd at least understand some of my questions.

"LOOK WHAT THE CAT DRAGGED IN," MAE SAID AS I LET myself into the dojo. River City Karate and Judo was a typical storefront kind of affair in a typical strip mall along Thirty-fourth Street. There were probably fifteen similar places dotted around the city. At least, the other places looked similar to an untrained eye. None of those other places had Mae, and Mae had been my lifeline from the moment I'd first laid eyes on her twenty years ago.

Back then, Mom had been thrilled I wanted to do something besides sit and talk to my imaginary friends. She didn't have a clue that it was one of those imaginary friends who had suggested that I study with Mae and had coached me on how to talk Mom into it.

Mom still doesn't know what I became that day when I slipped in the cool blue pool behind her. She's not stupid, however. She knows something's not quite right. I've done my best to shelter her and Dad and even my brat of a little brother, Patrick, from it, but I am not allowed to be fussy about my clientele. I've learned that the hard way, which is pretty much how I've learned everything else. The learning curve for Messengers is steep and unpredictable.

Mae used to be a Messenger. She sees all the stuff I see and hears all the stuff I hear and has had to deal with all the crap I've had to deal with. I'm not the first person that has been sent to her for training. There are a few of us around. We don't exactly hold conventions so I can't give you an exact number, but any place with a large population probably has a Messenger or two living there. Places like Montana? One Messenger might cover the whole state. New York City? I shudder to think about how many of us must be roaming around with boxes for banshees and envelopes for elves.

How did Mae get promoted up out of her Messenger gig into a training job? Mae won't say. When I ask, she smiles and tells me that I'll learn in time. It was the same thing she told me about the flying sidekick. She was right about that. I imagine she's right about this other thing, too. Still, it's hard to be patient. It's not in my nature. I will, however, persevere. Stubbornness is very much in my nature.

Mae has been my lifeline, my rock, my cheerleader and my mentor. I don't know what I'd do without her.

When I was little, Mae helped me not to be afraid of some

of the things that visited me, and she taught me how to defend myself. When I was older, she taught me to respect myself in ways that I might not have honored without her constant presence in my life. It sounds trite, but courtesy, integrity, perseverance, self-control and indomitable spirit are guiding principles that can get a person through some dark times. At the very least, I know I can count on myself.

Which is good, because a lot of the time, that's all I've got.

"Is that really a nice way to talk to someone who brought you chocolate-covered honeycomb from the co-op?" I asked as I walked into her little glassed-in office off the entry for the dojo.

"You didn't," she breathed, not moving. Mae has few vices, but sugar is one of them.

I handed over the chocolate-covered honeycomb. She lost no time in unwrapping it and taking a bite.

"What happened to your face?" she asked, leaning back in her chair and closing her eyes as if she were trying to find some way to fully savor the treat.

"A bunch of ninjas attacked me over by McClatchy."

She brought her chair down with a thump and opened her eyes. "Ninjas? Have you been watching those turtle movies again?"

"Okay. Maybe not ninjas, but some ninjalike guys."

"And they got the best of you?" She was actually surprised enough that she set the honeycomb down. I smiled. It's nice when your teacher has that much faith in you.

Too bad her faith was misplaced. I hung my head. "In a matter of seconds."

"They have throwing stars or something?" Mae picked up the honeycomb again. "Nunchakus?"

I shook my head. "Nope. Just their nasty old bare hands."

"How many?" Her eyebrows went up.

"Seven." I was pretty sure that was right. It's always tempting to exaggerate any account of a fight, whether you're on the losing end or the winning one. I wasn't looking for credit or sympathy at this point, though. Just information.

Mae shrugged. "Respectable. At least you didn't go down under, like, only two or three."

There was that. It didn't make my lip any less puffy, but it did take some of the sting from my pride. "Thing is, I didn't recognize their moves."

Mae's eyes opened wide again. "Not at all?"

"Well, maybe a little, but it wasn't something I've ever used."

"Live and learn," Mae said.

"With any luck," I said. In my book, the alternative doesn't look so great.

Mae finished the chocolate and brushed the crumbs off her hands. "Any idea why they attacked you?"

"They seemed to want the envelope I was delivering." At least, they had hightailed it out of there as soon as they got their hands on it.

"What was in it?"

I shrugged. "I don't have a clue. Alexander Bledsoe gave it to me for Aldo."

"Alex sent something to Aldo? Maybe some kind of poison-pen letter?" Mae snorted. Everyone knew that Alex and Aldo didn't get along.

"I guess I'll try to find out Sunday night. He should be working then, too."

Mae frowned. "I think you might want to contact him before then. He should know you didn't make the delivery."

"Do I have to?" Oops. That had come out a little whinier than I'd meant it to. I plopped down in the chair across from her.

"No, but you probably should. What's the big deal?"

I inspected my fingernails and tried to come up with words for how Alex made me feel. "He makes me uncomfortable."

"He's a vampire. He makes everybody uncomfortable." Mae shook her head. "Whether they know he's a vampire or not."

That wasn't entirely true. Either that or my uncomfortable was other women's horny. Come to think of it, that could be another reason I never went on any dates. "How about I try to find out who might have taken it so I have something to actually tell him? Maybe we could start with figuring out what the hell kind of martial art the guys who took the envelope from me were using?"

"Good enough." Mae said. "Show me some of their moves. I'll see if I can recognize them."

We went out on the mat. I stood in front of her, closed my eyes and tried to focus. I probably looked about like Mae did when she took that first bite of honeycomb. That made me smile. I brushed that thought away and focused on the ninjas. I remembered the first one dropping in front of me into a crouch, stepping sideways and then whirling his arms so I'd gotten an elbow right in the solar plexus. I tried the movement out for Mae in slow motion.

"Are you sure about that?" she asked.

Was I sure? I was sure-ish rather than completely sure. "No. It happened pretty fast."

"Anything else?"

I shut my eyes and thought again. The one who had slammed me on the point of my chin had stepped backward, pulled his elbows back and slammed forward with his hands raised. I did that and then opened my eyes.

Mae was shaking her head. "That looks like Rising White Crane. The first one looked like Repelling the Monkeys."

"Tai chi?" No way. Nobody used tai chi for self-defense anymore, or in this case, for attacking someone. Old people did tai chi. Grandma Rosie's friends at the Sunshine Assisted Living Facility did tai chi to improve their balance so they didn't fall and break their hips. Ninja guys didn't do tai chi after dropping out of trees to attack young women who were going about their business delivering envelopes to loser vampires who didn't even have the sense to move some place dark and foggy.

"I'm pretty sure." Mae crossed her arms over her chest. "So what are you going to do about it?"

That was the sixty-four-thousand-dollar question, now wasn't it? What was I going to do about it? I didn't relish the thought of telling Alex I hadn't delivered his envelope. Nor did I particularly relish finding out what the more karmic repercussions of that failure might be. Maybe I could find out who had taken the envelope and get it back by myself. It seemed worth a try. If I didn't have it back by Sunday night, I'd confess all to Alex and take my lumps, hopefully not literally. I rubbed my neck absently. "I think I better figure out who might be using tai chi as an actual martial art," I told Mae.

"Where are you going to start?" she asked.

Another excellent question. I thought for a moment. "I think I might go visit my grandmother and find out who teaches the tai chi classes at her assisted living facility. Maybe she'll know something helpful."

"Sounds like a plan," Mae said. "Keep me posted. Let me know if I can help."

The door opened and the first of our Little Dragons bounced in. "Ready for the really tough stuff?" Mae asked.

"Ready as I'll ever be," I replied.

Within five minutes, my students were all assembled. I went and took my place at the front of the dojo. "Who wants to practice their worm crawl?" I yelled out.

Seven Little Dragons screamed, "I do, Sensei!"

My head throbbed a little.

I AM NOT SURE A HUMAN BEING CAN EMIT A MORE PIERC-ing sound than that of a six-year-old girl screaming her lungs out to release her chi while attacking a hanging bag. I'm sure there are people who will argue with me. They might bring up roller coaster screams or haunted house squeals or even American Girl party trills. I beg to differ with them all. Maybe it wasn't really Ashley's chi. Maybe it was that my head still throbbed from my ninja beat down. All I knew was that if Ashley went after that hanging bag one more time, my eardrums were going to split.

"Excellent job, Little Dragons!" I yelled.

"Thank you, Sensei!" they yelled back.

My left eyelid twitched, but the Little Dragons skipped off the mat to their waiting parents. Everyone clapped. Hugs were exchanged. No one was bleeding unless there was a trickle coming out of my ear that I'd missed. Mission accomplished.

Mae came out of her office, and we stood on the edge of the mat together and exchanged the usual pleasantries with the parents. Mae was big on positive reinforcement for the kids and the parents. So we made sure to mention both how Hunter was doing so much better at waiting his turn and how nice it was to have him there for the whole class. We praised Caitlin for how bold she'd been and Sasha for paying attention. As the parents and the Little Dragons filed out, Mae's late afternoon judo class made up of mostly teenagers filed in. They might have spent their days at the junior high pushing and shoving, but here at the dojo, the kids filed in politely, bowing their heads and holding doors. It was like a bizarre church community where half the people could break your arms using only their pinky fingers.

I headed into the back room to change out of my *gi* and into my street clothes. When I came back, there was one person still in the waiting area, a young woman no more than sixteen at the oldest and probably a little younger than that, whom I hadn't seen before at the dojo. "Can I help you?" I asked.

"I'm not sure," she said. Her straight blonde hair fell over her face as she ducked her head.

"Are you a new student?" I asked.

"No," she said. "At least, not yet."

Got it. Prospective student. I watched her for a moment. There was something about her tentative manner. Not that a lot of prospective students weren't tentative. They were. The dojo could be an intimidating place when you first walked in. There's a lot of aggression in the air here. It's contained. It's controlled, but it's still aggression. People sense it. They may not know it, but they do.

Something about this young woman struck a chord with me, though. It wasn't exactly like the feeling I got when I knew Alex was behind me. Or even the shiver I got when I knew something dangerous was around a corner. Still, it felt familiar. I hoped she wasn't here to learn to defend herself because someone had already hurt her. I hated that. It felt too much like locking the barn door after the horses had already bolted. Which isn't to say it isn't worthwhile to make sure the horses never bolt again. I'm just saying that I'd rather keep them from ever bolting. Especially when it was a young girl. It just hit a little too close to home. "Any reason in particular you want to study here?"

She brushed her hair off her face and looked up at me. That's when I saw the scars. They ran from beneath her right ear, down her neck and under the collar of her T-shirt, like white rivers running through sand. "I heard this was a good place to learn."

So it was too late. Someone had already damaged this girl. I took a deep breath. "From whom?" I asked. We had an incentive program. We'd give someone a break on their monthly tuition if they brought in a new student for us. I also hoped I might be able to get the girl's story from whomever had referred her to us.

"Oh, no one in particular. I just heard it around."

I was completely familiar with the sensation I had right now. The girl was lying. I shrugged. There were no rules that said you had to reveal where you'd heard of River City Karate and Judo. Maybe she had a good reason for lying. It didn't seem like the best way to enter into the dojo, though. I glanced at my watch. I needed to get moving if I was going to visit Grandma Rosie before dinner.

"Well, it's nice to meet you . . . " I realized I hadn't gotten her name.

"Sophie," she said, taking the hand I offered.

"Melina," I said and gave her a smile. "Hope I see you around."

"I think you will," Sophie said.

GRANDMA ROSIE LIVES IN THE SUNSHINE RETIREMENT Center and Assisted Living Facility at Alhambra and J. She moved there about a year after Grandpa Ed moved into the Home of Peace Cemetery over on Stockton. Grandma definitely got the better deal. I parked in one of the visitor's spots. I eyed the circular drive that was for ten-minute stays only, but decided not to chance it. I didn't think they'd be chalking my tires, but why tempt fate? Last spring break, one of the residents called the cops on some kids who were "fishing" in the koi pond out front. Some people take the rules very seriously. Some of them have lots of time on their hands when they get old. Some of them have no sense of humor.

I checked my face in the vanity mirror again before I got out of the Buick. My lip was puffy, but the split had almost mended. My chin was a lovely shade of purple with a tinge of green around the edges. Ah, well, Grandma's eyesight wasn't what it used to be. Maybe she wouldn't notice. I snapped the mirror shut, got out of the car and headed toward the building.

I hadn't taken two steps when an unearthly wailing lifted

the hair on the back of my neck. I stopped and looked up. Perched on the windowsill of one of the upper apartments, a beautiful, pale young woman in a floating white dress opened her mouth and let out a mournful keen. I squinted. A banshee. She moaned again.

This was one of the downsides for me of visiting Grandma at the Sunshine Assisted Living Facility. The turnover in the clientele was high, and I more often than not ran into things I'd rather keep away from my family. A banshee on a windowsill? Well, sure as shooting, one of Grandma Rosie's friends was about to depart for that big bridge tournament up in the sky. Most likely, one of her friends with an *O* or a *Mac* at the beginning of his or her name.

As I walked below the banshee, I noticed a comb lying on the ground. It wasn't just any comb either. It was crusted with jewels and looked as delicate as a seashell. I looked up at the banshee again. She smiled. "Would you take that comb to someone for me?" she asked.

"What kind of someone?" She was just trying to get me to pick up the comb. I knew it. She knew it. I decided to play along anyway.

"Oh, almost anyone will do." She shrugged.

I kicked some loose leaves over the comb. Woe to the person who picked up that little piece of bling. She'd be back for them in no time at all.

The banshee gave me one last howl for good measure as I walked through the sliding doors into the facility. Inside, I signed in at the front desk—someone had meticulously taped plastic flowers around the pens so that the penholder looked like a pot of flowers—and headed down the hallway.

The Sunshine Retirement Center and Assisted Living Facility was a classy place. The halls never smelled like pee. There were two movie nights a week, one for new movies and one for classics. There were art classes, book clubs, exercise programs and a speaker series.

Grandma Rosie lived on the second floor. I took the stairs since I had never seen an elevator whose doors opened and closed more slowly than the one at Sunshine. The timing was set to accommodate people with walkers. I'm sure I'll be grateful for the extra time when it's my turn to cruise up and down the hallways with tennis balls on the legs of my aluminum walking contraption, but right now it made me nuts. I checked my watch. It was five fifteen already. I'd only barely catch Grandma before dinnertime. They eat early at Sunshine.

"Who is it?" Grandma called when I knocked.

For a moment I considered saying it was Little Red Riding Hood, but there are limits to what Grandma thinks is funny. "It's me, Grandma. Melina."

"Come in. Come in."

Grandma was ensconced in the recliner chair with the remote-control lift that we'd bought her for Chanukah. CNN blared from the TV. She grabbed the remote and clicked the mute button. I leaned in and gave her a kiss.

"Hi, Grandma," I said.

"Hello, sweetheart. To what do I owe the pleasure?"

I'd love to say that I visit my grandma all the time for no reason, but that wouldn't be precisely the truth. I do visit. Sometimes I don't have a reason. It just doesn't happen that way a lot. Yes. I suck. I drive her car every day but only manage to stop by when I need something. She deserves better. "I was hoping you could tell me about the tai chi instructor you guys have here," I said.

"Frank Liu?" Grandma asked, struggling up straighter in the recliner. "Why? Have you heard something?"

"Heard something? What would I have heard?"

"I thought maybe you might have heard where he's disappeared to," Grandma said. "We're all worried."

3

"YOUR TAI CHI INSTRUCTOR IS MISSING?" I SAT DOWN IN
the rocking chair across from Grandma's recliner.

"For three days now," she said, her eyes flickering to the
TV for a second. No one, and I mean no one, is as up-to-date
on current events as my grandma Rosie. I think she has CNN
on while she sleeps. "He hasn't shown up for two classes.
He was always so reliable, too. The Asians are like that, you
know. Reliable and polite."

I cringed. At least my grandmother's racism ran toward
positive stereotypes, but it still drove me a little crazy. I'm
positive there are lots of rude, good-for-nothing Asians out
there. They deserve to be recognized and not painted with
the polite and reliable brush for no reason. "He didn't call
or anything?"

"No and he hasn't answered our phone calls either. It's
so unlike him. I hope he's not ill or anything. When you
asked about him, I thought maybe you'd heard something
in one of your karate circles." She made a little karate-chop
motion with the side of her hand. I am often brought face-

to-face with how little my grandmother understands my everyday life. It makes me all the more grateful for that unconditional-love thing. And the Buick, too. I'm very grateful for the Buick. Have I mentioned how well its air conditioner works? It's like driving around in a refrigerated truck all summer. Delicious.

I shook my head. "Nope. I actually wanted to ask him a few questions about tai chi and who uses it."

Grandma patted my hand. "Always looking for something new to learn, aren't you? You're just like your mother that way." She beamed. My mom is totally Grandma's favorite. "If you have questions about tai chi, you should ask Lillian. She's made quite a study of it."

"Really?" I couldn't imagine Lillian would have the first clue as to who had dropped out of the live oak trees and opened a can of tai chi whoop ass on me, but I supposed it was worth talking to her. Plus, I doubted I could get out of it without being rude to Grandma about her friends. Lillian was one of her best buddies, a key member of her posse.

"Absolutely. Walk me to dinner. It's almost time. You can chat with her there. And by the way, what did you do to your face?"

Grandma, I thought, what big eyes you have. So much for counting on her crappy eyesight.

Walking Grandma downstairs and down the hall to dinner takes a surprisingly long time. Everything takes a little longer than it used to, from drawing the keys from the pocket of her elastic-waisted pants to her trembling ET-like finger extending itself toward the elevator buttons. I took deep cleansing breaths and managed not to throw her over my shoulder and run down the hallway, screaming like a banshee. See how that self-control thing comes in handy?

We eventually made it into the dining room. Lillian rolled in a few minutes after us. I mean that literally. She's using the wheelchair a lot more these days.

"Lillian," Grandma called out. "Melina wants to know about tai chi."

Lillian's cheeks went pink with delight. Lillian is a retired history professor from Sac State. For years, she lectured three times a week on the American Revolution and the War of 1812 and a bunch of stuff in between. Now, nobody wanted to listen to an old lady. To actually have someone ask her to explain something was an unexpected and delightful treat. It might also take three hours. I sighed, put it on my mental list of Things That Took Time I Will Never Get Back and submitted to my fate.

"*Tai chi* is actually Mandarin for 'supreme ultimate boxing' or 'boundless fist.' It's a very gentle discipline. The whole idea is to meet an incoming force with softness and to follow its motion. That way, the force of the attack exhausts itself and can be redirected. If you meet force with force, both sides will wind up getting hurt," Lillian said.

"Really?" My fingers went to my lip. There had been nothing soft about the hand that had connected with it earlier in the day. Maybe Mae was wrong.

"Lao-tzu wrote that the soft and the pliable will defeat the hard and the strong," she continued.

I nodded my head, but Lillian really didn't need the encouragement.

"It's still practiced in Taoist temples. Its whole basis is tied in with Taoist philosophy because it was created by a Taoist monk called Zhang Sanfeng in the twelfth century. He taught it to his disciples in the monasteries at Wu Tang Shan."

Now that caught my interest. "Is there a Taoist temple in Sacramento?" I asked.

"Right in Old Sacramento," she said.

Perfect, I thought. I could check out the temple and still maybe manage to have a margarita with normal people my own age. I stood up to leave.

"Would you like to stay for dinner?" Grandma asked.

I looked around at the faces of Grandma's tablemates. They were sweet, but the thought of sitting through an entire meal with them was enough to make the smallest crumbs of bread stick in my throat. "Thanks, Gram, but I've got to run."

"Are you sure? It's Friday. There'll be ice cream sundaes for dessert." She smiled up at me. Grandma knows my weakness for hot fudge. Still . . .

"Maybe another Friday," I said.

She patted my hand. "Of course," she said. "Another Friday."

The words echoed in my head. I'd heard them before. A few too many times before. I sat back down. "You know, I can't think of a better Friday than this one after all."

I PARKED THE BUICK ON I STREET, ACROSS FROM THE BOK Kai Temple in Old Sacramento.

Old Sacramento is the land of tacky souvenir shops, T-shirt stores and restaurants with *Olde* in the name, but that's just the surface. Old Sacramento is actually seriously old, at least by California standards. A lot of what's here has been here for more than a century. That alone would make it a magnet for all kinds of interesting things. In addition to that, however, there's a whole other world here that most people don't see. In the 1860s, the city raised the downtown one story to avoid flooding problems. The raised wooden boardwalks and buildings created a system of tunnels that are now home to a myriad of creatures both supernatural and of the "real" world that most ordinary citizens choose not to notice, not to mention the ghosts that haunt the place.

Most of the tunnels are blocked now, but for years underground access was used to smuggle everything from people to drugs in and out of the city and onto the river. The area

I was in now used to be Chinatown back in the day. Huge numbers of Chinese had immigrated to the United States during the Gold Rush. Even more followed to work on the railroads. Chinatowns sprung up in nearly every major city on the West Coast to supply the new immigrants with food and clothing and community. Then suddenly, the economy changed and nobody was so happy to see those Chinese immigrants anymore. The Chinese Exclusion Act of 1882 came soon after. People went underground. In Sacramento, they did it more literally than in other places what with those handy underground tunnels so readily available. Some people still refer to them as the Chinese Tunnels. Supposedly, opium dens and a healthy trade in contraband goods once thrived out of sight in the musty depths below the city.

Now? Well, I didn't know of any opium dens, but there was plenty going on in Old Sac beneath the picturesque planks of the sidewalks. You wouldn't know it watching the Bok Kai Temple, though. Nothing was happening there at all.

I glanced at my watch. It was eight o'clock. Shouldn't somebody be arriving for evening prayers? I hoped somebody did something soon. Norah had called me as I'd driven down here. Tanya and she would be hitting McClannigan's about now. I liked margaritas even better than I liked hot fudge sundaes, and I like hot fudge a lot. Damn Alexander Bledsoe anyway. Could I say no to anything tonight?

I rolled up the windows of the Buick and got out. If no one else was going into the temple, maybe I would take a look. It wouldn't be nice for it to be lonely, now would it?

I sauntered across the street. When I got closer, I could read the hand-lettered sign by the door. Closed for Renovation. Well, that explained the lack of faithful people coming to pray as the sun prepared to set. The place looked quiet, abandoned, but as I came closer to the door, I felt the familiar hum in the air that told me everything here was not as it seemed.

There was something in the temple that wasn't of this world.

I tried the door. Unlocked. My eyebrows shot up. That was unusual. Most places around here would keep their doors locked if only to keep the homeless from using it as a place to bed down for the night. I'm not saying it's right. I'm saying that's how it is.

I pushed the door open.

The air inside the temple was dank and musty. I could smell the tang of the river and something more. The hum in my head grew louder. I stepped inside.

I waited a few seconds to let my eyes adjust. I wanted to meet whatever was in there with all my senses working at their best. Whatever it was, it wasn't familiar. I stifled the urge to sing "Come out, come out, wherever you are." It wasn't wise to invite things you didn't understand out into the open unless you were sure you could get them to scuttle back into the shadows where they often belonged. One more lesson I've learned the hard way.

I walked a little farther into the temple. Nine steps rose before me, and I followed them up into the main sanctuary. The ceiling soared overhead. The place was a riot of color, but the dim light grayed everything. An altar at the far end held a tray of oranges and sticks of incense, but the incense wasn't lit and even from the doorway I could smell the beginnings of mold on the oranges. It's one of the curses of particularly acute senses. Fruit really has to be fresh for me to eat it.

Something was definitely going on, but I wasn't sure I would exactly call it renovation. Six big holes had been dug into the tiled floor of the temple. I get the whole breaking-eggs-to-make-an-omelet thing, but this didn't look like any demolition job I'd ever seen before.

This looked like somebody had been digging up graves.

As I crept farther into the temple, the hair on the back of my neck stood up. Something was coming toward me out of the gloom. According to my senses, however, this thing was decidedly human.

"Excuse me! Excuse me, miss!" A youngish-looking man in an orange robe approached me. "The temple is closed. You can't be here." He looked decidedly Asian, but his English was excellent.

When in doubt, play dumb. I'm sad to report how often it works for me. It must be something about my face. "Really?" I said. "Bummer."

"Uh, yes," the young man said. "Yes. A bummer. It's not safe for you here right now." He gestured to the holes in the floor. "Someone could get hurt. We're renovating."

"Oh," I said. "So no evening prayers?"

He flushed. "No. No evening prayers. No morning prayers tomorrow. We're closed for renovation."

"When will you reopen?" I asked.

"No time soon," he said quickly. "There's much to be done. We've only just started."

I peered around his shoulder at the holes. "Yeah, I can see that. What are you planning to do?"

His brow creased. "Planning to do?"

"What are you going to change?"

"Oh, everything. The floor. The walls. It will take a long, long time. Until then, you should go up to the Joss House in Weaverville. That's the closest one."

"So you're completely closed? No prayers? No classes?"

"Classes?"

"Yeah, like I thought maybe I might want to take tai chi or something. That's Taoist, isn't it? You all invented tai chi, right?"

"Plenty of tai chi classes in Sacramento without coming here." He moved forward, herding me back down the stairs. "Try the Y. Or the community college."

"Yeah," I said, allowing him to direct me toward the door. "Okay. The community college. I might try that."

"Great. Good luck." We were at the door now and he all but shoved me out.

The doors of the temple closed. This time I heard the lock click.

My senses are more tuned into things that aren't human than those that are. Most days, I find vampires and were-wolves easier to read than the guy sitting next to me on the bus. Sometimes, however, human emotion comes through loud and clear.

The young priest in the Bok Kai Temple was scared. I could smell it from a mile away.

I LEFT MY CAR ON I STREET AND WALKED OVER TO McClannigan's Olde Towne Pub. Norah had made an excellent choice. It was loud. It was noisy. The drinks were huge. Plus, I knew the bartender.

Norah and Tanya were already at a table. I spotted them almost as soon as I walked in. Norah tended to give off a glow. I think it's her innate goodness shining through. Either that or she has actually slathered so much sunscreen on her Nordic white skin that she's become translucent. I motioned to them that I was going to the bar to get a drink and then join them. They both waved and nodded, grinning broadly. I grinned myself. I was actually going out with friends on a Friday night. Maybe underneath it all I was a real girl. Now if I could only get rid of these strings that seemed to always be jerking me around.

I bellied up to the big wooden bar and waited to get Paul's attention. It didn't take long. I saw his head come up as he scented me.

I'm always amazed that Paul gets away with his bartender gig. It's not that he isn't good at it. He's amazing, like Tom Cruise in *Cocktail* amazing. I just keep waiting for someone to check and see how long he's been working at McClannigan's. Or to notice the photo.

Up and down the hallway that leads to the restrooms, there are a series of photos of Old Sacramento before it was Old Sacramento and it was just Sacramento. There's even an old sepia-toned photo of the inside of McClannigan's as it was in about 1912. The big wooden bar is there with the huge mirror behind it. Standing behind the bar is a broad-shouldered man with a ponytail and a beard. It's Paul.

The beard's a little fuller. The collar is way higher and a bazillion times starchier. Still, it's Paul and anyone who actually bothers to take a good hard look should notice. So far, apparently, no one has taken a good hard look. Or they're just too shit-faced on Paul's awesome gin and tonics to see straight.

Paul has been bartending at McClannigan's since around 1908. No wonder he's good. He's been practicing for a super-long time. Because of his seniority, he pretty much gets to pick his hours, too. Someday, I figure someone will also notice that Paul never works during a full moon. That's because he's busy then. He's out hunting with his pack in the Sierras. It's the werewolf thing to do.

"I didn't order a pickup," he growled at me.

I cocked my head in what I hoped was a coquettish manner. "No one said you did."

"Drop-off?" he asked, looking concerned, which is tough on a werewolf, even in human form.

I was often not the bearer of glad tidings. Still, it wouldn't hurt him to look a little happier to see me. I liked Paul as much as I liked any werewolf, which is more than I like vampires, but honestly, not by all that much. "Nope," I said.

"Oh," he said, his shoulders relaxing. "What can I get for you then?"

I smiled and he smiled back. Big mistake. He might be in human form right now, but I can see a wolfish grin a mile away. A shiver ran down my spine. "Margarita," I said.

He shook his head. "You shouldn't drink tequila. You need to stay sharp."

"Fine," I said. "How about a beer?"

"One Amstel Light coming up," he said, gliding down the bar.

"Hey," I called after him. "Is that a comment or something?"

He smiled at me. He really was a handsome man, and I was so not immune to that. He still had the broad shoulders and the long thick hair pulled back in a ponytail like he did in the photo. These days, the beard was kept trimmed to a neat goatee. There was something in the way he moved, an animal grace that promised both power and control and passion. I swallowed hard. I'm alone a lot and the shower attachment can keep a girl only so satisfied over the long haul.

Paul returned with my beer. I pulled out my wallet, and he waved my money away. "It's on the house. But just one, okay?"

Okay. There was the downside of all that power and control. He was all about power and control, and few things turn me off faster than that. Too many outside factors had control over my life as it was. I didn't need someone—least of all a werewolf—trying to dominate me in my own bed. "Thanks," I said and took the beer. There's no sense in being stupid about things either, now is there?

"So what brings you down here?" Paul asked, leaning forward on the bar. He smelled like fields of wheat that had been baking under the sun, and I could feel the heat pouring off of him. I leaned forward, too. My stomach fluttered a little.

"Does a girl have to have a reason to go out for a drink on a Friday night?" I looked around at the throngs of young women throughout the bar.

"No," he said evenly, standing up, withdrawing his heat and his scent from me. "But a Messenger usually does."

I sighed and twirled my beer around. Light beer. Would there even be any point to drinking it? "You know anything about the Taoist temple over on I Street?"

Paul leaned back in, eyebrows arched. "What about it? You getting all spiritual on me? Gonna start meditating and chanting?"

"Not exactly." I kept my eyes lowered. I didn't want him to see how keen I was for information, plus it's good form when you're talking to a werewolf. Staring them directly in the eye is often taken as a challenge whether you've meant it that way or not. "I wondered if you'd noticed anything about it, anything odd going on."

"Yeah," he said, his voice flat. "I've smelled it."

I looked up and then back down just as fast. "Do you know what it is?"

Paul wiped the bar with a towel and then slung it back over his shoulder. "Nope," he said. "Not a clue."

I did look up now. It was one thing for me not to recognize whatever it was. Paul had been around the block a few times, though. "Does it worry you?"

He braced his elbows on the bar and leaned toward me. "No. Not really. I told Chuck about it. He said it had nothing to do with us."

Chuck is the Sierra wolf pack's Alpha. His word is law for the pack, which is who Paul meant when he said *us*. There is only one kind of *us* for a werewolf and that is the pack. It is first and foremost, alpha and omega, chicken and egg.

Our faces were close now, inches apart. Paul smelled like sunshine and musk. I doubted any of it was cologne. My belly tightened. "And what do you think?" I asked, my voice unexpectedly thick.

"I think that if Chuck says to leave it alone, I leave it alone." Paul didn't budge. I didn't either. I wondered if Chuck had given any instructions regarding little ole me.

"Any interest in stopping by there later and checking it out with me? Sunset's not for a while yet," I said. I wasn't sure what was in there, but I'd be willing to bet that the chances of something crawling out of those holes in the floor would double once night fell.

He gave his head a fraction of a shake. "It's not pack business so it's not my business."

I sighed and stood up. Fine, then, I'd be on my own. What else was new? "Thanks for the beer," I said.

"Anytime," he said, grinning again. Then he was off to help the next customer, and I made my way over to Norah and Tanya.

I begged a stool off one of the other tables and pulled it up to where they were perched. They had margaritas. They were wearing pink and seafoam green halter tops with matching stripy skirts. I still had on my black tank top and jeans. Maybe I wasn't a real girl. I don't know why I kept bothering to pretend.

"So it looks like the bartender is totally into you," Tanya said. "He's totally still checking you out."

"You mean Paul?" I said. "He's just an old friend."

"Well, it looks like he wants to be an old friend with benefits," Norah said and laid her hand on my forearm.

I glanced over my shoulder. Paul was still watching me with a hungry look on his face. Therein lay the problem with getting involved with werewolves. I never quite knew whether they were planning on eating me, humping me or peeing on me. I'm not sure they knew half the time. Besides, Grandma Rosie always says that if you lie down with dogs, you'll wake up with fleas. Just thinking about it made me want to scratch.

4

THE SUN DOESN'T SET IN SACRAMENTO IN JUNE UNTIL nine o'clock. I chatted with Norah and Tanya and nursed my beer until eight forty-five. They'd already caught the attention of a couple of well-muscled young men. I didn't need to watch any more of the mating dance between the four of them. It was just too depressing. Hardly anyone even noticed when I left. Your life has gotten pretty pathetic when you can still feel lonely surrounded by people.

Paul gave me a little wave from behind the bar as I left. "Watch your back," he mouthed at me as I swung the door open.

Yeah, right. Like that was even possible.

I was back in the Buick, slouched low by the time the sun hit the horizon. It had been a long day, even for me, and my eyelids felt heavy. I blinked them open.

For the next half hour, I might as well have napped. It was toasty warm inside the Buick, and there was about as much action at the Bok Kai Temple as you'd expect on a Friday night. Those Taoists. They're quite the partiers. Not.

I was beginning to wonder if I was wasting my time. It was quite likely I was, but to be honest, I didn't know what else to do and I had to do something. Ninja dudes using tai chi had attacked me and taken my delivery. Taoist priests use tai chi. I couldn't help feeling my best course of action was to watch the local Taoists to see if anything shook loose, especially when the local Taoists clearly had something to hide.

At ten fifteen, I was rewarded for my efforts, if you consider having your life suddenly become a whole lot more complicated to somehow be rewarding. At any rate, three black Lincoln Navigators with tinted windows pulled up to the temple and then around back to the loading area closer to the river. I desperately wanted to sneak out and see what they were doing, but just when I got up the nerve to get out of the Buick, the Navigators pulled back around and turned left to head for the interstate.

I turned on the Buick's engine and followed.

I wasn't terribly thrilled with where we were headed. We got off I-5 and turned toward Fruitridge Road. Anybody who lives in Sacto can tell you that nothing good happens at night on Fruitridge Road. It's gang territory, and I'm not talking about any gang. I'm talking about the Norteños.

I routinely deal with some of the most evil, undead beings that walk our planet. Since I was three years old, dead people have stopped by to have chats with me. I'm not scared of much, but I'm scared of the Norteños. I dropped back a block or so behind the very shiny, highly conspicuous SUVs.

I was at least a block and a half back when the Navigators pulled up to a corner where a group of young men lounged in the balmy summer night. The Delta breeze had started to pick up, but it hadn't truly cooled anything off yet. I pulled over and rolled down my window. One of the young men detached himself from the group and sauntered up to the lead SUV. He had on a white wife-beater and baggy jeans that rode low enough on his hips to display a solid two inches of boxer shorts. Curse you, Marky Mark, for starting one of the stupidest fashion trends of modern times. The cholo said something to the driver in the SUV. From where I was, I couldn't make out the words. But you didn't really need to be able to hear to know what he meant. It wasn't a welcome.

Two Asian guys stepped out of the front of the lead Navigator, one from each side. They had on suits and ties. Their hair was short and neatly combed. They were not, however, office drones. I can appreciate what it means to be in fighting form, and no suit could disguise that these guys were in exactly that. Several more of the lounging young men on the corner stood up and approached the SUVs. Words were exchanged. Once again, I'm not sure exactly what was said. Body language alone told me it wasn't friendly. More Asian guys got out of the front seats of the other two Navigators. More words were exchanged. Sweat began to bead on my upper lip, and it wasn't just from the heat. Whatever was going to happen here wasn't going to be pretty.

The Asian guys opened the rear doors of the SUVs. For a moment, I could have sworn I heard the sound of bells ringing. Then things started hopping out of the vans.

I'm not sure really how to describe them. They sure as hell weren't people, although they clearly had been at one time. I mean, they were people shaped. They were no longer people colored, though, unless a sick greenish yellow was now the new beige and nobody had bothered to tell me.

They didn't move like people either. They hopped. When I say they hopped out of the cars, I mean it literally. They held their arms stiffly in front of them. Even from a block and a half away, I could see they had long, talonlike fingernails extending out from their fingertips. Their hair was long and matted. Long yellow strips of paper were attached to their foreheads.

They advanced toward the young Latino men on the corner, who were now doubled over with laughter.

That didn't last long.

The laughter pretty much stopped when the first of the creepy creatures grabbed one of the young men and bit into his neck like an escapee from a Weight Watchers meeting biting into a Krispy Kreme. Blood gushed from the wound, and the young man sank to his knees as the creature continued to rip strips of flesh from his chest with its teeth. That's basically when all hell broke loose.

I saw the glint of moonlight on steel. The Norteños had pulled knives. I watched as one approached one of the hopping things and shoved his blade deep into its belly. The thing paused for a moment, grabbed the gangbanger's arm and pulled it literally out of its socket. I fought back my gag reflex as the creature began to feast on the limb and the Norteño reeled away, shrieking. A gunshot went off. I don't know who fired it or where it hit. I do know that the hopping things kept advancing. Not one of them even paused. Another Norteño fell as one of the creatures bit into him.

The creatures kept advancing, kept grabbing young men and, in some cases, literally pulling them apart like overcooked chicken and feasting on them. I fought the wave of nausea that threatened to sweep me away.

Through it all, I thought I heard bells ringing.

For a few seconds, I didn't move. I don't think I could move. It was too shocking, too difficult for my brain to process what I was seeing. Two of the things converged on one young man and pulled him apart like a wishbone. Tendons stretched between them until they snapped. The air was ripped by the young man's screams. I had never seen anything like it, not even in my worst nightmares, and I've had some doozies.

It took me a few seconds more to come up with a plan. I'd passed a convenience store a few blocks back. Apparently, it was my day to appreciate 7-Elevens. There would be a pay phone. I'd call the cops. No way was I using my cell phone. No way did I want anyone to trace anything that had happened here tonight back to me. A nice anonymous pay phone would be just the ticket.

I whipped the Buick around as well as anyone can whip around a Buick, headed back to the 7-Eleven and made the call. I didn't stay to see if they'd come. I didn't wait to see what would happen if they did. I'd seen enough for one night. I didn't want to see anything more.

I drove back up I-5 to Richards, careful not to exceed the socially acceptable five to seven miles over the speed limit. I didn't need any more drama tonight. I'd had plenty. I was going to head home, make myself some hot chocolate, possibly with a healthy dose of Baileys in it and then crawl into my cozy bed and sleep, sleep, sleep. At least until a little before nine on Saturday morning, when I needed to be back at the dojo for another Little Dragons class.

Right now, the idea of being around all that fresh-faced innocence was helping me put one foot in front of the other. I did not luck out with parking and ended up two blocks away from the apartment. The walk was good for me, though. It gave me a few minutes to clear my head a bit. The Delta breeze had picked up more and the night had cooled. The air felt good against the hot skin of my face and made me a little less nauseous. What had those things been? I'd never seen anything like them. The ferocity of their attack made werewolves bringing down game look like kids playing ring-around-the-rosy—and, incidentally, that whole thing about ring-around-the-rosy being a rhyme about the plague? Total nonsense. Look it up.

I set my alarm for seven A.M. That would give me time for a shower and a leisurely cup of coffee—or as leisurely as a cup of coffee can be when you're being nagged about it while you drink it—before I had to face my Saturday morning Little Dragons. Unfortunately, it wasn't as easy as that.

Every time I shut my eyes, the scene at the park replayed

itself against the backdrop of my bloodred eyelids. All I could see were things that hopped, that looked like ridiculous characters from a B movie ripping apart young flesh and feasting on it. Young men screaming for mercy in Spanish. Others just screaming as blood gushed from ripped skin and places where limbs should still be attached. When I did finally fall asleep, I dreamed that I was sitting in the middle of the emergency room with battered, bleeding body parts surrounding me like piles of dirty laundry.

I opened my eyes from one dream to find none other than Alexander Bledsoe sitting in the corner of my room.

"How did you get in here?" I croaked. I knew I hadn't invited him in. Who had?

He didn't answer my question. "Stand up, Melina," he said.

My body obeyed him even though my mind screamed for it to stay safe under the blankets. I stood in front of him wearing only the panties and tank top I'd had on when I'd fallen into bed, exhausted and stricken.

"Come closer," he said. His voice was low and rough, setting off vibrations in me that I didn't want to ignore.

I took a step closer, unsure whether I was responding to his command or the needs of my own body or some truly unholy combination of the two. He rose from the chair and stood next to me, moving through the dark room like a shadow. His fingers traced the skin just above the neckline of my tank top. I felt as though I couldn't breathe. I felt like my skin was on fire and his icy fingers left trails of goose bumps behind them. He leaned down toward me, his lips cool and full only inches from mine, and a horrible screeching filled my ears.

My eyes flew open. I was alone in the room, still tucked safely beneath my blankets, morning light streaming in the windows and my alarm clock blaring from the bedside table.

No seductive vampire sat in the corner of my room. I sniffed the air. Not a sign of him.

I half crawled to the bathroom to take a very cold shower. I let the stinging drops beat against my skin as I tried to sort out which of the previous night's occurrences had been real and which had been all in my head. Maybe those hopping things had been figments of my imagination like my late-night visit from Alex. I could only hope so.

I was toweling off, still feeling like shit on a shingle, when the banging started on the apartment door. I threw on some shorts and a T-shirt and ran to answer it.

"Who is it?" I said, trying to peer through the peephole and getting just a blurry image of something blond on the other side.

"Police," the blond thing barked. "Open up."

HAVE I MENTIONED HOW I AM SO NOT A FAN OF DEALING with the police? Don't get me wrong. I am thrilled that they exist. I don't entirely get the mindset of people whose instincts make them run toward the sound of gunfire rather than away, but I'm happy they're around because I certainly don't want to be running toward the flying bullets. I heal fast but not fast enough for that. Plus, I'm not a big fan of pain.

Still, I don't want to have much to do with them. Cops like things to have labels, to be in neatly categorized little boxes. I exist in the margins. They seem to have a knee-jerk mistrust of me, so I try to make sure I don't come to their attention. It's occasionally tricky at the hospital where they're in and out of the emergency room all the time, but mainly I do a good job of not drawing attention to myself. I blend.

So why was Blond Surfer Cop at my doorway at seven thirty A.M.? And he *was* Blond Surfer Cop. He totally looked like he'd competed in Mavericks, dropped his board, brushed off the sand, donned a police uniform and driven to Sacramento right from the beach. His hair was all sun streaked, and even through the sliver-sized view the security chain allowed, I could see it wasn't one of those fakey highlight jobs.

"Hey," I said. "Keep it down. I've got neighbors, you know?"

He swore under his breath and then glanced around as if my neighbors might even now be dialing his superiors to complain. Satisfied that the hall was empty and quiet, he said in a half whisper, "Sorry. Are you Melina Markowitz?"

Bummer. I'd been hoping he had the wrong apartment. Although I'd also been hoping he wasn't here to visit Ben downstairs. I'd be okay with it if he was paying a visit to the skinny little dude across the hall. The guy looks like a ferret, and I am none too happy about the way he leers at Norah when she takes out the garbage. It skeeves me out, and consequently, I feel compelled to take out the garbage to protect her. It's not like me to willingly take on more household chores. "That's me," I said, trying to sound cheerful and unconcerned.

"May I come in?" he said.

I really didn't want him in the apartment, but I more didn't want him out in the hallway broadcasting whatever he was here about to all the neighbors. I sighed, shut the door and took the security chain off and then opened it. "Come on in," I said, feeling as though I should be humming a Grateful Dead song. I do like to get some sleep before I travel.

He stepped in and looked around, then he stuck out his hand. "Officer Ted Goodnight." He had a nice shake. He didn't try to break my hand, but he wasn't weird either. He was, however, tall. I was pretty much staring at the third button down on his uniform shirt.

"You're kidding," I said, shaking his hand.

"No. Not kidding. Why would I be kidding?"

Super. A cop with no sense of humor. At seven thirty A.M. He made up for it in the eye-candy category, though. The peephole had not done him justice. Gotta love that California-dude bronzed skin, and those pouty lips and sunshine-and-surf good looks. And he was solid. His uniform shirt clung to his shoulders and biceps in a way that left no doubt about what kind of shape this guy was in. Plus, he smelled good. I sniffed. I wasn't sure what it was, but it made me think of muffins and cookies.

Norah stumbled from her room in boxers and a tank top, her hair rumpled in a way that reminded me of a hair product ad. "Cops? In the morning?" She looked at me blearily and not a little affronted.

"I'm sure it's nothing, Norah. Go back to bed."

She nodded. "Don't tell him anything. You want Ned's business card?" Norah's cousin Ned had recently passed the bar and was constantly letting us know that he was available to deal with all our legal needs, should we have any. Since he could barely even parallel park his car, I wasn't sure he was who I'd want representing me in anything that came up, but the offer was kind.

"It's all right. I'm sure it's nothing." I shooed her back to her room, then turned back to Surfer Cop. He was cute enough to make me acutely aware of the fact that my hair was still wet and that I hadn't put on any makeup yet. At least I'd brushed my teeth, although maybe high-octane morning breath would get him to keep his distance. "It is nothing, right? I've got a parking ticket that I haven't paid or something?" Please, please, please let it be an unpaid parking ticket or a solicitation to buy a ticket to the annual picnic.

"Not exactly. Where were you at . . ." He pulled a little notebook out of his pocket and flipped it open. "Ten o'clock last night?"

I blinked. Where had I been at ten last night? Oh crap.

I'd been running away from where evil creatures were ripping cholos limb from limb and eating them like overcooked beef *machaca*. "I'm not exactly sure," I said.

"Let me refresh your memory," Officer Goodnight said. "Someone driving your car and looking a heck of a lot like you on the store's security camera made a 911 call from the 7-Eleven on Fruitridge regarding some kind of gang fight a few blocks over."

"Really?" I said. "Are you sure?"

Officer Goodnight all but rolled his pretty blue eyes. "I'm sure."

"Well," I said. "There you have it then."

"Not exactly," he said. "What were you doing there?"

"At the 7-Eleven? Being a good citizen and calling in a problem, obviously." I smiled brightly and cursed my do-gooder inclinations. What did I care about a bunch of gangbangers, right? I only spent the entire night having nightmares about their deaths and felt like there were stones in my chest every time I thought about them. That didn't constitute caring, right?

Now he did roll his eyes. "Ms. Markowitz," he said.

"Melina," I told him. Ms. Markowitz made me feel old. People call my mother Ms. Markowitz.

"Melina, look, I don't care why you were down there. Something pretty heinous happened there, and we're trying to get more information. No one down there is talking. We've got some dead kids and a lot of blood and a lot of people looking really scared. It would be helpful if you could stop playing games and cooperate a little. What exactly did you see?"

I tried to remember exactly what I'd said to the 911 operator. If I stuck to the script maybe I'd get out of this without being hauled off for psychological evaluation. "I saw a bunch of guys fighting. I heard gunshots. I didn't stick around to see or hear anything else. I hightailed it out of there and called you guys. I figured it was your job."

He nodded and jotted something down on his notepad. "You weren't involved with this group of guys you saw in any way?"

"No! Of course not! I'm an innocent bystander. I was driving by and tried to do what was right as a citizen." Who knows? Sometimes people back down in the face of self-righteous indignation. It was worth a shot.

"None of them were, say, your boyfriend?" Officer Goodnight seemed amazingly unimpressed with my righteous indignation. In fact, instead of backing off, he moved a little closer.

"No boyfriend," I said, perhaps a little too quickly. Have I mentioned my total lack of social life? Having a dream about Alex last night was the closest thing I'd had to a date in months and that was only a dream and it was about a guy who was undead. Admittedly, very sexy, but still completely undead. Although I have heard that vampire sex is supposed to be pretty damn good.

Officer Goodnight was trying not to smile. I bet a lot of girls managed to work their lack of a boyfriend into conversations with him. I bet those pouty lips set in that very square-chinned face had women of all ages telling him they were single. He sat down on one of the stools at our breakfast bar. Some of the starch left his shoulders, and he rubbed his hand across the back of his neck. Then he looked up at me, totally nailing me with those bright blue eyes. "Melina, if you're involved with this in some way, we can help. That's what we're here for."

I looked into his eyes and believed that he actually believed what he was saying. He really thought the police were here to protect and serve. Wow. How charmingly naïve. "I'm not involved," I repeated. I wasn't. Whatever was going down out there was none of my Messenger beeswax.

"If you're worried about retaliation, we can protect you." He had a nice voice, low with a touch of sand in it. A little scratchy, but not like a smoker's rasp. He put his hand on my forearm. His touch was warm and strong and very, very human.

I sighed. Pretty much the only human touch I got these days was at the dojo, and that generally didn't feel very good. This felt a little too good coupled with that scent of baked goods he seemed to carry with him. "I don't need protection," I said. Sadly, that was true. I could almost certainly do a better job of protecting myself from what I'd seen last night than any police force in the country, assuming they'd even acknowledge that there could be something like whatever it was I saw marauding around in their streets.

Too bad, though. I liked the way his hand felt on my arm, and I could easily start to imagine what it would feel like other places. Something inside me tingled, and it wasn't just the remnant of last night's dream. Nightmare, I reminded myself. Call it a nightmare.

He thought for a second and then took his hand away, which was a bummer. I wondered what I would have to do to get him to put it back. "Okay, Melina. Whatever you say." He reached into his pocket and pulled out his card. He jotted a few numbers on the back. "Here are all my numbers. Seriously, all of them. You can reach me day or night. If you change your mind, let me know." He stood up and headed back to the door to the apartment.

I glanced down at the card with its police department seal on it. That was enough to remind why I didn't want that hand on me or anywhere near me. Cops were trouble for someone like me. There was no way around it. "There's nothing to change," I said. "I'm telling you the truth."

"Yeah," he said, opening the door, looking faintly disappointed. "Sure. And flying unicorns are going by the window."

I knew that wasn't true. Unicorns can't fly. It's a common misconception. People seem to mix them up with Pegasus all the time.

"Hey." I stopped him. "The reports you're getting. What exactly do they say happened?"

He sighed. "You would not believe it if I told you."

Oh, if he only knew.

5

I MADE IT TO THE DOJO IN TIME TO OPEN IT FOR THE
Little Dragons class, but just barely. I managed to change
into my *gi* and be on the mat as they arrived. Mae teaches
the early morning adult classes during the week and the
Saturday afternoon classes, too, so she often has me take
the Saturday morning Little Dragon class on my own.

I wished she was here now, though. I would have liked
to have told her about what I'd seen the night before and
asked her what it all might mean. I wouldn't mind having a
little advice on what to do about Mr. Yummy Surfer Cop,
too. It would have to wait. Maybe I'd come back later in the
afternoon and tempt her with some turtle candies. Any
attempt at resistance withholding information would be
futile once I waved a combination of chocolate and caramel
in front of her.

The kids streamed in. Little dark-haired boys with cow-
licks sticking straight up. Little blonde girls in ponytails.
Brown kids. White kids. All wearing blazingly white *gi*s

and gap-toothed smiles. The heavy load in my heart began to lighten a little. There was still good in the world somewhere, and it was somewhere that I actually belonged. Like me, the dojo existed at some kind of strange juncture between a lot of different worlds. Like me, it didn't always look pretty and had taken a few knocks. There was no other place like it.

I started them racing across the padded floor doing a worm crawl. Marco Torres was the first one to make it to the mirror and back again to the wall. "Marco," I barked. "Step forward."

Marco did. I put a sticker on his chest. Before I could straighten back up, he threw his arms around my neck. "Thank you, Sensei," he lisped into my ear.

I was enveloped in the scents of green grass, bubblegum toothpaste and little boy. The load in my chest lightened that much more. "Thank you, Marco," I whispered back before I straightened up to teach the rest of the class, hoping that nobody would notice the sudden moisture in my eyes.

I TAUGHT BOTH THE LITTLE DRAGONS CLASSES. WE OFFER beginner and advanced kids' karate at River City. By the time I finished the second class, Mae had arrived. I waited with more patience than I thought I had in me as the kids left, and then I cornered Mae in her office.

The second the door was shut, I spilled everything. The release was incredible. Mae listened, her eyes slightly narrowed as she focused on what I said without interrupting. When I was done, she asked, "They hopped?"

"They hopped. Have you ever heard of anything like that?" I leaned my elbows on her desk, halfway exhausted from my recitation.

She shook her head. "And they had yellow things on their foreheads? And you think you heard bells?"

"Yep."

"And you didn't get kicked in the head during a sparring session recently?" She leaned back in her chair, looking at me with a frown on her face.

"Nope."

"I don't know, Melina. I'll look into it." She stood up and walked out of the office and into the dojo.

There wasn't much more I could ask. Well, there was one more thing. "What do you know about Frank Liu?" I asked, following her out.

"Frank Liu? Pretty much anybody teaching tai chi chuan in this city either learned it from him or from one of his students." Mae sat down on the mat, stretched her feet out as far as they would go to either side of her and laid her face down on the mat.

I sat down next to her. "He's missing," I said.

She sat up. "Frank Liu is missing? Where did you hear that?"

"From my grandmother," I said, stretching my legs in front of me, grabbing onto my toes and pulling my nose down to my knees.

Mae sank back down. "Are you sure she didn't just forget he was going someplace?"

I didn't even bother dignifying that one with an answer. Grandma Rosie may take forty-five minutes to walk two blocks these days, but there's nothing wrong with her mind. "Does he teach anyplace besides the retirement center that you know about?"

"I can find out," Mae offered. "Do you think it's connected to this other stuff?"

"I don't know," I said. "But it seems to me that it's got to be more than a coincidence that I get beat up by a bunch of dudes doing tai chi and the city's most prominent tai chi master is missing."

Mae nodded as best she could with her face pancaked

down on the floor. "I've got his home address if you want
to stop by there."

I looked across the mat and cocked my head at her. "You
couldn't have mentioned that earlier?"

I CALLED FRANK LIU'S HOME NUMBER BEFORE I LEFT
River City. No answer, just as Grandma Rosie had said. I
figured I'd try again later. I stopped for groceries on the way
home. Damn Norah anyway, I had actually developed a
craving for apples. I'd have to find something with high
fructose corn syrup in it to dip them in just to counteract
their innate goodness. I did not luck out in the parking space
lottery on the way home and had to struggle almost three
blocks with my two canvas bags (yes, Norah's influence
again) of items.

Ben was sitting on the front porch with another kid. A
girl. She looked familiar, but I couldn't quite place her at
first. Then it hit me like a bag of Granny Smiths. Sophie.
From the dojo.

"What are you doing here?" I asked when I finally put it
together. It came out sounding harsher than I'd intended it.
I don't like surprises. Generally, I've found they're not good.
In my life, surprises tend to run more toward ninjas jumping
out of trees and kicking my ass than friends jumping out
from behind sofas and giving me presents. Hence my reluc-
tance to welcome surprises with open arms.

Sophie let her hair fall back over the web of scars on her
face. "Ben and I go to the same high school," she said. "I
thought I'd say hello."

Almost no one stopped by to say hello to Ben. His old
friends weren't coming around anymore now that he wasn't
using, and he didn't have any new ones that I knew of. I don't
think it's any easier to switch cliques in high school now
than it was back in my day. If you're a stoner to start with,

a stoner you shall stay in everyone's eyes, even if you never touch weed again and all your stoner friends have dropped you like a hot bong with a broken carb. I'm afraid it left Ben alone most of the time. "I didn't know you were friends," I said, sounding like the lame adult I was.

Ben looked up at me, his hazel eyes slightly narrowed. "Well, we are."

You don't need to tell me twice when my interference isn't wanted. I toted my groceries up the stairs.

I tried Frank Liu's number again. Still no answer.

I started my laundry. My life is one glamour-packed moment after another.

Norah eventually stumbled out of her bedroom and plugged in *Grey's Anatomy* on DVD. Oh, how I wish half the doctors at Sacramento City Hospital were even a quarter as cute as the ones on TV. And half as promiscuous. It would make work so much more fun. The only hunkalicious doc we had was Alex, and while I suspected he was every bit as promiscuous as McSteamy, he tended to make sure his hunting grounds were far away from the hospital. Which was good, right? Hot vampire sex would be bad for me, right? Maybe if I kept telling myself that, I'd actually start believing it. Maybe if I kept telling myself that, I wouldn't dream about it again.

I tried Frank Liu's number again at about the time Mer looked at Der and said, "Choose me."

Still no answer.

"Who you calling?" Norah asked, stretching on the couch like a cat. All that yoga has made her disgustingly limber.

"My grandmother's tai chi instructor. She hasn't seen him in a few days and she's worried about him." There is simply nothing better than the truth. If one can get away with telling the truth or even truthiness, it is always the best choice.

Norah looked profoundly uninterested. "Tanya and I are going out with those guys we met at McClannigan's last night. Wanna come?"

I shook my head. It was a kind offer but not a tempting one. "No thanks."

"Where did you go last night anyway? I don't even remember you leaving."

"Tequila'll do that to you," I observed, truthinessing again. Tequila was a wicked inebriant.

Norah rolled her eyes. "Tell me about it. I swear, nothing but vodka tonight. I need to cleanse."

Ah, the vodka cleanse. That's my girl.

MAE HAD FRANK LIU'S HOME ADDRESS BECAUSE SHE'D been to his house the year before for some kind of big martial arts instructor potluck. I could only imagine. I mean, what would they bring? Flying Sidekick Pasta Salad? Kata Cold-cut Platters?

After Norah left for her date, I got in Grandma Rosie's Buick, hopped on the interstate and headed south to Florin Road. It was already getting dark. Liu lived in the Pocket. It's a little bulge of Sacramento that sticks out into the Sacramento River on the west side and is bordered by I-5 on the east. It's shaped like a *U*, hence the name. It's also a little pocket of residential saneness in a part of Sacramento that's begun to go insane.

I cruised past Liu's house once. It was a single-story cottage. There were no cars in the driveway and the blinds were closed. I couldn't see any light shining from the windows. If someone was home, they would have turned on the lights. It was dark enough for that now.

I went around the block and cruised past again. Nothing changed. I parked two houses down and on the other side of the street and considered my options. There was something to be said for the straightforward approach. I got out, walked up to the front door and rang the doorbell.

Nobody answered. I didn't hear or smell anyone inside the house, human or otherwise. There was a faint something in the air, though, a residue of power and conflict, but nothing I could really nail down.

I waited a few more minutes and pressed the button again. Still nothing.

It had gone from dusk to darkness. I glanced around. Lights had come on in most of the neighboring houses. A few TV sets, too. I went back to my car to contemplate my next move.

It was entirely possible that Frank Liu was only on vacation. Or out to dinner with friends. He may have simply forgotten about his class at the Sunshine Assisted Living Facility and been too busy to return my grandmother's phone calls. People forget about old people all the time. It's practically a national pastime.

It was also possible that something had happened to Mr. Liu and that he could be in trouble. I leaned my head back against the comforting plush of the Buick's headrest. I wished like hell I could figure out whom to go to to straighten this all out. I would have liked nothing more than to dump it in someone else's lap. But whose?

To figure that out, I needed more information. It was possible that some of that information was inside Frank Liu's quiet, darkened, empty house.

I looked around the neighborhood again. More lights had come on in more of the houses. People were home for the evening. The street was quiet. I got out of the Buick, walked in what I hoped was a nonchalant manner down the sidewalk and ducked down through Mr. Liu's side yard to the back of his house. If I was going to indulge in a little B and E, at least I could be discreet about it.

Walking into Frank Liu's backyard was like entering an enchanted garden. A stone path wound between raised beds. I could smell basil and cilantro and green tomatoes. I smelled rich, well-tended dirt. These gardens hadn't gone untended for long. Another few days of Sacramento summer and they'd be dry as a bone. For now, however, the ground still held a faint tinge of moisture. A fountain burbled somewhere, its sound a soothing tone over the whir of the neighbors' air-conditioning units. Faint light spilled from ankle-high lights along the path.

I stepped carefully, trying to be as quiet as possible. I had just gotten to the back door of the cottage when the beam of a high-powered flashlight spotlighted me against the wall.

"Hold it right there."

I took off like Peter Rabbit with Farmer Brown hot on his heels.

WHY HADN'T I HEARD HIM APPROACHING? GRANTED, I'D been near intoxicated by the smell of Frank Liu's garden. Still, I smelled him fine now and heard him even better as he charged toward me.

I broke to his right, jumped over a raised bed that I think might have had zucchini in it, stumbled a little on the path and headed for the back fence. My goal was to get over it, into the neighbor's yard and out onto the street before he got a good look at me. I sent up a little mental prayer. Please, by all that's holy and a few things that are not, don't let the neighbors have a dog. Dogs get one whiff of me and all the hair on the back of their necks stands straight up. It's not a pretty thing.

Now, I'm fast, but I didn't have a lot of maneuvering room and he was blocking most of it. I hit the back fence ahead of him, just not far enough ahead of him. I was halfway over when he grabbed my ankle and yanked me unceremoniously to the ground.

We tumbled in the soft grass. He landed on top of me and knocked most of the air out of my lungs. He was heavy as hell. Still, I managed to hook my ankle around his calf, knock his left hand out from under him and throw him. By that point I knew he had about six inches on me and quite a few pounds. Unfortunately, he also had me by the damn foot again before I could scramble away.

He dragged me back toward him. I scrabbled at the grass, but there was nothing I could catch hold of. I kicked hard and was rewarded with the sound of the air leaving his lungs, but he wouldn't let go of my foot. Tenacious bastard. His grip was hard and unyielding. He wasn't fooling around.

He pinned me beneath him. His chest pressed against my back. His thighs splayed over mine. His breath felt warm at the base of my neck, and, oh my, was that a gun or was he just happy to see me? And did I smell cookies?

My heart was pounding harder than it should have been with what little space I'd had to run. Damn adrenaline. It wasn't always my friend. I took a few deep breaths and tried to still its frantic tattoo. I let myself feel the cool soft grass beneath me. I focused on that in an effort to ignore the heat and hardness of the man's body on top of me. I'd need to be calm and collected to get out of this one.

He must have sensed the relaxation in my muscles because his weight shifted so he wasn't directly on me anymore.

"Turn over slowly," he said.

I did as I was told and got hit in the face with the full blast of a high-powered flashlight. I scooted back, sat up, shielded my eyes with my forearm and squinted into the light.

"Ms. Markowitz?" the voice behind the flashlight said.

I knew that voice. That voice came with the delicious smell of vanilla. "Officer Goodnight?" I said, feeling slightly incredulous.

He aimed the flashlight off to the side and out of my eyes. "What are you doing here?" he asked.

I was still blinking, trying to get my eyes to adjust to the sudden change. I do pretty well in darkness. I don't exactly see like a cat, but pretty damn close. It still takes me a few seconds to correct for big changes like that, though. I blinked for longer than it took me to adjust anyway. There was no need for Office Goodnight to know how good my night vision was. Plus, it gave me a little time to come up with a story. I opted to go with a slightly edited version of the truth, which all good lies are. "My grandmother's tai chi instructor hasn't been around for a while. She sent me over here to see if he was okay."

I heard Officer Goodnight inhale deeply, hold his breath for a second and then let it out with a whoosh. His breath smelled like cinnamon. Cozying up to this guy would be like climbing into a giant sticky bun. Not that I had any intention of cozying up to him. I just really like sticky buns. I know. I know. Put it on the list with margaritas and hot fudge sundaes. My weaknesses are legion. "What's your grandmother's tai chi instructor's name?"

I could hear wariness mixing with the cinnamon in his voice. What a surprise. He didn't trust me. "Frank Liu," I said. I love it when my lies work for me.

He shifted the flashlight back to my face. I ducked away. "If she was so worried about him, why didn't she call the police?"

That actually did make me smile a little. "You seriously want my grandmother to call the police on her tai chi instructor for not showing up for lessons at the retirement home? That would almost put her on a par with Mr. Moore. He's the one who called the cops on the kids who were playing in the pond out front. He wanted them arrested for koi rustling."

"Those fish can be expensive," Officer Goodnight said. He sounded a little defensive.

"Those fish get bought every other week from PETCO. She didn't want to be just another cranky old woman.

Besides, why should she call the police when she has a perfectly good granddaughter who owes her a ton of favors?"

The flashlight dropped and I could make out his features again. Damn, he was pretty. "It just seems kind of weird."

"Weird that my grandmother takes tai chi? I assure you, it's not. It's very popular in the senior population. Everybody who's anybody who might break a hip wants better balance." Perhaps inane chatter would distract him. Maybe I'd be able to waltz out of here yet.

"So why'd you run?" He crossed his arms over his chest. "Or whatever that move was that had you sailing over that zucchini bed. Way to get some air, by the way."

I bit my lip. Come on, Melina. Plausible lie. You can come up with a good one. It took a huge effort not to raise my hand and yell "I've got it!" when I came up with it. "I'm a woman alone at night in an unfamiliar place. You frightened me." Just how deep did that desire to protect and serve go?

His eyes narrowed. He still didn't want to buy it, but the sales pitch was definitely tempting him.

"Look," I said with just the slightest of catches in my voice. "My hands are still shaking. I've had kind of a rough week, you know." I held out my hand. With the right amount of focus, I can get it to tremble really well. It's one of the nice things about having a body that responds to mental commands. I wasn't sure he'd be able to see it in the light from the flashlight, but I threw in a little lip tremble for good measure anyway.

He heaved another sigh. More cinnamon. My stomach growled. "You're seriously here to check up on this Liu guy? You're not just pulling my leg." He sounded a teensy bit wistful. I started to wonder if it was hard to be the cutest patrol officer on the force. Did a lot of people not take him seriously?

"I'm seriously here to check up on the Liu guy." The

sincerity practically dripped from my voice. And why not? It wasn't a lie. Ah, my friend truthiness again.

"Well, come on then," he said. "I don't have all night."

That's when it finally dawned on me. "Hey," I asked. "Why are you here?"

6

"THE NEIGHBORS CALLED." OFFICER GOODNIGHT OFFERED
me a hand.

I took it and he lifted me to my feet without much of an
effort. "Freaking nosey neighbors," I grumbled.

"Gotta love 'em," he said. He grinned and I could see the
white of his teeth in the darkness. His mother must have
been an oral-hygiene freak, too.

"I was here about ten seconds before you showed up." I
dusted the grass off my jeans.

He shrugged. "They were already worried. He hadn't
taken in his newspaper for a couple of days. He usually tells
someone when he's leaving town. Apparently he pays the
neighbor kid two doors down to water his garden and stuff.
They were surprised he hadn't called."

"So what now?" I asked. If he hadn't been here, I would
have continued with my discreet B-and-E plan. I'm not great
with a lockpick, but I can shimmy through a second-story
window like nobody's business. It's kind of a catlike thing.
Maybe that's why dogs don't like me.

"We knock on the door and do a wellness check on Mr. Liu." Goodnight hitched up his pants and started toward the house.

"A what?" I squeaked. Wellness checks with my doctor generally require me to have my feet in stirrups. I thought this guy was cute, but I also thought he could at least take me to dinner and a movie first. I'm desperate, but I do have certain standards. Usually. I could probably be talked into making an exception. The dream that woke me up that morning still had my engine revving a little high.

"We'll knock on the door. See if he answers. Maybe take a look in the windows and see if anything's out of order. We already know the neighbors haven't seen him."

That was a big relief. I'd shaved my legs this morning but not all the way up, if you know what I mean. "He's not going to answer the door," I said, not moving. "I already tried that."

He looked over his shoulder at me. The moonlight shone on his blond hair. "Okay. Let's peek in the windows, then."

Ooh. I loved this guy! I trotted after him to the big picture windows across the back of the house.

I looked inside and my heart sank.

Frank Liu's place looked as though it had been hit by a cyclone. Wherever he'd gone, he hadn't gone without a fight.

OFFICER GOODNIGHT SWEPT ME BEHIND HIM WITH ONE arm as if to shield me from the sight of Liu's trashed living room. I can't remember the last time anyone tried to shield me from seeing something. Between the horror shows that routinely came through the ER and being a Messenger, I'd seen quite a bit. I wondered what he would have done if he'd been there when those creatures with the Post-it notes tacked to their foreheads had made the Norteños into their personal smorgasbord. Come to think of it, I wish he had been there. I would have liked not to have seen that.

He pulled his radio off his belt and started to talk.

"What are you doing?" I grabbed his arm and pulled the radio away from his mouth.

He looked down at me, brow furrowed. "I'm calling this in. I'm not sure I've seen too many clearer signs of foul play."

How could I have forgotten? Goodnight was a cop. He was doing cop stuff. What was I thinking? I needed to get out of here, not indulge in doctor-and-naughty-patient fantasies.

I was supposed to be doing Messenger stuff, except in this case, I wasn't sure exactly what that was. If my envelope from Alex was in the mess of broken lamps and overturned furniture that now filled Liu's living room, I doubted that I would find it with the cops watching. Without that, I didn't have a delivery to make.

Whatever had happened to Liu, he was a man, a 'Dane, a regular human. Surely it was the job of the very regular, very human, very 'Dane, very male cop in front of me to work on that.

"What is it, Ms. Markowitz?" he asked. He dropped his arm, but he was standing so close. I know I could have taken a step back, increased the distance between us so at least I wouldn't feel the heat of his skin on my own or practically hear the measured beat of his heart.

I sighed. "Melina. Please call me Melina."

"Only if you call me Ted." Those Chiclet white teeth flashed again.

"Ted," I said, "is there any way I could talk you into giving me just a few minutes lead before you call in your buddies?"

The grin disappeared. "Is there a reason you don't want to be seen by the police, Melina?"

Well, yeah, about a million of them, but none that I could explain to Mr. Cookie Breath. "I'm just nervous. You know, after last night and everything."

He nodded a little. "I guess I could see that."

"It's been a rough few days," I continued. Maybe if I could play on those protector instincts of his, I'd be able to walk out of here without giving a statement or ending up down at police headquarters. "It's not like you don't know where to find me, right? I just want to go home."

I swayed a little bit on my feet to give my words a little physical backup, and Goodnight reached out and caught me. Yep. The dude had a bona fide hero complex. He steadied me, his hands strong and large, easily encompassing my forearms. Then he pulled me to him.

Now, that I hadn't expected. My face was pressed against his wide strong chest, my stomach to his stomach, my hips to his hips. He was warm and solid, and his hand was at the small of my back, making me want to arch into him. "It's going to be all right," he murmured into my hair.

What the hell? Was he trying to . . . comfort me?

"Don't be frightened. We'll figure out what happened here. I won't let you get hurt." He held me for a moment longer, not even making an attempt to grab my ass while he did so, even though his hand was just a few agonizing inches away.

I didn't know what to do so I went with it. I let my body soften against his. Heat spread up through my body so fast that my knees really did feel a little bit weak. I clung a little tighter to him.

He groaned and pushed me away. "I can't do this right now. I've got to call this in, but I'll walk you to your car first. I'll tell the guys that I didn't see anyone back here, that whoever was back here was gone by the time I came."

I brushed my hair out of my eyes. "Thanks," I managed to whisper.

"My pleasure." The grin was back. "I just want one thing in return."

Oh, great. Nothing was ever free, was it? "What's that?"

"Can I call you?"

———

I WAS EXHAUSTED BY THE TIME I GOT HOME. OF COURSE, there were no good parking places close by. Three blocks away, I finally found a space big enough for me to parallel park the Buick. I'd had next to no sleep, and while I don't need a lot of sleep, I do need some. I am, after all, human. Or, at least, I think so. I'm never quite sure.

At first, my kind used to sort of spontaneously develop in places where we were needed. The best example I can give you is the sheephead. At least, that's how Mae explained it to me back when I was ten.

The sheephead is a fish indigenous to California. They're all born female. Once the need for a male arises, one of the sheephead switches teams, as it were. Scientists don't know for sure how the sheephead know to change, or what about that one fish makes it the one to change. They just do.

We don't really know why I was the one to become a Messenger twenty-some years ago. We're pretty sure the whole drowning thing had a lot to do with it, except I'm not the only girl in the Sacramento area who's had a near-death experience. Nor do I know exactly what was going on that made a Messenger necessary in Sacramento back in 1985, but something must have.

So why me? Why was I the one who got her life turned inside out and had to be a goblin gofer? What was there about me that made me the one who had to be a Messenger? It was another question Mae said I'd figure out when I was ready to know the answer. I hate it when she goes all Zen on me. Sometimes I think she does it on purpose just to irritate the crap out of me.

Regardless, I wanted my bed. I dragged myself up the stairs to my apartment, feeling each and every step, and focused solely on getting my sorry ass into something flannel and cozy. My key was already in the lock when I felt the hum. Someone—some thing—was in the apartment. Oh

God. Norah. I slammed the door open, crouched in the door frame, ready to fight. I wasn't watching any more death. I certainly wasn't going to watch something attack Norah.

Norah and Alexander Bledsoe looked up from where there were seated very cozily on the futon couch. Alex smiled and held up a glass full of red liquid. "Care for a drink, Melina?" he asked.

Norah smiled at me woozily. I glared at Alex. "That goddamn well better be wine," I said.

"YOU INVITED HIM IN," I SAID TO NORAH IN THE KITCHEN. I actually more hissed it. I knew she had. He couldn't have been here in my apartment otherwise. It's a handy tidbit of vampire lore to remember. They can't come in unless you invite them. Sadly, they're very charming when they feel like it and get themselves invited to the most amazing places and events. Now I was going to have to figure out how to uninvite a vampire into your home. Thank heavens for the Internet and old episodes of *Buffy*.

"He said he was your friend." Norah swayed slightly. "He said he needed to talk to you."

"Uh-huh." I crossed my arms over my chest. This must have been how my mother felt when I came home drunk from that party at Cynthia Clark's in tenth grade. I could see about a million consequences, all of which Norah was oblivious to.

"Plus," she said, giggling, "he's cute. Way cute."

It wasn't like I didn't know that. I suppose I should have warned Norah about him way before this, but seriously how do you tell someone that a vampire might stop by to chat and that you shouldn't let him in. I didn't like how glazed she looked right now. "Did he, uh, do anything to you?" Like bite your neck or your wrist or something? I added mentally. Another terribly awkward question.

Norah snorted, a completely out of character and very

unladylike noise for her. "No. I did have a few too many martinis earlier tonight though. I think I'm going to bed now." So much for the vodka cleanse.

"Good idea," I told her. "Fabulous, even."

Norah headed to her room, giving Alex a little finger wave as she passed by him. He blew her a kiss. I rolled my eyes.

I listened to her door click closed. "What did you do to her?"

Alex held his hands up as though I were robbing him. "Absolutely nothing. Vodka is strong stuff. People shouldn't mess with it if they can't handle it."

I rubbed my hand over my eyes. I was so tired. "What are you doing here?"

He raised his eyebrows. "Is that any way to greet a friend?"

"I'm not sure what we are, but I don't think it's friends," I said. I walked into the living room and curled up in the papasan chair across from the couch. I thought longingly of my bed. "I'm exhausted, Alex. I want to go to bed."

It took a while for the smile to spread completely across his face. He leaned back and crossed his long legs in front of himself. "Please, don't let me stop you. Would you like me to tuck you in?"

Another night, it would have been funny. Maybe even tempting. Tonight? Not so much. Between the ninja ass-kicking I'd taken, the gangbanger gore fest I'd witnessed and the run-in with Officer Goodnight I'd just returned from, all I wanted was the peace and solace of my bed. Alone. I looked blankly at Alex and didn't say anything.

He might have been undead, but Alex wasn't stupid. He set down his wineglass on a coaster on the coffee table. I wondered how many centuries it took to train a man to use a coaster. I'm betting my brother will have to be undead to have enough time to learn to use one. "I wanted to check on the envelope. Did Aldo say anything to you about it?"

"About that envelope," I said. "What the hell was in it?"

Alex raised an eyebrow. "You don't usually want to know."

"Yes, well, ninjas don't usually drop out of trees, kick the crap out of me and take off with whatever you've given me."

Alex sat bolt upright. "So you didn't make the delivery?"

I shook my head.

"Ninjas took it from you?"

I nodded my head. "Yes. And by the way, I'm fine, thanks. Just a little bumped and bruised."

Alex ran his hand through his hair. Okay. Definitely no product. "What kind of ninjas?"

"A weird kind. They were doing tai chi."

Alex threw his head back and asked the ceiling, "What did they do? Balance you to the ground?"

Wow. Maybe it was all the vampire pheromones in the air, but the strong column of his throat looked really tempting.

"No, as a matter of fact, they repelled-the-monkey'd me. And it hurt." I truly had no dignity left whatsoever.

"Pardon me. Who uses tai chi as self-defense anymore?"

"Apparently, Taoist priests," I said. "And furthermore, there is something seriously trippy going on down at the Bok Kai Temple."

I explained what I'd seen last night to Alex. He started to gnaw at the cuticle on his thumb. "They hopped," he repeated.

"They hopped," I confirmed.

"They had long yellow pieces of paper hanging off their foreheads, and you thought you heard bells ringing."

"I know. It sounds crazy. They looked like superlong Post-it notes. Maybe I was hallucinating. Maybe it was all the stress of seeing people getting killed. I mean, since when does 3M make tools for the supernatural?"

"No. There were bells and yellow pieces of paper. It's exactly what I was afraid of. We have to go talk to Aldo right now."

"I'm not going anywhere right now, but to my bed. Alone. I need to rest."

"This can't wait, Melina. Aldo has to know about it."

"Last I saw, your mouth worked just fine. You go tell Aldo about it."

Alex sighed and slumped back on the futon couch. "Yeah, about that. Remember I told you Aldo and I had a little falling-out. It's probably not completely safe for me to go on my own for a little tête-à-tête with Aldo. He'd probably dust me as soon as he looked at me."

"And this is my problem why?"

"It's your problem because you failed to make your delivery, Messenger. Now get your ass out of the papasan chair before I decide to show you exactly how well this mouth can work." Vampires are perfectly capable of talking in completely human tones that sound like everybody else. They also have a particularly persuasive voice they can use when they don't feel like being messed with. It's a little like that thing Liam Neeson did in *Star Wars* with the Jedi voice. Alex had just used his Jedi vampire voice on me.

I found I'd risen out of the chair without even being aware that I was doing it. "Crap," I said. "But I better be back here and in bed by two or you are going to have to explain to the Little Dragons why I can't teach class tomorrow."

"It's a deal," he said, back to his regular voice. "I'll drive. You don't look so hot."

"Thanks," I said, following him out of the apartment. I wished I could say the same for him.

IT WAS THE SECOND TIME I'D BEEN TO ALDO'S NEIGHBOR-hood in forty-eight hours. It must be some kind of record.

Aldo's house probably hadn't seen this much action since bell-bottoms were in style the first time around.

Alex pulled his guard red Porsche 944 Turbo up right in front. We were not exactly inconspicuous.

"Aldo hates it when we park in front of his house," I said from where I was sunk down so far in the leather seat that I could barely see over the dashboard.

"All the more reason to do it," Alex said, smiling.

I shook my head. "Do you want his help with this thing or do you want to piss him off?"

Alex thought for a moment before opening the door and angling his long legs out of the low-slung sports car. "A little of both."

I leaned back in the seat. It was even more comfortable than Grandma's Buick. I felt actually embraced by the leather. "Pull around to the 7-Eleven and park. I'll show you where the ninjas attacked me."

"Ooh, Melina," he cooed. "You know just what to say to make a guy putty in your hands."

If only.

He pulled around the corner, we got out and I directed him to where I'd been attacked. "Smart," he said. "Look at the sight lines. You can't see this spot from any of the stores or houses on this block."

I looked around. I hadn't considered that. "They were lucky, too, though, that no one was around."

Alex shrugged. "Midmorning on a weekday. It was a calculated risk, but most people would be at work at that time of day."

True enough.

"But how would they know I even had something they wanted? Or that I would take it here?" I stopped in the middle of the sidewalk, questions multiplying in my head faster than I could ask them.

Alex stopped, too, and turned around to face me. He

stuck his hands in his pockets and sighed. "My guess is that they had been shadowing you since you left the hospital, Melina."

I shook my head. "Nobody was following me. I would have sensed it. I'm sure. I can tell when you're within fifty yards of me, Bledsoe. I can't imagine that tai chi ninjas could have shadowed me for hours without me noticing."

"They're just men, Melina. Men with spiritual power and physical prowess, but still just men. They wouldn't have tripped your freaky sensors." Alex actually looked apologetic. "I should probably have warned you."

"Ya think?" I said, hands on my hips. I looked around the parking lot. It held pretty much the same kind of beater cars that it had held earlier. No shiny SUVs, though. I dropped my hands to my side in defeat. They had been shadowing me. How many SUVs had I seen between the hospital and here? I wasn't even sure. I knew there'd been one in this parking lot, though, and one by my apartment earlier, too. Could they have been the same ones that had driven the hopping things down to gang territory?

"Come on," Alex said. "This is fascinating, but we need to talk to Aldo."

I contemplated holding my ground and arguing more. It was definitely tempting. Bledsoe so deserved it. Why send me out with something that someone would try to take without a little advance notice? I'm not saying I could have taken the ninjas even if I'd been prepared, but I'd at least been able to hold my ground for more than thirty seconds. Bledsoe was already walking, though, and I suppose there was no use crying over spilled milk. Or, in this case, my own spilled blood. So as tempting as it was to watch him walk away— and the way his ass looked in those jeans made it very tempting indeed—I ran a few steps and caught up with him.

We walked the two blocks back to Aldo's house, marched up to the front door, rang the bell and waited. Then we waited some more. I felt the starch leaving my spine. If I were a flower—an ironic lily or a daisy—I would have wilted. "We should have called first, Alex," I said. "He's not home." My mother always says to call first, that dropping by unannounced is rude. I really should listen to her more often.

Occasionally, when I let myself contemplate it, I have to admit that I wouldn't be in this mess of a life if I'd listened to my mother at age three. Consequences are a bitch.

"He's home. I can smell him. I know you can sense him, too," Alex said. "Be patient."

He was right. I could feel the buzz in my flesh. Of course, I already had the buzz in more ways than one from standing next to Alex. It was stronger now, though. I swayed a little. I really was exhausted. An eternity later, the door swung open and Aldo stood in the frame in all his glory. He had on a purple velvet suit with a yellow shirt and an ascot. He looked like an extra from an Austin Powers movie. Alex winced. My eyes still felt seared from seeing the earlier massacre. Aldo barely registered. "Alex. Melina. What a pleasure. How may I help you?" he said, standing aside as though to make room for us to enter.

It was a good line, but I noticed he wasn't inviting Alex in. I also noticed the way he was staring at my throat. There was no way I was waltzing in there without somebody to watch my back, even if it was another vampire. Without an invitation, Alex would be stuck outside.

"We have a problem, Aldo. As master of the Sacramento Valley Seethe and a Council representative, I thought you should know about it," Alex said, his hands jammed into the pockets of his jeans.

"Really? You think there's something I should know about? Something I should inform the Council about?" Aldo looked off in the distance. "Were you not the very person who told Magdalena that I wouldn't know AB negative blood if it came in a labeled bottle? And that the Council was as effective as a vampire with gingivitis?"

I snorted but quickly tried to cover it with a pretend cough. "Allergies," I said. "I think it's the jasmine."

Aldo put on a look of mock concern. I say *mock* because I knew Aldo was never concerned about anything that didn't directly relate to Aldo.

"I may have said something along those lines," Alex admitted. "I was trying to impress Magdalena. You know how it is. You start to run your mouth and the most amazing things come out of it."

I looked over at Alex. He was no more concerned with impressing Magdalena than he was with impressing Aldo. He hated the entire vampire hierarchy and the Council, too, and steadfastly had as little to do with it as he could get away with. If he hadn't been so useful to all of them in the ER at the city hospital, they would have probably dusted his extremely fine ass decades ago.

Alex was like an undead canary in a coal mine, an early warning system for the vampires. He knew more about what was happening in the city than almost any other vampire and reported back on it when it started to get dangerous for the Seethe, who then reported it to the Council. In turn, they left him mainly alone. Mainly, but not entirely.

Aldo sighed. "What do you have to tell me, Alex?"

Alex nudged me. "Tell Aldo what you saw last night."

I did my recitation again. I described the hopping creatures with their long fingernails and their long yellow pieces of paper. I told how they'd massacred a group of young Latino men.

"And?" Aldo said when I was done.

"And I think they're *kiang shi*," Alex said. If we'd been in the movies, the music would have gone all ominous at that moment. Sadly, we had no musical accompaniment, and I had a feeling that neither Alex nor Aldo would appreciate me humming something. Wow. I really needed sleep.

"Kiang shi?" I looked over at him. "What the hell are *kiang shi*?"

"Chinese vampires," Alex answered.

Aldo shook his head. "They're not vampires. I'll concede the Chinese thing."

"They're undead. They drink blood." Alex was counting points out on his long, elegant fingers. "They'll turn to dust if they're out in the daylight or if they get staked in the heart. They're vampires."

"They're much more like zombies than they are like vampires." Aldo started to retreat into his house. "They have no intellect, no real will of their own. They're nothing but a murderous animal unless someone is controlling them. Then they're nothing more than someone's slave. They have nothing to do with us."

Alex started to follow him, pressing his attack, but came up short at the threshold. "They're stirring up trouble in the city. They've attacked before. I found one of their talismans clutched in someone's hand in the ER yesterday."

"Whose hand?" Aldo asked, seeming mildly interested.

Alex paused. "I'm not precisely sure. The arm it was on was no longer attached to anyone's body." He crossed his own arms over his chest.

I looked over at Alex. He shrugged. My stomach rolled. "Is that what I was carrying here earlier? Something you took out of a hand that was on the end of a severed arm?" I demanded. Why? Why did my mother have to have such a clean pool? I know she would have let a little mold grow if she'd known what she was getting me into.

"Pretty much," he said, inspecting his fingernails as if it were nothing out of the ordinary.

"Gross!" This was why I never wanted to know what was in the boxes and envelopes I delivered. I was much happier when I didn't know. Ignorance is totally bliss in these instances. I had the sudden urge to plug my ears with my fingers and sing "la, la, la" really loud.

Alex shook his head. "Get over it."

"What was it anyway?" I deserved to know that at least.

"I told you, it was a talisman. Though when I gave it to you, I wasn't sure. I knew the markings on it were in blood, chicken and not human. I knew it had some power." Alex continued to look as if he were talking about a recipe for a really good mojito.

"So you just scooted it over to me out of the shadows and sent me off with it?" I was starting to get really steamed now.

"What did you want me to do? Wrap it up and put a bow on it?" Apparently, Alex was starting to feel the heat as well.

"Are you two finished?" Aldo sighed.

"No, we're not finished," Alex said. "I want to know what we're going to do about it."

"Nothing." Aldo shrugged. "I told you. It doesn't have anything to do with us. They're not vampires, not like you and me. They're not my problem. It's a 'Dane thing."

"They're likely to become your problem if whoever's controlling them keeps this up." Alex bounced a little on the balls of his feet, like a fighter ready to jump into the center of the ring.

Aldo crossed his arms across his velvety fabulousness. "I doubt that."

"Oh yeah?" Alex said. "Do you remember how bad things were back in 1978? With Richard Trenton Chase? He wasn't really a vampire either as I recall."

"Who?" I said. "Richard Trenton what?"

"Chase," Alex and Aldo said in unison, and then they exchanged sour looks. I thought about yelling "jinx," but they didn't seem in the mood.

"Richard Trenton Chase was a seriously disturbed young man who decided that his own blood would turn to dust if he didn't drink other people's blood. He killed six people over four days. They caught him, but it created an anti-vampire hysteria in Sacramento that had us all ducking and covering for months," Alex explained.

"Longer than that," Aldo said with a sigh.

"So why don't you think we need to do something about these *kiang shi*?" Alex all but stamped his foot.

Aldo rolled his eyes and leaned against the doorjamb. "What would you have me do?"

"You could talk to the Council about it," I suggested. I mean, that's what they were there for, right? To keep the peace among the various factions that lived here. I mentioned already how many people came to Northern California during the Gold Rush. I mentioned, too, that they brought their gods and their demons with them. Well, all those various things didn't always get along, to put it mildly.

Let me put it this way, to paraphrase Tom Lehrer, the werewolves hate the vampires, the vampires hate the brujas and everyone hates a golem.

When a vampire hates or a werewolf hates . . . well, things tend to get violent. The American frontier was already a bloody and brutal place. The rivalries and feuds between the various supernatural factions had begun to make it noticeably bloodier.

Then someone got the bright idea to create the Council. Supposedly the Council exists to mediate between the different groups that live here. The idea is that if they're not all fighting each other, they'll be less noticeable to the general population, which is generally speaking a good thing for the continued health and well-being of my clientele. Remember the Salem witch trials? Nobody wanted a repeat of that kind of crap.

"Do you honestly think those things have a representative on the Council?" Aldo asked me, looking as if he were talking to a not particularly cute child. "It'd be like sending a rabid dog to a mediation. It simply wouldn't work."

"Isn't there somebody who can speak for them? Someone, I don't know, Chinese?" I asked.

This time Alex snorted a little. "It's not exactly like a United Nations over there."

I was not privy to the makeup of the Council or how representatives are chosen. So I didn't have much to say to that. "There has to be somebody to speak for them."

Aldo turned away from me. "I'll bring it up at the next Council meeting. I doubt anyone will be interested."

I looked over at Alex, who said nothing. His clenched jaw was communicative enough.

Aldo laughed. "From what Melina's saying, it sounds like someone's going after gangs. Perhaps we should give them a medal. Other than that, I see no reason for me to do anything about some blood-sucking zombies ripping limbs off soulless drug pushers."

I felt like I was hearing an echo of Paul's words last night. It has nothing to do with the pack, so it's not the pack's problem. It has nothing to do with the Council, so they would do nothing as well. It's rare that werewolves and vampires agree on anything. Perhaps I should have been grateful for this moment of peace between two groups who often made the supernatural world very uncomfortable with their tensions. There's a lot more out there than werewolves and vampires, but they represent two very large and powerful groups and can make life very unpleasant for everyone else when they're not getting along.

"Now, if that's all?" Aldo tilted his head to one side and smiled.

Alex stared at him for a few moments and then dropped his eyes to the ground. "That's all, Aldo. At least, for now. I doubt this is finished."

"Oh, it's finished all right," Aldo said, and then curtly added, "Good night," before closing the door.

I looked over at Alex, whose gaze was still riveted on his shoes. Finally, he took a deep breath and straightened. "Come on, Melina. I'll take you home. You'll be able to get your beauty rest."

He actually looked sad. I wondered if he was worried about possibly facing some bigger dragons in the near future.

———

ALEX WAS AS GOOD AS HIS WORD AND I WAS TUCKED INTO
bed by two A.M. I'm not sure the bed had ever felt so deli-
ciously flat and undemanding. No. It was more than undemanding. It was supportive. I'm not sure, but I think I might
actually want to date my bed. Sadly, it doesn't seem to have
much competition these days.

Which is not to say that Alex didn't make one last stab
when he dropped me off, but I could tell it was halfhearted
at best. He seemed oddly deflated by his encounter with
Aldo. I wasn't sure whether it was because he truly was
worried about limbless gangbangers or because he simply
didn't like Aldo to get the best of him. Or some vampirish
combination of the above. Whatever. If the pack didn't think
they had to do anything about it and the Seethe didn't think
they did either, why should a poor Messenger worry her
pretty little head about it? Especially when it was being so
lovingly cradled by her pillow.

7

I STARED AT THE HEADLINE EMBLAZONED ACROSS THE Sunday issue of the *Sacramento Bee*: "Gang Warfare Erupts."

I'd been looking forward to the Sunday sudoku and instead got blindsided by the front page's forty-eight-point type proclaiming Sacramento a war zone between the Norteños and the Black Dragons.

"What is it?" Norah asked from across the table. "You look like you've seen a ghost."

Usually it makes me laugh when Norah says that. She's been with me when I've seen ghosts and hasn't ever noticed. Once, I even watched her walk right through the faded spirit of the little old man who shows up now and then in the garden of the house two doors down. She was completely oblivious. This time, however, I knew what she meant. I felt as if all the blood had run out of my face.

Apparently, while I'd been practically mainlining the scent of Ted Goodnight in Frank Liu's backyard, the Norteños had decided to commit what the public information officer of the Sacramento Police Department called a retaliatory strike for recent attacks—which had to refer to the dudes in the black Lincoln Navigators and the *kiang shi*. The Norteños had struck deep in Black Dragon territory, mowing down at least four young Asian men and hitting two innocent bystanders with stray bullets.

"This has to stop," I said to Norah.

She took the paper from me and scanned the story. "It's a flare-up. They'll make it settle down. You know these things run in cycles."

She was right. They did seem to run in cycles. Gang activity would get out of hand. The police would crack down. Things would settle down for a bit, then something would make it flare up again. The police would crack down again, and the whole thing would start over.

This, however, wasn't the normal cycle and I knew it. I knew damn well that the Black Dragons weren't responsible for the attacks on the Norteños. I wasn't precisely sure who the men in the black SUVs were, but I knew they weren't from a typical Sacramento gang, and whatever the story was behind the *kiang shi*, they certainly weren't typical gang weapons.

Still, I suppose the Norteños had to hit back somewhere. The black SUV guys were clearly Asian. They must have decided to pick one of the more active Sacramento Asian gangs and hit 'em hard. At least they'd be sending a message.

The problem was, the message hadn't gone to anyone who had earned it. The Black Dragons weren't going to take what they would see as an unprovoked attack lying down. They would strike back, too. Pretty soon, the entire south section of the city would be unsafe. The blood of rash and foolish young men would flow in the streets. How many innocent bystanders would be lying bleeding beside them? Even one was too many, and it wasn't likely to stop there.

Whoever had attacked the Norteños using the *kiang shi*

had to know that the violence was going to snowball. Had they maybe planned it that way all along?

Something big was going on and no one seemed to care. I tried not to care either. Unfortunately, I kept having a mental replay of the Chinese vampires ripping the gang-bangers apart and feasting on their flesh.

It's hard not to care about that.

BY EIGHT THIRTY P.M. ON SUNDAY NIGHT, I WAS BACK outside the Bok Kai Temple on I Street. The sun would set by nine. If the dudes in the black Navigators were going to take the *kiang shi* on another outing into gang territory, they'd do it by nine thirty. I was hoping I could follow them, figure out a little more about what was going on and still make it to work by eleven when my shift started.

I slunk low in the Buick and watched the front door. The hand-lettered sign about the building being closed for reno-vations still hung there. I wished I could tell whether or not the door was locked, but I didn't want to risk anyone seeing me trying it. I'd made myself conspicuous enough already, thank you very much. Instead, I left the Buick on the street, walked down the block and cut back through the alley that ran behind the buildings on I Street. The Navigators had gone behind the building to load the *kiang shi* on Friday night. I figured there must be some sort of loading-dock entrance back there—an entrance that was likely to be as discrete and accessible for me as it had been for them.

The alley was already in shadow. The garbage in the Dumpsters that lined its length had spent the day baking in the sun, however, and the musky scent of the river nearby was overpowered by the smell of rotting garbage. I breathed shallowly through my mouth. It didn't help much.

The Dumpster behind the Bok Kai Temple was nearly empty. Whatever was going on in the temple didn't create a lot of garbage, apparently. I was grateful for that since the best way to get to the partially opened, second-floor window that I could see from the alley involved climbing onto the Dumpster and then making a short ascent up.

I was also grateful that I'd decided to show up wearing capri-length sweats and a tank top and had left the little flowered skirt and the twinset that I planned on wearing to work in a bag on the backseat of the Buick. Wall work in a skirt is just so unladylike. Plus, it always makes me feel good about myself when I've dressed appropriately. It happens so rarely.

I lowered the Dumpster's lid as quietly as possible, then stood with my back to the Dumpster, grasped the rail and did a reverse somersault onto it. The maneuver looks harder than it is, not that anyone was looking. Or, at least, I hoped no one was. I picked my way across the Dumpster to the wall, crouched low and launched myself at the window, catching it by its lower sill. I pulled myself up onto my elbows, the rough concrete scraping my forearms.

The window squeaked as I pushed it the rest of the way open and shimmied through. I dropped to the floor in a crouch, looking for something to hide behind in case someone came to investigate the noise. I was in an office of some kind. There was a battered metal desk that had clearly seen better days, a wheeled chair and a few metal filing cabinets. There weren't many choices for hiding places. I slid between the filing cabinet and the wall and hoped that if someone came, they wouldn't come all the way into the room.

I tried to slow my quickened breath as I listened for anyone's approach. It was only a few seconds before I heard soft footsteps in the hall. The door creaked open. I shut my eyes and crossed my fingers. If whoever it was stayed in the doorway, I'd be okay.

If they didn't . . . well, it'd be a toss-up as to who was going to end up okay and who wasn't. Now that I knew what to expect, I was pretty sure I'd know how to deal with the tai chi moves. But I didn't want to lay out whoever was there;

I was much more interested in finding out what they were up to than in beating the crap out of them. I am in many ways much more of a lover than a fighter. Still, if it came down to a choice, I was definitely going to choose me even if that meant fighting.

I could hear whoever it was in the doorway breathing. I smelled a faint scent of oranges and incense. I willed my body into stillness, finding the core of quiet deep within myself. I don't know how long I was there, but I heard the door creak shut again and the footsteps receded down the hallway.

I let out the breath I'd been holding.

I crept out of the office, careful to keep the door from making any noise that would bring back whoever was patrolling the place. Because that's what they were doing: patrolling. Now that I was inside, I could hear the footsteps as they passed back and forth in the space below. Each step made a faint slapping sound. Whoever was down there was barefoot and their feet were a little bit sweaty. I thought of the terrified young priest I'd encountered on Friday.

The doorway of the office opened onto a short hallway. I crept along it, pressed to the wall, as if that would stop anyone from seeing me if they came down the hallway. Somehow, it made me feel better to have the wall at my back. I tried to assure myself that it was a tactical maneuver. I was making sure no one could sneak up behind me. It had nothing to do with the fact that whatever was in the main hall below me was making the hair on my neck rise up and my flesh vibrate with the intensity of a Magic Fingers massage on a motel bed.

I slid as silently as I knew how down the hall. The smell of the river seemed to grow with every step. The sense of something old and tinged with a malignant magic grew with it. I swallowed hard and forced myself to keep creeping toward where the hallway opened onto the sanctuary.

It wasn't so much that I was scared of whatever was in

the sanctuary. At least, not really scared. There are repercussions if you hurt a Messenger. It's one of the few rules governing the different groups that make up the Council. I'm supposed to be protected.

I like that part of my job.

Unfortunately, following rules requires a being to be somewhat sentient. Whatever those things were that came out of the temple on Friday night, I kind of doubted they were sentient at all, let alone sentient enough to be aware of the rules protecting Messengers. I especially doubted that the guys in the black Navigators knew about the rules. They looked like the kind of guys who were used to making their own rules. They also looked like the kind of guys for whom protecting little white girls from harm was not a high priority.

I was to the end of the hall now. A wash of light from the high-ceiling sanctuary splashed at my feet. I skirted around it, sticking to the shadows, and slipped into the visitor's gallery that overlooked the main sanctuary. Down below me, the same priest who had shooed me away on Friday night stood nervously in the middle of the torn-apart space. I settled into an alcove that put me into even deeper shadow and waited.

The vibrations coming from the floor beneath me created a steady buzz in the back of my head. It echoed in my skull like the white noise of a television on a nonexistent station, all angry static and no sense at all.

While I waited, I started to wonder about what I was really doing there. I knew my role in the grand scheme of things and it did not include getting in the middle of a fight that wasn't mine. The problem was that I couldn't seem to figure out whose fight it was. If I could just decipher that little part of the problem, I'd know where to deliver my message of gloom and doom. I shifted a little and then had to stifle a sneeze from the dust I'd stirred around me.

In the end, I was no better than the vamps or the wolves.

I didn't want this to be my problem. I wanted to hand it off to someone else. Maybe Ted Goodnight. He'd be a possibility if I could determine who the dudes in the Navigators were.

I didn't have much more time to ponder. I had apparently timed my visit well. In less than forty minutes, I heard cars pulling up behind the temple. The men in black suits with their neatly combed jet black hair filed into the sanctuary, herding in front of them a group of men in orange robes. The robed men looked nervous. The suited men looked calm. One was even smoking a cigarette.

"Good evening, George," said the suited man who had walked in first.

"Good evening, Henry," replied the young priest who had kicked me out of the temple on Friday.

"How is my brother tonight?" Henry said. His tone was fake jovial, the kind that always sets my teeth on edge. Any second now he was going to ask if George was working hard or hardly working.

"I am well," George said. "Please stop this."

His voice was so even, so calm. Still, I could hear the urgency in his plea.

"You know I can't do that, brother," Henry answered. "I have a lot riding on this now, and it's all working out better than I could possibly have dreamed."

"Henry, these are people's lives that you are taking." George's voice had dropped almost to a whisper.

Henry snorted. "Lives? What lives? Do you know what the average life expectancy is of one of those cockroaches that I'm exterminating? Twenty-seven years. And most of that will be spent stealing, raping, lying and dealing drugs. That's not a life."

George's head bowed. "It is not our place to judge which lives are worthy enough to keep and which are not."

Henry shook his head and leaned against one of the intricately carved pillars that soared up to the ceiling of the sanctuary. "You are too soft, George. You always have been. That's your problem."

"And you, Henry, what is your problem?" George countered.

From up in my post, I could feel the rise in tension between the two brothers, but before Henry could answer, things began to stir in the dug-up areas of the sanctuary. I felt them more than I saw or heard them. The buzzing in my head had been reaching a crescendo during Henry and George's exchange. It was so loud now that I wanted to grab my head and hold my hands over my ears. As if that would help. I knew it wouldn't make any difference, but that didn't mean I didn't have the urge. I knew the *kiang shi* were on the move.

The smell of the river grew stronger, and I saw a greenish hand with long fingernails reach up out of one of the middle ditches. Henry nodded at one of the other men in suits. That man, in turn, nudged one of the monks forward with the gun he held in his hand. That man moved tremblingly forward. George had slunk back away from the gravelike holes in the floor.

As another greenish taloned hand emerged from the hole in the tile floor, the man in the orange robe pulled a long, thin yellow strip of paper from a teak box on the altar. As the creature in the hole came up out of its makeshift grave, the orange-robed man stuck the piece of yellow paper on the *kiang shi*'s forehead. The *kiang shi* froze.

As the five other *kiang shi* began to climb out of their graves, each one was met with a reluctant frightened-looking man in an orange robe bearing a long, thin yellow paper with red writing on it. Each one froze as the paper was affixed to its forehead.

Henry, still nonchalantly leaning against the pillar, looked over at George. "Brother?" he said quietly. It was phrased as a question, but I could hear the command behind it.

George shut his eyes.

Henry shook his head again as if at the foolishness of a child. He looked over at one of the men in suits and gave the slightest of nods. That man turned his gun around and with as much emotion as someone swatting a fly, pistol-whipped the robed man in front of him. The man made a strangled noise and sank to the floor, blood streaming from his temple.

No one moved. The man with the gun raised it again.

"Stop," George said, his voice half-strangled. "Stop."

Henry smiled. "It's entirely up to you, brother."

George pulled a bell from the sleeve of his robe and rang it. The *kiang shi* all turned as one and jumped. George rang the bell again. The *kiang shi* jumped again.

George kept ringing his damned little bell, and the *kiang shi* kept jumping toward the door. They would have been funny if I hadn't seen them feasting on human flesh. Somehow the memory of them massacring the Norteños leached all the humor from the situation.

I slipped from my alcove and slid back down the hallway to the office. I climbed back out the window, dropped to the Dumpster, ran down the alley and made it to the Buick as the Navigators pulled out from the alley behind the temple. I slid into traffic behind them and followed.

It was full dark now. The streetlights were on. Old Sacramento was starting to fill up with tourists and twenty-somethings all looking for a good time. There was enough traffic not to worry about the mean men in the shiny suits and the even shinier Navigators getting wise to the grandma car on their tail. I was relieved.

The next hour played out exactly the way it had the last time I'd followed the *kiang shi* and their masters. They drove to a street corner. This time it was down Highway 99. When we exited on Twelfth Avenue and then headed north on Thirty-sixth Street, I suspected we were headed for McClatchy Park. I wasn't disappointed. The Navigators pulled into the parking lot. A group of young men sat on the picnic benches under the live oak trees. I stayed across the street. My heart was in my throat. I knew what was going to happen next. I didn't need to stay around and see it. I slid the Buick into drive and hightailed it to the lights on Broadway, where I was sure I'd be able to find a phone. As I pulled away, I heard the faint tinkle of George's bell. Moments later, I heard the first agonized scream. I shoved the accelerator toward the floor, knowing that no matter how fast I went now, I was already too late.

OVER AT THE CIRCLE K ON BROADWAY, I GRABBED A BASE-ball cap off the floor of the Buick—there are advantages to never cleaning out your car—and pulled it low over my face. If I slunk up to the pay phone from the side, kept my back turned and the baseball cap pulled low, no one would be able to ID me from the security cameras this time. See? I'm totally teachable. I also grabbed a tissue from the box on the floor and used that as I held the phone and dialed. I didn't think Ted would go to the trouble of dusting the pay phone for prints, nor did I think he'd get a hit off mine, but I didn't want to take the chance.

I made my 911 call and went back to the park. My night was far from over.

The *kiang shi* were hopping back into the SUVs and I could hear the sirens off in the distance when I got back to the park. Even with my particularly acute eyesight (another benefit of the Messenger gig), I couldn't see much of what was left of the young men at the picnic benches. I could make out Henry standing, legs spread, hands joined behind his back as he surveyed what he had done. He watched the *kiang shi* hop back toward the Navigators, his expression smug. I could only barely make out George inside the first SUV. His cheeks shone as if they were wet. I think he may have been crying. Listening to the moans that came from the area by the trees, I wasn't sure if I wanted to be sick or cry with him.

I looked back at Henry and felt my anger rise.

This wasn't the *kiang shi*'s fault. They were just doing what came naturally to them. They were tools. You don't throw the hammer in jail when someone uses it to brain someone else. They didn't have much more control over themselves than hammers as far as I could see.

Henry, however, was a whole other piece of business.

Once the *kiang shi* had all hopped back inside, the SUVs pulled out of the parking lot. I swung a U-turn and followed them back toward the interstate. I was pretty sure they'd head back to the temple before going anyplace else, so I hung back. My heart was still beating too fast, and my breathing was still way too shallow and rapid. I needed to get hold of myself if I was going to accomplish the rest of what I needed to do tonight.

What I needed to know was who were the dudes in the SUVs? I looked at my watch. It was already past ten o'clock. I was going to be late for work. Again.

Up ahead, I could see the SUVs exiting on Richards. I flicked on my directional and changed lanes to the right. I decided there was nothing to be done about the late-for-work factor. In the grander scheme of things, I was pretty sure that stopping whoever was using the *kiang shi* to rip gang-bangers to shreds was more important than filing insurance forms and patient questionnaires. In the less-grand scheme of things, my supervisor, Doreen, was going to be none too pleased. Since that was pretty much her constant state of being, however, I could feel only so much guilt over that.

The SUVs turned down the alley behind the Bok Kai Temple. I cruised by in what I hoped appeared to be a case of extreme vehicular nonchalance. I went down the block and then made a series of left turns so I was positioned to follow the SUVs when they came out of the alley and either headed back toward the interstate or out onto the surface streets. I am nothing if not strategic.

I sat in the darkened Buick, slunk low in the seat, the baseball cap still pulled low over my face just in case, and waited. I didn't wait patiently though. I drummed my fingers on the steering wheel and tapped my foot. Exactly how long did it take to unload a bunch of Chinese vampires from some vans? And how many of them would it take to screw in a lightbulb? Or more to the point, how many did it take to start a gang war in Sacramento?

The answer to that question was apparently six.

Eventually the SUVs made their appearance at the mouth of the alley. I turned on the engine of the Buick, grateful for the low-key purr of its engine, but left the lights off until the SUVs had turned onto Third Street and wouldn't be surprised to see cars behind them. I merged into the traffic heading back to the interstate with them, and then followed them as they headed south on I-5.

I didn't have the luxury of following loosely this time. I had no idea where we were going. I was grateful they hadn't gotten on I-80 and headed into the Bay area. I'd have lost them for sure there.

Instead, we headed south through the suburbs that string along I-5 like so many pink-stuccoed, red-tile-roofed pearls on a string. In my continuing run of luck, since the SUVs were traveling in a caravan, they were even easier to follow.

The lead SUV began to move to the right at Laguna Road and then exited onto Elk Grove Boulevard. We all turned left off the exit ramp. We still weren't alone. A Toyota Camry, a Ford Escape and a late-model sedan in a baby-shit brown color that should have been illegal all exited at the same time, and we all headed toward the strip malls that lined Elk Grove Boulevard on both sides.

The boulevard is wide. It has two lanes in each direction with right- and left-turn lanes at the lights and a well-landscaped median in between. The SUVs hung in the left lane. I stayed a car behind them and in the right lane as we passed by drive-thrus and chain stores and nail salons and into a heavily residential area. As a result, I missed the turn when they swung into a subdivision on the left. Cursing, I sped up and made a U-turn as soon as I could. By the time I'd swung around, the SUVs had already pulled through. I watched the gate to the community swing shut. I pounded my dashboard in frustration.

Okay. Deep breaths, I told myself. There's a way through this. I pulled up to the gate and contemplated the panel in front of me. I hit the button to bring up the subdivision directory and selected a name at random.

"Hello?" said a sleepy female voice after four rings.

"Hey, it's Julie," I said, trying to sound cheery.

"Who?" the voice asked.

"Julie. From the meeting the other night," I said, attempting to maintain that bright tone. It so does not come naturally to me.

"I don't . . . I mean, I'm not sure . . ." the voice continued, confused.

"You didn't mean it when you said we should get together?" I tried to make my voice sound hurt now.

"Oh, no. Sorry. You just caught me off guard." The intercom made a buzzing noise and the gate slid open. I drove the Buick through.

It's amazing how often people don't want to be rude. You can't count on it, but it often comes in handy.

The subdivision was basically one big well-lit, wide-streeted, carefully landscaped squarish loop with a cul-de-sac off each corner of the square. The houses were huge with Palladian windows, three-car garages, approximately six inches between lots and front yards the size of postage stamps. That was okay. The ten-foot fences would keep the yards private and, of course, give all who entered the feeling of being in a prison or perhaps a cattle pen. There were at least seventy houses, but it would take less than ten minutes to cover the whole place, even driving at a Buick-appropriate fifteen miles per hour. I considered turning off my headlights but decided it would make me more conspicuous rather than less.

I found the SUVs parked in front of one of the McMansions on the second cul-de-sac. It was a completely unremarkable house, exactly like its neighbors. Even the black SUVs parked in the driveway didn't distinguish it. The house to the right of it had a black Ford F-150 on its driveway, and the one on its left had a white Yukon Denali. I had no idea what sort of off-road experience these people were expecting in the wilds of the suburbs of Sacramento, but they were definitely prepared. I wondered if they had bottled drinking water and emergency rations in the back. It's not the cockroaches that will survive nuclear holocaust, it's the soccer moms. They're some tough cookies.

I cruised on past the house. No one appeared to be keeping watch, but it was better to be safe than sorry. All the shutters were closed in the front of the house, but light spilled out from between the slats. Someone was there. That was for sure.

I rounded the cul-de-sac, pulled the Buick over across the street and toward the corner leading back into the main subdivision traffic loop and cut the engine. I sat with the windows rolled down, listening. The neighborhood was impressively silent. Traffic on Elk Grove Boulevard was nothing but a background swish from here. It almost sounded like those atmosphere CDs of ocean noises that are supposed to help people sleep. The blue light of television sets flickered out of living room windows up and down the block, but I couldn't hear anything. They probably all had their windows closed and the air-conditioning on.

I slid down in the seat again, but I didn't bother with the baseball cap. It was already dark and I really didn't think anyone was watching. I had about fifteen minutes that I could sit here and watch the house before I'd have to take off to maybe be on time for work at the hospital.

Nothing happened. The SUVs sat in the driveway. Light shone through the shutters. Crickets chirped in the darkness. Everything seemed normal. Too normal. It was like going to Aldo's place. The normality of it all made it way more creepy and, I suspected, way more dangerous.

I finally started the Buick and left for the hospital, knowing that I'd found something important and still wondering what the hell I was supposed to do about it.

8

I SKIDDED INTO THE EMPLOYEE PARKING GARAGE PRACTI-
cally on two wheels, which is a pretty mean driving feat in a
moving sofa. I'd changed into my skirt and twinset as I'd
driven up Highway 99 from Elk Grove, but even with that
time-saving maneuver, I was close to half an hour late. The
idea that I might slide into my little cubicle in the processing
department unobserved went out of my pretty little head the
second the double doors whooshed open to let me in.

The ER waiting room was total chaos. Every seat was
filled. Boys of various shades of brown lined the walls,
blood-soaked ice packs pressed to various body parts. I
shuddered to think of what the people being treated ahead
of them had looked like. Four security guards patrolled the
room.

I headed to the registration area where I was supposed
to have been checking in people for the past thirty minutes
or so.

"Damn it, Melina, where the hell have you been?" My
boss, Doreen Hughes, rolled back in her chair and glared at

me. Doreen is in her late forties. She battles her weight, her teenaged children, her lazy-ass husband and the fecklessness of the night staff at Sacramento City Hospital personified largely by me. She's not bad as far as bosses go, but she's still a boss.

I gave an apologetic shrug. "Sorry. Car trouble." I felt a slight twinge of guilt for maligning the Buick. It had never once given me a moment of unease or trouble, but I blamed it for everything. If it ever became real like the Velveteen Rabbit (and I damn near loved it enough to make it so), I was going to have a lot of 'splaining to do.

Doreen's already creased mouth pursed down even smaller, threatening to disappear all together. "Just get started. We've all got lines about a mile long."

The first person to sit down in front of me at my desk was Bao Nguyen. He had bloody gashes on his cheek that looked like they needed stitches even to me, a left arm that hung down at a funny angle and, bless his pea-picking heart, active health insurance. He was replaced by Enrico Torres, who had shallow knife wounds on his forearm. The parade went on through Canh Ngo, Huynh Tran, Franco Rodriguez and Jorge Ramos. Notice a trend? That's right. All Vietnamese boys or Latinos from the 'hoods, most of them sporting gang tats.

Then Alicia Alvarez huddled down in front of my desk, her dirty gray hoodie pulled around her. She looked about nineteen. There was blood on her jacket and tears staining her cheeks. She didn't, however, seem to be injured. I took her name, address and phone number, and then I asked what had brought her to the ER.

"It's not me. It's Maricela. My baby girl."

"How old is Maricela?" I asked.

"She'll be six months next week." Alicia's voice faltered.

I looked up from my computer. The way she hunched forward cradling her stomach, I wondered if she was pregnant again already. She barely looked old enough to be out of high school. "What seems to be the problem?"

"Jaime, my brother, he got shot."

Okayyyy. That wasn't good, but it didn't get me any closer to hearing why Alicia thought Maricela needed to be seen or even where the baby was now.

"They just shot right into the apartment, right through the window." Her voice caught. She swallowed hard and went on. "I drove him here, but I didn't have no one to leave the baby with, so I brought her, too. She fussed the whole way here. Wouldn't stop screaming. I figured I'd feed her when I got here."

"And?" I leaned forward.

"She wouldn't eat. They took Jaime in, and I tried to nurse her, but she wouldn't eat. She stopped screaming then, too."

"Okay. Why do you think she needs to be seen by a doctor?"

Alicia leaned back and opened her hoodie. A perfectly beautiful baby girl with skin the color of caramel and jet black curls against her cheek, lay in her lap. "I think she needs to be seen 'cause I can't get her to wake up no more."

I froze. Something was not right with that baby. Now that Alicia had opened her hoodie, I could smell it. A fetid rotten smell came off the perfect little angel baby in Alicia's lap. "Alicia, is there any blood on her? Did she get hit by the bullet? Or by, I don't know, a piece of glass or something?"

She lifted Maricela's shirt and showed me a tiny pinprick of blood on her smooth, round little tummy. "Just this."

I leaned forward and sniffed. The smell was even stronger. It was hard to detect over the disinfectant smell of the hospital that tended to scorch my nostrils with its harshness. Now that I was seeking it out, though, I could smell it and it did not smell good. Something was seriously wrong with that baby.

The tears welled up in Alicia's eyes. "She was just sleeping in her crib." Alicia wrapped her arms around herself and her baby and began to rock. "I shouldn't have put the crib by the window. I shouldn't have. It was so hot in the apartment. I thought she'd get some air. Oh God, what did I do? Why did I put her there?"

"Wait right here," I said. I shoved my chair back, hit the button to go into the emergency room through the back door and ran.

I found Alex in one of the bays, assessing a knife wound. "Dr. Bledsoe, there's a baby at my window. Someone's got to see her now."

Alex didn't even look up. "If triage sent the baby to be seen by you first, then she doesn't need to be seen right away. Just because it's a baby, doesn't mean that she hops the line. You know the drill, Melina."

I dropped my voice low and tried to speak slowly. If I panicked, he'd blow me off entirely, but I had to get him to listen. Why the hell didn't I have a vampire command voice? "There's something wrong, Alex. Something really wrong. Someone's got to see her now."

The tone in my voice must have gotten through to him because he looked up at me. "Are you sure? Because I'm not exactly playing Hungry Hungry Hippos here," he said, stepping back so I could see the nasty gash across the young man's arm.

I sniffed. I didn't smell the horrid combination of blood and bowel that I'd smelled from Maricela. I bit my lip and nodded my head up and down. "I'm sure."

He stood. "All right, then. Show me."

I ran back to my desk with Alex striding behind me. Alicia had pulled her hoodie back around Maricela. Alex looked at me quizzically.

"Show him, Alicia," I said. "Show him the baby and the mark on her tummy."

Alicia unveiled the baby again, and I saw Alex come to attention. He knew it, too. Something wasn't right. Alicia lifted Maricela's shirt. Alex's eyes narrowed as he looked at the tiny dot of blood. He pressed against the baby's stomach. Maricela's eyes flew open and she screamed.

In two seconds, Alex had snatched Maricela from Alicia's arms and had taken off at a run into the ER. "Take care of the mother, Melina. Phone upstairs. We need an OR stat."

BY THE TIME ALL THE PAPERWORK HAD BEEN FILED AND most of the young men had been ushered into various parts of the ER, I was numb. I felt as though I were hallucinating, I'd seen so much pain and heartache. Through it all, over the smell of sweat and blood and the sour tang of fear, I kept thinking I smelled cinnamon coffee cake, too. I was clearly losing it. Yet I knew that I had seen the least of it. The boys that had been really hurt didn't come through my area. They got checked in by the nurses as best as they could. The unending parade of damaged young men that had trampled through my office was only the tip of the iceberg.

Alex came in through the door that connects our area with the treatment area. "Hey." He looked tired. His skin was even whiter than usual and there were circles under his eyes.

"How is she?" I didn't bother with formalities. He knew who I was asking about.

"She's still in surgery." He leaned one hip against my desk. I pushed my chair back. My cubicle isn't that big, and for a guy who didn't need to breathe, he seemed to be taking up more than his fair share of oxygen.

I glanced up at the clock. It had been hours since Alex had raced out of the ER with the baby tucked under his arm like Larry Fitzgerald running for the end zone. "Is she going to be all right?"

He rubbed his hand across his face and nodded. "Thanks to your nose, yeah, she is."

"What was wrong with her?" I scooted my chair closer.

I felt so cold. I wanted to be close to someone, something to warm me. Unfortunately, Alex doesn't give off any body heat.

"A piece of shrapnel nicked her colon. She was bleeding to death in her mother's arms." His voice was flat, his words matter-of-fact. I looked up into his face. If he felt anything, he wasn't showing it to me.

A baby. Caught in the crossfire. This had to stop. Someone had to make this end. It was bad enough to see all these young men ruined, but a baby? What could a baby have done to deserve being shot while she slept in her crib by an open window on a warm summer night? I didn't trust myself to speak.

Alex patted me on the back. "She'll be fine. We caught it in time. I'd give Celeste a wide berth for a while, though. I think she's taking it personally." Celeste was the triage nurse who'd sent Maricela out to the waiting room to bleed to death while someone stitched up her uncle. She wasn't exactly my favorite person under the best of circumstances anyway. I found I didn't much care if she was pissed at me or not. I was so numb right now, though, that Norah could have stopped speaking to me and I probably wouldn't have cared.

Alex stood up and started to walk away. He stopped after two steps and turned back to me. He cupped my chin in his hand and ran a chilly finger down my cheek. My breath caught in my lungs. I looked up at him, directly into his eyes.

"You did a good thing tonight, Melina. Try to hold onto that."

Then he was gone.

When the supply of maimed and damaged boys slowed from a roaring stream to a trickle, I pushed my rolling chair back from my desk. The line of us on my side of the glass didn't look a whole lot better than what I'd seen come through the ER. Oh, we weren't bloody. No one was going to need surgery. But my coworkers all had the same shell-shocked look that I supposed was on my frozen-feeling face. Even Doreen, who had been through more than a few battle-fields in her day, looked like hell.

"I need a break," I declared to anyone who might be listening.

Doreen waved her hand in permission. I headed to the ambulance bay. The smell of cinnamon got stronger. "Hey, Melina," a voice said from the shadows.

I turned in time to catch the flash of white teeth as he grinned in the darkness.

Officer Goodnight. No wonder I'd been smelling baked goods. I wondered if it was his cologne. Maybe Calvin Klein actually made "Cookies on a Winter Day" scent. If he doesn't, he should. Forget Gwyneth Paltrow playing with puppies on green grass. The cookie thing would sell like crazy.

"You're not stalking me, are you? Because that could get old." I leaned against the cement wall. It still held some warmth from the heat of the day, and the scratchiness against my back reminded me that I probably would be able to feel something again some day.

He walked over and leaned next to me. "No stalking. I'm here to take statements. Pretty much everyone is here taking statements. It's going to take all night." His voice broke a little. "There are so many of them." His hand brushed mine as are our arms dangled between us. His fingers were warm. It made me even more aware of how cold mine were.

"I work here." I felt I needed to explain my presence, too.

"I know." He didn't move. He just stood there and let his hand brush against mine again. My heart started to beat faster. "I looked you up."

"That's a little creepy," I said. "Are you sure you're not stalking me?"

He snorted a little. "Not completely. I was thinking I was checking out a witness when I did it, but I suppose I might

have had ulterior motives on a subconscious level that I was
unwilling to acknowledge to myself."

"Pretty fancy talk for a beat cop," I said.

"I'm full of surprises."

"There was a baby, a little girl." My voice shook a little.
I took a deep breath. "She was sleeping in her crib. She got
hit by a piece of shrapnel."

I don't know why I said it. Maybe I needed to tell someone. Maybe I needed to tell someone who had seen what I'd
seen tonight and more, someone who would understand.
What good it would do, I didn't know. Probably none. Telling someone wouldn't get the shrapnel out of that tiny body.

"I know," he said. Then he took my hand and laced his
fingers through mine. We stood in silence and watched the
sun rise over the city.

I'D EVENTUALLY HAD TO GO BACK INTO THE HOSPITAL IF
only to clock out for the day. I was happy to get out of there,
away from the groans and calls for help, the chill of the
hallways and the ever-present smell of death with the cop-
pery tang of blood beneath it.

I went home and showered under the hottest water I could
stand, and when I got out, I called my aunt.

"Aunt Kitty? It's Melina." I took a deep breath, held the
phone away from my ear and waited for the ear-piercing
squeal to be over. Aunt Kitty is my mother's younger sister.
She's only five years younger than my mother chronologi-
cally. Maturitywise, she's younger than me. I think her emotional development arrested somewhere around fourteen.

I wanted to follow up on the McMansions, and I knew the
best place to start would be with Aunt Kitty. I knew she'd be
likely to be home, getting reorganized after a busy weekend
of showing houses and wheeling and dealing, and that if
anyone could get the information I wanted, it would be her.

"Melina, sweetheart! How are you? How's work?"

"I'm fine. Work's fine." That wasn't entirely true, but nobody really wants the truth when they ask those questions. "I'm just curious about something and wanted to see if you could help me."

"Of course, darling. Anything for you. You know that." Aunt Kitty is the kind of aunt who takes you shopping and buys you makeup when you're twelve, lets you rent R-rated movies when you're staying at her house when you're fifteen and proclaims "Dessert First" night every so often just for the hell of it. She's like a teenager but with all the rights of a grown-up. The only thing more dangerous that I can imagine would be cats with opposable thumbs.

"Can you look up an address and figure out who owns the house?" I asked. Aunt Kitty is a real estate agent. She's a pussycat of an aunt but a tiger when it comes to buying and selling houses. She always makes it high enough on the board at her office to park in one of the nice spaces in the underground parking garage. In real estate speak, we're talking rock star.

"Of course I can. Is there some place you're interested in? Are you thinking of buying?" Bless her pea-picking heart, but Aunt Kitty managed not to sound incredulous at the idea. I am as likely to have enough money to make a down payment on a house in Northern California as I am to grow wings and fly.

Actually, the flying thing might be a teensy bit more likely. I'm never quite sure what new things I will discover about being a Messenger. Maybe that's right around the corner for me.

"No. I'm just curious as to who owns this one house."

She sighed. "I'm probably not supposed to ask why."

"Probably not."

Aunt Kitty has always hoped that the makeup purchases, the R-rated movie rentals and the Dessert First nights would gain her some special entrée into my life. She's right. They have. There are just some things I'm better off not telling anyone no matter how much I want to share. It's been tough for her to deal with, but she tries. She really is an awesome aunt. She sighed again. "What's the address?"

I gave her the number of the McMansion the *kiang shi*'s handlers had gone to the night before and listened to her fingers tippy-tapping at her computer keyboard. "So are you seeing anyone?" she asked.

"Do I have to answer that to find out who owns that house?" I countered.

"No. It's just a conversational topic to kill time while I wait for the search results to come up."

"No. I'm not seeing anyone," I said.

"There's a young man at my office who just started . . ."

"Aunt Kitty," I said. "We've been through this before." I am not cut out to date real estate agents. Or maybe they're not cut out to date me. I'm not exactly sure. I do know we scare each other. Sadly, I think they scare me more than I scare them. Real estate agents are fearless.

"Here it is," she said brightly. "The owner of the house is Edwin Ho. Oh, that's interesting."

"What is?" Goodie. There was something interesting about the house. Maybe it would help me figure out what the hell was going on.

"Well, I thought the agent who brokered the sale was retired. I didn't know he was still in the business." Aunt Kitty prides herself on being tapped in to all the good info that's out there. Missing a detail like that would rankle her, I was sure.

"What's his name?" I asked.

"Winston Chung." I could hear Aunt Kitty's fingers furiously typing. "Look at that. I guess I must have gotten my wires crossed. He's brokered at least ten sales in Elk Grove over the past three months." She tapped some more. "Now that's odd."

"What's odd, Aunt Kitty?" I felt a little like Jay Leno's audience. Next thing I knew I'd be screaming, "How odd is it?"

"All these properties have their mortgage from the same bank."

"Is that really that weird?" I knew for a fact that Aunt Kitty had banks she preferred to work with and steered her clients that way. I bet easily seventy percent of Kitty's clients ended up financing their homes with her friend Lavonda at the Second Northern Bank of California.

"It's weird enough that I want to do some checking, and that's going to take some time," she said. "Can I call you back?"

I told her she could call me back anytime, which is pretty much true—I don't sleep much—and we hung up.

I gathered up my karate gear and headed out the door to go to the dojo. The teen sparring class was this afternoon. It took both Mae and me together to contain the raging hormones that flooded the place during those. Ben was in his usual place on the stoop as I left. He had on a pair of skintight red plaid pants that seemed to have the legs from the knees down attached by a combination of fishing wire and safety pins.

"No Sophie today?" I asked as I stepped around him.

He leaned back on his hands and looked up at me. "At least, not for me," he said.

"How long have you two been friends?" I asked.

He shrugged. "I'm not sure we're friends now. She stopped by. We chilled. That's all."

I nodded. She stopped by and they chilled. Of course. How could I have been so dense? "What's her story?"

"You mean the scars?" He looked up at me. It was good to see his eyes clear and not red and puffy.

"Yeah, I guess so." I sat down next to him.

"Car accident. At least, that's what I heard. She doesn't talk about it." He picked at the safety pins holding his pants legs together. "Somebody said she actually died and they brought her back. Cool, huh?"

"Yeah," I said, not meeting his eyes. "Cool."

I chewed over what he'd just told me as I drove to the

dojo. Someone who had died and been resuscitated. Now she was hanging around Mae and me.

I was spectacularly unsurprised to find Sophie at River City Karate and Judo when I walked in. She, on the other hand, looked a little apprehensive as I walked in. Her eyes widened and she ducked behind her hair.

"Hi, Sophie," I said. "Care to tell me who you really are?"

"I TOLD YOU SHE'D BE UPSET," SOPHIE WAILED, PRACTI-cally hiding behind Mae, which was not so easy since she had about four inches on her.

"I'm. Not. Angry," I said through gritted teeth. "I just want to know what's going on and I want to know now."

I'd found the two of them working out on the mats in the dojo. Sophie was dressed in a beginner's *gi* and white belt. Her skinny ankles stuck out the bottom of the too short pants. Her toenails were painted pink, but the polish had chipped.

Mae was, well . . . Mae.

"That's not possible." Mae smiled at me the same way she smiles at the Little Dragons when they want candy.

In response, I came damn close to stamping my foot when I asked why.

"Because I don't know and neither does Sophie," she said.

"What *do* you and Sophie know?" I asked, trying to unclench my jaw while I said it. I slung my backpack down in the tiled waiting area, bowed slightly and walked onto the mat.

There's something about the sensation of that scratchy mat under my feet that makes me feel like I'm home. Tension runs out of my body like saline out of a leaky IV bag. I don't feel it at my apartment. I don't feel it at my parents' place. I don't feel it at the hospital. I feel it at the River City Karate and Judo.

I am so screwed up.

"I know that ever since I came out of my coma, I see things that nobody else sees and hear stuff that nobody else hears," Sophie said, her head now held high as if she were defying someone or something by saying those things out loud.

I looked over at Mae. She shrugged.

"What kind of things?" I asked.

She let her hair fall in front of her face again. "Stuff," she said.

"Stuff," I repeated. "You're seeing and hearing stuff. There are medications for that, you know?"

"I do know," she said softly. "Don't you think I've considered that? That maybe I got knocked hard enough on the head that I'm crazy now?"

That did actually make me feel a little bad. I'd never had to go through that. Three years old is too young to consider that you may be becoming delusional or schizophrenic or bipolar or whatever the popular diagnosis of the day is. Everyone else around me may have wondered, but I was blissfully without that concern.

"Oh," I said. "So did Mae tell you that if they told you to come here, the voices were probably real?"

She sighed. "Yeah. I can't decide if that's good news or bad."

I patted her on her skinny shoulder as I walked past her to retrieve my backpack and go change. "Welcome to the club, kiddo. Welcome to the club."

9

I LAY EXHAUSTED ON THE MAT. I WAS PRETTY SURE I WAS going to have a heck of a bruise on my right bicep and would probably be limping for at least a day. As usual, the sparring class lived up to its name and reputation. The kids might bow and say a respectful "sir" or "ma'am" as they walked in the door, but once we were on the mats, they were ready to rumble. It felt so good. It was a good clean pain, not that murky ache in my stomach every time I thought about little Maricela and her weeping mother.

The kids had gone and I was trying to fill Mae in on what I'd learned so far.

"They're called *kiang shi*." I was talking to Mae but kept Sophie in view. Was she ready to hear this stuff? She'd been a Messenger for what? About a nanosecond? If that even was what she really was. Was she really ready to hear about hopping undead Asians feasting on the living flesh of Latino gang members? I'd been a Messenger for twenty-three years and I wasn't particularly ready for it. She seemed calm enough, though.

"Never heard of 'em," Mae said.

"Me neither, but both Alex and Aldo knew what they were." And had a big argument about them, but with Alex and Aldo that pretty much went without saying.

"What are they going to do about them?" Sophie asked.

I shook my head. "Nothing as far as I can figure out. Aldo says they're not the Seethe's problem, and I can't see Alex taking on a community improvement project."

"What about the guys in the SUVs? Are they *kiang shi*?" Sophie scooted closer to me on the mat.

"No. They're human. At least, they're as human as you can be if you're the kind of person who would sic a vampire on a human being."

"How are they controlling them?" She picked at the peeling polish on her big toe.

"Hell if I know."

Mae stood up and stretched. "It sounds like there's an awful lot you don't know."

Wasn't that always the case? The one thing I was constantly sure of was that there was a hell of a lot of unknown stuff coming at me in unexpected ways. "I'm not sure I really need to know anything more. It's not really my business. I don't have a delivery to make. Nobody is asking me to take anything anywhere." I sat up on the mat.

"But people are getting hurt." Sophie sounded indignant.

"People are always getting hurt somewhere. It's not really my job to protect them." I knew that sounded heartless. Maybe it was heartless, but it was also true.

"Whose job is it then?" she demanded.

I looked over to Mae for some help. She looked right back at me and didn't say a word.

"What am I supposed to do?" I stood up and did a last few stretches.

"Maybe you could start by tracking down some of the stuff you don't know," Mae suggested.

"And do what with the information? Aldo doesn't want it. Paul doesn't want it. Alex doesn't want it." I was starting to get a little steamed. How the hell did this become my problem?

"Once you know more, maybe that will be clear." Mae smiled at me.

I glared back. "Fine," I said, marching off the mat and grabbing my clothes. "I'll get right on that."

"You can't keep living like this, Melina."

I'd thought the same thing to myself about a hundred times a week, but I wasn't sure what Mae meant by that. "Which this? The this where I work three jobs and have no personal life? Or only doing the one job that doesn't pay and makes me a walking oddity worthy of my own basic-cable reality show?"

She walked off the mat and stood beside me. "Neither. Or maybe both. I'm talking about the one where you don't take responsibility for anything."

I felt like I'd been slapped. "What am I supposed to be responsible for? I take the things I'm supposed to take to where I'm supposed to take them. That's my job. I do it despite the fact that no one ever asked me if wanted to do it or not."

Mae flung up her hands. "That's right. Poor Melina. She's stuck in a situation that she doesn't like. I've been hearing this song since you were seven years old. It's time to drop it. Do something. Stop just reacting. If you don't like the status quo, change it."

"How precisely am I supposed to do that?"

"I don't know." Mae shook her head. "I just know that if you stay on this path, you'll end up bitter and alone. Is that really what you want?"

Sure. Isn't that what every girl dreams of? A solitary life with an ill-tempered cat? Maybe I'd spend my time sitting on the front porch yelling at kids to get off my lawn.

Of course that wasn't what I wanted. I wanted what all

the other girls my age wanted. Fun and romance and following dreams. It wasn't, however, the hand I'd been dealt. I'd tried. I'd been slapped down over and over.

What hurt most was that Mae had always been the one who understood that. For the past nineteen years, she'd been the only person I could talk to and be completely honest with. She was the only one who knew who I really was and what it all really meant. She'd been my shoulder to cry on. Now, suddenly, she was telling me that she didn't want to be that person anymore.

"You know it's not what I want."

"Then do something about it besides complain, Melina. Take charge of your life. Do it before it's too late."

Too late? What the hell did that mean? "Mae, do you know something about what's coming?"

She looked down. "You don't have to be prescient to see what road you're on, Melina."

That hadn't been what I'd meant and she knew it. I began to wonder if Sophie's appearance in our lives had a much more sinister overtone than I'd considered before, but if Mae knew anything, she wasn't saying. She just stood there and looked at me.

I let the door to the dojo slam behind me.

I TOOK A SECOND HOT SHOWER. I STOOD UNDER THE spray until the water started to turn cold, grateful that our water was included in our rent. When I got out, I put on my jammies. I was so done for the day. I was going nowhere, no how. Wanna know how done I was? Stick a fork in me.

Sadly, that was only a fantasy. I'd have to leave for work at the hospital in a few hours. I could pretend, though, right? I could pretend to be a regular girl who was going to spend the evening watching DVDs in her pj's.

I flipped open my laptop. I had a rather long list of things I didn't know, and the Internet seemed like a good place to start. My first hurdle was figuring out how to spell *kiang shi*. It turned out there were probably about five different ways of spelling it in English, but they all brought up pretty much the same set of Web sites, all of which had pretty much the same information.

A *kiang shi* is a Chinese vampire, the first site said. Well, duh, that I knew already. Next was a lengthy explanation about the two souls that the Chinese believe inhabit the body. Long story short: there's the superior soul or the *hun* and the inferior soul or the *p'o*. *Kiang shi* are created when the inferior soul remains in a body after death for too long, usually because of a violent death or too much time between death and burial.

The hopping thing? It's because they're stuck in rigor mortis. They aren't fully dead, so the muscles can't relax. They're stiff so they have to hop. Who knew?

Then I hit an explanation for the Post-its on their foreheads. Well, not Post-its, talismans. Again, who knew? The talisman was a yellow piece of paper with symbols drawn on it in chicken blood by Taoist priests. Suddenly everything was starting to come together. That's why Henry, whoever the hell he was, needed his brother George and his buddies. He couldn't control the *kiang shi*, only a Taoist priest could. How lucky for Henry to have one in the family. His mother must be so proud.

At least I knew what I was dealing with now. Except, I really didn't want to deal with them. Those dudes were nasty.

I read on anyway. *Kiang shi* are nocturnal. I'd pretty much gotten that. Oh, and apparently they are rapists. I guessed the cholos were lucky that the *kiang shi* were straight, otherwise they might have been subject to even more indignities than just being torn limb from limb and munched on like Kentucky Fried Gangstas.

Here was a frightening thought: as they feed on more people—and Alex was wrong; they might drink blood, but they actually feed on people's chi—they become more powerful. Instead of just being able to rip people apart, they would be able to stab people with their swordlike fingernails and lasso them with superlong eyebrow hairs. Seriously, eyebrow hairs! I knew I could use a trip to the salon for a little wax and trim, but I couldn't imagine how long they'd have to be to lasso someone. Thinking of them sucking the chi out of me made me place my hands over my abdomen, the center of the chi, almost reflexively.

I moved on to more important items, namely, how to fight the suckers. Supposedly they're blind and track you by following your breath. I can hold my breath for a long time, but I wasn't sure I could fight and hold my breath. Part of a good fist strike or a kick is the timed release of energy. Breathing is big part of that. That's why we teach seven-year-old girls to shriek as they kick and punch. It certainly isn't for the health of our eardrums. Still, good to know. Until they've killed enough people to start to fly, *kiang shi* can only hop. A barrier across a threshold of about six inches or so can keep them out. I guessed that stairs would be a problem, too, and gave a mental thanks for having a third-floor apartment. I don't always feel that way after grocery shopping for the week, but it seemed like a happy thing at the moment.

I'll take what happy I can get where I can get it.

Kiang shi also can't cross running water or—get this—a line of glutinous rice. I love sticky rice! I'd have to keep some around. In fact, Norah might have some in the cupboard leftover from an ill-advised attempt at making her own vegetarian sushi. It's harder than it looks.

You can apparently also stun them with one of those eight-sided feng shui mirrors. I'd have to ask Norah, but I was pretty sure she had one of those. I remembered her mapping out the quadrants of our apartment when we were moving in.

So . . . mirrors and Post-its and sticky rice. It seemed

pretty easy to arm yourself against these things, if you knew what you needed. How many people would know that, though? Despite having spent the majority of my life as a 'Cane, I'd never even heard of *kiang shi* much less figured out how to protect myself from them until now.

And how were you supposed to kill them? I saw lots of information on slowing them down, freezing them in their tracks, containing them, but nothing on how to kill them.

I clicked through another page of search results. Half of the entries had the same information as the first page I'd clicked on. Finally, on the third page of results, I found it.

How to kill a *kiang shi*? You have to decapitate it and then burn it. That seemed a little trickier. Maybe I'd stick to sticky rice and eight-sided mirrors.

I yawned and stretched and shut down the computer. These things weren't hard to defend yourself against if you knew how, but you had to know how. Which meant that you had to know what you were defending yourself against in the first place. I doubted the Norteños were home googling *kiang shi*, because they had no idea what to google. They had no idea what they were fighting, and that put them at a serious disadvantage.

They certainly didn't know they were battling something supernatural. Why would they? People can and will ignore almost anything if it doesn't fit in with what they expect. There was one case where people kept walking into a subway station that was on fire because the belching smoke didn't fit into what they expected. They ignored the smoke and many of them died. Smoke was natural, normal. If people could ignore it, they could definitely ignore Chinese vampires.

Although, come to think of it, what I really wanted to know was why? Why were people siccing Chinese vampires on a Latino gang? What could they possibly gain from that? And who were they? I glanced at the clock. It was after ten. I'd call Aunt Kitty tomorrow. Right now, I needed to get to work at the hospital. I changed into a pair of black dress slacks and a button-front shirt and headed out for the hospital.

I WALKED INTO THE HOSPITAL AND MADE MY WAY TO MY desk. As I walked past my fellow office workers, each one stood up. It was the weirdest thing. I'd gotten past about two of them, when the first one, Jenny Brown, began to clap in a slow rhythmic beat. Next to her, Rachel Green joined in. The front desk volunteer turned around and started clapping, too. Pretty soon about a dozen of my coworkers were just standing there clapping. I stopped and looked all around me. I couldn't figure out what the hell they were applauding.

Doreen walked over and patted me on the back. Literally patted me on the back. "Good job last night with that baby."

I was seriously confused. "But I didn't do anything." It was Alex that had rushed Maricela into the OR. It was Dr. Perry from pediatrics who had done the surgery. I'd filed an insurance claim with California's Healthy Families. I didn't think it warranted applause.

"That's not what Dr. Bledsoe says," Arlene, the front desk volunteer, said. "Dr. Bledsoe says that if it wasn't for you, that little baby would have probably died in our waiting room and the hospital would be facing a massive lawsuit."

We can't have that. God forbid there should be a massive lawsuit. Oh, the dead baby would have been bad, too. There's nothing that will make you lose respect for human life faster than working in an urban emergency room. "Anybody would have caught it."

"I don't think I would have," Jenny said. "We were so busy. I wouldn't have even looked at that baby much less noticed anything was wrong. You're a hero, Melina."

They surrounded me. They patted my arms and back. They even brought cupcakes. I damn near cried. I worked with these women night after night. It wasn't like I never talked to any of them, but not really. They knew nothing about who I really was and beyond who was married and who was single and who had kids and who didn't, I really didn't know a damn thing about them.

Now here they were, bringing me baked goods and calling me a hero. I felt like one of the gang. I couldn't remember ever feeling like that anywhere. Even at the dojo, I'm a little bit of an oddity. The men don't like me much because I'm hard on their egos. Martial arts tend to attract powerful, dominant men, alpha males. Alpha males don't much like it when someone smaller than they are takes them down. They hate it when that person is also female. It's not a pretty thing to say and maybe it even sounds sexist, but it's true. I find it a bit ironic that the one place in the world where I actually feel at home, I'm not well liked or even appreciated by a big section of people.

Here at the hospital, I try to keep my head down and do my job. In the 'Dane world, if someone is noticing me, it usually means that something weird is going on that they shouldn't see. On this particular night, however, they were noticing me and it was for something good. They thought I was a hero. It would almost have felt good if I hadn't known how wrong they were.

Maricela had a piece of shrapnel in her belly because I hadn't done enough to stop what was shaping up to be open gang warfare. I was the only one who knew and cared about who had really started this fight, and all I'd done so far to stop it was make a couple of anonymous phone calls.

The thought made the cupcake turn to glue against the roof of my mouth.

The rest of the evening was blessedly quiet. I suppose even gangbangers had to take days of rest from killing each other. We had huge stacks of filing to catch up on from the rushes of the previous nights, but I'll take filing over looking into the eyes of another boy with a knife wound any night.

In my heart, I'm way more of a lover than a fighter. I just somehow can't seem to arrange my life to represent that.

I ran into Alex in the hallway on my way to the cafeteria to grab a cup of weak, putrid coffee. "Ms. Markowitz," he said with a slight incline of his head. "Congratulations."

"Very funny, Alex. I know you're the one spreading it around that I'm some kind of hero. We both know better."

He shrugged. "I only told people what happened. That baby owes you her life."

Wow. Way to twist the knife. "That baby owes no one anything. If anything, we all owe her something. She shouldn't have to live in a place where gunfire can erupt while she sleeps in her crib."

"Always looking on the bright side, aren't you, Melina?"

I decided to ignore that crack since it came from someone who would die an immediate and painful death if he ever decided to actually walk on the sunny side of the street, and shifted toward the wall to let the traffic in the hallway move past us. "About the other night . . ."

"There's nothing to discuss about the other night." His face looked a little grim.

I pressed on anyway. I mean, what was he going to do? Throw me over his arm and suck my blood in the middle of the hallway? I didn't think so. "I did a little research on the, um, special people we were discussing." It didn't seem wise to actually say *kiang shi* or *Chinese vampire* or whatever with people walking by us. No one was really trying to eavesdrop, but people did seem to look whenever Alex was around. It can't be helped. I'd like to say it's another one of those vampire things, like the voice and all that. It isn't. Alex has a certain charisma. Watching him walk through a crowd is like watching a magnet being passed over iron filings. Things just gravitate toward him.

He crossed his arms over his chest and leaned against the wall, looking like a *GQ* ad for scrubs. The man could totally rock a pair of drawstrings. "Those special people are none of my business, as you know, and they are certainly none of yours."

Fine, fine. Aldo had been dismissive and now Alex had his undies in a bunch. I knew that. I knew Alex wasn't any happier with the situation than I was, but that's why we needed to figure out whom to dump it on. "That's the thing, though. Who exactly was it driving those special people around? Do you know?"

"I don't know. I don't care. What's more, I suspect that caring could get a person in a lot of trouble." He leaned toward me now, looking into my eyes as if he could make his point better by staring it into me.

He might be right about that. I suddenly had to swallow really hard. "But someone should care, right? Then we wouldn't have to. If we figured out who that person, or persons, is, then we wouldn't have to worry about caring."

"I'm not worried about caring, Melina," he said softly. "I'm getting a little worried about you caring. You need to drop this. It's not safe."

"Who's going to know? I'm nobody. I'll just poke around a little and figure out who needs a message about it. Then I'll deliver the message. That is my job, you know." It was a mistake to stare into his eyes. I felt a little dizzy, and the sounds of the hallway around me seemed distant.

His hand touched my arm, steadying me. His touch, cool on my skin, made me shiver. He cocked his head. I swallowed hard again, trying to get the hammering of my heart under control, trying to work up the ability to tell him to back away. That's what I wanted, wasn't it? I was sure it was what I wanted. Except that I felt as though I were about to burst into flames.

"Leave this alone, Melina. Walk away and leave it alone. Either it will go away on its own or it will come to the attention of someone who will deal with it."

"And how many kids will end up in our emergency room

by the time that happens? How many people will die?"
Damn it. Tears were welling in my eyes. I hated that, but
that parade of wounded young men kept marching by in my
mind. And Maricela. Don't forget Maricela. "How many
babies, Alex? How many of them will be shot?"

He shrugged and backed away, breaking the spell. "I
don't know. Another ten. Another one hundred. What difference does it make?"

I knew he didn't mean it. I'd seen the way he'd raced
through the ER, cradling Maricela to him. It still pissed me
off, though. I wrenched my arm from him. "It makes a difference. It makes a difference to me."

He chucked me under the chin. "You're so cute when
you're mad!"

Now I knew he was just trying to piss me off. I hated that
condescending bullshit. I knocked his hand away. "You don't
know the half of it. And while we're talking about cute, stay
out of my damn dreams, will you?"

"Your dreams?" He cocked an eyebrow at me. "You
dreamed about me? One of *those* dreams?"

I felt the flush spread from my neck all the way up to my
hairline. "You didn't do it on purpose?"

"Do what?" He was laughing now. "Make you have some
kind of hot sex dream about me?"

"Forget it." I pushed off from the wall and walked down
the hall, followed all the way to the cafeteria by the sound
of his laughter.

I STOPPED IN TO SEE TO MARICELA. THEY'D MOVED HER
to the regular pediatrics ward from the ICU. I figured that
was a good sign. I peeked into the room. There was no one
with her. She looked so small in the crib, so tiny. She barely
made a bump under the sheet. It took a second for me to be
sure her chest was rising and falling as it should. Then I

could focus in on the whisper of her breath going in and out over all the other hospital noises, the buzzers and beeps and clicks and whirrs that filled the halls day and night.

I sniffed. The smell of decay and blood was gone from her. She smelled like talcum powder and lotion and antiseptic.

I didn't come in from the hallway. I just peered around the corner. Frankly, I couldn't bear to get any closer. The sight of her tiny fist curled in on itself on the sheet was enough to undo me. I didn't know what getting close would do.

I did know that despite the smell of decay I'd gotten from her the previous night, there was something I hadn't smelled from Maricela. I hadn't smelled evil. I hadn't smelled sin.

In the typical goings-on of my not-so-typical life, I try to keep myself on the straight and narrow, but it's hard to do. Since becoming a grown-up, I've discovered there are a lot more gray areas in the world than there seemed to be when I was a kid. Sometimes, no matter how I try to keep my feet on the right path, they stray. Some of it's temptation. Some of it's ignorance.

Some of it is my job.

But as I stood in that doorway, I knew that whatever might have clung to my shoes when I'd wandered in the wrong direction, I didn't want to track it anywhere near that little baby. Enough evil had come into her life without her doing anything to deserve it. I wouldn't be the bearer of any more.

"Keep breathing," I whispered, and then I went home.

10

I FELL INTO BED WITHOUT TAKING A SHOWER FIRST. USU-
ally I can't stand the idea of rubbing whatever's clung to me
at the hospital onto my own sheets, but I was beyond caring.
The past few days had been a gauntlet, physically and emotionally. I closed my eyes and wondered if there was some
special incantation a person could do to keep a certain vampire out of her dreams. The fact that the source of the dreams
seemed to be internal rather than external made the incantation idea seem even less likely. Apparently, I didn't need to
worry. My sleep was black and dreamless.

I woke up in the early afternoon, disgusted with the smell
of my own skin. I almost ran into the shower. I didn't see
the message from Aunt Kitty until I'd gotten out. I braced
myself for the phone squeal and dialed her digits.

"Hey, Aunt Kitty, what's the haps?"

"I don't know, dear. What is the haps?"

I smiled. She knew perfectly well what I meant. Sometimes she plays clueless just for my entertainment. "Did you

find out anything more about the houses that your friend sold in Elk Grove?"

"I found out a little. To be honest, Melina, I'm not sure what's going on. I have a funny feeling about it."

That was hardly a surprise. There had to be something hinky going on. Whatever was happening at those houses wasn't a typical real estate deal. "What kind of funny feeling?"

"The kind of funny feeling that tells me there's something not quite kosher going on with my buddy Winston. He hasn't done more than a deal or two every few months for several years. I think he steps in for friends who need someone to deal with the paperwork now and then. Nothing more than that. Now, all of the sudden he's brokered seven deals in Elk Grove in a period of a few weeks, and they're all financed by the United Bank of Hong Kong in San Francisco through the same mortgage broker. I can't find any record of him ever having worked with that bank before."

"How close are the other houses to the one I asked you about?" Were they all in a cluster? Maybe a whole family wanted to buy houses near each other. It was definitely a buyer's market in Elk Grove these days. The foreclosure wave had washed through that area like a tsunami.

"Not that close. Not that far."

That was informative. "Can you give me the addresses?" Maybe I'd stop by a few of them tonight before I left for work and see if I could see anything else that connected them besides an aging real estate agent.

"Sure. I'll give you the names of the new owners, too." Aunt Kitty paused for a second. "They're all Asian, you know."

I hadn't known. "Hmm."

"It's not that unusual. Winston has an in with the Asian community and he uses it. We all do things like that. I make a lot of deals because of people I've met at temple. I'd say half my clients are Jewish."

"I wasn't judging, Aunt Kitty."

"I know, sweetheart. I just know it looks odd. I wanted you to understand."

I understood better than she did, apparently. "Got it. Nothing weird about all the deals for these houses going to people with Asian names and being financed by the United Bank of Hong Kong in San Francisco with the same mortgage broker."

"When you say it like that it sounds suspicious." Aunt Kitty didn't sound suspicious. She sounded troubled.

There are few things worse than a troubled aunt. Troubled aunts sometimes become meddlesome aunts. I didn't need that. "That's just my voice, Aunt Kitty. I can make 'Old McDonald' sound suspicious. I mean, why did he need that many different animals anyway?"

Aunt Kitty laughed, but I could tell she was still a little anxious. "Fine. Here's the addresses and the names." She rattled off seven addresses, then paused again. "That's interesting."

"What is?"

"Meet me for coffee this week and we can talk about it more."

I could recognize an aunt angling for some niece time. We set a date and a time. "See you then," I said.

I SAT IN THE BUICK, THE MAPS I'D PRINTED OUT FROM the Internet splayed out on the front seat next to me. Aunt Kitty was right. The houses weren't too close and they weren't too far. None of them were in the same subdivision, but all the subdivisions were in the same area. I had parked a few blocks away from the first one. I'd put on nylon shorts, a Dri-Fit tank top and sneakers. I popped my iPod earbuds into my ears, got out of the car and jogged away, looking like any other suburban jogger, I hoped.

The house was essentially a cookie-cutter copy of every

other house on the street: a pinkish beige stucco with a red-tiled roof. The grass was green and mowed. The curtains were drawn, but lots of people didn't want everyone walking by to be able to see into their living room.

I stopped to tie my shoe so I could take a longer look.

Nope. Nothing strange that I could see from the sidewalk. There was kind of a smell, though. It was strong, almost skunklike, and I thought I could hear a humming noise.

I glanced around. The sidewalks were empty. No one was out mowing their lawn or gardening. I stood up, brushed off my knees and sauntered up the driveway to the side of the house.

The smell grew stronger. So did the humming noise. I didn't get very far. Entry into the backyard was blocked by a big metal fence. It's not so strange for backyards in California to be gated, especially backyards in decent subdivisions. A lot of people have pools around here and pools mean gates. I'm all for it, most of the time. I'm sensitive to the whole little-kid-drowning-in-backyard-pool thing for obvious reasons. This gate, however, looked extra solid. And the lock? I'm not exactly the world's best at picking locks, but I've jimmied a few in my day. No way was I getting past this one. Well, at least not by picking it.

It wouldn't have taken much for me to climb the fence. All I'd have to do was back up a couple steps and get a running start. I jump way better than most. The idea made me nervous, though. Who knew what was on the other side?

There could be a dog, and that simply would not do. I sniffed. I didn't smell a dog, but then that skunky smell masked pretty much any other smell that might be there. It was enough to make my head swim.

I jogged down the driveway and the few blocks back to my car.

I repeated the process at four of the other houses. I was starting to get nervous. There was more traffic coming in and out of the neighborhoods. People were getting home from work. Kids were coming home from school and activities. It was that time of day. So far, all I had was five houses that smelled funny and hummed more than their neighboring houses and had fairly intense security gates. On the last house, I decided to hop the gate.

I listened for a long time. I didn't hear any growls or snufflings or clicking nails or any other doggie noises. I didn't hear people either or feel the presence of anything supernatural. It was now or never. I took my running start and was over the fence in one bounce.

I landed in a crouch and immediately backed into the corner. It might make it difficult to maneuver if something came at me, but at least I knew what was at my back. I stayed there for a second or two, getting my bearings.

The skunklike smell had grown stronger, making my nose twitch. It was starting to smell familiar, but I still hadn't placed it. The humming noise had grown louder, too. That was familiar as well, and even better, I knew what it was. The hum of electricity. Somewhere around here a generator was running. The hospital had several that came on whenever there was a power interruption, so I recognized the sound. Temporary power outages simply won't do in a hospital. Apparently, they wouldn't do at certain houses in Elk Grove either.

Slowly I came out of my corner. I stuck close to the wall, though, just in case. Something strange was happening here. I didn't know what it was, but I knew I'd better be prepared for who knew what to leap out at me from somewhere.

I sidled along the wall, the rough stucco scraping against my back. I came to the first of three windows on that side of the house. It was just as tightly curtained as the one in front. The fence I had jumped over was easily seven feet high. Why bother pulling the curtains on a window that no one could see in? I shrugged and moved on. Maybe it was a bedroom and the person liked to sleep late. Or had migraines. Or was allergic to the sun.

I checked my sense again but still didn't catch the familiar hum of anything of the other realms. If whatever was in there was allergic to the sun, it was a real allergy, not a characteristic of their supernatural nature.

The situation was the same at the next window and the next. Not a pinpoint of light coming out or going in.

As I peered around the corner of the house, I spotted the generator in the backyard. It wasn't exactly a feat of sleuthing. The thing was huge and red and noisy as hell. But it was neatly hidden away inside a little structure, which muffled the racket down to a hum.

I could see a system of wires and pipes coming from the generator shed, leading to the other side of the house. I hesitated before I went to follow it, though. In California, most houses like this one opened onto the backyard. That was where the pool was for family playtime and the patio for family barbecues and the swing set for kiddie playdates. Usually the back side of the house featured a lot of glass—sliding glass doors and big picture windows—to unify the indoors and the outdoors. At least, that's how Aunt Kitty always put it.

This backyard didn't exactly look played in. The pool had been drained and was being used as a garbage pit by whoever lived here. No barbecue, no swing set. Of course, that didn't mean there wasn't someone sitting inside the house looking out the window and admiring the generator.

I sidled around the corner, careful to check sight lines. So far I didn't see anyone, and the windows on the back side of the house were as completely covered as all the others. I crept a little farther, stopping every step or two to listen for any sign of human occupation.

There wasn't any. Nothing I could see or hear at least, and the blasted skunk smell masked anything I might pick up with my nose.

I crept farther, back flat against the wall. I reached the

edge of the wall. I braced myself and took a quick peek around the corner.

More curtains.

I took a deep breath and relaxed a little. Whoever lived here—if anybody was actually living here—sure did value privacy.

I made my way across the backyard. I didn't exactly saunter, but I wasn't creeping along the walls like a spider anymore. I followed the pipes and wires from the generator to the other side of the house. Surprise, surprise. That was where the meter was.

I am not an electrician. That hasn't been one of the areas that Mae felt I needed education in. Nevertheless, I looked at that mess of wires and black plastic and knew with certainty that Pacific Gas and Electric had nothing to do with the way the generator in the backyard was wired into the house.

Something was so definitely not right here, yet I really wasn't sure what it was. I was pretty sure, however, that it was time to go. I took my running steps back and prepared to bounce over the fence again.

That's when I noticed the security cameras.

IF IT IS POSSIBLE TO KICK ONE'S OWN ASS FROM ONE SIDE of town to the other, that is precisely what I did. There was a huge fence. There were tightly curtained windows. Would it have killed me to look up for a security camera? I was reasonably sure I had been out of the camera sight lines for most of my trip around the house. I'd stuck pretty close to the walls and would have had the scratches on my back from the stucco to prove it, but they'd already healed, leaving a prickly sensation across my back, but no blood.

I was pretty sure, however, that I'd been right in the line of sight of the last camera before I cleared the wall and that

I'd looked right up into it, giving anyone who might be watching a very clear view of my face.

On the bright side, I didn't have a lot of identifying marks. No moles. No scars. No tattoos with my name and birth date on my neck. My car had been parked blocks away. If someone had been watching—and that struck me now as a pretty big if since no one had come charging out with guns blazing or hopping out ready to eat my flesh with undead glee—how would they figure out who I was?

The fact that they'd followed me to Aldo's and taken the envelope from me left me feeling uneasy, but it was possible that they still didn't know who—or what—I was.

By the time I reached I-5, I was breathing normally and my heart no longer pounded in a hummingbird kind of cadence.

I did, however, damn near pee my pants when my cell phone rang. The number was restricted, but I jammed the earbud of my headset into my ear and answered anyway. "Hello?"

"Are you driving?"

I recognized the voice instantly, even without the scent of cinnamon. Although oddly, I thought I could smell snickerdoodles once Ted Goodnight started talking to me, even over the phone. "I am."

"Are you using a hands-free device?"

I smiled. Boy, he was bossy. Good thing he was so cute, even if he was a 'Dane. "I am, as a matter of fact."

"Good."

He didn't say anything for a second.

"Is that why you called? To make sure I was obeying the cell phone law?" I finally asked. "I'm not texting or drinking either, in case you were worried about me breaking those laws, too. I did change lanes in an intersection earlier. I don't want you to think I'm some kind of Goody Two-shoes."

"I don't think that, and I didn't call to check to see if you were breaking laws." Another pause.

"So you called for another reason?" I prompted. Conversation was not going to be this guy's strong point, obviously, which was probably okay since I can pretty much talk the hind leg off a donkey when I'm nervous and this guy definitely made me a little antsy.

I heard the breath of his sigh from the other end of the phone. "I had a crappy day and I suddenly wanted to hear your voice. What time do you get off work?"

I mentally took back the crack about him being a lousy conversationalist. Those two sentences pretty much melted my hard little heart. I glanced in my rearview mirror. For a second, I could have sworn I'd seen a black SUV behind me. Either it changed lanes or was a figment of my somewhat paranoid imagination. After I saw *I Am Legend*, I spent two weeks convinced there were undead vampire dogs around every corner. I turned my attention back to Ted. "Seven tomorrow morning. I work the night shift."

"Oh." His disappointment was palpable. Then in a brighter tone, he said, "How about breakfast?"

Now it was my turn to pause. What exactly was I flirting with here? I mean, besides the obvious answer that I was flirting with a broad-shouldered, slim-hipped man with sun-kissed skin and hair that would make a supermodel weep? I was flirting with a cop. Oh, sure, we'd held hands and watched the sunrise together—another thing that was way too sweet to be real. He was still a cop and did all kinds of cop-type things, like arrest people. And lecture them about driving and talking on their cell phones. How long would it be until something happened that I wouldn't be able to explain away? What would he do then? How would I be forced to respond? "Is this a date?" I asked.

"Breakfast doesn't seem very datelike," he said. "Could it just be, you know, breakfast?"

"Just, you know, breakfast sounds great." It wasn't a date. I could do that. I knew I was walking a dangerous line, but damn it, I love snickerdoodles. "So, as long as we're chitchatting here on my hands-free device, hypothetically speaking, can you think of a reason why a house would have a generator in the backyard, a funny smell and a lot of security around it?"

He paused again. "Where is this house?" He didn't sound all funny and tongue-tied anymore. He sounded a little angry and back to bossy. See? Cop stuff.

"Nowhere," I lied. Lying comes very naturally to me. I've been doing it a long time. I don't think it can be taught. It's sort of a Zen thing. You have to be one with whatever untruth you're putting out in the universe. "I was just curious."

"That's a pretty specific set of things to be curious about. Are you sure you didn't see a house like that? Is it in your neighborhood? Or near the hospital?" Wow. He could get serious fast.

"I'm sure I haven't seen a house like that," I said. "It's just a hypothetical question."

"Hypothetically speaking, then," he said after another pause, "I would say that a house like that was a grow house."

There was a flash of black in my rearview mirror again. I glanced but didn't see anything. "A what?"

"A grow house. A house where someone is growing marijuana, a lot of marijuana."

I let my head fall back against the velour headrest. The skunky smell made sense now. Geez, was I ever an idiot. There was a reason they called it skunk weed.

I've got nothing against weed. If you ask me, they should legalize the damn stuff and then tax the holy hell out of it just like they do with booze. Think of the millions of dollars in revenue that could be generated, the school programs that could be supported, the highways that could be paved and the hospitals that could be built. That said, it isn't legal now, and buying it and using it therefore demand that one associate with people who don't mind breaking the law in bigger ways than lighting up the occasional doobie. Plus, if it was legal, they could regulate it a little better. It's one thing if a forty-year-old wants to have a puff or two after a hard week. It's an entirely different thing when a fourteen-year-old is lighting up behind the gym between classes. I realize plenty of underage kids drink. I just think there are a lot fewer of them than there would be if there was no regulation at all.

I was still a little confused. "Why would they grow it in a house?"

"Because we've been cracking down on outdoor cultivation and because they can grow it faster and stronger inside with hydroponics. Plus, with all the foreclosures, if they can get financing, they can snap up houses damn cheap right now." I liked his voice. I'd spent so much time focusing on how good he smelled every time we'd been together that I hadn't noticed his voice. I liked the little bit of a rumble it had. I bet it would feel great whispering in my ear when it wasn't coming through a hands-free device.

"Who's they?" What the hell had I stumbled on? A network of grow houses? What would marijuana farmers have to do with Chinese vampires?

"The usual suspects. Gangs. Mafia. Tongs."

That was it. I was done. We had just gone outside my comfort zone. I pulled off the freeway and headed toward home. "That they."

"Yeah, Melina. That they. A they you should seriously consider staying very far away from. Are you sure you don't want to tell me where you saw this house?"

"I'm telling you, there's no house." And I'm having cocktails with the Easter Bunny later today.

"Is it connected to the reason you were in the area at that gang fight?" he pressed.

"Nothing's connected to that. It was a coincidence. I just happened to be in the wrong place at the wrong time." Geez, did he ever let go of anything? Were we going to be rocking on the porch in our golden years with him still asking me about that? Dear Lord, why was I thinking about rocking on a porch with him when I was an old lady?

He sighed again. "Right. We'll talk more at breakfast, okay?"

Not really, but the idea of free pancakes won me over. "You betcha."

11

DOREEN FLIPPED A WALLET ONTO MY DESK. "CAN YOU GET this guy's paperwork started? I think everything you need is in there."

"Is he truly hurt too much to sit in the chair?" I gestured with my chin at the rolling chair across the counter. I don't like going through people's wallets. First of all, you never know what might be lurking in one. People keep crazy shit in their wallets. Second, it makes them too human, too real. It's a lot easier to do my job if the person is just an injury and a set of numbers. Once you've seen pictures of their grandkids or their membership card in PFLAG, they begin to become actual people. Way too many actual people come through the emergency room. Recognizing them as people makes my job harder and slower. It really does no one any good.

Doreen's laugh was completely without mirth. "Way too bad. It looks like someone went after him with a machete."

That made me shove my chair back and look up at her. "Who attacks someone with a machete?"

"You got me, girlfriend, but somebody hacked him up good. He's going to lose one of his hands. I don't see any way they can save it."

We are not doctors. We are admitting clerks. Most of us have no medical training whatsoever, but after a year or two of watching people come through the emergency room, we begin to have a sense of who's going to make it and who isn't. I cringed. "I'll get him checked in."

I picked up the wallet. It was leather and well-worn. My grandmother would have appreciated it and pointed out that if you buy something of quality, it lasts a long time. I would have pointed out that my attention span is short and I don't want to carry the same wallet for my entire adult life. I flipped it open and pried the driver's license out. That would give me most of the basic information I needed to start with like full name, address and all that.

I peered at the picture of the older Asian man, and then I read the name. The guy who was about to lose his hand because of a machete attack was Frank Liu.

For a few minutes, I toyed with the idea that it could be a different Frank Liu, but then I looked at the address. Nope. It was my grandmother's Frank Liu. That was the address of the house I'd been to in the Pocket. At least he wasn't missing anymore. I thought about calling Ted to let him know his missing persons case was no longer that, but I figured that news of a machete attack would probably reach his ears soon enough.

Plus, I needed to figure out what this meant. I hadn't even figured out why Frank had gone missing. Now he was back, or at least most of him was. I winced again as I thought about what Doreen had said about Liu's hand.

I had no doubt he was headed into surgery now. Maybe I'd be able to talk to him before my shift ended, to ask a few questions that didn't necessarily have to do with his insurance coverage.

AT THE END OF MY SHIFT, I SLIPPED QUIETLY INTO FRANK
Liu's hospital room. Throughout the course of the night,
I'd been keeping tabs on him via the hospital's computer
system. His surgery had been short, which was either a
very good sign or a very bad one. His stay in recovery had
been brief. Chances were, he wouldn't remember it. Most
people don't. Blessed be modern pharmaceuticals and their
memory-erasing properties. He'd been transferred to a semi-
private room on the fifth floor about an hour ago. I figured
he'd be all settled in now and the nurses would be done
poking him and prodding him for the moment.

The room was dim but not dark. Hospital rooms almost
never are. There's always light from the hallway seeping in
somewhere, and all the different machines cast their own
spectral glow. I glanced at the screen displaying Frank Liu's
vital signs. At least to a layperson's eyes, he was looking
okay. His oxygen saturation was ninety-eight percent, and
his heart rate was steady and regular.

He looked small in the bed and very, very still. Not quite
as small as Maricela but still way smaller than I thought he
should.

There was someone in the chair next to the bed. My first
reaction was that I was glad that Frank wasn't alone. The
second was a little bit of panic when the person raised his
head from where it rested on the bed and asked, "What are
you doing here?"

I felt I could easily ask George, the priest from the Bok
Kai Temple, the same question. What indeed was he doing
here?

"I, uh, just wanted to check on Mr. Liu," I stammered
instead. I don't know why I'm so bad at conversational con-
frontation. Really, if he'd jumped up and aimed a roundhouse kick at my head, I would have known exactly what to

do, how to deflect it, how to set up my own attack. This talky-talky stuff? I suck at it. I recover faster from a fist strike to the jaw than someone saying something mean to me.

"He'll survive," the priest said, a trace of bitterness in his voice. "They made sure of that."

I took another step into the room. "Who are they? What do they want?"

George rose up in his chair. "You need to leave. You've done enough damage already."

Me? What had I done? "I assure you, I had nothing to do with what's happened to Mr. Liu."

George snorted. "Really? Then exactly whom was he sent here to warn? It wasn't me. I've had warnings enough. I don't need any others."

"He was sent here? Like a message?" Who would do that to a person to send a message? And why to me? I didn't even know anything, although I'm not sure I'd ever seen a clearer indicator that I was close to learning something important than the very still body of the man under the bed sheets.

"Of course he was. That's why they made sure he'd stay alive. A dead man is only a warning for a little while. People forget him after a while. A living maimed man? He acts as a warning for a long, long time. Now, please, miss, whoever you are . . . whatever you are . . . go away and don't come back."

I squinted at George. What exactly did he mean by *whatever you are*? Did he have an inkling that I wasn't quite what I seemed? "How can you be sure this is a warning to me when you don't even know my name?"

He shook his head slowly. "Do you think it's a coincidence that you're the only one who's been poking around the temple and that you happen to work in the very hospital where they dumped Mr. Liu's body?"

When he put it like that, it did seem like a heck of a

mash-up. "Okay. So they're trying to warn me. What are they trying to warn me about, and who are they?"

He stood and advanced toward me. "You don't need to know any of that. All you need to know is that it's time for you to mind your own business."

I left the room, wondering if he knew how much I wanted to do precisely that.

OFFICER TED GOODNIGHT WAS LEANING AGAINST MY grandmother's Buick, long legs crossed at the ankle in front of him and arms crossed over his chest, looking very un-officerlike, when I walked into the employee parking garage. He had on faded blue jeans and a King Crimson T-shirt with an unbuttoned chambray shirt over it that did little to disguise the bulge of his biceps or the muscles across his chest. My heart did an embarrassing little flip-flop that reminded me way too much of the first time I'd seen Leonardo DiCaprio in *Titanic*. I think Aunt Kitty and I went to that movie about seven times, despite my brother yelling after us on our way out the door that, in the end, the boat was still going to sink. Boys. They don't understand anything.

Then I noticed that the chambray shirt didn't fully hide the shoulder holster and sidearm underneath it. I'm not a big fan of guns. I don't understand them, so they make me a little nervous. "How'd you know which car was mine?" I asked, stopping a few feet away from him.

He smiled when he saw me, and little crinkles formed at the corners of his cornflower blue eyes. My heart did the flip-flop thing again. Maybe I needed to have an EKG. That couldn't possibly be normal. "I have make, model and license plate on the police report from the first night you called in the gang fight. Not too many Buicks of this vintage parked around here. It didn't take long to find it."

Cute and resourceful, too, but a warning bell sounded in

the back of my mind. Police report. He was still a cop and I still needed to tread carefully. I was playing with fire here. Plus, did he say first night I called in the gang fight? Did he know about the second one? Before I could ask a question, however, he said, "Do you want to leave your car here? Or should I follow you home and we can leave from there?" He stood up and jammed his hands in his pockets.

I decided on the latter. I had no desire to come back to the hospital until I had to come back for my shift at eleven. I had no desire to see Frank Liu's way-too-still body or the very pissed-off priest who was keeping guard at his bedside. If Frank Liu was indeed some kind of warning message from someone to yours truly, it didn't seem so terrible to have a police escort home either. I found a parking spot relatively close to my place, hopped out of the Buick and into his pickup truck. "Nice," I said as I looked around the inside.

"It's not fancy, but it gets me from place to place." He sounded nonchalant, but I saw a little blush on his cheeks.

This was bad, very bad. Not only was he a cop, but he was sweet. He blushed when I complimented his ride. I had a terrible feeling that he would be the kind of guy who took off his suit jacket and put it around a girl's shoulders on a cold night, the kind of guy who would remember Valentine's Day, the kind of guy that I used to watch in movies and sigh over until I realized that no guy like that would ever be able to withstand dating a girl whose schedule was regularly interrupted by elves, goblins, werewolves and fairies.

I almost asked him to turn the car around right there, but my stomach growled and I decided I'd stay for the free pancakes.

Really. He held no other interest for me whatsoever.

IN THE END, I DIDN'T ORDER PANCAKES. WE WENT TO THE Tower Café and frankly, there's no point in having breakfast there if you aren't having the custard-soaked French toast with a side of crispy bacon and lots of hot black coffee. Mmm. Mmm. Mmm.

Ted waited until I was in a custard-and-carbohydrate-induced state of nirvana before he asked, "So where exactly is the grow house?"

I choked.

It's not that I didn't expect him to ask. I knew he would ask. I just expected he would sidle up to it and sneak it in, not give it to me bold-faced like that.

An episode of back-slapping and several sips of water later, I gasped out, "What grow house?"

"Whatever one you saw yesterday." He leaned back in his chair and smiled at me as if it were the most innocuous of questions, like maybe he was asking where I bought my earrings or what kind of movies I liked. For the record, the answers are craft fairs and romantic comedies.

"Hypothetical, remember?" I croaked, setting down my fork. This is where hanging out with cops gets tricky. He knew I was lying. Contrary to what one sees on TV, cops are not stupid, they won't sell their souls for a bear claw and a lot of them have learned how to spot a liar faster than they can pull their weapons.

"Melina," he said, reaching across the table to take my hand.

His touch sent an instant warmth racing up my arm. I squinted at him. Had I missed something? Was there something about him from another realm? Was he an itsy bit 'Cane? No matter how hard I looked, I saw nothing but man. I'd been spending way too much time hobnobbing with hobgoblins. I couldn't even recognize normal when it was holding my hand.

"You don't have to be afraid. I can protect you," he said.

Wow. A girl could get used to this. Someone to protect me? I couldn't remember the last time anyone even offered. Sadly, it was pointless anyway. He had no idea what he was up against and could no more protect me from the *kiang shi* than my grandmother could. Grandma Rosie could balance the hell out of a Rising Crane position, but I didn't think she had the skills to contain those killing machines. "Why do you think I need protecting?"

He looked incredulous. "Do you remember how we met, Melina?"

Oh yeah, we met over me witnessing the brutal slaying of several gang members. "I told you. I was just driving by. I wanted to be a good citizen." I all but batted my eyes at him.

He let go of my hand and looked down at his coffee. "Okay. You don't want to tell me what's going on. We haven't known each other that long, and maybe you're still trying to decide if you can trust me or not. I get that. I can wait. But, Melina, please don't wait too long. I don't know what you've got yourself into, but I do know it's got you brushing up against some pretty unpleasant people. I can help. Remember that. I want to help. No judgments."

The sincerity in his voice almost broke me. It was on the tip of my tongue to tell him exactly where those grow houses were and let him take care of it. I desperately wanted to tell someone about Frank Liu, too. It almost made sense to tell him. He was a cop. He'd have the resources to find out who owned those houses and investigate them more quickly and more thoroughly than I would.

But how to explain the other part? The pesky part that dealt with undead Asians marauding through the most gang-afflicted portions of Sacramento. Could I explain one piece without the other? I didn't see how, but I owed him something, especially for that part about no judgments.

"I'll think about it." I reached my hand across the table for his this time. He lifted it to his lips and kissed my knuckles. I damn near slid off my chair. Instead, I said, "They found Frank Liu."

———

TED WALKED ME TO THE DOOR OF MY APARTMENT AND stood behind me, his hands jammed into the pockets of his jeans, while I undid the locks. I opened the door and turned around. "I'd invite you in for a cup of coffee, but we just drank about a gallon of the stuff."

He laughed. "That's okay. I know this is probably your only time to sleep, and my shift starts soon. I should get going." He took a step closer to me and looked down into my eyes.

"Thanks for breakfast. It was great." My voice came out a little bit squeaky. I swallowed and tried to clear my throat.

"Yeah, it was." His gaze had traveled down to my lips. He took another step closer. "We should do it again sometime."

"Sure," I said. Now my voice was all breathy. Fabulous. I was becoming Betty Boopenstein.

He slid his arm around my waist and pulled me against him. My hands settled on his chest. I mean, what else was I supposed to do with them? But it set off some kind of reaction in him, because the muscles under my hands rippled and he pulled me even closer.

"Soon," he said, his voice a husky whisper.

"Uh-huh" was all I managed to get out this time, but that was okay, because then he was kissing me.

I'd known he was going to kiss me from the second his gaze had focused on my mouth. I'm not exactly Paris Hilton, but this isn't my first rodeo either. I'd thought I was prepared. Hoo, boy, did I have that wrong.

His lips claimed mine, warm and smooth and sweet. His hands slid lower, pulling our bodies closer, leaving me without the slightest doubt that he was very happy to see me. His tongue swept against mine, probing and teasing, then slipped away as he sucked my lower lip between his teeth.

He lifted his head and looked down into my eyes, and I

wanted it all again, the warmth of his mouth, the scrape of his beard against my cheek, his hard body pressed into my softness, his heat against my heat.

"You taste like maple syrup," he said, a smile quirking at the corner of his lips.

"You taste like cinnamon and vanilla," I replied.

I reached behind his neck and pulled his mouth down to mine again and lost myself in his kiss.

I often feel small. My life constantly reminds me of how insignificant I am. I can barely go a day without some reminder of the fact that my problems don't amount to a hill of beans in this crazy mixed-up world. So it was no surprise that I felt small when pulled against the broad chest of this golden warrior of a man. The surprise was that I felt so incredibly safe.

Until something pulled at my pant leg.

I glanced down and caught a glimpse of a tail as something darted into my apartment.

Ted shifted against me and my attention veered back to him. Maybe I hadn't really seen what I thought I'd seen. Maybe it had been a figment of my imagination. I hadn't felt the buzz of a supernatural being nearby, but of course, that could have been masked by the fact that my entire body was buzzing with an entirely different sensation at the moment, one that was one hundred percent human.

It pulled at my pant leg again. Damn. It was still there and it was an imp. There are few things peskier than an imp, and I grew up with a younger brother, so I know about pesky.

I slid my hand down and held up one finger, trying to communicate to give me a minute.

Apparently, imps don't understand sign language. He pulled on my pants again. Too many more tugs and I was going to end up dropping trou right there in the hallway. I kicked at him. Not a hard kick, just a little let-me-go kick.

The little bastard bit me.

I squeaked. It wasn't a hard bite. It was like being nipped by a kitten with those tiny needle-sharp teeth, but it was enough to let me know he was going nowhere. It was also enough to make Ted straighten up.

"Are you okay?"

"I . . . uh . . . I just . . ." I just have an imp gnawing at my ankle and probably really need to see what he wants. There was no way I was telling him that.

Ted moved away from me and I felt suddenly cold, not so easy on a warm summer morning in Sacramento. He raised his hands. "I know."

"You do?" Had he seen the imp? Most people couldn't. Had I managed to stumble on another human being that saw what I saw, but had managed to not be sucked into doing the bidding of whatever supernatural force happened to drop by? How cool would that be?

"I do, Melina. I don't want to rush this anymore than you do. You're right. I'll go now." He caressed my cheek.

That was so not what I wanted, but considering the mischievous little fairy that had darted back into my apartment, it was probably the right thing to do. I hated doing the right thing.

Ted's hands were back in his pockets. He looked bashful again. "I'll call you later, okay?"

"Okay," I managed to squeak out as he walked down the stairs. I waited until I heard the front door open and close. Then I walked into my apartment and hissed, "What the hell do you want?"

THE IMP HELD UP A FLUTE. "COULD YOU TAKE THIS TO someone for me?" he asked, his voice squeakier than mine had been out in the hallway right before Ted kissed me.

Oh yeah, Ted had kissed me. Wow. I'd kissed a cop. Of all the weird things I'd done in my short time on earth, that might have been the weirdest. Cop kissing. What would be next? Lawyer licking? Was it really alliterative if the first letters just sounded the same?

"Listen, you," I started to scold and then realized I didn't know the thing's name. I hated when creatures called me "woman" or "girl" or just "human." It felt disrespectful. I didn't like to make anything else feel the same way. Damn my mother and those early Golden Rule lessons. "What's your name anyway?"

The imp smiled a crooked little close-mouthed smile. "You can call me Joe."

"Joe the Imp? Seriously? Are you on the campaign trail?" That's just what the Republican Party needed. Actual hell creatures making their party platform.

Joe rolled his eyes. I mean that literally. He could really make his eyes do total circles in their sockets. That totally skeeved me out. "You wouldn't be able to pronounce my real name."

"Try me." I was so sick of things patronizing me. Enough already.

"Fine, then." He then emitted a series of whistles and clicks and grunts.

I conceded defeat. "Joe it is."

He made a little bow.

I suppressed the urge to curtsey. "Listen, Joe, I was in the middle of a moment back there and I kind of resent the interruption. Could you not wait just a minute or two? I'm sure you've heard that patience is a virtue."

"A moment? Is that what you humans are calling it these days? I remember when it was just referred to as fornication. You certainly have come a long way, baby." He chuckled, which came out like a bad George Bush imitation. It was very unpleasant.

I took the flute from the imp and turned it over in my hands. It wasn't anything fancy. A person could walk right by it on a shelf in a thrift store, but this flute would never end up at a thrift store. I recognized this flute. "How'd you end up with Kokopelli's flute?" I turned it over again, wondering why it didn't give off any sign of being an instrument of power. Maybe sometimes a flute was just a flute.

The imp shrugged its bony shoulders, making his leathery wings stretch a little as he did so. "I borrowed it for a little while. I thought he might want it back."

I nodded. "So you stole it and you want it returned before he finds you and beats the snot out of you."

Joe drew himself up to his full height, which was only about three feet, if that. "My dear lady, how dare you suggest that I came about this flute through dishonest means?"

I waved away his protests. "Save it for someone who cares, bat breath. I'll take it. Can it wait until tonight?"

"Probably." He inspected his fingernails.

"What is that supposed to mean?"

"Sooner would probably be better than later."

"He's looking for you already?"

The imp's wings sagged. "Pretty much."

I was tired. I'd kissed a cop. My grandmother's tai chi instructor was lying maimed in a hospital bed. I wasn't anxious to be caught up in some imp's drama. "Where is he?" I asked.

The imp gave me some general directions that would take me toward Amador County. I'd gone worse places on less sleep. I sighed. A girl's gotta do what a girl's gotta do, and apparently this girl's gotta take musical instruments to Native American deities on this particular day.

I opened the window to usher out the imp. I wasn't sure how he got in, and sometimes it was best not to ask questions like that. I sure as snot wasn't walking him out the front door of the apartment building, though. The imp had wings. He could use them.

"Why'd you take it?" I asked as Joe hopped up onto the windowsill, curiosity getting the better of me.

He smiled up at me. Not a pretty sight. He had sharp little

teeth and a lipless mouth and the smile looked more like a grimace on his nasty little face than an expression of anything nice. "It was shiny," he said and flew away.

'Nough said.

12

I WASHED MY FACE, BRUSHED MY TEETH AND GAVE Grandma Rosie a call. If there's anything her people—and by her people I meant senior Americans—knew how to do, it was to help out someone in the hospital. I knew that by noon there'd be an entire brigade assembled to send cards, deliver flowers and visit when Frank Liu was ready.

"I think I need to get my hearing aids checked," she said. "I could have sworn you said someone attacked him with a machete."

"No problem with the hearing aids, Grandma. That's what I said." Which was a good thing, because the last time I'd taken her for a hearing-aid check, I'd almost gone insane in that little booth at the Costco. The hearing-aid dude there is seriously strange, and he doesn't have anything supernatural to blame it on.

Grandma muttered, "What is this world coming to?"

I didn't have an answer, or at least not one that I was prepared to share with my grandmother. I sometimes wondered what would happen if I just blurted out that Chinese vampires living under the streets of Old Sacramento were being used to attack gang members or something like that. I was taking no chances of ending up back in the little hearing-aid booth at Costco, though, so I kept my big trap shut.

Then I got back into her Buick. Amador wasn't far and the route was scenic, but I wasn't looking forward to the drive or the company I was going to keep. I might as well get it over with.

If all you know about Kokopelli is the cute little flute player from the T-shirts and key chains everyone brings back from their vacations in Scottsdale, the real deal can be quite a surprise. I'd crossed paths with the flute player before, so I knew what I was getting into this time.

I wondered what had brought him so far north, although if he was going to be this far north I supposed Amador County, with its acres of chaparral, made sense. At least he'd be at home in the landscape. Plus, the name Amador supposedly means "one who loves." What could be more perfect for a fertility god? The general answer for what brought Kokopelli anywhere was, however, usually a girl and not the beauties of the countryside. He was a major horndog, perhaps the biggest horndog I had met personally. It was wise for a young woman to keep her distance from him unless she wanted to end up knocked up. I hoped to hell it wasn't some nice Miwok girl he was after. The tribes had enough trouble as it was.

I looked at the flute sitting on the seat next to me, seeming all innocent and inanimate and everything, and wondered if I should just toss it out the window and go home. It was tempting, but I knew I wouldn't do it. I don't know what the adult equivalent of getting a huge zit on the end of your nose is, but I really don't want to find out either.

I'd gotten to the general area that the imp had sent me to and the nonfat latte I'd gotten at the drive-thru Starbucks on my way out of town was beginning to have an uncomfortable effect on me. There was nothing around but chaparral.

I pulled off the road, figuring I could relieve myself behind some handy bush and then resume searching for my Anasazi friend.

This was how a lot of my deliveries went. Not necessarily the fresh-air-peeing part, but the not-knowing-exactly-where-I-was-going part. Sometimes I got specific instructions like Alex's request to take that blasted envelope to Aldo's house. More often, though, it was like this. Some little creature would give me some little items that it wanted to go somewhere. I'd show up in the general area and somehow the thing I was delivering to would find me. It was time-consuming and sometimes boring, and I pretty much always had a paperback book in the Buick to while away time during long waits.

I found a likely pull-off area and a likely bush. When I came out from behind the bush, still putting myself back together, Kokopelli was leaning against my car with a lazy grin across his face.

"Don't bother buttoning up for me, sweetheart," he said. He wasn't exactly handsome. His face was too craggy for that, but there was something about him. He had a certain charisma that was hard to deny. He also had a beautiful head of thick dark hair brushed off his high forehead and a profile so sharp you could cut glass with it.

I finished zipping up anyway. "I've got something for you."

"And I have something for you, darling." He grabbed at his crotch. I know, real smooth, right? Sadly, it probably worked for him nine times out of ten. I was happy, however, to be the tenth. I so did not want to get near this guy. One of the things a person wouldn't know about Kokopelli if all they knew was the sanitized version popular at tourist traps, is that he is hung like a celestial stallion. Seriously, I'm surprised he can find pants with enough room for that thing. Check out all the old petroglyphs of him. He's had a serious *schwanzstucker* since forever.

I ignored the comment and his outrageous bulge. "It's in the car," I said.

He smiled wider. "So come and get it."

I shook my head. I wasn't getting that close to him, that damn pack on his back or his crazy knob. Whatever seeds he wanted to sow could land in someone else's fertile plains. A baby was about the last thing I needed at this point in my life. "I'll come and get it as soon as you move away from the car."

"Don't do me like that. Come give this weary old traveler a hug." He spread his arms wide, the bulge in his pants twitching as if it had a life of its own.

"Not in a million years. If you want the flute, you'll step away from the Buick." I crossed my arms across my chest, feeling naked under his gaze anyway.

He brushed his long hair back from his forehead. "All right, then. I need the flute and there's always pussy somewhere," he said and walked several yards away from my car.

I considered whacking him over the head with the damn thing for that last comment, but I knew it was as much about pride as insulting me. Kokopelli didn't get turned down much. So instead I put the flute on a rock halfway between us and then backed away.

As I did, he cocked his head and gave me a strange look. "So that's how it is."

"How what is?" I asked, happy to have the solid bulk of the Buick behind me.

"You're in love. You should have told me, *Guapa*. I wouldn't have been so mean." He grinned. "I love love."

I could feel my face getting hot. "Who said I was in love?"

"No one had to say it. I can smell it on you." He smacked his lips. "It's strong, too. I'm surprised you don't have packs of dogs after you."

Now there was a charming thought. "You're making this up. So I turned you down. Get over yourself."

He laughed outright now. "Whatever you say, sweetheart, but old Kokopelli knows the truth and so do you."

"It's been a pleasure," I said, opening the door of the car.

"It certainly could have been," he cooed, retrieving the flute and running his hands over it. He had long fingers and they danced along the instrument in a way that made me start to breathe a little faster. He smiled at me and lifted the instrument to his full, sensuous lips. Blood pounded in my ears.

I slammed the door closed with a thunk and took off, shooting gravel out from underneath my tires.

Love. What the hell did love have to do with it?

AS DELIVERIES WENT, THAT ONE WAS PRETTY EASY. I probably wouldn't rest completely easy until I got my next period, but I didn't think even Kokopelli could knock a girl up from that kind of distance. I got home, barely able to keep my eyes open. There was no way that I could teach karate. I called the dojo but got the answering machine. Mae was probably warming up. She didn't often answer the phone when she was stretching. I left her a message explaining that I wouldn't be in that afternoon and that I'd fill her in on why later.

One of the great things about working for Mae was that she understood my sudden and inexplicable absences. The hospital? Not so crazy about those.

It bothered me that Mae and I hadn't spoken since our spat the other day. I wanted to talk to her. I wanted to ask her how to handle the Ted situation, because after the kiss he gave me in the hallway that morning it was definitely a situation. I wanted to ask her what to do about the grow houses and Frank Liu. I wanted the comfort of knowing that she would help me and guide me.

I couldn't quite let go of hearing her tell me that I should grow up and take some responsibility for a change, though. That still stung.

It didn't sting enough to keep me out of my bed. I toppled in without showering again and dreamed about cinnamon rolls.

I WOKE UP WITH JUST ENOUGH TIME TO SHOWER AND head off to work. It was already dark outside. I paused at the doorway before I left the apartment building. Someone had sent me a warning in the form of a horribly disfigured man. Would they be out there? Waiting for me in the dark?

I don't scare that easily. Maybe it's having died once already. Maybe it's dealing day after day with so many different kinds of creatures.

Maybe I'm just not so crazy in love with this life that I can't imagine it ending.

Still, I wasn't crazy about becoming Messenger dim sum for a gang of *kiang shi* or being chopped up like a piece of fish in a Ginsu knife demonstration.

The Buick was less than a block away. I couldn't quite see it from inside the building, but it wasn't far. Could I make it to the car if *kiang shi* were hopping after me to the tune of ringing bells? As long as I didn't do something totally horror-movie appropriate like drop my keys or get my foot stuck in a grate I was pretty sure I could outrun even the best hopper among them. Except the stuff I'd read on the Internet said that they got stronger with each feeding. They'd been feeding plenty on a gangbanger smorgasbord. How strong were they now? How far could they jump? How fast?

What if there was another "warning" waiting for me?

That I didn't think I could take. Another man hacked at with a machete lying on the sidewalk, a bloody cipher to be unencrypted by only a few? No thank you.

I had to go, though. Mae had drilled into me from a very young age the importance of maintaining every shred of normalcy that I could. Part of being normal was having a job. My mouth felt dry.

I didn't know what was out there. I didn't know what was gunning for me. I did know that I couldn't live like this. Tomorrow morning after work, I was starting Operation Figure It Out.

I took a deep breath, held it and walked out the door. I heard nothing and smelled nothing. Nothing made my flesh buzz with supernatural awareness. I can hold my breath for a long time. I didn't have to take another one until I was at the Buick. What I saw there, though, made me blow out the breath I was holding.

Someone had gouged a triangle into the paint on the side of my car. A triangle. Not a pentagram. Not any kind of obscenity. Just a simple three-sided geometric figure.

What the hell did that mean?

MY CELL PHONE RANG ABOUT HALFWAY THROUGH MY shift. Now normally, taking a personal call during work hours would earn me a glare or two from my coworkers and definitely from Doreen. Apparently, my hero status was like an amulet that warded off glares. A couple of people glanced my way, but no one stared for long as I answered it after checking the caller ID.

"Hey, you, hungry for more pancakes?" I asked.

Ted chuckled. "Hungry, but maybe not for pancakes."

Didn't that set off a little thrill in my girliest parts? "What'd you have in mind?"

"Maybe dinner next time."

"Dinner sounds more like a date than breakfast."

"It does." He didn't sound nearly as shy and tongue-tied as he had before. One good French kiss and the guy was bold as brass. "Maybe we could do it after you file your vandalism report."

That stopped all the tingling and fast. "What vandalism report?"

"The one where you report how someone keyed your car."

My eyes narrowed even though he wasn't here to squint at. "How do you know about that?"

"I saw it tonight in the hospital parking lot. It's kind of hard to miss."

"What were you doing at the hospital?"

"How much trouble will I be in if I say I was checking on you?"

What an excellent question. Another excellent question was why was it that the first guy who really interested me in years had to be a cop? I know I'm a little on the self-destructive side—yet another side effect of the whole near-death experience, in my humble opinion—but this was suicide. What was I doing? "Probably more trouble than you want to be in."

"Okay, then, what if I was dropping off a dude who'd gotten knocked off his bicycle by a drunk and checking up on you was just a fringe benefit?"

"Slightly less trouble but still not home free, Goodnight."

He sighed. "I'm doing it for my own protection as well as yours, Melina. I know you're into something you shouldn't be. I know you're probably in over your head whether you want to admit it or not. I also know that I haven't had enough years on the force to have them look the other way if I get tangled up in something. I like you, Melina. I like you a lot. But I've wanted to be a cop since I was eight years old."

How did he do that? How did he put his heart out there on a platter like that? Didn't he know how dangerous that was? I'd sooner parachute into a pit of vipers than tell someone my hopes and dreams. Of course, being a little unsure of what those hopes and dreams were, made that kind of a moot point, but still! "I get it. If I told you that I have no idea what that triangle means or who did it, would that help?"

I heard him suck in his breath. "A triangle? Are you sure?"

"Yeah, I'm sure. I thought you saw it."

"I drove past it. I didn't get a good look at it."

"It's definitely a triangle. Math was not my strong suit in high school, but I'm pretty sure those three-sided geometrical figures are triangles."

He didn't speak for a second. Then he asked, "Melina, have you gotten yourself mixed up with a Triad?"

I SPENT THE REST OF MY SHIFT CHEWING OVER THAT question. Had I gotten myself mixed up with a Triad? Those dudes in the suits with the shiny Navigators could totally be Triad members. A Triad is kind of like a Chinese version of the Mafia. It seems like every ethnicity has one. They traffic drugs, they launder money, they run prostitution rings. Any major city with a large Chinese population probably has a Triad or two in its midst. I hadn't heard of any in Sacramento before. San Francisco, sure. But not Sacramento. The police had their hands full with the Russian mob in Sacramento.

I gathered my stuff from my desk drawer and went to clock out. Alex just happened to be loitering near where we kept our time cards. He lounged against the wall, looking nonchalant.

"Good morning, Dr. Bledsoe," I said.

"Melina," he said. His eyes darted up and down the hallway. A CNA bustled past us. I headed toward the exit and the parking garage. Alex followed me. When the CNA was out of earshot, he said, "Hurrying off for breakfast with your new cop friend?"

"What do you know about my cop friend? And how?" I

kept walking. He wouldn't be able to stick with me long. The double doors that led outside were already in sight.

"It's really sort of a toss up as to which gossip travels faster, hospital gossip or underworld gossip. I can never tell." He matched me stride for stride. I thought about running, but that seemed cowardly.

"So which one did you hear about my cop friend from? And for the record, his name is Ted."

"We need to talk." He hustled me into a waiting room with no one waiting in it. You'd be surprised how often the waiting rooms are empty. At least, of corporeal presence. I don't venture in them very often, because even if no one is actually around, those rooms are full, mainly of emotion. I could barely walk through the miasma of fear, tension and despair that fog these areas of the hospital. A lot of panic swirls around the emergency room, but I've learned how to block that out.

Alex marched right in and flung himself down into one of the chairs, long legs stretched out in front of him, hands steepled across his broad chest.

I hesitated at the doorway.

"Come in and sit, Melina. I won't bite." He smiled at me, letting me see just the tiniest bit of fang.

"Is there a reason that you're torturing me?" I asked. Seriously, enough was enough.

His smile grew. So did his fangs, but just the tiniest bit. "Sweetheart, you have no idea what kind of torture I can cook up. I could have you begging for mercy in five different languages in a New York minute. Now come into the room, sit your sweet little ass down in the chair and let's talk."

I took a step back from the door.

"Melina, sit down," he said using his command voice and there my ass was in the chair. Damn him. Damn him. Damn him.

"Fine. I'm here. Happy?"

"Ecstatic." He looked at me over his long, steepled fingers. He didn't look ecstatic. He looked a little hungry.

"I heard about him from both. The nurses and staff are talking, and there are rumblings from other places as well. You're playing with fire, Melina. I don't know what's gotten into you. Leave the 'Danes alone. Play with someone your own size. I, for instance, am almost always available."

I wasn't sure if I knew what had gotten into me either, but that didn't mean I was going to stop. I stood back up and walked toward the door. "I'm not playing with anything. I had breakfast with someone. It wasn't even a date."

Alex was between me and the exit in a blur. "You watched the sunrise, holding hands." Alex scowled.

"Who told you that?" I'd find whatever little gnome passed that tidbit on and stomp him. Even a Messenger was entitled to a little privacy every now and then.

"I heard it from Marian, the surgical tech with the big . . . uh, eyes." Alex smiled and all but licked his lips.

I thought for a second. I was pretty sure I knew who he was talking about, and while she might have had big eyes, that wasn't what was making his grin so wolfish. "So what? I'd had a rough night."

Alex's smile faded. "He can't find out who or what you are."

"I have no intention of telling him what I am. I'm not exactly looking for a one-way ticket into the loony bin. What do you care anyway?"

"I care because I have a vested interest in keeping stakes out of my heart." He backed me toward the wall.

I looked out toward the hallway. It was deserted. Where was the snoopy surgical tech with the big "eyes" when I needed her? "Who said anything about anybody staking you?"

"Nobody has to say anything. I know what happens if someone with a little authority finds out about our kind. I've

seen the witch hunts. I've watched werewolves rounded up.
I've witnessed them exterminating pixies like garden pests.
It's done quietly and mercilessly. There's no public outcry,
because the public doesn't know. I have no desire to see that
happen. We have a good thing going here in Sacramento.
We don't bother anybody and nobody bothers us. I want to
keep it that way." He pressed further forward.

I tried to keep my ground, but he was right against me.
I took a step back and the wall stopped me. "Nobody's talking about changing any of that, Alex. I'm not going to tell
him that I'm a Messenger."

He cocked his head. He was so close to me now. "How
long do you think you can keep pretending you're a regular
girl? He's going to figure it out and what then? It won't be
just your skin on the line. If you're exposed, then a lot of us
are exposed. All the 'Canes have a vested interest in this."

I wanted to push him away, but at the same time, I didn't
want to touch him. His lips were close to my ear, and his
words set off a cool tingle that ran down my spine. "What
does he have that I don't have?" Alex leaned in even closer.

"Uh, let's see. A heartbeat for one? The ability to attend
a family barbecue without turning into a pile of ashes?
Those strike me as good qualities."

"Superficial at best, Melina, and you know it. You don't
even like your family."

"Not true! I love my family," I protested.

"That is not the same as liking them," Alex said, leaning
in farther still.

I leaned in closer to him as well. It was like coming too
close to a magnet. I felt myself swaying. "I don't like you
either, you know."

Alex smiled. I could see that his fangs had fully extended.
You wouldn't even notice if you hadn't been looking for it.
I was, though. I knew better than to get this close, and yet
here I was. Too close. Too drawn. Too needy. "He'll never
be able to understand what you are. He'll never be able to

completely accept it. He's not part of the same world you are."

"And you are?"

"You know I am."

I shook my head. I didn't know any such thing. What I did know was that I seemed forever stuck between these two worlds: the one everyone else knew about and the one a lot of people suspected but couldn't prove. I didn't fully belong in either. How was I supposed to make a life like that?

I put my hands on his chest and shoved. It was like trying to move a tank. He waited for a second, long enough to let me know that he wasn't going anywhere unless he wanted to, and then stepped back.

I brushed my hair back from my face and straightened my top.

"So are you off for another breakfast with him?" Alex looked at me through narrowed eyes.

"No," I said. "As a matter of fact, I'm having coffee with my aunt."

13

AUNT KITTY SHOWED UP AT STARBUCKS IN ONE OF HER real-estate-agent suits. Coffee with me was clearly just one stop among many in her busy day. I'd be willing to bet she had appointments stacked up from now until well into the early evening. You could tell what kind of day Aunt Kitty was planning on having based on her wardrobe choices. She's a bit of a chameleon. I've seen her show up for coffee or even lunch wearing yoga pants and a tank top. Scrubbed free of makeup, she honestly doesn't look all that much older than Norah and me.

If asked, she will tell you she owes it to a combination of good genes, no smoking of any substance and a good clean Citron martini once a week whether she needs it or not.

She's also likely to show up at a Starbucks like she had today, in an Ann Taylor suit with two-toned Ferragamo pumps with a matching bag and her hair sculpted into something that wouldn't move in a hurricane.

"Busy day?" I asked, scooting in next to her, inhaling the rich dark aroma of my latte as though it were crack.

"It's not easy out in the jungle these days," she said. Sacramento real estate had gone from boom to bust in a precipitous fall that still had the region reeling. Somehow Aunt Kitty was weathering it better than most. I wasn't entirely sure how, and I didn't ask too many questions. I'd learned the hard way that asking questions about her work got Aunt Kitty thinking that I wanted to be a real estate agent just like her.

I could just imagine what would happen if I tried to show houses with imps turning up with stolen flutes and vampires hanging around with mysterious envelopes. I'm sure it'd be just great for sales. On the other hand, maybe I could make a specialty out of haunted houses. I knew where all the best ones were. People love that kind of stuff for reasons that I can never quite figure out. If they could see how often the other world actually crept into their own without calling it up at all, they'd be way less likely to mess around with the creepy stuff in the first place.

"It's good to see you," I said.

She smiled, kissed my cheek and then rubbed the lipstick mark away with her thumb. "It's good to see you, sweetheart. I don't get to see you often enough. Neither does your mother. She said so the other day."

I sighed. There was the real reason for the coffee invitation. I hadn't called home in a while. I supposed I was overdue. This was so typically my mom. She said that she didn't like to meddle in my life, so instead of just picking up the phone and demanding that I show up for a Friday night dinner with the family, she'd send cryptic little messages to me through my aunt or my grandmother. "I'll call her today," I said.

Kitty patted my hand. "Excellent."

"So about whatever was so interesting . . ." I prompted, giving her my best ingratiating smile. Luckily, Aunt Kitty didn't require much ingratiation to hand over the goods.

She reached into her purse, pulled a slip of paper off of one of her ubiquitous notepads and handed it to me. Aunt

Kitty always had a little notepad in her purse. They were always pretty, and it was nice to know you could always find something to give her as a little gift that she'd actually like and use. "The addresses for the tax bills, although I don't think it's going to help you much."

"They're not the addresses of the houses?" I asked before looking at the paper.

"No, but that's not terribly unusual. Some people have those sent to an accountant or a business office."

"So what's so weird?"

"All the tax bills for these houses are being sent to the same address. Different suite numbers, but one address."

"Is it an apartment building or an office building with suite numbers or something?"

"You wish," she replied. "It's one of those mailbox places. You know, where you can ship packages and get a passport photo taken? They also rent post office boxes. Those are all box numbers."

"How can you tell?"

"I looked up the address on Google Maps and hit street view." She looked at me as if I were dim. "You can read the street sign.

"Do you want me to look into this further, Melina? I'm sure something's not right here. All the paperwork looks legal. I just have a bad feeling about it. The way things have been going, there's a lot of real estate fraud happening. Maybe I should report this to someone."

That was a thought. Maybe the regular authorities could take care of this. But then again, I still didn't know precisely what we were dealing with. I'd keep it in mind, but for now I just wanted to check out the addresses and see what I could see. Finally, I said, "No, Aunt Kitty, I think you should leave it alone. You don't need to get in the middle of it."

"I don't think you should be in the middle of it either, honey. I don't like this one bit."

I didn't either.

———

I HIT THE SHOWER BEFORE I DID ANYTHING ELSE. NORAH was in the kitchen packing her lunch when I got out.

"Hey, stranger," she said, smiling. "What have you been up to?"

I ran through the list of possible answers: tracking down places to grow marijuana in suburban Sacramento, returning flutes to Native American deities, being warned in the person of a mutilated Asian man about things I didn't understand. I went with, "The usual."

She nodded and held out a piece of apple for me. I took it and got the peanut butter out of the refrigerator. Norah insists on the grind-your-own variety from the co-op. After years of dining on Skippy and Jiff it was a tough transition for me, but I've learned to adjust. It's crazy. The stuff actually tastes like peanuts.

"Are you sleeping at all?" she asked.

I busied myself with the peanut butter, spreading it just so on my slice of apple. "Some."

Then she hugged me. This is how Norah totally undoes me. She walked over and put her arms around me and held me for moment. Then she went back to packing her lunch. No questions that I couldn't answer. No warnings that I couldn't heed. No guilt and no demands. Just a little tiny dose of unconditional girl love. Could a girl have a better roommate? I don't think so.

"Have you seen Ben around?" I asked, thinking about other recipients of Norah's unconditional love.

She shook her head and then smiled. "I think he has a girlfriend."

I raised my eyebrows. "Really?"

"Yeah. She seems a little shy, always ducking so her hair hangs over her face. But shy's okay. Her name is Sophie." She shoved her lunch into her ginormous hobo bag and slung it over her shoulder. "I'll catch you later, okay?"

"You bet."

She paused at the door. "Remember to be gentle with yourself, Melina." The second she opened the door, I felt the buzz. I ran to grab her, but I was too late. I was at least a step too slow. I needed to get more sleep. My defenses were down and my reflexes were too sluggish.

I heard her say, "Can I help you?"

Then I heard a very male voice with just a hint of an accent say, "Absolutely."

"STAY AWAY FROM HER," I TOLD KOKOPELLI. "I MEAN IT."

"Jealous, little bird? You don't have to be. There's plenty of me to go around." He grinned and looked back and forth between Norah and me as if he were already imagining himself as the filling in a girl sandwich.

Norah looked at me, one eyebrow raised. I shook my head and said, "Don't worry about it. Go to work. I'll see you tonight."

"Are you sure?" Norah's brow furrowed with concern.

"Absolutely." The last thing I needed was Norah raising one of Kokopelli's little bastards. I'd never get rid of him then.

She trotted off down the stairs. Kokopelli watched her go, smacking his lips as he leaned over the banister to watch her all the way out the door. Then he turned back to me. "You are bound and determined to ruin all my fun, aren't you?"

"Nope," I said. "It's a fringe benefit. What are you doing here?"

"Has anyone told you that you're cold, Messenger? It's not becoming in a woman to be cold." He smiled at me.

"I have been given lists of how I'm unbecoming. I really don't think you can come up with anything new at this point. Now what do you want?"

"Fine, then." He pouted for a second and then pulled his

flute out of his pack and held it out to me. "This isn't my flute."

I didn't take it. "Then whose flute is it?"

"Hell if I know. It's old. It's the right material. It's just not my flute. It's got no power."

I remembered how innocent the flute had seemed sitting on the bench seat of the Buick. And it hadn't given off any buzz at all when I'd held it in my hand. "You're sure it just doesn't need to be charged up or something?"

"It's not an iPod, sweet cheeks. It's a sacred object. Well, it's not a sacred object. It's a piece of crap. My flute is a sacred object and I want it back."

"Exactly how am I supposed to do that?" This is not how this was supposed to work. Someone or something was supposed to give me something that I took to someone else. Occasionally I had to fetch something from one place to another, but it was always set up in advance.

"I don't know. Find the rat bastard who gave you this one and get mine back. He probably still has it."

"And if he doesn't want to give me back the real one?"

"Then tell him that this is what I'm going to do when I find him." Kokopelli then proceeded to describe doing something with the fake flute that I was relatively sure was anatomically impossible. I am not, however, an expert in imp physiology and decided to take him at his word.

"Okay, then," I said and took the fake flute. "How do you want me to get in touch when I have the real one?"

"Don't worry about it. I'll figure it out." Kokopelli slung his pack back over his shoulder and headed down the stairs, leaving me holding the flute and wondering how to go about finding Joe the Imp.

I WENT BACK INTO THE APARTMENT, STILL NOT QUITE sure what to do with the flute, and took Aunt Kitty's list of seven names and started plugging them into various search engines. Sadly, there really isn't any such thing as privacy anymore. At least, there isn't on the Internet.

My big problem was that the names weren't that uncommon. Li, Chin, Zhang. You get the picture. There's more than a few people around with those surnames. Narrowing it down to San Francisco didn't exactly help loads either.

Doggedly, I scrolled through page after page of results, hoping to find some common thread besides the post office boxes in San Francisco and the grow houses in Elk Grove. One didn't exactly advertise the latter on the Internet anyway.

I looked again at the address of the post office boxes. It was on Stockton Street near Chinatown. On a whim, I typed in *Chester Li Chinatown*. The third entry was for the San Francisco Sino-American Association. He was on the board of directors. I typed in *Mark Chin*. His announcement that he had joined the board of directors of the San Francisco Sino-American Association was the second Google entry for him. I went down the list. All seven people who owned grow houses in Elk Grove financed by the United Bank of Hong Kong were members of the board of directors of the San Francisco Sino-American Association. I googled the association. Lord love a duck, they had an online newsletter.

I clicked on it and waited for the page to load, drumming my fingers on the edge of my desk.

It took a few seconds, but it came up. A photo of a ribbon-cutting ceremony for their new headquarters dominated the front page of the newsletter. Seven men stood gathered around one man holding a giant pair of silly scissors. I zoomed in on the face of the guy with the scissors and sucked in my breath.

The guy with the scissors was the guy who had seemed to be running the show at the temple, the one who had ordered the one priest pistol-whipped with a flick of his fingers, the one who had called the priest at the temple "brother." His name was Henry Zhang, and he was the founder of the San Francisco Sino-American Association.

I might not know what to do with a sacred flute, but I knew where my next stop was.

BEN WAS IN HIS USUAL POST ON THE FRONT STOOP WHEN I was leaving.

"Hey, Melina." He stood up when I walked out the door. He was a lot taller than me now. When he and his mom had moved in, we'd been eye to eye. Now we were more like eye to Adam's apple.

"Hey, Ben," I answered.

I watched his Adam's apple bob up and down a couple of times. "So are you headed over to the dojo?" he finally spit out.

"Not right now." I hadn't known it was possible to look both relieved and wildly anxious at the same time before. Ben sighed and sat back down.

I sat down next to him. "You've been seeing a lot of Sophie." I said it just like that. Like a fact. Which is what it was. I figured the only reason he wanted to go to the dojo was to see her. I wasn't born yesterday.

"Yep." Ben leaned back. "I have."

"I'm not sure that's such a great idea."

His eyes narrowed. "Well, I do."

"Ben, you don't understand what you're getting into here."

He slumped lower.

"There are things going on in Sophie's life right now that you can't possibly understand." Seriously, Sophie didn't understand what an incredible U-turn her life had just taken, but I did. She might have thought her chances of having a normal adolescence disappeared into the car wreck she'd survived, but she had no idea how much weirder things were going to get now that she'd been called to be a Messenger.

There wasn't going to be any junior prom or homecoming dances for her. There weren't going to be any of the normal teenaged coming-of-age rituals. For crying out loud, I'd taken my driving test with an angry pixie buzzing in the backseat. The examiner had kept turning around, trying to find the bee he was sure was in the car. When he couldn't find it, he almost flunked me for having a car that wasn't up to standard.

I'd tried to do some of those things and had finally given up after having to explain one too many times some weird happening. Too many eyes had stared at me. It was too easy to become conspicuous, something I couldn't afford to do and that Sophie wasn't going to be able to afford to do either.

Ben could, though. Sure, he'd already painted himself into a corner with the bad-boy behavior at the high school, but that wouldn't last much longer. Contrary to how it feels at the time, high school does not last forever; he'd be able to start over with a clean slate someplace new.

Unless he kept hanging out with Sophie.

"Sophie's different," I started, trying to figure out how to explain some of this to Ben without explaining too much or even just enough that he'd decide I was completely loony tunes and needed to be locked up.

"I get that," he interrupted. "That's why I like her. She's different. She's not like anybody else. Why would I want to be with someone who's like everybody else when I can be with someone special?"

And for that, I had no answer.

I TRIED THE FRONT DOOR OF THE TEMPLE AND GOT NO joy. It was securely locked. I probably could have busted it in, but discretion is the better part of valor and I didn't want my presence to be that obvious to anyone. Yet.

I wasn't sure what strategy I was going to need to take. I'd leave bursting in, guns blazing, causing shock and awe

for a later date if I needed it. I've never actually done shock
and awe. I'm more of a quick-kick-to-the-kneecap-and-then-
hightail-it-away-from-danger kind of gal, but this whole
situation was taking me entirely out of my element. Who
knew what would be next? I might start wearing pink and
lime green, and, of course, unicorns might fly.

I ducked around to my favorite Dumpster in back. I was
surprised that it didn't smell worse. I peeked inside. It was
nearly empty, just like last time.

Undead men apparently didn't make much garbage.

I retraced the same route I'd taken a few nights before,
but dispensed with the part where I ducked behind the file
cabinet. I wanted to be found today. I wanted to have a little
chat with the frightened young man in the orange robe.

I found him downstairs, sitting in the lotus position in front
of the altar. He'd changed out the oranges, for which I was
grateful, but the incense he burned made me want to sneeze.

I saw the slightest twitch of the fingers of his right hand.
The rest of him didn't move, however. I was pretty sure he
knew I was there. The twitch was what poker players would
call a tell, a little something he did that gave himself away.
He probably wasn't even aware that he'd done it.

I settled down on the floor a few yards away to wait. I
didn't know much about Taoist prayers, but I figured it would
be more respectful not to interrupt. Whatever he was doing,
it didn't take long to finish. He untucked his legs and stood
up in one fluid movement, not such an easy thing to do after
sitting in lotus position for a while. I'm pretty limber, but
the side of my right foot always ends up going to sleep when
I sit like that, and then I tip like a chair with a short leg when
I stand up.

"Get out," he said.

I'll admit, I'm not always greeted with open arms wherever I go. Sometimes people don't want the messages I'm
delivering or the gifts that I've brought them. Sometimes
people take it out on the Messenger, although everyone

knows how patently unfair that is. Still, they generally wait for me to get a word out before they tell me to leave.

"Nice to see you, too," I said, always ready with a witty comeback.

"Please, Ms. Markowitz, just go. It will be safer for you. It will be safer for me. It will be better for everyone." There was a note of desperation in his voice. He almost sounded as if he was pleading.

"How do you know my name?" I asked. I was reasonably sure I hadn't handed over an engraved business card to anyone at this point.

He shook his head. "These are smart men you are dealing with. They have ways of finding things out. They have ways of knowing things. They'll know you've been here, for instance, and someone will suffer for it."

My stomach turned. "The way you said Frank Liu suffered? To send me a warning?"

He nodded.

My first instinct was to run. If this guy didn't want me to help, then what the hell was I doing here? Maybe Aldo was right. This wasn't our problem. Then I thought of Maricela, the way her still body had lain against the pillow, so tiny that she almost hadn't made a dent. If that wasn't everyone's problem, I didn't know what was.

"I can't," I said. "I can't let this continue."

He turned and walked away from me. "You have no control over this situation. Any involvement from you can only make things worse. It already has made things worse."

"It's going to keep getting worse unless we stop it," I said. I wasn't sure of much, but I was sure of that. These men would keep on pushing until they demolished whatever was blocking their path. They had to be stopped, yet no one but me seemed willing to do it.

"And how do you suggest we do that?" He stopped and turned to face me, eyebrows arched with sarcasm.

"For starters, we could get rid of those things." I pointed

over to the holes in the floor where the *kiang shi* rested. Granted, it was a little like gun control. *Kiang shi* didn't kill people. People who controlled *kiang shi* killed people. Still, take away the *kiang shi* and Henry Zhang and his buddies would be back to having to use more conventional weaponry and more conventional authority figures could figure out what to do about it.

His face twisted. "Those things, as you call them, were men once. They didn't become what they are through any fault of their own."

Again, to use the gun analogy, I didn't care how they were made any more than I cared how a 9mm was made. You pointed a gun at someone and pulled a trigger and someone got hurt. You pointed a *kiang shi* at someone, rang a little bell and someone got hurt. Those were the basics I felt I needed to know. "They are what they are. I don't care how they got that way," I said.

"Maybe you should," he countered.

I crossed my arms over my chest. If giving me a lesson on the origins of Chinese vampires would get him on my side, I was willing to listen. At least, for a few moments. Besides, knowing how they came to be might give me some hints as to how to make them go away. "Fine. Fire away."

"Ever hear of the Drytown Mine Massacre?" he asked.

I shook my head.

"I figured. They don't exactly teach that in school." He sat down again on his mat.

I sat down in front of him and settled in for my history lesson.

"On May 15, 1878, fifteen white men went to the Drytown Mine and rounded up at gunpoint all the Chinese men working there."

I shook my head. "Why?"

The monk snorted. "Do you think they needed a reason beyond that those men were Chinese? They really don't teach you your history around here, do they?"

I bowed my head a little and bit my lip. Interrupting with questions was only going to make this take longer.

"It was a rich vein. The white men wanted it for themselves. The fact that the Chinese men had already been working it was irrelevant. So they rounded them up at gunpoint." He paused.

I had a fair idea of what was going to happen next in the story. I just hoped whatever the men had suffered had been brief.

Hope springs eternal. So does the evil that men perpetrate on each other with excuses of skin color and religion and a million other tiny differences that never make any one person less human than the next.

"They herded the men back to their camp. It was a prosperous place. A few of the men had actually been able to bring their wives over. They had thought themselves lucky. Perhaps that was their sin. The hubris of thinking they were special, that they deserved their luck."

Did pride goeth before a fall in every culture? It seemed so. I didn't want to hear what came next, but he wasn't going to stop now.

"They raped the women in front of their husbands and their children." His voice was almost without inflection now. It made the horror of his words all the more stark. "One man tried to stop them. They slit his throat. Unfortunately, their knives weren't very sharp. It took him over an hour to bleed to death."

I felt frozen. I wanted to leave. I knew that I couldn't. I had to listen to this recitation. If I had a prayer of getting this man's help, I had to understand how he saw the situation.

"After they were finished taking turns with the women, they beat the men to death with their rifle butts. No need to waste a bullet on a China man when you could just bust in his skull and watch him writhe on the ground in agony as he died while you ate his food and drank his whiskey. Then they hung their bodies from the trees for the crows."

"What happened to the women and children?" I asked.

"They ran. The white men burned their tents and whatever they didn't steal. Not all of the women survived, but enough of them did to tell the story, to warn others to stay away from that mine. They didn't dare come back for the bodies until much later. They let them rot for days, hanging in the trees." He cocked his head and looked straight at me, almost as if he was surprised that I was still there. "Do you know how a *kiang shi* is made, Ms. Markowitz?"

I did, from my earlier Internet research, but I shook my head anyway.

"It can be any number of factors, but the most common ones are when a person dies a horrific and violent death and when a person isn't buried properly. When those things happen, a man's upper spirit ascends, but his lower spirit is stuck in his body. These men had a double curse upon them, violent death and improper burial. By the time their families returned to bury them, it was too late."

"How did they end up here, buried in your floor?"

He sighed and rubbed the back of his neck. "As near as we can tell, Wen Cai, the first priest of this temple, heard the stories of walking corpses. He made talismans to control them and brought them here to the temple that was being built, and buried them under the floor. No one knew until we started the renovation and found them, along with scrolls that told their stories."

I leaned forward. "And then what, George? How did they end up being used to kill gangbangers in McClatchy Park?"

George's face crumpled. "That part is my fault. All of this, it is my doing." His shoulders dropped.

"What did you do, George? How is it your fault?"

"I thought it was so interesting. I thought it was a piece of our history. I thought the knowledge of it was something worth preserving. I thought it was something we should understand now so we could make sure that it never happened again." His voice ascended into something close to a wail.

Whatever I may be now, and trust me, I am not sure of what that is, I was raised Jewish. With that comes a very steady diet of "we shall never forget." From the time I was in grade school, I knew about the Holocaust. I had the gas chambers explained to me and was shown pictures from the work camps. Sweet, kind and gentle Grandma Rosie wouldn't speak to the German exchange student next door and would sooner poke herself in the eye with a sharp stick than ride in a Volkswagen. Why? Because we had to make sure it never happened again. I understood exactly what George was talking about. "You were right, George. It is important. It is worth understanding," I said quietly.

He shook his head. "I went about it in the wrong way. I contacted my brother. I thought the Sino-American Association would be interested. Part of their mission is supposed to be the preservation of our culture." Bitterness twisted his words.

"Your brother, Henry," I said.

He nodded his confirmation. "And now we are all in terrible danger. Henry will do anything to get what he wants, and he will kill anyone who gets in his way. He has taken my brother priests hostage and uses them to force me to do unspeakable things."

I didn't doubt him. I had seen firsthand what Henry was capable of. "But why?" I asked. "Why is he doing this? It makes no sense."

"When does violence ever make sense? All I know is that more violence to people I love will happen if you don't leave this alone. If I don't do what he says, they will kill my brother priests. Do you understand? These are gentle men, men who have dedicated themselves to living spiritual lives. Get out of here, Melina Markowitz. Get out and stay out."

14

I WENT FOR A RUN BEFORE I WENT TO THE DOJO. I HAD
to clear my mind, which was clicking and buzzing and
grinding like an old computer trying to link up with the
Internet. What did I know?

I knew that George and Henry Zhang were brothers. I
learned that George was the one who had discovered the
kiang shi buried under the temple floor and had told his
brother. I knew that his brother looked for all the world like
a successful Asian American businessman intent on giving
back to his community through a service organization. I
knew that the seven members of that organization's board
of directors had all purchased homes in Elk Grove using the
same real estate agent and getting loans from the same bank.
I knew that all those homes were being used as grow houses.

I also knew that Henry was forcing his brother to make
the *kiang shi* attack Latino gang members in some of the
worst neighborhoods in Sacramento by holding his fellow
priests hostage. Then those Latino gangs had retaliated by
attacking an Asian gang, and a good portion of the city was

now shooting at each other and babies were ending up in my emergency room.

Basically, I knew enough to make my head swim. It was already well over eighty degrees, and after about four miles, I was drenched with sweat and no smarter than I was when I started. There's a reason I don't run much. I hit the shower back at the apartment and headed to the dojo to talk to Mae.

If there was anyone who could help me make sense of this mess, she was it.

The dojo was quiet, dark and locked when I arrived. It wasn't what I'd expected, but it wasn't crazy weird either. Mae did have a life out of the karate studio. She just didn't spend all that much time leading that particular life. I was used to her always being right there when I needed her or just wanted her.

I was pretty sure that present circumstances represented need much more than want. I unlocked the door and started stretching out. I didn't bother turning on the lights. More than enough daylight streamed through the big plate glass windows at the front of the studio for me to see what I needed to see, and there was something restful and tranquil about the semidarkness. It was . . . crepuscular and I liked it.

The second I walked onto the mat, I felt that sense of grounding that I so often experience at the dojo and nowhere else. I hoped that Mae and I were past whatever had made her snap at me the other day. If I understood better what it was, I'd apologize for it. Right now, I was afraid that bringing it up would bring it back. Grandma Rosie always says, "Least said, soonest mended." I hoped it would be true for Mae and me right now. I'd be lost without her guidance. In fact, I was lost. I needed her shining like my bright North Star to bring me home.

I knew she was there before she got to the door. Her presence felt like a slight warming of my blood, not quite the full-fledged buzz that vibrated through me in the presence

of something truly supernatural, but still a disturbance in
the field, if you will. Except that with Mae it was more of a
comfort than a disturbance.

Even though I knew she was coming in, I stayed still on
the floor, willing myself not to move or react first.

"You're here early," she said, her voice normal and calm,
as if the last thing she said to me hadn't been a harsh
indictment.

"A little," I said. "I needed to stretch. I went for a run
today and it left me feeling tight."

She nodded. "Good idea." Then she went into the office
and locked her purse in her desk drawer. We may pound the
idea of integrity into the head of every student who walked
through the door, but not all of them catch on right away.
It's best to keep wallets and things locked away.

Then she went into the back room to change. I folded
myself into a lotus position and waited for her to come out,
trying to figure out how to ask for her help. I'd never had to
ask Mae for help. Her help had always just been there. It
wasn't like she even offered it to me; it was just a constant
presence in my life, there for me to use whenever I needed it.

Moments later, Mae joined me on the mat. "You hate
running, especially in the heat. What's up?" she said as she
began to stretch herself.

I nearly wept with relief.

I poured it all out to her, the whole enchilada, gooey
undead cheese and spicy Native American sauce and all.
She sat still and listened, nodding occasionally, never interrupting. I knew I'd missed talking to her the past few days,
but I'd had no idea how much until I experienced the relief
of laying my problem out before her on the dojo mat as I'd
done so many times before with problems big and small.

"So what are you going to do?" she asked when I was
finally done.

"I'm not sure what to do." I had no idea where to turn

next. I didn't know what it all meant or what I was supposed
to do about any of it. "I'm not sure it's really my problem.
It's definitely way above my pay grade."

Mae looked at me sharply. "There are all kinds of ways
to be compensated."

Oh brother, had we ever had this talk before, and I was
so not interested in rehashing it. Yes, there were perks that
came with being a Messenger. The being superfast and
extrastrong thing was nice. The healing quickly thing had
its moments as well, as did the part where I didn't need much
sleep.

The part where any chance of leading a normal life rode
off into the sunset without me? That part required more
compensation than all of those other things plus an occasional winning lottery number combined.

But like I said, I wasn't interested in having that conversation again. We weren't going to see eye to eye, and I didn't
want to have another argument so soon after the last one. "I
know. It's just a phrase. You know what I mean, though,
don't you?"

"More than you realize," she said.

I wasn't sure I was going to have the patience for Mae to
go all Master and Grasshopper with me. Truly, I hated that
stuff. It's bad enough that I have to do this job. They could
at least make it straightforward for me. There was the problem of knowing who the *they* were. It had never been fully
explained to me, but I knew something was out there. "So
what do I do now?"

"You make a decision," she said as if it were as easy as
deciding between New York Super Fudge Chunk and Cherry
Garcia in my grocery's freezer section. Come to think of it,
that decision isn't all that easy either.

"If I knew what decision to make, I wouldn't have had
to spend forty-five minutes pounding on the pavement in
eighty-degree heat," I pointed out. Eighty degrees doesn't

sound like much, but you can pretty much add twenty degrees to the actual temperature after about a mile. It was hot.

She smiled and placed one cool hand on my arm. "I know. It's time, though. You can't keep floating along the surface of things, letting the current take you where it goes. It's time to decide your own direction, for once. Make a choice. Build a dam. Or get out of the stream all together. Decide and do it."

"Won't you even talk it over with me?" I was trying to keep my temper, but I was losing that battle fast.

"I am talking it over with you," she said.

Okay. That was an opening if ever there was one. "So do you think I should go back to Aldo?"

"Aldo's not going to help you."

What were my other options? "What about Paul, then? Or Alex?"

She considered that for a moment. "They'd make good allies, but they're not going to take action on their own."

"Well, neither am I," I exclaimed. I was a Messenger, damn it. I carried and toted. I bowed and scraped. Was I suddenly supposed to morph into Joan of freaking Arc and lead some kind of holy battle?

"If you don't, then no one will, Melina." She seemed completely calm.

I wanted to shake her. "Why won't you help me?"

"That's what I'm trying to do."

I stood up from the mat. "It sure as hell doesn't feel like it."

I knew I sounded petulant. I didn't care. I was sick of this. I was sick of Mae not helping. I was sick of no one doing anything to stop Henry Zhang. I was sick of little babies getting hit by stray bullets while they slept in their cribs.

I was sick of just about everything.

AS I DROVE HOME IN A HUFF, I FIGURED I MIGHT AS WELL deal with my flute problem this afternoon. Apparently I was going to have some time free since I was in the middle of a temper tantrum and was unwilling to teach. I hadn't a clue how to summon an imp. Well, actually, I had a clue and the clue was that I didn't have the skills.

I can't actually do magic. I don't know how to cast spells or create hedge circles or ward doorways and windows. I've tried and I don't have the skills. Not everyone does. It takes an openness to the world that I can't seem to muster. It used to frustrate me, especially in moments like this one when being able to cast a summoning spell could really come in handy.

I knew a couple witches who could probably do it. The one that irritated me least was a woman named Meredith, but her services didn't come cheap.

Yet another drawback of being a Messenger, there was no one to whom I could submit an expense report to get reimbursement. I spent what I spent.

I called her as soon as I got home. "Hey, Meredith, how are you?"

"What do you want, Melina?" She sounded rude, but it was nice to deal with someone who wasn't playing games with me for once. I'll take rude over manipulative any day.

"I need an imp summoned." Oh, to be direct and to ask for what one needs. My heart sang a little song.

"Do you need a specific imp or will just any old imp do in a pinch?" Meredith asked.

"A specific one."

"Got a name?"

"Joe."

There was a pause on the other end of the line. "You've got to be kidding."

"You have no idea how much I wish I was." If that wasn't the understatement of the year, I didn't know what was.

She chuckled. Meredith had a low throaty voice and her chuckle sounded sexy even to boringly straight me. "I have an inkling. Imps are pains in the ass."

Amen to that sister. Still . . . "Can you do it?"

She sighed. "Do you have any hair or talon clippings? Anything he might have touched and held?"

Talon clippings? Eww! Who would keep imp talon clippings around? I did, however, have a flute that he must have handled at least a little bit. "As a matter of fact, I do have an object that belongs to him."

"Well, that will make it easier. Are you in a hurry?"

I certainly didn't want Kokopelli making any more unscheduled visits to my apartment. That kind of trouble I did not need. "Kind of."

"Will tomorrow night do?"

"Absolutely."

"Meet me at McClannigan's at eight."

Uh-oh. Now we were treading on some thin ice. "Meredith . . ."

"Do you want your imp or not?"

That was an easy question to answer. "I want him."

"Then be there at eight and bring some folding money, if you know what I mean."

I knew what she meant. Meredith likes to get her drink on. I wouldn't go quite so far as to call her a drunk, but only because I wasn't keen on being judged myself. She didn't even have what my mother and her friends refer to as "a problem." My mother's friend with "a problem" was picked up by the police when she ran down our street naked screaming that the Israelis were out to get her, exposing her drinking problem, her lily white ass and an extremely unattractive anti-Semitic streak all at the same time. You would never have known if you'd met her at bridge club. Well, you would have known about the drinking problem because she generally smelled of booze by ten in the morning and you could probably have guessed about the lily white ass, but she kept the anti-Semitic thing nicely under wraps most of the time.

In contrast, Meredith tends to get a little sloppy, and the already somewhat low necklines of her blouses tend to get a little lower yet, especially if Paul is around. Paul was undoubtedly why we were meeting at McClannigan's. Rumor has it that Meredith and Paul hooked up one night a year or two ago and Meredith has been lobbying for an encore ever since.

Part of me didn't want to be involved and part of me wanted a ringside seat to what was bound to be a gossip-worthy event. I agreed to the time and place and we hung up.

I SPENT FRIDAY SLEEPING AND LICKING MY WOUNDS. IT was beautifully quiet and uneventful, and I was ridiculously grateful for it. Paul did not seem overjoyed to see me when I walked into the bar, however. In fact, he scowled, rolled his eyes and then turned his back on me.

"Well, it's a pleasure to see you, too," I said.

"I don't want anything to do with it," he said.

"Do with what?"

"Whatever it is that brought you here."

So unfair. So judgmental. That was just so totally werewolf. "You don't even know what it is! It could be fun."

"It's not going to be fun. Nothing you've gotten yourself involved with lately is fun."

Alex was right. My business was on the underworld gossip hotline. This was not a pretty turn of events. "What do you know about it?"

"More than I want to." If he polished that glass much more, it would disintegrate.

"Can I have a beer to go with the lecture and the disdain? Or do I have to dry swallow it?"

He scowled some more, but he did pull me another Amstel Light. I was going to have to take a good long look at my behind the next time I was at the dojo. Maybe Paul was trying to tell me something.

"I want a lemon drop." Meredith plopped down on the stool next to mine.

If I thought Paul was scowling at me, that was because I had not yet seen the look he was going to give to Meredith. I was surprised she didn't fall back off her stool. He then turned to me and gave me a wide-eyed what-gives sort of stare.

"Meredith and I have some business to transact," I told him.

"And you had to transact it here? In my bar?" He actually sounded a little panicky.

"Apparently," I said. "Now could you make her a lemon drop, please?"

"Those things are pretty strong." A furrow developed between his brows. It took me a second to place the look. He looked worried. Honestly, there's something kind of comical about a worried werewolf. I tried to hide my smile. Judging from the way Paul glared at me, I wasn't entirely successful.

Meredith leaned forward on the bar, plumping her breasts on her folded arms and said, "That's okay. I like things strong."

I could swear that Paul gulped.

To be polite about it, Meredith is a bit of a bombshell. She's not quite as young as she used to be, but in all fairness, Paul is easily two or three hundred years old. Tonight she had on a pair of tight jeans, a low-cut purple blouse that had something sparkly woven into it and a pair of high-heeled sandals. Norah would have called her a cougar, and to be honest, she was practically purring. Maybe it wasn't such a bad label for her.

I once again had on jeans and a black tank top. Maybe it

was time to go shopping. I glanced around and counted about five guys who were covertly checking Meredith out, despite the fact that she had ten to fifteen years on each and every one of them. Maybe it was time to have Meredith take me shopping.

She reached across the bar into the little tray where Paul kept the drink garnishes and grabbed a Maraschino cherry. Holding it by the stem, she ran it across her lower lip and then put it into her mouth, pulling the stem out with an audible pop.

Paul dropped the glass he was holding and it shattered on the floor. He let loose a string of obscenities and went off to get a broom.

"Do you do that to him on purpose?" I asked, turning to her.

She smiled. "Do what?"

Paul came back and managed to make Meredith's drink without smashing anymore stemware. He set it down in front of her without a word and moved to the opposite end of the bar. Meredith smiled again.

"So show me this object you've brought to help summon your imp."

I pulled the flute out of my backpack, unwrapped it from the cloth that I'd put around it and set it in front of her on the bar. From the corner of the bar, I saw Paul's head come up as he tried to scent it. It's a tricky thing with metal. I have trouble with it, too.

Meredith drained half her lemon drop. "Kokopelli's flute?"

"Look again." I sipped demurely at my Amstel Light. One of us had better stay at least a little bit in control.

She picked it up and turned it in her hands, running her long fingers up and down its length. "I'm getting something from it, but it isn't nearly as strong as it should be."

I resisted suggesting that she pucker up and blow. Paul, on the other hand, seemed to be turning a really interesting shade of purple. He strode over from his end of the bar, snatched the flute out of her hands and said, "Set that down before you get arrested."

"For holding a flute in public?" Meredith's eyes were wide and she was clearly amused.

"For public indecency." He set the flute down on the bar and stalked away again.

"I've never seen him like that." I turned back to Meredith.

She shrugged. "I have a knack. That, by the way, is not Kokopelli's flute."

"So I've been told."

"It's got some magic but not nearly enough, and not of the right kind either. That one might be Greek, but I'm not sure. I'd have to spend some more time with it."

"I don't really care about that one. I need the real one back." I explained about the imp and how I ended up with the fake flute.

Meredith nodded and drained the rest of her lemon drop. "Hey, Paul, mix me another one," she called, leaning over the bar again.

Tight-lipped and stiff-legged, he mixed up another lemon drop and brought it over. "Anything else?" He didn't sound as though he really wanted to get us anything else, but Meredith ignored his sarcasm.

"Give me some of those pretzels, too. Melina and I are going to be in back for a little bit. Can you make sure we're not disturbed?"

Paul rolled his eyes again. "Do you have to do that stuff here?"

"You know why I do it here."

His shoulders sagged. He brought us the pretzels and he shooed us away. "Go on, then. Get it over with. And clean up after yourselves," he called after us as we walked toward the back of the bar where the storeroom was.

"Why do you do it here?" I asked as I walked alongside

Meredith. Meredith didn't so much walk as stride. She was shorter than me, but she still managed to make it look like her legs were about a mile longer than mine.

"There's this spot in the storeroom. It has . . . power." A slow smile spread across her face, and I wondered exactly what kind of power the spot possessed.

"Is that what you use on Paul? Did you cast a spell on him, because I've never seen him act this way around a woman." And I'd seen Paul on the prowl.

Meredith smiled wider. "Not all of my powers are magical."

We walked through the Staff Only door and into the storeroom. Meredith gestured to a broom leaning against the wall. "Grab that, Melina. Now, do me a favor and sweep that spot over there under the hanging lamp."

There wasn't much on the floor, but I swept it anyway. While I was doing that, Meredith started pulling items from the giant hobo bag she had set down in the corner.

She strode into the center of the pool of light from the hanging bulb and placed the flute, the lemon drop and the pretzels on the floor directly beneath the bulb. I'd watched Meredith cast circles a few times and always wondered how much of it was really necessary and how much of it was theatrics. It always seemed a little bit cheesy to me, but it worked. The few times I'd tried to cast a circle, well, let's just say that geometry was not my strong point.

Meredith closed her eyes and let her head fall back, her arms hanging loose at her sides. I watched the rise and fall of her chest as she breathed in and out, three times. A stillness came over the room. The noises of the bar seemed to come from far away now. She opened her eyes and lifted her arms over her head. Her long hair crackled with energy. She walked the perimeter of her circle for the first time.

She held her hand out to me. I'd seen it done often enough that I knew what she wanted. I grabbed the sage smudge stick and handed it to her. She held it in front of her. I lit it with one of the matches that had been lying next to it on the floor. I was rewarded with a small smile.

Meredith walked the circle again. This time I could see a faint glow in the wake of her footsteps. She handed the smudge stick back to me and held out her hand again. I gave her the small sack I knew she expected. She walked the circle again, this time sprinkling salt from the sack after her as she went. The glow grew brighter, burning a pale blue.

She moved to the center of the circle and chanted, "Three times round the circle is cast. I stand between the worlds at last."

The circle glowed on its own now, flickering from blue to green and back again. She pulled a piece of chalk from her jeans pocket and crouched to the floor. She sketched a pentagram on the floor within the circle, keeping the flute, the lemon drop and the pretzels at the center of the pentagram.

Then she started to call Joe, and that's when things got weird.

Remember that Eagles song, "Witchy Woman"? The raven hair? The ruby lips? The sparks flying from her fingertips? Well, that is precisely what was going down in the back of McClannigan's Olde Towne Pub. Meredith's hair floated like a dark nimbus around her head and crackled with blue light. As she turned slowly in the center of the pentagram, arms outstretched to her sides, her fingers left a glow of energy behind them.

"Joe," she said. "Joe, I have something of yours. You have something of another's. Come to me, Joe."

Then she stopped and closed her eyes. Joe appeared in the center of the pentagram with an audible pop.

Joe whirled around, searching the room and spotted me. His leather eyelids lowered over his eyes. "You," he said. "What do you want?"

"I'm pretty sure you know," I said.

He scowled.

Meredith knelt down next to him and lifted the lemon drop. "Are you thirsty, Joe? Did you come a long way?"

"Long enough," he said, eyeing the glass. "I am a little parched. Maybe just a sip."

Meredith handed him the glass, his nails clinking against it. He took a sip and his eyes widened. "Tasty!"

She took the lemon drop back and offered him a pretzel, which he took and nibbled in a manner way more delicate than I would have predicted. I'd figured Joe for a cram-it-in-his-mouth kind of guy. He finished the pretzel and reached for the drink, licking his lips with a lizardlike forked tongue.

After he'd finished most of the drink and about half the pretzels, Meredith said, "You know you have to give it back, right?"

His shoulders slumped. "He didn't want the one I sent."

"It's not his, Joe. He wants his back." Meredith scratched the back of his neck with her long fingernails.

Joe stared up at Meredith with a look of adoration on his face and shivered with delight. "I can see that. Perhaps we could work out a deal?"

I chimed in. "I think it's too late for that. He's kind of pissed at this point. If you hand it over now, I can get it to him and we can all put this behind us."

"It's not like I have it on me." He glanced at me.

"Is it far?"

His head drooped and he shook it. "No. Not too far. We're in Old Sac, right?"

"Yep."

He nodded. "I can take you there now."

I looked at Meredith. She'd have to release the circle. She nodded and stood back up. Walking backward around the circle, the glowing edges receded more and more until she'd been around three times. She knelt again. "It was nice to meet you, Joe. Merry meet and merry part and merry meet again."

"A pleasure to meet you as well, Witch."

I opened my backpack and Joe hopped in. It was going to be stuffy, but there was no way that he could walk through McClannigan's without someone raising a ruckus or thinking they were having a psychotic break, both outcomes to be avoided. As I headed out of the storeroom, Meredith called out to me, "Send Paul back here, would you, Melina? Tell him there's something I want to show him."

I smiled and shook my head. I could only imagine.

15

WHEN WE GOT OUT OF THE BAR, I ASKED JOE WHERE WE were going.

"Down the block. Look for a set of white wooden stairs leading down and some columns." His high voice was muffled but still easy to hear through the backpack.

I started walking. Sure enough, toward the end of the block was a set of stairs leading down from the street. That wasn't all that unusual. Sacramento is, after all, a raised city. The weird thing was, the stairs didn't really lead to anything. I'm not saying there was an abyss at the bottom, but it was just a vacant area. Grass had grown up through what little had been paved. A few columns still stood, but several were down on the ground in various stages of disintegration. I peered at the top of one of the fallen capitals. Sacramento Ironworks 1860.

I wondered what the area had been. Some kind of patio or promenade, maybe? I ducked underneath the stairs out of view of the street above or the alleyway that ran alongside. We were invisible or might as well have been. I could hear people walking by on the sidewalk, but I couldn't see them.

I set the backpack down on the ground as gently as I could, although I heard a little grunt from inside anyway. I unzipped it, and Joe hopped out and shook out his wings. "Have you ever considered, I don't know, washing that thing? It smells like cheese in there and not in a good way."

Everybody's a critic. "Sorry. I don't usually use it as a form of transport. Now where's the flute?"

"This way." Joe twitched his head in the direction of a cellar door that hadn't been visible from the street.

I tried the handle, but it was locked. Joe shook his head and shoved at my knees to push me aside. Using his talons like a set of lock picks, he had the door open in a matter of seconds. "How do you get along with those sausage-sized fingers?" he asked, shaking his head as he led the way into the dank, dirty-floored space that the open door revealed.

I followed more slowly. The smell of the river reminded me of the *kiang shi*. We were only a few blocks from the temple and their resting place, and the sun was getting ready to set.

"You're complaining about the smell inside my backpack when you hang out in this place?" Along with the scent of the river, I detected the pungent odor of sweat and a faint undertone of decaying garbage.

Joe shot me a dirty look over his shoulder. "I don't hang out here. It's convenient for storage. That's all. Help me move those boxes." He pointed to a stack of cardboard moving boxes against the far wall.

An arched entrance behind them had been bricked up at some point. The original brick arch was an elegant thing, but the bricks that had been used to fill the space were a more haphazard affair. Clearly, people don't take the same pride in their work as they used to. I glanced around. All the walls were brick, and while some of the material was crumbling, it was easy to see the pattern that had been set and followed.

I started moving boxes. After the second one, I realized

that Joe was just standing there, skinny arms crossed over pigeon breast. "Yo, I said I'd help, not do the whole thing."

Joe grumbled something about lazy humans and put his slight bulk into shoving away one of the boxes I'd uncovered at the bottom of the pile.

It took us a few minutes, but we finally shifted all the boxes away from the wall, exposing a metal grate on the floor. Joe flicked out a talon and undid the screws on each of the grate's corners. I'd have to rethink my position on having talons. They were handier than they seemed at first glance.

He reached inside and pulled out a cloth-covered bundle. He shoved it toward me and said, "Take it already."

I squatted down to look him in the eye. "So tell the truth, Joe. Why'd you really take it?"

He sighed, ruffling his wings. "There's this woman . . ."

I should have known. I glanced down at the flute. "Did it help?"

"I didn't have the nerve to even try. I did all this for nothing." He looked at the floor, scraping at the dirt with one of his nasty little toes.

I stood back up, thinking about what had actually reached through all my defenses to touch my heart recently. "If you want my advice, forget the magic and the sacred objects. Tell her your hopes and dreams. Put your heart out there on the table. If that doesn't get to her, nothing will."

He looked up, one eye screwed tight shut as if considering. "You are one strange human, Messenger."

I sighed. "So I've been told. So I've been told."

I SPOTTED BEN AND SOPHIE FROM HALF A BLOCK AWAY. They were sitting on the front stoop. Ben was leaned back on his elbows, more relaxed than I'd seen him in a long time. Sophie laughed at something he said and tossed her hair back over her shoulder. Ah, young love. A twinge of jealousy made me wince. It was followed rapidly by a stab of concern. It bugged me a little that it happened in that order, but as Popeye would say, I yam what I yam.

I checked to make sure Kokopelli's flute was tucked safely in my backpack. I didn't really have to look. I could feel its buzz against my backbone. But it was bad enough to have a budding Messenger hanging out on my front stoop with my charming ne'er-do-well downstairs neighbor. It was another thing entirely to contribute in any way to getting her knocked up by him.

Young love wasn't exactly something I'd ever gotten to experience. I was having my doubts that I'd even get to have old love. Messengers weren't the safest people to be around. It was hard enough to keep myself safe without having to worry about someone else. Most days, I didn't feel like I had the energy for even one more thing.

Besides, how was I supposed to explain my job to someone? It certainly wasn't first-date material. "Hi, my name's Melina. I hang out with the arcane. Do you have a hobby?"

Sophie placed her hand on Ben's arm, and he looked up at her with an expression I'd never seen before on his face. It damn near stopped my heart. Oh, crap. The two of them were actually falling in love.

Had Sophie told him what she was? How could she? She barely knew what she was herself.

The question that truly stopped me in my tracks, however, was, had Sophie told Ben what I was?

I had never told anyone what I was. Maybe it was becoming a Messenger at such a young age. By the time I knew that I was different from everybody else, it was too late to tell anyone. I'd spent years being told to keep my imagination under control and to not make up stories. When I finally had words to describe what my life had become, no one even wanted to hear about it. At least, no one I wanted to tell about it.

I'd had Mae. Although apparently, I didn't even have her anymore.

Sophie would have some advantages that way. Sixteen was far from grown up, but it was a lot more mature than three. Her life in the normal world was much more established. Maybe she could find a way to integrate being a normal teenager with being a Messenger. I sure hadn't been able to do it, though.

I was well aware of the possible ramifications of telling people what I was, and they were none too appealing. Spending time in a padded room wearing the special jacket with the extralong wraparound sleeves was not my idea of a rockin' time. Neither was a lifelong dependency on heavy-duty psychotropic drugs. I didn't know what the ramifications might be for someone I told, especially if that person actually believed me.

If Sophie had told Ben what we were, would he believe her? What would happen if he did?

I hadn't a clue.

I sauntered up to the steps.

"Hey, Melina, how's it going?" Ben smiled up at me with an expression that could almost be thought of as sunny.

I held up my hand to quiet him. Something was coming. I wasn't sure which I sensed first, the smell of the river or that all-too-familiar tingling in my flesh, but they were both followed rapidly by the sound of a bell. "Get inside," I said.

"What?" Ben asked. "Why?"

"Just do it." I turned to Sophie. She was frozen, a look of horror on her face. Whatever she'd already seen, she must not have felt evil before.

Her hands went to her face. "What is it? What is that?"

"I don't know yet, for sure. Please go inside." So I lied. I was pretty sure I knew exactly what was coming.

Sophie looked at me, confused and still not moving. I heard the bell ring again. "I'll explain later. Please, both of you, go inside."

Sophie's look of confusion changed to one of horror. Ben's eyes went round and he said, "What the hell . . . ?"

I turned. *Kiang shi* at nine o'clock, hopping up my sidewalk. I grabbed both Ben and Sophie by the shoulders and manhandled them into the foyer of the apartment building. I pointed at Ben's apartment door. "Get inside. Do it now and stay there until I tell you it's safe to come out."

For a second, I didn't think Ben was going to be able to open his apartment door. His hands shook so hard he couldn't get the key in the lock. It finally slid home and the two of them slipped inside.

They were safe, for the moment. At least I only had to worry about me.

The *kiang shi* were at the steps. They jumped them easily. Damn it all. They were becoming more powerful. According to what I'd read, they could only hop so high at first. The more they killed, the more powerful they became and the higher they could jump. I needed something to block the door, something higher than a step, and I needed it fast.

I spotted Valerie's herb planters. By themselves, they probably weren't tall enough, but stacked? That might do it. The *kiang shi* were right there, though. Think, Melina, think. Okay. The *kiang shi* were blind. They found their victims by their breath. If I held my breath, I might as well be invisible.

I took a couple deep breaths, blowing them out of my lungs as completely as possible, sucked in a big one, held it and threw open the door to the building. The first *kiang shi* had cleared the steps. As horrible as they had looked from a distance as they ripped apart gangbangers, they were much worse close up.

Flesh hung off his face, green and rotting. The smell of the river was overpowered by the stench of decomposition. Arms held in front of him, his long nails were stained with blood.

I grabbed the planters, but they were heavier than they looked. A grunt escaped my lungs, and the *kiang shi* turned to look at me. The one in the lead reached for me, raking my arm with his long nails. I heaved and lifted the planters, but the effort caused me to expel another breath.

This time the lead *kiang shi* grabbed hold of my arm and tugged. I knew what was coming next and no way was I going to stand still for it. The last thing I wanted was for Alex to be looking to see what my hand might be holding when it was no longer attached to my body. I whirled and planted a side kick on the *kiang shi*'s chin. He tumbled backward, letting go of my arm, but not before he managed to sink his teeth into my forearm. He righted himself almost immediately.

I made the mistake of glancing at my arm. The *kiang shi* had taken a chunk of me with him when he had fallen. There was no time to do anything about it. If I didn't stop them, it wouldn't matter anyway. I'd be dead in minutes.

I gulped in another breath, stacked the planters at the threshold of the building and leaped over them inside. I stood, literally holding my breath, to see if they could clear the obstacle.

The bell rang. The *kiang shi* hopped. The lead *kiang shi* hit the planters and fell back, knocking into the *kiang shi* behind him.

I would have laughed except that I didn't want them to be able to sense me and I knew how very unfunny it would be if this didn't work.

The bell rang again. The *kiang shi* jumped again, in unison, like a horrid undead drill team. Again, the lead *kiang shi* knocked into the planters and fell back.

My lungs burned and my eyes watered. I wasn't sure how much longer I could hold my breath. Would it empower them if they could sense me? If they knew their prey was just over the obstacle in front of them, would it provide the incentive they needed to clear the herb planters? I didn't dare find out. I didn't want to end up like a dismembered cholo on an emergency room gurney.

The bell rang. They hopped. Again, they knocked into

the planters. The world began to turn a little gray around its edges.

I slid into a crouched position, ready to fight if they made it over the planters.

The bell rang, but in a different rhythm this time. The *kiang shi* turned. It rang again and they began to hop away from the apartment building. I still held my breath. I leaned against the wall to keep my balance. The world narrowed down to a pinpoint.

The bell rang again. The *kiang shi* were off the stoop. I couldn't stand it anymore. I sucked in a deep breath. The bell rang yet again and the *kiang shi* began to hop away, but not before one of them turned his nasty, rotting head and hissed at me.

I felt his cold fetid breath even yards away and gagged. The bell rang and it continued to hop away. When they were finally out of sight, I knocked on Ben's door.

Sophie flung the door open and caught me as I stumbled inside.

Ben stared at me. "What the hell were those things?"

I didn't have a good lie ready. I didn't even have a bad lie ready.

I'd been caught in plenty of situations that required explanations before. There was the lovesick Sasquatch who needed me to deliver a love letter on the Girl Scout camping trip. I had to explain away a lot of destruction after that episode, and while I've no doubt that my taking responsibility for all of it seemed highly suspect, Ms. Bernard already thought me a little bit odd and was happy to accept my mea culpa if it meant she didn't have to deal with me anymore.

That was different, though. Ms. Bernard hadn't actually seen Big Foot, although I now really wonder whether even that would have mussed her hair. I think she had one entire backpack dedicated to her supply of Aqua Net. Ben had seen the *kiang shi*. I don't know whether I could have made a case for him having some kind of acid flashback, but I do

know I couldn't have looked him in the eye ever again if I'd
tried. Lying was out this time. More's the pity.

Then there was the matter of Sophie. She still hadn't
spoken. She looked shell-shocked. It's one thing to have
someone tell you that you're going to be a supernatural
errand girl, it's a whole other thing altogether to have the
supernatural hop up onto the stoop where you're pitching
woo with your boyfriend and try to eat your flesh.

This was the kind of situation that I usually hashed over
with Mae. Just thinking about her made my eyes sting. I was
still more than a little miffed at her. So I was supposed to
step up and take some responsibility? Fine. I'd make my
own decision about this.

"They were *kiang shi*," I said.

Ben sat down on the couch and ran his hands through
his already very messy hair. "What the hell are *kiang shi*?"

"Chinese vampires, *mas o menos*." I followed him in and
sat down in the chair across from him. Sophie still hovered
by the door, glancing back and forth from Ben to me as if
one of us might suddenly sprout fangs and jump at her.

Ben's head shot up and he stared at me. "Are you kidding
me?"

"Do I look like I'm laughing?" I stared right back at him.

"What the hell is going on?" he asked.

Now that was an excellent question.

IT TOOK ABOUT AN HOUR FOR SOPHIE TO FINALLY START
talking. I was beginning to get worried. Once the dam
broke, however, I sort of wished she'd revert to silent-shock
mode.

"Those are the things you were telling Mae about?"

"Yep. Those would be the very things." I'd brought
Sophie up to my apartment and sent Ben off to replant his
mother's herb garden before she came home. I was hoping
she wouldn't notice. If she did, we'd have to come up with

something clever. I might be able to get away with telling Ben the truth. I didn't think Valerie would take it anywhere near as well.

Ah, the flexibility of youth.

"What are we going to do about them? Do we have to kill them?" Sophie sat on the kitchen counter and drummed her heels against the cabinet doors.

"I don't know," I said as I filled the teakettle and put it on a burner. It was a reasonable question. However, it was one I hadn't had time to even consider. "I haven't exactly sat down to chat with them, but they seem kind of tricky to reason with when they're trying to eat my flesh."

Sophie stopped drumming her feet long enough to give me a slightly dirty look. "I just thought you might know."

I shook my head. "These are my first *kiang shi*. I didn't even know they existed until last week." And to think, I'd thought things were bad then, what with the vampires and werewolves and elves and gnomes and all. I didn't know when I had it good, did I?

"What do they want with you?"

Ben came back in then, still brushing dirt off his hands, and saved me from having to answer.

"Planters all planted?" I asked.

He nodded. "She might notice. She might not. We'll see."

It would have to do. With everything I had on my plate, I didn't think I could make Valerie's basil a priority at that moment despite my deep affection for a good fresh pesto.

A few moments later, the teakettle began to whistle, and I dropped a tea bag in a mug, poured hot water over it and handed the drink to Sophie. Then I checked my arm again. It hurt. The *kiang shi* had more ripped my flesh than bitten it, and the wound wasn't healing the way I was used to healing. I'd gotten the bleeding to stop, but the edges of the wound were still ragged, and frankly, it didn't smell too good.

Ben hopped up onto the counter next to Sophie. He'd

taken off the hooded sweatshirt. Sitting next to Sophie in my kitchen, he looked younger somehow. Maybe it was the scare we'd all had.

"So what do we do now?" he asked.

I glanced at the clock. Alex should be in the ER. "I go to work."

"What about us?" Sophie asked, holding the mug of hot tea between her hands as if she was still cold.

"I guess you guys stay inside and practice holding your breath."

16

MY ARM WAS ON FIRE BY THE TIME I GOT TO THE HOSPI-
tal. It felt as if fire ants were crawling inside my veins. Someone needed to look at it, but I couldn't show it to just
anybody. Alex was the only person who would have both
the medical knowledge and the arcane knowledge necessary
to know what to do. I knew he was on duty, so I figured it
wouldn't be so hard to nudge him into an empty exam room
somewhere and have him take a quick peek. Plus, I wanted
to talk to him about what was going on to see if he had any
ideas about what I was supposed to do next.

I bandaged the wound up as best as I could and wore a
long-sleeve cardigan to cover my arm.

Have you ever noticed how when you're trying to avoid
someone, that person seems to be lurking around every corner, but when you *want* to run into someone, you never see
them?

I wanted to run into Alex. So, of course, he was nowhere
to be found. Every time I walked through the ER, he had
just gone somewhere else.

I finally tracked him down as he was striding through the double doors that went from the ER to the open corridor.

I scurried after him. He turned down the corridor past a gurney that a little boy who'd fallen out of a tree had been lying in earlier. It still needed to be cleaned. As he went past, Alex trailed his index finger through the blood pooled along the edge, like a kid might trail his finger through chocolate icing. Then he licked his hand clean. "Mmm," he murmured. "B positive. My favorite."

I would have been totally grossed out if I hadn't known he'd done it half for effect. He'd known I was behind him. He had better senses than I did. He'd probably smelled me twenty paces back. Plus, my arm hurt too much for me to be grossed out. My head felt hot and my eyeballs felt scratchy.

"Nice," I said. "Thinking of having the blood of a baby for dessert?"

He licked his lips and smiled, his mouth still too red from the blood he'd just consumed. "Yummy. Baby. There's a treat I haven't had for a long time." He turned to look at me. His eyes had changed from deep chocolate brown to the golden color of a cat's eye.

I felt a chill. Every once in a while, I forgot that Alex was the real deal. He might keep his vampire urges under garlic lock and key better than most, but those urges were still very real and very present. I knew he was saying it to make me uncomfortable, to make me squirm, but I also knew he knew what it was to be a vampire.

I gulped. "I wanted to show you something."

He smiled. "Dear *Penthouse*, I never thought anything like this would happen to me . . ."

I slugged his shoulder with my good arm. "You wish."

He shrugged. "You're the one having the dreams."

I blushed. Stupid dreams. Stupid big mouth that told about the dreams. Stupid vampire. I shoved up my sleeve and unwrapped part of the bandage. It looked worse than it had when I'd left the apartment. Purple streaks ran up my arm from the wound, and the flesh around it had started to turn a color I really didn't associate with my skin. "I wanted you to look at this."

He grabbed my arm and turned it to get a better look. The cool of his fingers felt good against my skin. Maybe I should have iced it. "What the hell happened?"

I explained about the *kiang shi* attack on my porch.

He gritted his teeth together. Hard. I actually heard them squeak. I shivered a little. Vampire teeth gritting is worse than chalk on a blackboard. "They attacked at your house? How did you get away?"

"By stacking the herb planters on my porch high enough that they couldn't jump over them and holding my breath."

He looked up from my arm. "How did you know to do that?"

"I googled them."

He nodded, a twitch of a smile at his lips. "Nice work. Does it hurt?"

I nodded.

"A lot?"

I nodded again.

He looked at me closer now, eyes squinted as he appraised my condition. "You're running a fever, too. How long ago did this happen?"

"It's been a couple of hours."

"Dammit, Melina, you should have come to me sooner."

"I tried! You were impossible to find."

He looked a little ashamed. I was glad. He was the one who'd gotten me into this mess in the first place. The least he could do was treat my undead bite wounds.

"Fine. Fine. What we need now is some sticky rice. Is anybody in admitting getting take-out Chinese?"

I shook my head. "They're all doing South Beach right now and treat carbs like they are the devil's own enticement." There was a funny buzzing in my head.

"We need to send someone out for rice, but it has to be the right kind. We need the kind that they use at the sushi places. Is there anyone you can call?"

A few days ago, I would have called Mae without a second's hesitation. Now thinking about asking her for help made me press my lips together in a hard straight line. Ben didn't have a drivers' license. Sophie apparently did, but I didn't think I wanted either of them leaving the safety of the apartment right now.

The only person I could think of was Ted. He'd said to call when I was ready to accept his help, hadn't he? Plus, didn't that kiss earn me enough points that I could call him for a rice delivery. "Let me get my cell phone."

I extricated myself from Alex's grasp, but that turned out to be a mistake. My legs were no longer steady. My knees buckled. Alex caught me before I hit the ground.

"The toxin is spreading. We need to get you treated fast. I'll go get your cell phone. While I'm there, I'll let Doreen know you're sick. You wait here." He hustled me into an empty exam room and lifted me onto the gurney.

I stared at the ceiling. The patterns in the tiles started to swirl on me. What exactly had Alex said about toxins? I didn't remember reading anything about toxins on the Internet.

Before I could formulate in my slightly foggy mind what I wanted to ask, Alex was back with my purse. I pulled out my cell phone and called Ted. He sounded groggy.

"Did I wake you?" I asked.

"Melina? Is that you? Are you okay?" Wow. He woke up fast. My mom was like that. She could sleep through the loudest movie with massive explosions and car chases, but if a small voice at her side said the word "Mommy," she was wide awake in a nanosecond.

"Not exactly. I need a favor."

"Name it."

That was amazing. Just like that. No bartering or bargaining. No trying to figure out what was in it for him. Just name it. "I need some sticky rice from a sushi place."

"Tell him to get it from Zen Toro," Alex said.

"Is there someone there with you?"

"Alex Bledsoe. One of the emergency room doctors. I have this, well, this boo-boo, and Alex says I need sticky rice to treat it." Had I really just referred to the place on my arm that had been ripped open by an undead Chinese zombie vampire thing as a boo-boo? Yep. I had. Apparently having *kiang shi* toxins race through your system was a little like being drunk. "He says to get it from Zen Toro."

"I'll be there in twenty minutes."

I hung up my phone and turned to Alex. "He's on his way."

He took my wrist and checked my pulse. "You should rest until he gets here."

I closed my eyes, but my mind remained restless. Finally, I said, "What would *kiang shi* want with a lot of marijuana?"

He turned a chair around and straddled it, resting his arms on the back of the chair. "Is this a riddle? Like why did the zombie cross the road?"

Everyone knew the answer to that one: for *brains*!!! I thought about my question. Was it a riddle? It was certainly some kind of enigma. "No. It's not a joke. I followed the guys in the SUV to a house in Elk Grove. My aunt did some checking, and the same real estate agent sold a bunch of houses in Elk Grove all at the same time."

"Isn't that kind of what real estate agents do? Sell houses?" I felt his cold touch on my arm and glanced down, but he was only taking my pulse.

"Yeah, but this guy is mainly retired." I explained about all the buyers using the same bank as well.

"Okay. So what else makes you think these houses have anything to do with marijuana?"

"I think they're grow houses, Alex." I explained about

the security systems and the funny smell. "Have you seen those news reports about the extrastrong marijuana that's started circulating around here?"

Alex doesn't get pale. He doesn't flush. His heart doesn't race. He's dead so there's no blood coursing through his veins to make that stuff happen. He can, apparently, look entirely dumbfounded. "Did they see you?" he finally asked after staring at me for several long seconds.

"Maybe."

"What does maybe mean in this particular context?" His voice was damn near as icy as his hands.

I explained about the security cameras, catching glimpses of black SUVs on my ride home. "So I'm figuring the grow houses and the Chinese vampires and the gang warfare on the streets are all connected, but I can't quite figure out how. I thought you might be able to piece it together for me," I said brightly, hoping a little sugar would take me a little further with him.

"It does make a certain kind of sick sense," he murmured.

"What does?" I had a feeling Alex would see a pattern here. One thing about living for a long, long time, there's not much new under the moon.

"I think it might be all about drugs, Melina." He straightened up and brushed that thick hair off his forehead and stretched.

I swallowed hard. "Drugs?" I squeaked. "You mean the marijuana?"

He nodded. "I do mean the marijuana. Think about it. Who controls the drug trade around here? Especially the weed."

It was an easy question. "Gangs."

"You bet. Any idea which gangs might have the biggest drug territories?"

I shook my head.

"The Norteños and the Black Dragons."

What a coincidence. Those just happened to be the two gangs that were trying to mutually destroy each other with a little help from our undead Chinese friends.

"So who might profit from having those two gangs at each other's throats?"

This was interesting. I tried to struggle into a sitting position. "Someone looking to break into the drug trade in Sacramento?"

"I told you to lie still and rest." He pressed me back down. "Close but not quite. You wouldn't need to weaken both the Black Dragons and the Norteños to do that. You could find some little corner of the city to do your business. Right now, though, supply is disrupted because of the gang fights and both gangs are only looking at each other. How about someone looking to *take over* the drug trade in Sacramento? Wouldn't this be the perfect time to try something like that?"

"Do you think this is that big?"

"I don't know what to think," he said, rubbing a thumb at his forehead. Could vampires get headaches? "I do know that you need to stay out of it."

"Kind of hard to do at this point, don't you think? They seem to know where I live."

He frowned. "There is that."

"They're more than just Chinese American businessmen, Alex." That was another piece to the puzzle that frightened me. Whoever those men were, they were scary dudes, scarier than the *kiang shi* in a lot of ways. Who would have the hubris to use a supernatural tool like that to do something as mundanely criminal as take over Sacramento's marijuana trade? That set off another idea.

"We need to have someone take this to the Council," I said.

Alex cocked his head and regarded me with those dark, dark eyes. "I'm pretty sure you were standing next to me when we had our little chat with Aldo. No one's taking this to the Council. No one cares."

I stared at him. "Some group of criminals is using supernatural beings for nefarious purposes and the Council doesn't care?"

"Looks that way," Alex said pleasantly.

I leaned toward him. "They used supernatural beings to threaten a Messenger." Which, to be sure, truly rankled me.

Alex thought for a moment. "You might be able to get some traction there. Talk to Mae about it."

"Will you talk to Aldo?" I pressed.

Alex stood up. "Nope. I did my bit. I've done all that's required of me. I'm pretty much done."

"Except for trying to stitch up the bits and pieces of the young men they bring in here. Except for trying to get a baby to breathe again."

Alex's expression turned serious. "Yeah, except that part and stitching you up, too. Other than that, I'm done with this, and you should try to be done with it, too, Melina."

I waved him away with my good hand. He grabbed it.

"Listen to me, Melina. Listen carefully. I have not lived this long without learning a few things. There are fights that you cannot win. This feels like one of them. I'm not crazy about the parade of broken boys that comes through this emergency room during times like these. I think they should all be home studying for their SATs, but they are not my problem. When you come in here . . ."

He paused and gritted his teeth again.

"When you com in here, wounded and poisoned, it's a whole different thing. Think this through, Melina. It takes a serious amount of evil in a human soul to use something like a *kiang shi* for monetary gain. These are not people you want to play with."

As if I hadn't already figured that out all by myself.

TED SHOWED UP WITH THE STICKY RICE. HE CALLED MY cell, and I told him where to find us in the hospital. "Hey," he said, coming in and brushing the hair off my forehead. "How's it going?"

"I've been better," I said, but I still couldn't stop myself from smiling up at him. His hand was soft and warm.

He frowned back, his hand still on my forehead. "You're burning up."

"Yeah, she is. We need to get this going." Alex stood up from his chair and held out his hand.

Ted handed over the take-out bag. He didn't say a word to Alex, but his appraising look was plenty loud.

Alex opened the bag, took out the container of rice and then started taking the bandage off my arm.

"What the hell happened to you?" The alarm on Ted's face was easy to read.

"I got bitten." It was the best explanation I had, and the truth seemed the easiest course of action. My brain was in way too much of a whirl to lie well. My Zen lying place was totally unreachable.

"By what? You need to report things like this, Melina. Animal control should be taking this animal into custody."

There was a thought. Animal control. Maybe they would deal with the *kiang shi*. Alex snorted as he packed the wound with sticky rice.

"Is that stuff sterile?" Ted asked, staring at Alex.

"They boil it, don't they?" Alex said, not looking up from what he was doing.

Ted's frown deepened. "That doesn't seem like enough."

"Trust me." Alex looked up now and smiled a little. His voice altered just a little bit, not enough to be a full command voice, but enough to be way more persuasive than any normal person's voice. "It's an old wives' tale, but it works every time. What she really needs now is to go home and rest. Can you take care of that part?"

Ted nodded.

"Are you armed?" he asked.

Ted nodded again.

Alex turned to me now. "You need to lie low for a while, Melina. I mean it. I can't protect you." He jerked his head in Ted's direction. "Neither can he. Not really."

"I'd love to. But I don't think it's an option."

He shook his head. "Change that dressing every four hours and call me if it's not getting better. You kids scoot along now."

I COULD ACTUALLY FEEL THE TOXINS BEING SUCKED BACK out of my system. By the time we got to Ted's truck, the fiery pain was down from a four-alarm to a three-alarm. I still had that weird spinning feeling in my head, the one I usually associate with tequila shots. Ted helped me into the car and buckled me into my seat. I took a good, deep whiff of him as he leaned across me.

He smiled. "Are you sniffing me?"

"Yep."

"You are a very strange girl." He shook his head and started to back out of the car, but I reached up with my good arm and pulled him toward me for a kiss. He tasted every bit as good as he smelled.

"Is that the fever? Or you?" he asked, pulling away to look down into my eyes.

"I think it's me, but it's a little tough to be sure. Does it really matter?" What kind of guy passed on making time with a girl because of a little fever?

He shut my door, went around and got in on his side. "I'm not sure what the rules are about this." He turned the key and the pickup growled to life. I love the sound of a solid old truck. I wriggled in my seat.

"There are rules?"

"Sure there are. There are always rules." He glanced over at me with what looked like real concern creasing his brow. "If you were drunk, you'd be totally off-limits right now. I'm not sure about feverish, though."

"First of all, I'm getting less feverish by the second." It was true. That Alex, he sure knew how to treat an other-worldly bite. "Second, I don't have such good luck with rules. I pretty much ignore them these days."

"I've noticed." He stopped smiling.

"Hey, it's not my fault. It's not that I don't want to follow them. It's just that circumstances seem to force me in other directions." That was a hell of an understatement.

He glanced back at me again, his head cocked to one side, his expression way too intelligent for someone who was also that cute. "It's a choice, Melina."

"I wish." Like anyone had ever given me a choice about any of this.

He went back to focusing on his driving. "You can't just wish. You have to do it."

"You have no idea," I said and leaned my head back against the seat rest.

He reached over and took my hand as he drove. "No," he said. "I don't. I wish that you would explain some of it so that I would. I think I could help."

I didn't have a snappy comeback for that one. It wasn't anything that anyone had ever offered me before.

17

WHEN WE GOT TO MY DOOR, THIS TIME I WAS ACTUALLY ready for his kiss. I knew it was coming because he kept looking at my mouth and then snapping his attention back to my eyes. I knew it was going to shake me again, too. I couldn't afford to have something sneak up on me again. It might not be as benevolent as a kleptomaniac imp this time. As we got to the door, I closed my eyes and opened my senses. Nope. Nothing weird in the apartment this time. No imps were going to tug at my pant leg in the middle of our lip-lock.

My back was pressed against the wall, just the way I like it. There aren't many things that can sneak up on you with a nice solid expanse of plaster at your back. I looked up at Ted and he looked down at me. I didn't even realize that I'd started biting my lower lip until he brushed his thumb over it and said, "Nervous?"

"A little," I admitted in an uncharacteristic show of candor.

He lowered his head and rested his forehead against mine. "Me, too. This feels like a big deal."

"We don't have to . . ." I started to say.

He lifted his head and cupped my chin with his hand. "Do you really think you're getting out of this that easy?"

Then I didn't know what to say. I wasn't entirely sure I could say anything. My throat felt constricted. Maybe it was because my heart was beating so very fast. The air between us seemed to heat to a nearly scorching level. For a moment, nobody moved.

But it was only a moment. I'm not sure who started kissing whom first, but suddenly our lips were touching and our tongues were tangling and our bodies were pressed together, except our clothes were in the way. I needed his body against mine without anything in between us.

I opened the door to the apartment and we stumbled through, our lips still pressed together.

"Well, hello, there," Norah said from the living room.

What was she doing home? Surely she was out on a date or something. She was always out on a date or something.

We broke apart like high school kids caught necking in the afternoon on the living room couch.

"Uh, hey," I said, trying to tuck my shirt back in.

Ted's arm snaked around my waist and pulled me back against him. At first I thought it was a gesture of solidarity, but then I realized he was probably trying to hide what felt like a Kokopelli-worthy bulge in the front of his jeans. "Hi," he said from behind me, his voice a little rough.

Norah's eyes narrowed as she looked hard at him. "Hey, aren't you that cop that was here the other morning?"

"That would be me," he said. "Here to serve and protect."

I fought a giggle.

Norah shifted her focus to me. "Really, Melina, a cop?" She heaved a great sigh, shook her head, snapped off the TV set and marched off to her room.

Ted let out his breath. "I take it she's not a fan of the police." He turned me toward him and pulled me up close to him again, and I found I didn't really care what my room-mate thought.

"She has issues with authority figures," I said, sounding breathy since he had started kissing his way down the side of my neck. Amazing. Norah would let a vampire in, serve him red wine while he stared with naked hunger at the pulse beat in her alabaster neck, but she was off in a huff over me invit-ing in a cop. My roommate was nuts.

He lifted me up and set me on the kitchen counter. As his hands slid underneath the loose bottom of my top, the question of my roommate's sanity left my mind entirely.

In fact, any question I ever had probably left my mind. My worries over my arm, the *kiang shi*, what to buy my mother for her birthday . . . all gone.

His lips trailed across my chest. He looked up at me now, eyes steady and gaze open. I wrapped my legs around his waist and pulled him closer. His head fell back. I leaned down and nipped at his exposed throat. He growled. "Do you have a room?" he asked. "Preferably one with a door and possibly soundproofing?"

"Yes on the door. No on the soundproofing."

"Could we go there now?"

I slid off the counter, my body rubbing against his as my feet came to the floor. "Right this way," I said.

We kissed our way down the hallway, unbuttoning but-tons as we went. We made it inside my room and he kicked the door shut behind us, lifting my shirt off as he did it. I slid his shirt off his shoulders and ran my hands over the smooth muscles of his chest. He made that growling sound again. No wonder he'd weighed a ton when he'd pinned me down in Frank Liu's garden. The man was pure muscle.

He undid my jeans and I wriggled them off and kicked them away, thanking every intuition that had led me to shave my legs and wear a pair of panties that matched my bra that morning. For once in my life, I felt I was dressed appropriately. Who cared that it only happened when I was half-undressed?

He ran his hands down my waist to my hips, leaving a trail of goose bumps behind him. Then his arms encircled me and pulled me against him.

The shock of feeling his overheated skin against my own made me gasp. His mouth found mine again and I lost myself in that sensation as well. I felt like I was floating, then realized that he was laying me down on my bed. Oh, what miracles, I'd actually made the damn thing today so it wasn't its usual cyclone of sheets and blankets, but a smooth, inviting surface.

He followed me onto the bed. I reached between us, undid his belt and started to work on the buttons of his jeans, my fingers clumsy with urgency. Oh, 501s, how can you be so damn sexy and so nearly impossible to deal with when I want to have sex? Are the denim gods laughing at me as we speak?

He laughed and stood back up to shuck them away. He stood there for a moment, beautiful and naked, looking down on me with an expression on his face that made me feel more beautiful than I'd ever felt in my life. I wanted him to stay there so I could continue to feel like that, and I wanted him back with his skin on my skin, too. He looked just as torn.

Apparently, skin won out. He covered my body with his, settling his erection so it rubbed in just the right place. His fingers trailed over the tops of my breasts, tracing the edges of my bra, then reached lower to circle my nipples. He snapped open the front clasp of my bra, exposing me to the air, to his gaze, to his seeking and searching tongue. The heat at my core rose a few more degrees. Much more, and the sheets were going to burst into flames.

His fingers trailed lower, across my belly, to trace along the top of my panties. I think I stopped breathing for a moment.

"You okay?" he asked.

I nodded, wordless and breathless. Then my panties were gone, skimmed down my legs and tossed to the floor. His fingers explored me, gentle and teasing, thick and strong. I gave myself over to the sensations rushing through me, losing myself in the pleasure. Tension coiled inside me, my back arched. I whispered his name.

His hands left me and my eyes flew open. He was getting a condom from his wallet. He grinned at me. "I thought it was wishful thinking when I put it in there tonight. I'm glad I wished."

I was glad, too. It had been so long since I'd had sex with anyone, I wasn't even sure I remembered how the damn things were supposed to go on. Luckily, he took care of that, then pulled me over on top of him.

If I'd thought he'd set me on fire before, I had no idea what he was capable of. He slid me onto him, filling me in one smooth thrust. Then with his hands on my hips he set a slow and steady rhythm that had me gasping. Once we'd found our groove, his hands were free to roam, though. From my breasts to my spread thighs, over my belly and down to the very center of me.

Our rhythm picked up, faster and more urgent. He whispered words of encouragement. "Yes, like that, beautiful girl. Yes, Melina. Come for me, baby. I'm right behind you. Come for me."

For once in my life, I opted to be obedient.

TED SLEPT SPRAWLED ON HIS BACK. I TEND TO HUDDLE more, curling in on myself as if I was protecting vital organs. I suppose I actually might be. Things show up at night to talk to me. There's a reason supernatural beings are so often referred to as things that go bump in the night. That is when they tend to show up. Some bump more than others. It's a matter of personal preference on their parts pretty much. Protecting parts I don't want to get bumped is pretty much all on me.

So he sprawled and I curled up with my head resting on his chest. He still smelled like cookies, except now he smelled like cookies with sex frosting. I let my hands glide over his chest, appreciating its definition as if by Braille. He stirred, pulled me closer and kissed the top of my head. I felt something unspool deep inside me.

I ran my hands down to his belly and let my fingers dance down the trail of hair below his belly button. He nudged me, but he wasn't using his hands. He kissed me on top of the head again and then asked, "Do you have to be anywhere this morning?"

"Not for hours," I said.

"Good." He rolled me onto my back and made me forget all about baked goods. No man has ever done that before.

"YOU HAVE NOTHING TO EAT IN THIS REFRIGERATOR except tofu and apples." Ted didn't sound particularly happy.

"Norah says that an apple provides the same amount of help in waking you up as coffee." I scooped coffee into the filter anyway.

He straightened up and stared at me. "I don't even care if that's true or not. I still want the coffee."

"Me, too." I felt the smile spread across my face. It was the oddest sensation. I don't think I could have even stopped it if I'd wanted to. The totally weird thing was, I didn't want to. I wanted to smile. I couldn't remember the last time I'd felt that way either.

I sliced up an apple and handed him half the sections. "Do you want peanut butter on yours?"

"No, thanks."

I peeked under the bandages on my arm to check my bite wound. It was practically healed and was more than a little itchy. I wanted to take the dressing off, but I didn't want Ted to see how much better it looked. That would require explanations I wasn't ready to give.

I did think I was ready for one explanation, though. "So does this trust thing run both ways? If I trust you with something, will you trust me and not ask questions?"

He pulled me into the circle of his arms. It felt so good to rest my head against his chest. It felt so safe. I wished it wasn't just an illusion. No place was safe now. Whoever Henry Zhang really was, whatever he really wanted, he knew who I was and no place would be safe for me anymore. Unless and until Henry Zhang was no longer in the picture. If he was here to take over Sacramento's drug trade, perhaps the easiest way to get rid of him would be to disrupt his supply of drugs.

Ted kissed the top of my head yet again. "Of course it does."

I pushed away from him, and never taking my gaze off his face, I pulled the list of the grow house addresses out of the back pocket of my jeans and handed it to him.

He unfolded the paper, looked it over and then looked back at me, head cocked to one side, eyes slightly narrowed. "What are these, Melina?"

"Addresses," I said. I am nothing if not helpful.

He snorted. "I can see that. What are they the addresses of?"

I blew out a breath. How much should I tell him? How much could I tell him? This was uncharted territory. I wasn't telling him about the *kiang shi* or anything else from the world that most people didn't see. The grow houses were the work of humans, and if a cop didn't represent human authority, I didn't know what did. "They're the addresses of seven houses that smell funny and have very advanced security systems."

His eyes went wide. "How did you . . . ?"

I pressed my fingers against his lips and shook my head. "Don't even ask."

He took my hand in his, kissed the palm and moved it away from his mouth. "I have to ask."

"No." I shook my head. "No, you don't. You have to trust me. Or don't. Drive by them yourself. I figure you'll have to do some investigating on your own to get the search warrants and stuff."

Concern furrowed his brow. "How are you connected to these houses, Melina? Tell me so I can make sure to protect you."

There it was. That protection thing again. Sure, it was great when it meant that he was the one who remembered to put on a condom, but it was going to get in the way of this relationship damned fast.

I'm not saying I didn't like it. Quite honestly, I ate it up with a spoon. The idea that someone somewhere was watching my back was decidedly appealing. It was also a total pipe dream.

I tried to reassure him. "I'm not connected in any way that the police will see. I promise you, my name will not come up."

"Try me." He was so sincere, I was half-tempted to go ahead and spill the whole thing. I couldn't, though. Really, how could I? Where would I start? With my mother's battle against mold and mildew on pool tile? Or fast forward to the here and now and try to explain about Chinese vampires and massacres at mines?

At best, he'd think I was pulling his leg and be pissed off. At worst, he'd think I was crazy. There was nowhere on the spectrum in between that I wanted to exist either.

"Please, I don't have anyone else to turn to and I can't explain. I'm trusting you with information. You're going to have to trust me back and not ask how I got it."

He cupped my chin and ran his thumb along my jawline. It felt so nice. I wanted to grab him by the front of his shirt and drag him down the hallway to my bedroom and have him spoon around me and stay that way for the rest of the day and into the night. I didn't, though. I looked up at him.

He heaved a sigh. "Okay. If you change your mind . . ."

"I know," I said. "I'll call."

He walked out the door, leaving me with a feeling of unease. It was true. I had nowhere else to turn. Aldo wouldn't do anything about it and neither would Chuck. Alex wasn't going to help, nor would Paul. Let's face it. George Zhang didn't want my help. He'd made that clear enough. Mae said to chart my own course, to make the decision I thought was best. This was it. Hand it off to someone who at least wanted to do something about it. Nobody else did. I hoped I wasn't sending Ted into something unprepared. I hadn't sensed anything paranormal at the grow houses, though.

Plus, he was a cop. He was prepared. He'd have backup. What was that like anyway?

TED CALLED A COUPLE OF HOURS LATER. "MELINA, WHAT are you involved with?"

"Why? What's going on?"

"We're getting the search warrants ready now. This is big, Melina. Huge, even. These houses are the source of the BC Bud that's been turning up around here. How did you know about them?"

"Let's just say I stumbled across them, okay?"

"Not okay. If you're mixed up with these people, you're going to need protection. Mark my words, by the time they finish with this thing, its roots are going to go all the way back to Hong Kong."

The whole point was that I wasn't going to need protection. With the grow houses shut down, Henry Zhang and his buddies wouldn't have any more reason to hang around Sacramento. Abracadabra voila! My problem would be solved. "It's going to be fine now, Ted. I'm sure of it."

————

"HOW'S THE ARM?" PAUL ASKED AS I SLID UP TO THE BAR.

I didn't bother to ask him how he knew. "Better." I flexed it. It was feeling better, almost as good as new. "How's Meredith?"

He blushed. "Irritating." He handed me a Diet Coke.

"I didn't even order yet."

"You shouldn't drink while you've got a wound like that. It interferes with the healing process. Did Alex put you on antibiotics?"

I shook my head.

Paul rolled his eyes. "I'll talk to him. Who knows where those things' mouths have been?"

Who knew indeed? I really didn't want to. "How have things been over at the temple?"

"Quiet."

"Good. I could use some quiet."

Paul poured himself a beer and knocked his glass against mine. "Amen, little sister. Amen."

I finished my soda, left a tip on the bar and waved good-bye to Paul. I sauntered over to the temple, not bothering with sneaking in the back way. I figured the least I could do was let George Zhang know that the trouble was over. I figured it would be best to do it before nightfall so he could do what needed to be done to keep the *kiang shi* from rising.

I walked right up to the front door and knocked. I had to wait awhile and knock a few more times, but I knew he was in there. I could hear movement coming from inside. One of the big double doors finally creaked open a fraction.

"Hey, George, what's up?"

His eyes widened and he grabbed me by the arm, hustling me inside the temple. "Not again! Why won't you leave me alone?"

I grabbed my arm back and rubbed it. The wound looked healed, but it was still tender. "A girl could develop a complex being greeted like that, George. You're awfully hard on my self-esteem."

"I am less concerned about your self-esteem than I am in trying to help you stay alive," he hissed at me, eyes darting around the temple as if someone might be hiding in its spare interior.

"That's almost sweet, George. I guess I'll forgive you for the less than enthusiastic greeting. I only wanted to stop by to tell you that it's over. It's going to be okay now."

His eyes narrowed. "What do you mean that it's over? How is it over?"

"You should be able to turn on the ten o'clock news and have Edie Lambert tell you about how the grow houses in Elk Grove were busted today. Without the BC Bud, there's no reason for your brother and his friends to stay here in Sacramento and make trouble."

George covered his eyes with his hand and shook his head. "Unbelievable. Could you be more naïve? More stupid?"

That was completely unfair. I'd figured out what was going on and stopped it. Granted, I'd had some help along the way, but I'd called the shots. I'd done exactly what Mae had told me to do. I'd made a decision and followed it through. "Hey! Watch it with the name-calling, dome head."

"Can you ever be serious?"

"Of course. I'm serious as a heart attack. It's going to be okay. It may take the police a little while, but they'll trace those grow houses back to your brother eventually. It's over. He may as well clear out. If he doesn't understand it, you can explain it to him." I was sure once I'd connected the dots for George, he'd have an attitude adjustment.

"My brother does not care for explanations from others. You haven't shut down his operation, but you have probably made him angry. You're in serious danger, Ms. Markowitz. Please stop meddling in this before you get hurt."

I shoved up my sleeve so he could see my bandaged arm. "They already tried to hurt me and they've already failed. I can take them. I know how."

He shook his head slowly. "You don't understand how the Triad works. If they can't get you, they'll get someone close to you. If they can't get that person, they'll get someone else. Someone is going to get hurt, and it will be way worse than a bite on the arm."

18

GEORGE HAD WAY HARSHED MY VICTORY BUZZ, AND I
didn't appreciate it one bit. It had been a tough few days, and
I thought he'd be happy to hear that I'd managed to resolve
what was happening even without his help. Some people
simply didn't know when they had a good thing going.

I wanted to tell someone what I'd done, someone who'd
appreciate it. I doubted Alex would give me a pat on the
back. Nor would Paul. I couldn't really tell Ted much of
anything that I hadn't already told him.

There was one person who would understand. One person who might even give me a pat on the back for charting
my own course. That was Mae.

I sighed. I hated how things were between us. I decided
to drive by the studio. It was late, but she might still be there.

My cell phone rang as I drove toward the dojo. It was Ted.

"Hey," he said. "Where are you?"

"I dropped in on some friends and now I'm on my way
home." I would be on my way home soon. Just as soon as
I'd done a longing stalkerish drive-by of River City Karate.

"I thought you were supposed to be resting."

"It didn't bother you that I didn't rest that much last night," I teased.

"Yeah, well, I was thinking we could do some not resting again tonight if you felt up to it."

The warm rumble of his voice sent a charge running through me. For once, it wasn't unwelcome. Oh, Lord help me, I liked this guy. I was pretty sure that way lay insanity for me. "Ted, where are you right now?"

He paused. "Outside your apartment."

"You're sure you're not stalking me?"

Another pause. "I'm not as sure about that anymore. How long 'til you get here?"

"Five minutes. Ten at the most." I was practically at River City now.

Our last class at River City ends at nine o'clock. It's a sparring class for the adult students. Occasionally, some of them end up staying a little late and gabbing, but Mae usually sends everyone packing by ten thirty at the latest. After all, she has to be there to open the doors for the six A.M. advanced adult class. Granted, she doesn't need as much sleep as most people, but she still likes some time away from the dojo.

All that is to explain why there shouldn't have been cars in the parking lot. None of the other businesses in our strip mall stayed open that late. Not the nail salon. Not the sushi joint. Not the consignment shop. I pulled into the lot, just to make sure everything was okay.

"I'm going to stop and see if Mae is still at the dojo. I, uh, haven't been around as much as I usually am and want to check on my schedule."

"How about I meet you there and we can neck in the parking lot?"

"Making me an offer I can't refuse, are you?"

"You come to me on the day of my daughter's wedding," he mumbled.

"That is probably the worst Marlon Brando imitation I have ever heard."

"Wait until you hear my Jimmy Cagney."

He was an old movie buff. Everything new I learned about him felt like a major revelation. I'd heard about this part of a relationship before. I'd heard Norah talk about how fun and exciting it was to discover everything about a new lover. I'd never experienced it before. I felt like Columbus discovering America, except without the unpleasant racial-dominance overtones. "Geez, Goodnight, have you seen any movies made in this century? Have you heard there are these things called talkies now?"

He chuckled. The sound of it made me smile. What had I gone and done? I wasn't positive, but it seemed like I might have fallen in love. "My dad was a major insomniac. The TV was on all night long constantly. I think I picked up half the movies in my sleep."

Wow. Another tidbit. An insomniac dad. "What about your mom? Was she an insomniac, too?"

There was a hesitation now. "She wasn't really in the picture. At least, not after I was about seven. I can't really tell you about her sleep habits."

Uh-oh. I'd blundered into something deep, at least deeper than I'd intended. "I'm sorry."

"No worries. It was what it was, and it was a long time ago."

"Still want to make out in the parking lot on your break?"

"Absolutely. I'll see you in ten."

Everything was most definitely not okay. The three cars in the parking lot were shiny black Lincoln Navigators.

"Can you make it five? Something is not right here."

I screeched into the parking lot, ripping off my seat belt and leaping out of the car. I felt the buzz then. They were here. The *kiang shi* were here.

I ran to the door of the dojo.

I SLIPPED UP TO THE BIG PLATE GLASS WINDOW AT THE front of the dojo. Every instinct told me to rush in, proverbial guns blazing, but I knew that was wrong. I needed to be smart. I needed to assess the scene before I burst in.

What I saw sickened me. Two *kiang shi* had Mae cornered on the far side of the dojo. It wasn't a bad place to be. It was the corner where we keep most of our sparring weapons. In fact, she was using one of the kendo sticks to fend them off. She swept it around, coming in hard at the sides of their faces, forcing them to move back, and then sweeping up to smack them over their nasty heads. They couldn't sneak up behind her because she had the wall at her back. Still, they kept swiping at her with their long clawlike fingers, barely daunted by the hard cracks they were taking to their heads and shoulders.

My heart clenched. She didn't know what I'd learned on the Internet. She didn't know they were after her chi or that she needed to hold her breath. I had to get to her.

The other four *kiang shi* stood still as statues not far from George Zhang, who cowered by the door to the dojo office, ringing his bell with tears streaming down his face. Henry and four of his henchmen hovered next to George. I'd have to get past them somehow.

I sidled closer to the door.

One of the henchmen, a bald-headed guy with a neck as thick as one of my thighs, said, "She's lasting longer than I expected. Twenty dollars says she doesn't make it another five minutes, though."

"I'll take a piece of that action," said a younger man with a broad nose and a low ponytail. "I say she makes it seven."

They were laying bets on how long Mae would live. I wanted to break their necks with my bare hands.

Henry said, "One hundred dollars says that she makes it ten."

Mae's kendo stick snapped; without taking her eyes off the constantly advancing *kiang shi*, she grabbed another from the wall behind her.

The third of the henchmen, this one taller with a trendier haircut that swooped over his forehead, said, "I give her less than two."

As they dug for their wallets, I made my move.

There are ways for a woman my size to take down someone bigger than she is. It's a little tough when there's a group. What I wanted to do—what I needed to do—was to get to Mae. If I could tip her off on how to evade the *kiang shi* and we could somehow get to the changing room, we could escape out the back. There was a heavy bench against the wall in the back room. With two of us, we could drag it to the door and hope it was high enough to at least slow the *kiang shi* down.

I crashed open the door and Henry's henchmen whirled around at the noise. As I'd hoped, two of them—Baldy and Ponytail—rushed me. I dropped low and took them both out together with a leg sweep. As they sprawled to their faces, I leaped over them and somersaulted into the middle of the mat, landing on my feet.

The other two henchmen were already advancing. I ducked behind the row of Wavemasters—essentially free-standing heavy bags on water-filled pedestals—we keep against the wall opposite from where Mae was still holding off the *kiang shi*. Over and over, they lunged for her abdomen, giving her the opportunity to smack them both over their heads and under their chins. Of course, they fed on chi and they were going for the center of hers.

"Mae," I yelled. "Hold your breath. They locate you by your breath."

"Got it," she answered.

I didn't have time to say anymore or even see what she would do with the information. The henchmen were on me and one had pulled a knife.

He was fast, but I was faster. He lunged. I grabbed the Wavemaster and tipped it on its water-filled pedestal. He ended up stabbing the Wavemaster with enough force that the knife stuck.

The second man was coming from the other direction. I let go of the Wavemaster, allowing it to right itself, and ducked behind the one next to it. The man feinted left, then right, then right again. I stayed behind the Wavemaster. Without a weapon of some sort, he wasn't going to be able to reach me behind the bag. I waited until he was directly in front of the bag and then rammed into it as hard as I could with my shoulder.

The bag, with my weight behind it, struck him full force in the forehead; he went down, the Wavemaster landing squarely on his chest, knocking the wind out of him.

By that time, Knife Boy had gotten unstuck from the first Wavemaster. He was coming at me again, leaving me no time to duck behind anything. I crouched low, leaped up with my right leg tucked against my chest, then straightened the leg and came down on his knife arm with an ax kick. The knife skittered away. The man howled and clutched his arm to his chest. I hoped I'd broken it.

I turned toward Mae. Sweat beaded her upper lip, and her shoulders had begun to tremble. She wasn't going to be able to keep fighting for much longer.

As one of the *kiang shi* lunged for her center again, I ducked beneath his arm. I blocked his lunge with both my forearms, grabbed hold of his arm, ducked beneath him again and pirouetted behind him, locking the elbow as I went. I wrenched the arm up behind him.

Instead of forcing the *kiang shi* to the floor as I'd intended, it was like taking the wing off an overcooked turkey. I felt the joint snap. The decomposing flesh on his arm wasn't enough to keep it attached to his body. The arm snapped free in my hand.

I took my impromptu club and swung it like a baseball

bat at the head of the other *kiang shi* as he lunged toward
Mae. I caught him in the side of the head, spinning him
around. As the jagged edge of the bone scraped across his
face, it caught the edge of the talisman and pulled it free.

Baldy and Ponytail were now up off the ground and heading toward Mae and me in the corner. The *kiang shi* who'd
lost his talisman advanced on Baldy and Ponytail.

"Stop it," Henry screamed at George.

"I can't. Not without the talisman." George stopped ringing his bell. The *kiang shi* threatening Mae froze, but the
one advancing on the henchmen kept moving. It grabbed
Ponytail by the arm. Ponytail screamed as the *kiang shi*
pulled him toward it.

"Then get the talisman," Henry yelled. "Now."

Taking advantage of my inattention, Baldy got in a palm
strike to my jaw that spun my head back toward Mae. If I
know I'm going to be in a fight, I never wear a ponytail high
on the back of my head. I'll braid it low. It's better to have
it loose than to have it in a high ponytail. Unfortunately, I
hadn't thought about my hair when I'd charged into the dojo.
As my head spun, my ponytail practically leaped into
Baldy's hand. He yanked it downward. Hard. I went down.
All the air left my lungs, and for a moment, I could do nothing but lie there, gasping. I could not have been more vulnerable, on my back unable to move.

I heard George's bell start to ring again. He must have
managed to put the talisman back on the marauding *kiang
shi*'s forehead. I saw Baldy gathering himself for a strike.
If I were him, I'd come down on my throat and collarbone
and crush my windpipe. It looked as though that was precisely what he was going to do.

In the second before he made his strike, Mae came crash-
ing from the side. She leaped in the air and spun, thrust out
her foot and caught him in the chin. He crumpled to the
ground, but then the *kiang shi* were on her. Now that she

was out of her protective corner, they could go at her from both sides. She didn't stand a chance.

I struggled to my feet. I had to get to Mae. I had to stop the *kiang shi* from tearing her to bits, but there were four men between her and me. There's a point in a fight when adrenaline takes over. The red haze envelops my brain and all I see are targets and I strike them as hard and fast as I can. I spun and kicked one man in the gut and used the momentum from the strike to snap another's head back with a palm strike under the jaw. They got in a few licks of their own, but I barely felt the kick to my ribs or the blow to my shoulder.

Then over the ringing bells and shouts and screams, I heard the whoop of a single police car siren. The bells stopped. The *kiang shi* froze.

"Get them," shrieked George. "Get them to the cars. Get all of them."

They retreated and fast.

TED WAS THROUGH THE DOOR ALMOST THE SECOND THEY left. He checked me first. "Are you okay?"

"I'll be fine. Mae. Check Mae." When I could finally get to my feet, I ran to where Mae lay on the mat in a pool of blood.

Ted knelt down next to her. "Get some towels or something. Anything we can use to stop the bleeding," he barked at me.

I ran to the back room where we kept a stack of towels in a cupboard. I raced out with them. Ted had ripped away much of Mae's *gi*, at least what was left of it. My stomach rolled when I saw the wounds. Huge chunks of her flesh had been torn away. It hung in shreds from her arms and her rib cage.

Ted grabbed some towels and began pressing them

against the wounds. "Move, Melina, now," he barked again. "Direct pressure against any wounds you can find. We have to stop the bleeding or she won't last until the ambulance gets here."

I grabbed towels, too. She was bleeding in too many places. I couldn't figure out where to press to try to staunch the flow. She'd been bitten and slashed.

I looked up to find Ted staring at me. "What the hell were those things?"

There was no time to explain. "Call for help. Get an ambulance."

"It's already done. A bus and backup are on the way." He brushed the blood-matted hair off Mae's face. "Hold on, Mae. They're on their way," he told her. "We'll hear the sirens any second now."

"Stay with me, Mae. Stay with me," I whispered to her. "Do not leave me. Stay here."

"Trying," she said, her voice so low I almost couldn't hear it.

"Melina," Ted turned to me, hands still busy trying to make makeshift bandages out of cheap Costco towels. "I need to know. What were those things? How did you do some of those things you did? Did I really see what I thought I saw? They're going to be here any minute. I need to know what to say."

"I don't care what you say, Ted." I didn't either. All I cared about was getting Mae to the hospital and getting her help. "You saw what you saw. Believe what you want to believe." I'd tried to protect him. There was no time for that now.

"I don't want to believe any of it, but I can't help you if you won't help me. Was that some kind of act or something?"

"An act? Does this look like an act?" I nodded toward the blood-streaked mat. "Does Mae look like she's pretending?"

His jaw tightened. "No, but what I saw couldn't have been real. Those things couldn't be real. What you did couldn't be real."

"Trust me. It's as real as it gets." I finally heard the sirens in the background. "They're coming, Mae. Hold on."

"Alex," she whispered.

"Absolutely," I said. "I'll call him first thing. He'll be waiting for you at the hospital."

"Now," she whispered. "Call him now."

I looked up and Ted was staring at me again. "You heard those sirens a full five seconds before I did. What is going on here? What are you?"

And there it was. I could see it in his eyes. He finally started to get it. I wasn't what he thought I was, not even close. I had to get him away and keep him away before he really figured it out. In my whole life, there was one person who knew what I was and accepted me for it without asking anything back and she was bleeding to death in my arms. "I'm sorry, Ted," I whispered. Then I turned my back to him and tried to keep Mae's lifeblood from leaking away forever.

Thirty seconds later, the door burst open and the EMTs ran into the dojo. I was thrust aside as they went to work, starting IVs, taking blood pressure, calling into the hospital. They shoved Ted in the opposite direction, toward the back of the dojo.

I looked at him across the mat and then walked out the door. I pulled my cell phone out of my pocket and dialed Alex. He answered on the second ring. "Hello, Melina."

"Alex," I said. "Mae needs you."

Then I said the hardest thing there is for me to say. "I need you."

THEY WOULDN'T LET ME STAY WITH MAE. I WANTED TO ride in the ambulance with her, but not as a patient. Arguing

with the EMTs was wasting precious moments. She needed
to get to the hospital and she needed to get there fast. I
decided to drive myself. The decision wasn't exactly
endorsed wholeheartedly by the EMTs, but since I outran
them to my car, they didn't argue. Besides, they knew how
critical it was to get Mae to a trauma center. They were going
to waste only so much time with someone who could still
run on her own two feet.

I didn't manage to outrun Ted. "I'll drive you," he said,
trying to usher me to his car.

I pulled my arm away from him and almost screamed at
the pain that ran up my side. "I'm fine," I hissed between
gritted teeth.

"Yeah," he said. "I can see that. I see exactly how fine
you are. Now come on and let me drive you."

I got into the Buick and slammed the door shut behind
me. I watched him grow smaller in my rearview mirror as
I fishtailed out of the parking lot and sped away, hot on the
trail of the ambulance. I'd seen the look in his eye. He would
never again look at me the way he had the night before. I
didn't think I could bear the change.

Fat lot of good it did me. Once I got to the hospital, I was
shuffled off into my own bay of the emergency room. I
couldn't even get them to tell me where they'd taken Mae.

Being a patient in a hospital in which you work is a special kind of hell. I knew how to get the information I wanted,
but I couldn't access a computer without someone seeing
me. The fact that I was dripping blood, my own and other
people's, made me somewhat conspicuous; no one was going
to let me get close to any piece of hospital equipment.

They kept assuring me they were doing everything they
could for her. I knew that was true. These were, for the most
part, good people. There are a couple of doctors who think
God speaks directly into their ears and a few nurses who I
think might be closet dominatrixes, but mainly, these were
people who'd chosen their professions with a sincere desire

to help their fellow man or woman or whatever. Unfortunately, I also knew everything they could do wrong. Hospital error is terrifying and way more prevalent than anyone wants to admit.

I knew what I had to say to get released quickly. Nothing hurt too much. I wasn't seeing double. I could move my arms and wiggle my fingers. The only reason I didn't bolt was I knew the cops were going to have questions and I had no idea what I was going to say to them. I felt a momentary stab of pity for Ted. He'd have to figure it out on his own. The less contact he had with me, the better.

After about forty-five minutes, Alex came in, sat down on the plastic chair in my charming little bay of the ER and said, "They took Mae into surgery. She'll be in there for at least four or five hours. You might as well let them treat you."

"I want you to do it." The words were out before I knew I wanted to say them. I stole a quick look at him. Based on the surprised expression on his face, I knew it wasn't a thought he'd planted in my head and forced me to say with some weird vampire power.

"It's not always a good idea for a doctor to treat someone he's emotionally involved with." Alex stood and walked over to my bed. He took my hand, his skin cool against the fevered heat of my own.

It wasn't comforting in the usual way I might find someone else's touch comforting. It was nothing like the night Ted stood beside me while we watched the sunrise and we held hands for the first time.

It was nothing like when Ted had held me close and murmured in my hair. On the other hand, Alex didn't look at me like I was a freak because through some accident of birth and genetics and timing, I am what I am. No, I'm not like other girls. No, I probably don't need protection, but I do need some comfort now and then. The cold touch of an undead emergency room doctor might be all I could get, and for the moment it would have to do.

"We're not emotionally involved," I said.

He looked down at me with something an awful lot like pity in his eyes. Or maybe it was regret. "We're not?"

"No. We're not. Now check to see if my goddamn rib is broken, will you?"

He sighed and began to examine my rib cage with his chilly hands.

Cold comfort indeed.

ALEX GOT THEM TO RELEASE ME. I COULD TELL NONE OF the nurses thought it was a good idea, but none of them seemed to want to argue with Alex tonight. Maybe he'd shown them a little fang. It was just as well. I wasn't staying there any longer anyway. I shambled out of the ER through the double doors into the hallway, clutching a fistful of prescriptions and a thick stack of papers that I'd never look at again.

"Which waiting room?" I asked.

"I'll walk you." He took my arm. I tried to shake him off, but it hurt too much, so instead I ended up walking docilely beside him to a waiting room on the second floor in the east wing. It was practically identical to the one we'd sat in just the other day, except the desperation and fear that threatened to choke me in this one was my own, not the faded imprint of someone else's emotions.

"How bad is she?" I finally asked, wanting and not wanting to hear the answer.

"Pretty bad." He didn't look at me. I was glad. I didn't want to see the pity in his eyes, and I didn't want him to see the tears in mine. I couldn't lose Mae. I didn't know how I'd go on without her. I felt as if my throat were swelling shut every time I thought about her lying on the mat, so broken and so helpless.

"Who's doing the surgery?"

"Valdez."

That was good. Valdez was one of the best. If anyone could piece Mae back together, it would be him.

"Where's your boyfriend?" Alex asked, still not looking at me, studying his fingernails instead.

I shrugged and then winced. There wasn't a place on my body that didn't feel bruised and battered. "I don't know, and I don't think he's my boyfriend. At least, not anymore. I guess, he, uh, saw me . . . in action."

Alex nodded. "I see. Freaked him out, did you?"

"It appears so." I didn't bother mentioning that I'd shoved Ted away before he could fully figure out what he'd seen.

"He'll be back. He seemed . . . okay for a mundane."

High praise coming from Alex, but still not enough. Alex hadn't seen the look on Ted's face. "I don't think so. I don't think he should. It's not safe." The only reason Mae was lying in an operating room, bleeding from a hundred different places, was because of me.

Alex finagled a pillow and a blanket for me from one of the nurses; I took them and curled up on the couch. He handed me two tablets and a little paper cup of water.

"I don't want any pills. I'll be fine."

He shook his head. "Get over yourself. They're just Tylenol. They won't dull your amazing Messenger senses; they'll barely take the edge off those bruises."

I took the pills from him without looking at him and tossed them back. "You'll wake me up if something happens?"

"Yeah, but I'm out of here by five A.M. You're on your own after that."

I nodded. For all practical purposes, I was on my own now. Having a vampire watch over me for the night didn't exactly make me feel like anyone had my back.

IT WAS THREE THIRTY IN THE MORNING WHEN VALDEZ walked into the waiting room and flung himself down into one of the chairs.

I sat bolt upright. Alex straightened in his chair, too. Valdez rubbed his eyes. "I'm sorry," he said. "We did everything we could. Her injuries were simply too overwhelming."

Then the universe opened up and swallowed me whole.

19

ALEX GOT ME HOME, BLESS HIS SILENT, UNDEAD, PEA-
picking heart. I remember him starting to lift me off the
couch and me landing a pretty decent upper right in the area
of his kidney. No one was carrying me out of the hospital,
not until they actually had to.

"Still in there, are you, little one?" he'd asked, leaning
over me. "That's good. Get up and walk, then."

If I saw anyone I knew on my way out of the hospital, it
didn't register. I remember the too-bright lights, the antiseptic smell. It was so familiar, the terrain of my everyday
life, and now it seemed like some kind of bizarre foreign
landscape. Putting one foot in front of the other to walk
down the corridor took all my focus and concentration.

Then we were in the elevator. The sudden rush away of
the floor made my knees buckle.

"Hang on there," Alex said. "Hang on. Just a little
longer."

I registered what he was saying. I even nodded, but I

didn't understand. What was there to hang on to? Mae was gone. She was what I'd hung on to since I could remember.

Alex led me out of the elevator into the parking garage. The fluorescent lights buzzed. Their flickering light made shadows dance around the columns and in the corners. At any other time, I'd be on my guard now. This was the kind of place where it would suck to be attacked. The quarters were confined, and there were too many hard surfaces someone could bounce your head on or pin you against. Right now, however, I couldn't have cared less.

A strange urge to laugh started in my chest. This was where bad things were supposed to happen. Isn't that where the heroine in the movie was always attacked, as she walked through the gloom in the parking garage? Bad things weren't supposed to happen in brightly lit dojos.

Alex gave me a little shake. "Not yet, Melina. I'll have you home as fast as I can. Hold it together until then."

Home? Home was the dojo. Home was the scratchy old mat where I'd broken Trevor Shelton's nose before I learned to pull my palm strikes. Home was the changing room in the back where the wooden finish had been worn off the floor by years of bare feet. Home was where Mae knew when to give me a hug and when to drop me to the floor with a scissor kick.

He opened the door of his car and folded me into the seat. The smell of expensive leather surrounded me, and I suddenly realized that Alex had no smell. None. It must be a vampire thing. He would never smell like cookies. The world of cookies and men who protected you wasn't my world anyway. I'm sure that eventually, I wouldn't miss it at all.

The rock on my chest got a little heavier.

Once he'd started the car, I rolled down the windows as we sped through the city. The streets were practically deserted at this time of day. It was too late even for the night owls and way too early for regular folk. I let the wind play across my face and whip my hair across my eyes. There was nothing to see out there anyway.

He parked in front of my apartment building. I was surprised when he got out of the car with me. "You don't need to come in. I'm fine," I said.

"Right," he said. "You're peachy. Is your roommate home?"

"You mean Norah?"

"Whoever. The limber blond."

I shot him a look, and he held up his hands in a gesture of truce.

"Probably," I said. "I don't know where else she would be."

"Good."

"Why? Are you hungry?" I stopped on the porch.

"Just open the door, Melina." He didn't look hungry. He looked sad and weary.

I let us in the front door and clambered up the stairs. I didn't remember there being so many of them. I unlocked the door to the apartment and walked in, turning back toward Alex standing at the threshold. "You might as well come in," I said.

He stepped in. "Let's get you to bed."

I gave him a baleful look.

He gave me a disgusted one back. "Not even I'm that low. You need rest, Melina. You've been through an ordeal, physically and emotionally. You need to sleep."

"I'm going to take a shower." I still had blood streaked all over my arms. It was probably in my hair and on my face, too. I didn't even know whose blood it was anymore. Mine? Mae's? Henry Zhang's men's? Did the *kiang shi* bleed?

"Probably a good idea." Alex nodded his head and only then did I realize how difficult it must have been for him to stand there talking to me, to have me in his car, to hold me while I was covered with blood and not even take the tiniest little lick.

I couldn't come up with words to say what I wanted to tell him about that, so I nodded, too, and headed into the bathroom. I heard Norah's bedroom door open as I turned on the shower. I left the door to the bathroom open a crack. Alex was keeping his distance from me, but his willpower had to have taken a beating tonight. I didn't want him to slip up with my best friend and not because I would be jealous if he did. I didn't want her exposed to any of that ugliness ever, if I could help it.

"Hey, Alex," she said. "What's going on? Where's Melina?"

I peeked through the cracked door. Alex took Norah's hands and I saw surprise register on her face as she looked down on his hands on hers. His cold flesh must have shocked her a little. She looked back up at his face, a quizzical expression on her own.

"Melina's had a bad night. Mae was attacked at the dojo. Melina got there at the end of the attack."

Norah's eyes widened. "Is Mae okay? Will she be all right?"

"Mae is dead, Norah."

Norah pulled her hands away from Alex and clutched them in front of her chest, her face blank for a moment. "Dead? Mae is dead? Is Melina okay?"

"Physically, yes. She took a beating, but she'll be okay. Emotionally? I don't know. She's going to need our help."

"What can I do?"

Tears filled my eyes as my friend asked that question without a second's hesitation.

Alex grabbed the stack of prescriptions I'd left on the kitchen counter. "There's an all-night pharmacy over at Arden Way and Howe. Can you fill these for her? Have them call me if they give you any grief, okay?"

"You bet. Let me pull on a pair of jeans and I'll be out of here." She turned and headed back to her bedroom.

"Hurry, Norah," Alex said. "I can't stay here any later

than five A.M. and I don't want her to be left alone for the next day or two."

Norah turned and nodded once. Three minutes later, she was out the door with her purse over her shoulder and I stepped into the shower.

The hot water stung. I was more scraped up then I'd realized. I didn't flinch away. There was a comfort in the pain. Alex was right. At least I was feeling something. I bowed my head and watched until the rust-swirled water turned clear.

I got out of the shower, put on a pair of sweats and walked out into the living room. Everything felt strange. The scratch of the hardwood floor against my feet, the glide of material against my skin. I felt like an alien that had been dropped onto a new planet, one without Mae. I shuffled into the kitchen, pulled a bottle of whiskey out of the cabinet and started to pour.

"Whoa, there." Alex took the bottle out of my hands.

I turned and glared at him. "I think I've earned a drink. I'm not carrying messages for anyone tonight."

"And I think you'll be better off with the heavy-duty pharmaceuticals that will be arriving in a few minutes. I definitely think that those won't mix well with booze, and I'm the one with a medical degree." He put the top back on the bottle and put it back on the shelf.

"A medical degree that's like a couple hundred years old," I muttered.

"It still counts." He took me by the shoulders and pulled me to his chest. "You'll get through this, Melina, but it's going to take some time. Alcohol is not going to be the answer."

My face felt flushed and the chill of his hand was oddly comforting. Maybe this was right. I'd resisted Alex's flirtations for so long, I never really thought anymore about why. It was just the dance that the two of us did together, him pursuing and me twisting away. Maybe I could feel something besides pain tonight. Maybe it would remind me that I was still alive.

I lifted my head and looked up into his eyes, really looked, straight on. No sidelong glance. No skittering away. He looked back. His eyes were deep, dark pools, filled with shadows and longing. His hand slid along my jawline to the nape of my neck, leaving a trail of goose bumps behind it. Then he lowered his head toward mine and kissed me.

It wasn't like any kiss I'd ever had before, not that I was such an expert at kissing, but I wasn't totally new at it either. I'd expected the temperature difference. I'd known this wouldn't be the hot, moist rush of the fevered kisses I'd shared with Ted a few nights before. I simply hadn't expected what that would mean. It was like kissing someone who'd just drank a glass of ice water, except that the ice water was somehow electric. It was crazy. It was strange. It was totally different and I kind of liked it. What good had all that heat done for me? It was just a reminder of what I couldn't have. It wasn't safe to be near me, at least not for humans. We were too fragile. We broke too easily. Humans, I feared, were overrated.

Alex's cool swirled through my heat as his tongue swept between my lips. His chill spiraled down along my nerve endings, leaving them humming and throbbing and burning for more. His cold made the tips of my breasts ignite in flame. I slid my hands up his chest and wrapped my arms around his neck, pressing myself against him, wanting to feel like that everywhere.

He groaned and pushed me away. "Melina, no, not now. Not like this." His voice was a deep rasp that made me shudder against him.

"I'm pretty sure that's exactly how it's done." I was breathing hard and my whole body was trembling.

He shoved his hair off his forehead, his jaw clenched hard enough for me to see the muscles bunch. "Sex is no more the answer for you right now than booze is."

I leaned back against the cabinets. "Then what is, Alex? Since you're such an expert on what I need and don't need right now, what is it?"

For a second, I thought he might reach for me again, but instead he clenched his fists at his sides. "Time. You're going to need time."

We were still staring at each other across the three-foot expanse of my galley kitchen when Norah returned from the pharmacy. Alex apparently wanted me literally at arm's length.

"Did they give you everything?" he asked Norah as she handed him the bag.

"They were short on a couple of things, but they had at least some of everything." She came over and put her arms around me. Her heat felt so strange, so fragile in its humanity. She brushed my wet hair behind my ear. "Do you want me to braid your hair for you?"

I almost started to cry. It was such a Norah offer. It meant nothing. It would change nothing. It was offering to take care of such a superficial thing, and yet I knew her touch and the stroke of the brush was going to give me all the comfort I could stand for now. I nodded.

She was back in a moment with a brush and an elastic band. Alex shook out a couple of pills and handed them to me with a glass of water. "She can have two more of these and one more of those in four to six hours," he told Norah.

"I'm right here," I said. No one answered me. Instead, Norah led me to the living room, settled me on a cushion on the floor and began brushing out my hair.

Nobody spoke. Norah hummed a little bit while she brushed. Suddenly, exhaustion overwhelmed me. I wasn't sure how many hours I'd been up, when the last time I'd slept was or for how long. As she wound the plaits of my hair, my eyes began to close and I began to sway.

I must have finally dozed off. I woke up as I was swept in the air. My response was immediate, instinctive. I threw an elbow and swung with my fist. It didn't do any good. It was like trying to spar with an iceberg. "No, little one, it's okay this time." Alex's words swept over me like a cool breeze. "Let me do this for you."

I let him carry me into my bedroom and put me in the bed that Norah was turning down. They settled me in like parents of a toddler who'd fallen asleep in the car on the way home, and I let them. There was no more fight left in me. Maybe when I woke I'd have some again, but not now.

"I have to go," I heard Alex tell Norah.

"I know," she said, her voice steady. I wondered what she'd do if she really did know how urgent it was for Alex to get home before sunrise. Maybe I was fooling myself, though; maybe her ignorance wouldn't keep her safe.

"Stay with her," he said

"I will."

I heard Alex leave. "You don't have to stay," I told her.

"I want to."

I couldn't keep my eyes open. They weighed a thousand pounds apiece. The blackness was just on the other side and I wanted to be there, but I had to warn Norah first. "You don't understand. It might not be safe."

I felt the bed shift as she sat down next to me. Her warm hand stroked my back. "I understand way more than you give me credit for, and I always have."

I DON'T KNOW WHAT THE PILLS THAT ALEX GAVE ME were, but I'd never slept that deep, dark and dreamless of a sleep before. I glanced at the clock when I finally opened my eyes. It was nearly noon. I considered getting out of bed but then decided against it. It took me a moment to register what had woken me.

Someone was knocking at the door. Whatever they were selling, I wasn't buying.

I heard it open anyway. Norah must be here. She must

have stayed home from work. I let my head fall back onto the pillow. She should have gone to work. She should have gotten as far away from me as she possibly could. She should probably move out.

"Oh," Norah said. "It's you. I'll see if she's in."

A few seconds later, the door to my room cracked open. "It's the cop," she said flatly, disapproval clear in her voice and the expression on her face. "Do you want to see him?"

I lifted my head far enough to shake it.

"Good girl," she said.

Then I heard her say, "She's not here." And the door slammed.

THE NEXT TIME I WOKE UP, ALEX WAS SITTING IN THE chair in the corner of my bedroom. I gave myself a discreet pinch to see if I was dreaming. No such luck.

"Hungry?" he asked, rising from the chair.

I shrugged. My stomach felt empty, but the thought of food didn't particularly appeal. "Maybe a little. You?"

"On some level or another, always." He sat down on the bed.

"Where's Norah?"

He shrugged. "I sent her to bed. She was exhausted, but she didn't want to leave you. I gave her a little nudge."

My eyes narrowed. "What kind of nudge?"

He rolled his eyes. "Nothing like that, Miss Priss. I used my voice. It didn't take much. She wanted to go to bed. She just didn't want to leave you. You're lucky. She's a good friend."

I nodded. It was true. Too bad it wasn't lucky for Norah.

"You need to eat," he said. "What do you want?"

I didn't want anything, but I knew he was right. I would eat. I would sleep. I would keep putting one foot in front of the other. It would dishonor Mae if I didn't. She hadn't trained me to be a quitter. "Grilled cheese and tomato soup."

"Coming up."

While he went into the kitchen, I headed to the bathroom to scrape the fuzz off my teeth and wash my face. By the time I was done, I could smell the butter melting in the pan. Alex didn't mess around.

I sat down at the counter and watched as he deftly flipped my sandwich and heated up the soup without burning it. I tend to burn both when I make this meal. It is what my mother used to make for my lunch on cold rainy days, and it always speaks to me of comfort and love. It had been a long time since I'd sat and watched someone prepare it for me, though. My mother probably still would, if I gave her the chance. I just hadn't wanted to open myself up to that in quite a while. Grilled cheese sandwiches could have strings attached.

I assiduously avoided strings as best I could at all times. Nothing that had happened in the last twenty-four hours would change that either. If anything, I would need to stay farther away than ever from my family. Strings were connections, and connections to me were not good for people's health.

Alex set a plate down in front of me. I looked at the toasted bread and gooey cheese and wondered if there were strings attached to this sandwich as well. I wasn't entirely certain who had started last night's kiss. My stomach growled, though, so I took a bite, expecting it to taste like cardboard, to stick to the roof of my mouth. It didn't. It was delicious. I couldn't help it. I moaned a little. "That's really good," I said.

He crossed his arms over his chest and said, "Glad to be of service." Then he leaned down on the counter across from me and looked very steadily into my eyes. "You're going to be okay, Melina."

I set my sandwich down and took a spoonful of soup. "So you keep saying."

"I've watched a lot of people go through a lot of terrible

things. You get to know which ones are going to make it after a while. You will."

I looked up into the deep, dark pools of his eyes and got lost there once again. I used to avoid looking into Alex's eyes. Looking into a vampire's eyes isn't as unsafe as staring directly into a werewolf's eyes, but it still was an unnecessary chance to take. I had been pretty good at not taking unnecessary chances until recently. I hadn't really thought I was taking chances now. Apparently, I'd been wrong.

I set the sandwich down. Ted had been an unnecessary chance. That was done now. At least he'd be safe. What sort of unnecessary chances caused the shadows in Alex's eyes?

"How many people have you lost? Ones that you actually cared about?"

"More than I want to count." He didn't blink or look away, and I could see the pain down in his eyes.

"It must suck to be you," I said. The double entendre was out before I realized I'd made one. The subconscious is a fascinating thing.

"Good one. Nice to see you still have your sense of humor."

"I didn't really mean it that way." I put my hand on his arm and, for once, didn't flinch away at the marblelike chill of his flesh.

"I know." He put his hand over mine.

"How do you do it? How do you keep going? It hurts so much. I feel like there's a rock on my chest the size of Montana and I can't get it off."

"The undead thing takes care of some of that, you know."

I shot him a look. He might have been undead, but he wasn't immortal. He could be killed permanently. If he wanted to, he could waltz out of the hospital on a beautiful summer morning and turn himself to dust in the rays of the early morning sun. "I'm pretty sure I know better. So how do you live with it?"

Without his eyes leaving mine, Alex lifted my hand off

his arm and placed it back in my own lap. "You don't know. The fact that I'm not really living in the first place does take care of some of it. Once you've settled for half of an existence, it's almost a relief to feel something, even if it's pain."

"I'm so sorry," I whispered. I could only imagine what he was talking about. Would I get to a place someday that my own survival was so without joy that I would welcome feeling like this?

"Don't be. But remember this: you can't feel this pain unless you've felt the joy also. When you've lived as long as I have, you learn to be careful. The grief isn't worth it unless the love before it was truly grand. I've learned to be stingy with my emotions. Otherwise I think I would end it."

I understood what he was saying. I recognized it, even. Hadn't I been doing the same thing for the past few years? I avoided my family. I didn't make new friends. And it still hadn't kept me safe. I'd lost one of the only people I'd allowed myself to love. "Fate sucks," I said.

He shook his head. "It's not fate. There is no such thing. Don't fool yourself. There's no plan. Who would make a plan that looks like this? It's all a random series of chance occurrences."

I knew the argument to make, that the plan was too big and too complex for us to see. I couldn't bring myself to say it. "So what's the point? Why even bother?"

He straightened up. "I thought you'd figured that out. The point is to somehow leave the room a slightly better place than it was before you walked in."

I was having trouble believing that a vampire was telling me that, but then again, I'd always known that Alex wasn't your run-of-the-mill vampire. I was going to comment on that, but my doorbell rang and broke the moment.

Alex started for the door, but I shook my head. "I'll get it." I had a feeling I knew who it was.

Sure enough, I could practically smell the cookies through the door. I peeked through the fish-eye lens anyway to make sure. I wasn't in the mood to take any chances. I'd yet to see Henry Zhang or his gang of Chinese vampires to knock politely, but the past few days had been full of unpleasant firsts for me and I didn't want any more of them.

It wasn't Henry Zhang, though. Or *kiang shi*. Or mutilated tai chi masters. It was Ted. I suddenly felt immensely tired. I did not have the energy for this right now. I didn't think I ever would, to be honest, but definitely not now.

I undid the locks and the security chain anyway and opened the door. "As I live and breathe," I said. "If it isn't Officer Ted Goodnight. To what do I owe the pleasure?"

20

"WHAT ARE YOU? AND WHAT WERE THOSE THINGS?"

He looked as if he hadn't slept. His clothes were rumpled and his eyes were bloodshot.

I took a step back and crossed my arms over my chest. "I'm what I've always been."

Ted shook his head. "Don't dodge behind semantics with me, Melina. Tell me what you are."

Alex made a funny throat-clearing noise from the kitchen. I sighed. The two of these men in the same room wasn't going to be a pretty thing. "Officer Goodnight, you've met Dr. Bledsoe."

I turned on my heel, walked into the living room, curled up in the papasan chair and prepared to watch the two of them do battle over who had biggest swinging dick of them all.

Ted's eyes narrowed. "I didn't know you guys made house calls."

Alex leaned one hip against the counter. "I think there might be several things you don't know, Officer Goodnight.

Are you here as a cop or a friend?" Alex moved into the living room and sat down on the couch. It was as near to me as he could get. I looked at him and shook my head.

Ted looked over at me. Pain shadowed the confusion and anger I'd seen there before. "What exactly is going on here?"

"Alex is my . . ." What the hell was Alex to me? My friend? Not exactly. He'd never make it onto the guest list for Latkepalooza, my mother's annual Chanukah party. My coworker? True enough, but that didn't exactly explain why he was here at my house in the middle of the night. My favorite vampire? Having seen the look on Ted's face after the *kiang shi* and their handlers took off, I wasn't sure how well that was going to go over.

"Her advisor," Alex filled in for me.

"Advisor on what?" Ted followed us into the living room. He didn't sit down. You would have thought that would leave Alex at a disadvantage. Ted was a big man; having to look up at him from a seated position would be difficult. But somehow, Alex slouched back and made it seem as though he preferred it that way.

"Whatever she needs advising on." Alex smiled. I checked him for fang, but there didn't seem to be any showing. Whatever game he was playing, I didn't get it.

Ted didn't seem to get it either, but he did seem upset. He'd clenched his hands in fists at his side despite the relaxed position he was standing in. As a fighter myself, I appreciated the stance. He looked loose at first glance, but then I saw the fists, the clenched jaw and the way he balanced on the balls of his feet. He'd shifted. He could go in any direction. He was ready for a threat. He just had no real idea of what he was getting himself into, and I thought it was best to keep it that way.

My heart did a little tattoo, though. Damn, he was good. Too bad being in any way associated with me might get him killed. "Maybe you could advise her to tell me the truth. I'd like to know what's going on before anyone else gets hurt, especially her. What is she?" His gaze narrowed in on Alex. "What are you? I don't for a second buy that you're a regular ER doc anymore."

"Excuse me, I'm right here," I said, not completely appreciating being spoken about in the third person. "And I can take pretty good care of myself, thank you very much."

Ted swung his gaze back toward me, and the look of concern on his face hurt me almost as much as my cracked rib. "I saw that. That's one of the things I'm hoping you'll explain to me."

I didn't have anything to say to that, and I couldn't hold his gaze any longer. I looked down at my toes instead. My pedicure was completely ruined.

"Why don't you tell me your questions and we'll see what we can do for you," Alex broke in.

Ted sat down then, across from Alex. Great. I was going to be ping-ponging back and forth between the two of them as though I were watching a tennis match. "How about we start with what those things were at the karate studio?"

"Good starting point." Alex nodded. "Those, my friend, were *kiang shi* or Chinese vampires."

"Alex!" I couldn't believe what I'd heard. What the hell was he doing?

Ted's eyes narrowed. "Very funny." Once again, he turned back to me. "Melina?"

Now what? Lie? Tell him they weren't *kiang shi*? It wouldn't be the first lie I'd told someone about something they'd seen. People don't really want to believe in the supernatural. Oh, they may want to read a book about vampires or go see a movie about zombies, but they don't want them to really exist. The world is dangerous enough all on its own without adding in other dimensions. Most people know that at some level. It's what makes those fantasies fun. They can't possibly be real.

"I think you should trust him," Alex said quietly.

Trust. That was an interesting concept. Did I trust Ted?

He sat there on my couch, muscled forearms braced on powerful thighs. I could smell his vanilla and cinnamon scent from where I sat. If I had conjured up a hero for myself from whole cloth, I'm not sure I could have done a better job. I didn't know if I'd ever wanted to trust someone more. "Me trusting him isn't really the problem, is it?"

Alex's eyebrows arched. "Interesting point. How about you, Ted? Are you willing to trust Melina?"

Ted flung himself back on the couch. "Have I been doing anything but trusting her since the second I've met her? I know she lied to me about why she was near that gang fight in the first place. I know she lied to me about why she was asking about grow houses. If I hadn't been able to verify her name and address through the police databases, I wouldn't be sure she wasn't lying to me about her name. And here I am, sitting on her couch in the middle of the night playing patty-cake with you, who lies to me about what he's doing here. Right now, I don't trust anybody." He rubbed his hands across his face. "I don't even trust myself. For all I know, I'm turning into my old man and starting to see things."

"Your father was a psychic?" Alex asked, clearly interested.

"No. A schizophrenic. One that didn't always stick to his medication regime exactly how it was prescribed. It was all fun and games until his voices would tell him to get naked at the mall or trim the shrubs at the public park into animal shapes. Then things would get interesting." He smiled, but it didn't reach his eyes.

A clearer picture of my hero was starting to form. "Where was your mom?"

"She took off when I was seven." He shrugged. "When she married him, she thought she could handle it. She thought true love would find a way. What can I say? She was young."

"And she left you there to deal with your mentally ill dad?" Now I was leaning forward.

Ted held up his hands to stop me. "Can we have the Ted Goodnight therapy session some other day? Right now, I'm more interested in figuring out what exactly went down at that karate studio and how the hell it connects with gang fights and grow houses and figuring out what and who you are, Melina."

We. He wanted to know what we were dealing with. I didn't think I could allow that. I didn't think I could let there be a we. I looked over at Alex, who smiled back at me complacently. Maybe he was being more clever than I'd realized. Maybe the best thing to do was to tell Ted the truth. Let him think we were crazy like his father. Or messing with him. Or whatever. I didn't care. I just needed him out of harm's way.

Damn it all to hell, this caring about other people really sucked.

"They were Chinese vampires. They were discovered during renovation work at the Bok Kai Temple in Old Sacramento. One of the priests there told his brother about them. The brother's whatever the Chinese version of mobbed up is. Alex here thinks he's using them to distract the Norteños and the Black Dragons long enough to take over the marijuana trade in Sacramento using the stuff they're making in a bunch of grow houses in Elk Grove."

Ted stared at me. "And will the Chinese vampires be joined by legions of Korean werewolves who have been cooking meth in trailer parks in Truckee?"

"No. The werewolves are refusing to get involved. Trust me, I've tried to talk them into helping. They'll have nothing to do with it." I sat back in my chair and folded my legs up.

Ted shook his head. "You two are a piece of work, you know that?" He stood up and slung his jacket over his shoulder. "When you're ready to let me in on your little secret, let me know. I'll still be here, Melina. No matter what. When you're ready to accept my help, I'm just a phone call away."

He walked to the door of the apartment.

Alex got there before him.

"What the hell?" Ted looked back to where Alex had been sitting, clearly trying to figure out how he'd gotten to the door so fast. I'd seen him go, a kind of blur of motion sweeping past me. It wasn't the easiest thing to get used to, but a person eventually accepted that vampires were crazy fast.

"I think you should stay a little longer." Alex stared full into Ted's face.

Ted stared right back. Then he slugged him. It was a reasonably nice upper right to the jaw, and he didn't pull it either. Ted must have been pretty steamed because if Alex hadn't been a vampire, I'm pretty sure he'd have a broken jaw now. As it was, Alex barely flinched.

"I said, I think you should stay a little longer." Alex smiled. This time, he showed a little fang.

I so didn't have the time or the inclination to deal with this, but I had a bad feeling that if I didn't, one or both of these men were going to end up needing medical attention. I got up and stood between them at the door. "What the hell are you doing?" I asked Alex.

"Taking his side, are you? He punched me pretty hard you know." Alex rubbed at his jaw.

"You provoked it. On purpose." I felt like a schoolteacher with two naughty boys in a schoolyard fight. I turned to Ted, who was shaking out his hand. "Do you need ice for that?"

"No. What the hell is going on here? For a second, I thought he had . . . fangs."

I took his hand. It was already swelling and starting to turn purple. "I hope you didn't break it."

"I do have fangs," Alex confirmed. "Although I cannot turn into a bat and fly away. It's the one part of the vampire myth that I really wish was true."

Ted looked down at me. "What is he talking about?"

"Ignore him," I said, releasing his hand. "Just go."

Alex put his hand on the door. "He needs to stay, Melina. You can't deal with this alone."

"Then you'll help me." I turned to face him now, Ted at my back.

Alex's face softened. "I can't help you. Neither can Paul. You need someone on the human side. These are mundanes, Melina. They're doing evil things, but they're regular men and they're subject to the laws of regular men and you need a regular man to deal with them."

"Not this one." I crossed my arms over my chest and shook my head. "He's off-limits."

"But he's so convenient. He's right here," he wheedled.

"If you need help with something, Melina, he's right. I'm right here." He put his hands on my shoulders and turned me around to face him. "I do not have even the slightest idea of what is going on here, but I know you're in trouble. Let me help you. Please."

"Help her do what?" Norah asked from the door of her bedroom.

"I don't have proof yet, but I believe she has to take down a Triad that's using Chinese vampires to take out their rivals in the local drug trade." Alex turned to Norah and gave her a big smile. "And how are you tonight, Ms. Norah?"

Norah tossed her hair. "I'm fine, Alex. How's Melina?"

"Better."

"What's he doing here?" Norah asked, her eyes narrowing to slits as she gestured at Ted.

"Apparently attempting to be chivalrous and protect his Lady Fair." Both Alex and Norah laughed.

"He doesn't know her that well, does he?" Norah came in and folded herself into a lotus position in the papasan chair. Dammit. That was my spot.

Alex took a long slow sniff of us both. "He might know her a little better than we think."

"I didn't mean biblically. There's knowing and then there's knowing." Norah nodded her head.

"You have a point." Alex sat down on the couch.

I barely followed what they were saying. The electric

buzz, my arcane warning system, had started to buzz. I slid between Ted and the door.

"What is it?" he asked.

"I don't know yet." I lowered slightly, shifting my center of balance to be ready for whatever might come through the door. "There's something out there."

"How do you know? I didn't hear anything." Ted laid his hand on my shoulder.

I didn't shake him off, but I didn't have time for long explanations either. "I'll tell you later."

I heard breathing on the other side. I inhaled, but it was hard to sense what was there with all the other smells surrounding me, and hard to differentiate the buzz I was feeling with Alex and Ted messing with my systems the way they did.

I looked through the peephole and decided the surprise route might be best. I flung open the door.

Paul stumbled through, with Meredith right after him holding a covered dish. "Melina," Paul said. "I came as soon as I heard. Are you all right?"

THIS WAS A NIGHTMARE. AN ABSOLUTE FREAKING NIGHT-mare. Ted, Alex, Paul, Meredith and Norah were sitting around in my living room, eating some kind of casserole made from brown rice with sunflower seeds sprinkled across the top and discussing my options for dealing with the *kiang shi*. Okay. In all fairness, Alex wasn't eating. He and I were the only ones. He didn't need to eat, and I was still full from the grilled cheese.

"The first thing we have to do is figure out who this Henry Zhang guy is and how connected he is," Ted was saying. "Mark my words. When we're done, we may well trace this thing all the way back to Hong Kong. And by the way, this is darn tasty." He gestured at his plate with his fork.

Norah giggled and pointed to our window onto the street. "If this was a movie, that window would shatter in a hail of gunfire right now. And he's right. I really like this. Can I have the recipe?"

"Of course." Meredith smiled. "It's sort of a variation on a dish my mother used to make all the time. I changed it up a little bit with more organic and whole grain ingredients."

"I can't believe you knew about me," I said to Norah, ignoring the fact that she seemed to be taking as much delight in the situation as she was in the spinach and rice casserole. Had they all lost their minds?

"I can't believe you didn't know that I knew. How stupid do you think I am?" She was curled up in the papasan chair now, leaving me to sit on our love seat next to Ted.

I huddled in the corner, probably looking as miserable as I felt. He took up more than his fair share of the space, physically and metaphorically. The 'Dane in the room. It was worse than the gorilla or the elephant or whatever the hell the metaphor is. "Not stupid. Naïve, maybe, but never stupid."

She shook her head. "You didn't think I was very observant either. Did you really think I wouldn't notice a Big Foot on a Girl Scout camping trip? Or that dude out on the landing the other morning? He was sort of hard to miss."

I put my head in my hands. I didn't think I could stand much more of this. It had been bizarre enough listening to Alex explain to Ted what and who I was. Honestly, I don't think I'd ever heard it explained before. At least, not in words. No one had explained it to me. I just was what I was. I hadn't heard Mae explain it to Sophie either. I'd missed that conversation.

Oh no, Sophie. I closed my eyes. Maybe they wouldn't be onto her yet. She might well be safer if I left her alone. I certainly wasn't anywhere near as slick as I thought I was.

Listening to Norah chiming in with anecdotes about brushes with goblins and fairies leaving packages on our doorstep and a bunch of other events that I thought I'd done a marvelous job of covering up was humiliating. She'd been humoring me for fifteen years while I'd thought I was protecting her. I wasn't sure whether I was more pissed off about the condescension or the waste of the energy I'd put into my efforts. It was a little like finding out you were sterile after being on birth control pills for years.

And then there was Ted, sitting there and taking up space. I could not even begin to count the ways I didn't want him involved with this. I couldn't believe I'd let it come to this. I knew better than to get emotionally involved and here I was all tangled up in blue.

It wasn't just him, though. I didn't want any one of them involved in this.

"You're the one with the resources to find out about Henry and about the grow houses," Alex was saying to Ted. "Especially now that the grow houses are busted. Half of Sacramento PD must be working on this right now. You could do some clever digging and no one would think it was out of the ordinary."

"No, no, no." I put up my hands. "It's not safe. Are you forgetting what they did to Mae? What is he supposed to do if they sic the *kiang shi* on him? I am not watching another person I care about die."

Ted's big square hand covered mine. "That's what you're there for. You and Alex and Paul, I guess. To take care of those . . . things." How the hell was he supposed to fight this fight if he couldn't even say the names?

The truth was, this wasn't his fight. I looked around the room. The fight didn't belong to any of them. Henry Zhang wasn't going after Alex or Ted or Paul, at least not yet. I'd thought that busting the grow houses would slow him down, but instead, it had just made him angry. I was the one who had poked the hornet's nest with a stick.

"It will take months for the police to trace those grow houses back to Henry," I said. "They may never be able to do it legally."

"So we don't wait for that," Paul said. "We take them down now and let the police figure it out after we leave their bodies on the doorstep."

Meredith looked up at him with big gooey eyes. Was she squeezing her thighs together? I think this whole thing turned her on.

It wasn't turning me on. Not one bit. In fact, it was making me sick to my stomach. It wasn't hard for me to imagine Paul ripped apart and bleeding, the way Mae had been.

The second any one of them threw down in this fight, Henry Zhang would turn on them in a New York minute. It would be their fight, too, then. I wasn't going to let that happen.

I stared at my feet for a few more minutes and then I got up and went back to bed.

21

"ARE YOU OKAY?" TED BRUSHED THE HAIR OFF MY FORE-
head. It was hard to believe that hands that big could be that
gentle. Maybe he was more magical than he knew.

"I'm just tired." I wasn't okay, though. I might never be
okay again. I hadn't even realized how okay I had been
before until I'd lost that okayness. Mae was gone. It kept
repeating in my brain. For a second or two, I would forget.
I'd get swept up in thinking about George and Henry Zhang
and the *kiang shi* and the grow houses and the gangs and
I'd forget. Then it would flood back into my brain like a
screaming siren. Mae was dead. I'd never sit on the mat at
River City Karate and stretch with her again. I'd never spar
with her or watch the way her eyes closed when she ate
chocolate. She was gone.

I talked to ghosts every now and then, so I knew there
was a chance, albeit a slim one, that I'd see her again, but
she wouldn't really be her. At least, not all of her. There's a
reason they call them shades. They're only shadows of who
they were in life.

"I'll be back tomorrow," he said and pulled the covers up over my shoulder.

"Ted, have Alex or Paul walk you to your car," I murmured.

He stiffened. "I don't need a babysitter."

"I didn't mean to imply that. These things, they're dangerous. You don't know what you're getting yourself into. You should run screaming in the other direction."

He sat back down on my bed. "I sort of did that already. When I saw you . . . and them . . . back at the dojo. I'm sorry, Melina. I thought I'd lost my mind. I thought I was turning into my father, except for instead of hearing voices, I was seeing things. Schizophrenia destroyed his life. He was going to be an architect. Instead, he ended up walking around San Leandro in his slippers, talking to people nobody else saw and covering our front windows with aluminum foil."

"What made you decide you weren't crazy?" I'd certainly felt crazy enough more than a few times living the life I was leading and neither of my parents were nuts.

"Wikipedia."

I lay back down on the bed. "Stop messing with me."

He grinned. "It's true. I looked up schizophrenia to see what the early onset symptoms are. I mean, I don't really remember when my dad started acting loopy. I was only a little kid. I don't think I really knew how bad it was until my mom took off. Anyway, it turns out, with schizophrenia, you only have auditory hallucinations. You don't see things, you hear them. My dad never saw anybody, he just heard the voices telling him Bill Clinton needed him to stay up all night to keep an eye on the neighbors in case they were collaborating with Monica Lewinsky."

"So the fact that you actually saw the *kiang shi* made you realize that you weren't crazy?" How was that for some whacked-out logic?

"Pretty much." He kissed my forehead. "Go to sleep.

We'll figure this out together tomorrow. We don't need to involve any of those clowns out there if you don't want to."

I kept my eyes closed as he left the room. My heart ached. Those clowns were a million times better prepared for what needed to be faced than Ted was and I still wasn't going to take them with me.

How much longer would I have to keep up this charade? Norah was checking on me every fifteen minutes, too. I needed them to believe I was asleep and safe so they would leave me the hell alone so I could get down to business.

I had to find Henry Zhang and I had to kill him. Henry was the head of the snake. If I cut off the head, the rest of the animal would wither and die. Without the grow houses supplying product and without Henry to lead them, I was certain that the Triad would pack its bags and go back to San Francisco where it belonged and leave me the hell alone.

Alone. The way I belonged.

IT WAS NEARLY DAWN WHEN ALEX LEFT. HE WAS DEFI-nitely pushing his luck. I guessed the tint on the windows of his Porsche must block UV light, otherwise he was going to be smoking by the time he got back to his apartment.

Paul and Meredith left at about the same time, although not before Meredith snuck into my room, slipped some kind of amulet under my pillow, muttered something in Latin and tiptoed back out. Norah peeked in at me one last time before she went to bed. It wasn't hard to fool her into thinking that I was deeply asleep.

I waited for five minutes after she started making the little humming noise she makes as she falls asleep. Then I got up and dressed. I pulled on a pair of yoga pants with a lot of stretch to them, a sports bra and a tank top. I threw a hoodie on over it. It wasn't exactly high style, but nothing would restrict my movements. I unlocked the bottom drawer of my desk. I don't own a lot of weapons. Mainly, I am a weapon. I pretty much can kill someone with my pinky finger. Generally, I choose not to brag about that. Letting others know would only draw out people who want to prove me wrong. It is, however, still true. Still, these weren't what passed even for my idea of normal times, and I definitely needed something beyond normal measures.

I don't own any guns. I do, however, have a fair number of knives. The thick-handled hunting knife wasn't what I needed. It was too big and only sharp on one side. Instead, I selected a thin-bladed dagger that I strapped to my ankle. I braided my hair low on my head and walked out the door.

My first stop was to the Bok Kai Temple. Dawn had broken. It was light enough that the *kiang shi* had to be back in their graves. At least I didn't have to worry about them. I took the back alleyway into the temple, though. I didn't want to chance Henry having posted guards to watch his brother.

George wasn't in the temple. He was nearby. I was sure of that. I could smell his fear and anxiety throughout the sanctuary, but he wasn't in the temple proper. I slipped down the stairway, the sanctuary looking strangely innocent in the dawn light. I couldn't help myself, I walked over to the *kiang shi*'s graves.

The smell of rotting flesh was strong, even stronger than the scent of the river. Had they decomposed more? I peeked over the edge of one of the graves at one of the *kiang shi*. He didn't appear to be any more rotten than before, but I'd never really had a good close-up look at any of them. I'd been either wanting not to look or fighting them off.

Whoever he had been in his former life, he was disgusting now. Death did not become him. I suppose it doesn't really become anyone, but some certainly handle it more graciously than others. He lay there, like his five brethren, arms crossed over his chest. No talismans hung from any of their foreheads.

I remembered now. They rose without the talismans and

the priests had to put them on. They had to do it damn fast, too. They must need to be faster and faster as time went on, too.

I shook my head and went in search of George Zhang.

I found him asleep on a cot in the small apartment attached to the temple. It wasn't much. In fact, it made Norah's and my place look downright opulent. The floor was bare. Nothing hung on the walls. The only furniture besides George's cot was a scarred wooden table with two straight-backed wooden chairs.

I shook him awake. Shockingly, he was no happier to see me this morning than he'd been on any other of my visits.

"No," he said, rubbing his face as he struggled to a sitting position. "No. Not you. Not again."

"I'm putting a stop to this, George, and I'm doing it today. I need your help."

He shook his head. "No. I won't do it. I won't put any more of the people I love at risk. The only way to do that is to cooperate with my brother. I'll do what he says. Eventually, he'll have what he wants and he will leave us alone."

"Well, that's the problem, George. I won't let any more of the people I love be at risk either. That means not cooperating with your brother. In fact, it means taking your brother down."

"It's not possible."

I shrugged. "Then I'll die trying." It wasn't my preferred solution for the situation, but it would resolve it. I was pretty sure that with me out of the way, Henry Zhang would leave my family and friends alone. "Where is he?"

"Leave it alone. Maybe if you stop interfering, he'll leave you alone."

"Not a chance I'm willing to take, George. Cough it up. Where's big brother bunking?"

He pressed his lips together in a tight line and said nothing.

I sat back on my haunches, unsure of what to do next. I

could pull my knife and threaten to torture him, but I'd seen what motivated George Zhang. If his brother had threatened to harm him, he would never have put the *kiang shi* in motion to attack the gangbangers. It was watching his brother's henchmen beat up one of his brother priests that had broken him.

"Come on, George. I want you to meet somebody."

HOSPITALS ARE NEVER ACTUALLY QUIET. THEIR PACE MAY slow at certain times, but it never stops. There is, however, a little something called shift change. If you want to slip into a hospital room unnoticed, try to do it at seven in the morning, three in the afternoon or eleven at night. That's when the nurses and doctors from the shift before are giving the nurses and doctors from the next shift the straight lowdown.

I ushered George down the hall of the pediatrics ward, past the empty nurses' station and into Maricela's room.

In addition to the IV tube, she had a feeding tube running into her stomach. She was sprawled on her back. Little mittens were on both her hands, and her wrists were secured to the sides of the crib.

"Why is she tied down like that? She's just a baby," George whispered.

"That's the problem. She's only a baby. She doesn't understand what's going on. They have to restrain her so she doesn't pull out her IV or her feeding tube," I explained.

George took a tentative step into the room. "What happened to her?"

"Shrapnel," I said. "When the Black Dragons started shooting at the Norteños, there was what they call collateral damage. Maricela is collateral damage."

"Why is she all alone?"

"Well, George, her mom has to work. If she doesn't show up for her shift at the Styrofoam factory, she'll lose her job.

If she loses her job, Maricela has no home to go home to and no food to eat when she doesn't get there. My doctor friends tell me she'll be fine, but she almost died. She's still not entirely out of the woods."

George turned away and leaned against the wall outside Maricela's room. "This is wrong."

"True that," I said. "She won't be the last either, George. You know your brother doesn't care who gets hurt as he barrels along to whatever goal he's set for himself. The Maricelas of the world mean nothing to him. He has to be stopped. Tell me where he is."

George bowed his head. "He and his men are staying at the Omni on Capitol Plaza now that the grow houses are busted."

I SHOULD HAVE LET GEORGE SLEEP. IF I'D DONE A GRID search of the area around the temple, I would have found the Navigators parked in a neat little row in the hotel parking lot. It was barely two blocks away. Conveniently located for creating mayhem. Continental breakfast included.

Daylight had started to burn. I wondered how long I had before Henry went after someone else I cared about. Was it enough that he'd killed Mae? Would he go after my family next?

This had to end now, and the way to end it was clear: either Henry Zhang had to die, or I did.

I am not a killer. Or, I suppose I should say, up until that point, I'd never been a killer. I'd never taken a life, human or otherwise. I have no doubt that I'd occasionally delivered something that might have contributed to someone's end, but I'd never ended anyone's life myself.

I fingered the knife at my ankle and shoved down the fear that rose up in my throat like bile. There was, after all, a first time for everything.

The Omni on Capitol Plaza is huge. It's thirty-five stories

and has close to five hundred rooms. Even with a nose like mine, it was going to be impossible to sniff out exactly where Henry Zhang and his friends were staying. I figured, however, that they would come out eventually. Unlike their friends the *kiang shi*, they weren't nocturnal and would probably want to eat something besides hotel food at some point. Nor did they look like the kind of guys who were going to walk. What seemed to make the best sense was to watch the cars. I wouldn't even have to follow the cars when they left, which was a good thing. If these men knew who I was, and obviously they did, they also knew what I drove. I love Grandma Rosie's Buick to death, but inconspicuous it is not.

No. All I needed to do was watch for when they came back and then follow them into the hotel. I circled the block until a space opened up on the street. Finally, I had a stroke of luck. I'd be behind enough shrubs that they wouldn't see me, but I had enough of a slice of view of the SUVs that I'd be able to see when they moved. I'd have to reposition at that point anyway.

For now, I hunkered down in the front seat of the Buick and settled in to wait.

HENRY ZHANG MIGHT NOT HAVE BEEN NOCTURNAL, BUT he wasn't exactly diurnal either. It was getting close to noon when he and his band of merry men finally came out of the hotel, looking freshly showered and shined. They loaded into one of the Navigators and took off.

It was about time. I had a cramp in my leg, I had to pee wicked bad and my butt felt bruised from sitting too long. Now that I was sure they were gone, it was time to scope out the lobby for a place to position myself to watch for the return of my prey.

That was the way I had to think of them. They were prey. I was the hunter. It was as impersonal as that.

I brushed my hair back into its braid, put on my jacket

and grabbed my duffel bag from the backseat of the Buick.
I kept an eye out for anything unusual as I marched into the
lobby of the hotel. I didn't think Henry had left a guard, but
it was better to be safe than sorry.

I'd seen nothing out of the ordinary by the time I made
it to the registration desk. It only took a few minutes to rent
a room. It wasn't like I was actually going to stay in it, but
once you're a guest, you're free to loiter in the lobby so long
as you don't make a scene.

A scene was the last thing I needed to create. Once I was
checked in, I bought a newspaper and sat down in one of
the chairs behind a potted fern. I wouldn't be visible by
anyone walking in the front entrance and going straight to
the elevators. It was possible that Henry would go in a side
entrance, but he seemed like a front-door man to me.

I settled in to wait some more.

HENRY APPARENTLY WASN'T ONE TO DAWDLE OVER HIS
lunch. He and his men came walking in at around two
o'clock. I stayed very still in my chair behind the fern as
they marched through the lobby. His men definitely had his
back. They were watching. If I'd moved, they probably
would have spotted me right away. It wasn't easy sitting
there, watching my target wait for the elevator, head tilted
back and throat vulnerable and exposed, but now was not
the time.

Henry and I would need some privacy for what I had
planned.

I moved quickly as soon as the elevator doors closed. I
needed to see what floor they were on. With that narrowed
down, I should be able to sniff out their rooms.

I watched as the numbers over the door lit up, one by one.
They stopped at twenty-three. Bingo.

Now I had to figure out how to get to Henry when he was
alone.

Hotels are not entirely unlike hospitals. They're big. They're impersonal. They both profess to care about your comfort when they're really all about making money. For my purposes at that moment, the most important thing was that they both have shift changes.

Oh, sure, the office staff might work nine to five, but the cleaning and maintenance crews were on 24/7, 365 days a year, and that has to be done in shifts. At three o'clock, the daytime maid shift was leaving and the evening shift was reporting for duty. Just like in the hospital, it was the perfect time to slip in unnoticed. They didn't exactly have a meeting where they sat down and exchanged information about different rooms and guests, the way they do at the hospital, but they did have a nice gossip in the changing room.

It hadn't been too hard to figure out where the changing room was. I'd done a little reconnaissance of the basement after I'd figured out which floor Henry and his buddies were chilling on. It also wasn't all that hard to find a uniform still in its dry cleaning bag, hung on a rack. This made me very happy because my plan hinged on me looking like a maid and I really didn't want to club one of them on the head to steal her clothes. Their lives were hard enough without getting involved with my *meshugass*. I figured I'd leave the uniform in some easy-to-find location with a twenty tucked into the pocket to make up for whatever inconvenience I was causing by stealing it. Call me hypersensitive, but I hate to be inconvenienced, and my mother's upbringing with her emphasis on the Golden Rule does come through at the oddest moments.

By three thirty, I was armed with a linen cart and a uniform. There's a reason that people are always waltzing into places unnoticed in TV shows and movies by wearing a uniform and carrying a clipboard. It works. Still, for my purposes, it wasn't going to be enough to sneak into Henry's room. For what I needed to do, he was going to have to be alone.

I took my laundry cart up to twenty-three. Now that I knew what floor Henry was staying on, the job of determining which room he was in would be easier, though not necessarily a slam dunk. My nose is good, really good. But still, it wasn't like I'd ever been really close to him, and most of the time that I'd been around Henry, the *kiang shi* had dominated my senses.

I pushed the cart slowly along, wondering whether I'd be able to sniff him out. About halfway down the hallway, I had my answer. I smelled it. That strange combination of river and rot that I smelled whenever the *kiang shi* were near. I slowed my steps. It was definitely strongest right outside room 2318, and there was a whiff of it outside 2320. I did another pass to make sure. Yep. The smell was definitely coming from 2318. It must be some kind of olfactory version of the theory of transference. If a person can't come or go from a place without taking some of it with them and leaving something behind, apparently they can't spend a lot of time with brutally murdered undead Chinese miners without picking up a bit of their perfume.

I made my way farther down the hall to the alcove with the ice and vending machines where I could duck out of view for a while. I wasn't sure how long I'd have before someone came looking for the linen cart I'd made off with. Plus, I needed to get this over with before I lost what little courage I had.

I pulled out my cell phone and dialed the hotel's phone number and punched in 2-3-1-8 when prompted by the electronic voice that answered the phone.

I heard the phone ring down the hall in Henry's room.

"Hello?" the voice said over my cell phone.

"Hi, this is the front desk. We have a package for a Mr. Henry Zhang in Room 2318."

"Hold on for a moment," the voice said. Then as if a hand had been placed over the receiver, I heard a muffled exchange. "Are we expecting a package?"

"Here?"

"They say there's a package for Mr. Zhang at the front desk."

"Who even knows we're here?"

"I don't know. That's why I'm asking. Should I have them send it up?"

"No. Take Wen and go down and check it out."

The voice came back to me. "We'll be right down to pick it up."

"Thank you, sir," I said and hung up. I scooted my linen cart quickly out into the hallway and then returned to a more plodding pace with my head down. Two of Henry's men came out of the door and headed for the elevators. Damn. That meant there were still two more inside.

At least I'd improved my odds. I pushed my cart to room 2318 and knocked on the door. "Housekeeping."

One of Henry's men opened the door. It was the bald guy with the thick neck. I kept my head tilted down, but it wasn't necessary. He didn't even look at my face. He took in the uniform and the cart and that was all. And to think, I'd planted my heel in this guy's solar plexus only two days before. You think you've made a connection with someone, then bam, you realize you were nothing but a nasty side kick to them. "You already made the beds."

"We wanted to bring more towels." I picked up a stack from the cart and marched past him. I mean, who doesn't need more towels when they're staying at a hotel? There's never enough for your hair. Of course, I generally prefer my towels without a dagger tucked inside the stack, but today was different.

Today I was a killer and I liked my dagger just fine.

Sure enough, he stood aside.

As I suspected, Henry and his men had two adjoined rooms. Henry was in the next one. I went into the bathroom and began straightening the toiletries next to the sink. I heard Henry answer his cell phone. "Tell them that they're the ones who called us about the package." He lowered the phone. "Jimmy, what was the name of the person who called from the front desk about the package?"

Jimmy, or at least the guy I presumed to be Jimmy, said, "They didn't say a name. They just said the front desk."

Henry lifted the cell phone back to his ear. "Give them five more minutes and then come back up."

I didn't have much time. I slid the dagger up the sleeve of my maid's uniform and left the stack of towels in the bathroom.

I moved into the main area of the hotel room. Baldy and Jimmy were both in this room with Henry propped on pillows in the next. I picked up the phone and pretended to wipe down the desk beneath it. Instead, I unplugged it. I turned around still holding the phone. Neither man was watching me.

I wrapped the cord around the neck of one and smashed the phone into the head of the other. They went down in a heap. "I think it's for you," I said brightly.

I leaped the bodies, barrel-rolled through the open adjoining door and was in Henry's room with the connecting door slammed behind me before Henry even registered that anything had happened. He was just looking up from his newspaper when I leaped onto the bed, pinned him by his throat to the bed with my left forearm and pressed the dagger against his throat with my right hand.

I watched a series of emotions pass across Henry's face. I saw surprise, confusion and then recognition. I didn't see fear. Why the hell not? He should have been afraid. Hell, I was afraid and I was the one with the knife.

"Hello, Ms. Markowitz." Henry smiled at me. "Are you surprised that I know your name?"

"No, Henry, I'm not surprised. Are you surprised that I know yours?" He flinched a bit when I said his name. Score one for Melina.

"You are a very clever young lady. Nothing you do would

surprise me anymore." He settled his head back against the pillow.

I made sure my knife followed his movements. "Maybe this will. I'm going to stop your Triad from moving into my town. I'm going to cut off the head of the snake, Henry, and that would be you."

He laughed, which actually impressed me. Not many people would be able to muster up a chuckle with a sharp knife at their throat. I knew what it meant to be able to do that. It meant that death meant nothing to you. Henry was as cold-blooded as they come. "Oh, you poor mistaken little girl, a Triad is not like a snake. You can't cut off the head and kill it. We would have been hunted out of existence long ago if that were the case. A Triad is like a hydra. Cut off the head, and two will grow back in its place."

I pulled back for a second, reassessing. Was it possible? Would I end up killing Henry and not have anything to show for it but a stain on my soul that would never wash off?

"Sacramento is ripe for picking. I can't believe it's taken us so long. I suppose no one wants to leave San Francisco for a backwater like this. Still, better to be king in a backwater than someone else's knight in a paradise. I may be the first one to try it, but I won't be the last." Henry tilted his head, again moving his neck a little bit away from my knife.

Again I followed his movement. That argument wasn't going to hold water at the moment. At least, not for me. "The Triads can do whatever they want. It's when you started bringing the *kiang shi* into it that I had to get involved."

Henry shook his head ever so slightly. Anymore of a shake and he would have sliced his own throat.

"That was not it, Melina. You were ready to leave that alone. It was the baby, wasn't it?"

He knew about Maricela? My shock must have shown on my face.

"You and my brother are too softhearted. You put too much value on other people's lives, especially the lives of those you deem to be innocent. Innocence is overrated if it exists at all."

"What sin can Maricela have possibly committed? She's six months old."

"And she is a greedy, self-centered being. All children are until we teach them to pretend to be otherwise. What is she going to become anyway? Look at her mother. A stupid whore. What precisely do you think she'll teach her? How to give a twenty-five-dollar blow job?"

I leaned forward and the knife cut a little bit into Henry's skin. His eyes went wide for a fraction of a second, not long, but long enough for me to see it. He wasn't as cool as he made out to be. "Let's leave the baby out of this. I'm past caring about much because of you. All I really care about is making sure you can't hurt any more of the people I love, and I figure there's only one way to do that. That's to kill the one person you love, Henry. I figure that would be you."

"A very pretty speech, Ms. Markowitz. I know I should feel terrible about my selfishness, but that selfishness is what has made me into the successful businessman I am today. So successful that there are men who are willing to die for me."

That's when I heard the door to the adjoining room click open. I had made the classic mistake. I had not acted decisively. I'd let Mae down once again. I hadn't been able to chart my course and stick with it. I had wavered. I had let Henry talk me into waiting, into hesitating, and now, truly, all might be lost.

Once you've died once, you become a little more used to the idea. Death always wins in the end. There's a certain amount of relief in knowing that. If you lose, it's because the inevitable has finally happened. It's not your fault. It's bound to happen sooner or later. I leaped off the bed, spun and slammed the heel of my foot into one of Henry's men's larynx, and figured that if my day was today, so be it.

While I was still in the air, the one next to him lowered

his shoulder and took me out with a tackle that crashed me
into the table and chairs. I rolled and bunched up my legs,
ready to send him reeling back with a kick to the chest. I
never got the chance. The third man dropped an ax kick on
my solar plexus and then hit two pressure points at the base
of my skull.

Everything went black.

22

WHEN I CAME TO, I WAS TIED TO A CHAIR. THE CHAIR WAS set in the middle of the floor.

Henry sat behind his table and gestured with his hand. One of the men brought him a cup of tea. "Forgive my lack of hospitality. I'd offer you tea, but I know you can't drink it with your hands bound behind your back that way."

Plus, if they gave me a cup of anything, I'd throw it in their faces. I was in that kind of mood. Being smacked on the back of the head and tied up does that to me. I was, however, working at the knots I could reach as fast as I could without letting them know what I was doing. Somebody here was either a Boy Scout or a sailor. Either way, they knew their knots. "I'll take a rain check," I said.

He smiled again and shook his head. "So clever. Always so clever. How is it, Ms. Markowitz, that you came to be so clever?"

I shrugged as well as I could. "A happy nexus of genetics and opportunity, I guess."

"Ah, opportunity. I'm glad you brought that up. That is

precisely what I wanted to talk to you about." He set down his cup of tea and folded his hands in front of him.

His movements were so measured and controlled. It made what he said even more menacing, and I already felt pretty darn menaced what with the being bound to the chair and all the guys with guns under their jackets. It was the strange lack of emotion that made him so scary. Henry Zhang didn't feel any of this. I twisted my hands harder and was rewarded only with a trickle of blood dripping down my hand. "What kind of opportunity?"

"A business opportunity. We don't have to be adversaries, Ms. Markowitz. We've simply gotten off on the wrong foot. We could join forces."

I shook my head. I took my cue from Nancy Reagan— which would have killed my lifelong Democratic mother— and just said no. "I don't think that would be possible, Henry. Kind of you to offer, though."

"Who says it wouldn't be possible?" He leaned forward over the table. "Who controls you? Tell me. You would be surprised at the many ways I have of taking care of little problems like that."

I shook my head again. "You misunderstand me. No one is controlling me."

He leaned back in his chair and shook his head. "It's hard to try and make some kind of accommodation with each other if you won't be honest with me. You can't have done this on your own."

"And why is that?" That plain annoyed me. So I hadn't figured out everything on my own. I'd had Alex and Paul and Norah and Mae and Ted, not to mention Aunt Kitty, all contributing pieces of the puzzle, but I would have figured it out on my own eventually. Probably. At some point. Maybe.

Henry waved my question aside. "It doesn't matter. What matters is whether or not you're willing to come and work for me."

"Not only no, but hell no," I said.

"Don't be so hasty. Think of the benefits. This is a very lucrative business. You wouldn't have to share a rundown apartment. You could buy a house. Forget the filing job at the hospital. It wouldn't be necessary. You could be free to pursue other interests." He stood and walked around his desk, stopping directly in front of me to lean against it.

It did sound nice. "And what exactly would I have to do to get all this money and free time?"

He smiled his crocodile smile again. "Besides stay out of my way?"

I nodded.

"The occasional errand." He shrugged. "Think about it, Melina. Money. Comfort. Join us."

I thought for about a nanosecond, and then I spit at him. It landed on his cheek. He stared at me and then very slowly and deliberately removed a handkerchief and wiped his face. Without ever taking his gaze from my face, he stood. "Take her out to the rail yard and kill her," he said and walked out of the room.

IT HAD GOTTEN DARK OUTSIDE. I WAS SURPRISED. IT WAS easily close to ten o'clock. My how time flies when you're tied up in a hotel closet.

There had been a fair amount of discussion on how to get me out of the hotel unseen. In the end, I had been hoisted by my own petard. Damn Shakespeare anyway. His phrasing is often too apt.

Henry's men had jammed me into the linen cart that I'd used to worm my way into the room and had hauled me out via the service elevator at the end of the hall. It was a hop, skip and a jump to the loading dock and into one of their stupid Navigators from there.

The rail yards in Sacramento are infamous. It's a pretty decent section of real estate in a prime location. It took an eon or two for the appropriate authorities to write environmental impact reports and then development stalled. Truly, they have no idea what's in there. They think there might be a Chinese cemetery or two from the height of the railroad-building boom on the edge of the China Slough, a wetlands area that was filled in a long time ago. They also think there might be a buried locomotive or two. Apparently, back in the day, when the railroad officials didn't know what to do with something that didn't work anymore, they'd just drive it out into the slough and let it sink.

Don't even get me started on the toxic chemicals.

There's actually a bike path that runs around it and along the river on the way to Discovery Park. In the daytime, there are joggers and bikers and young mothers pushing strollers.

The sun wasn't shining now, though. There was nothing but shadow as Baldy, Jimmy, Ponytail and the guy I took to be Wen shoved me along. I wondered how you picked where to execute a person. Is there some kind of etiquette? Worse yet, is there some sort of final humiliation? I'd never been to an execution before. Just my luck that my first one would be my own.

They marched me across the overgrown and desolate field. I could make out the old shop buildings on my right. I knew Old Sacramento was behind me. I felt that familiar buzz and wondered what else might be out here in the rail yard. Maybe it was the accumulation of many dead bodies, their spirits possibly hovering nearby. I'd never had that happen before, but there's a first time for everything, isn't there?

Of course, it didn't look as though I was going to be having too many more first times. I tried to look for someplace I could run to hide or something I could use as a weapon, but there was nothing.

We walked out into the unmown grass. It was already up to my waist. By midsummer, it would turn brown and die and be a fire hazard. Now it was green and fresh and still growing.

Baldy shoved me forward. I tripped and landed on my knees. "Any last words, Ms. Markowitz?" he asked.

I heard him click the safety off the gun. He was breathing faster now. Was he frightened? Or did the idea of putting a bullet in the back of my skull excite him?

Kneeling on the ground, the hum of the presence of something supernatural got stronger. It was probably something in the ground.

He inhaled deeply. This was going to be it. He was steadying himself, making sure his kill shot was sure and smooth. He'd let his breath out and before he inhaled again, he'd pull the trigger. I bowed my head and tried not to be afraid, but it was impossible. This was it.

Something huge and hairy came streaking at us from the right. Baldy pulled back as it hit him from the side, taking him down in one powerful lunge. The monster stood over him and snarled. A werewolf. The buzz I'd been getting hadn't been from dead bodies or old deities. It had been from an approaching werewolf. I really needed a better system, like when you get a certain ringtone on your cell phone when a particular person calls.

Baldy pumped three shots into the werewolf's chest. The werewolf recoiled, pushed back by the percussion of the bullets, and Baldy started to scramble away. Within seconds, however, the werewolf was back over him snarling. Unless the bullets were silver, they were only going to make him madder. He turned his face toward me and growled. Baldy might be down and no longer able to put a bullet in the back of my skull, but I was still kneeling here on the ground almost eye to eye with an angry werewolf.

I dropped my own gaze to the ground and tried to still the frantic beating of my heart. My fear would only drive him further into his bloodlust.

The other three men turned and ran.

Another streak came from the right. This one was shaped like a man. It took Jimmy down and pinned him within seconds. The other two kept running.

Vampire. Nothing else could move that fast. I heard Jimmy scream as the vampire started to feed. I couldn't bear to look. Next to me, the werewolf lifted Baldy and shook him, the way a dog might shake a squirrel or a rabbit. I heard Baldy's neck snap, and the werewolf dropped him to the ground.

The vampire was still feeding on Jimmy. He was going to drain him. That much was clear to me. Was I going to be next? And for which one? Would I be Purina Werewolf Chow? Or Vampire V-8? Or some very unpleasant buffet for the two of them?

I could feel the werewolf's hot breath on my neck. He was right behind me. He began to circle me, coming around to face me. Then he licked my face. I lifted my face and looked right into his eyes. "Paul?"

He licked me again. I should have known.

"Jesus, you guys are fast." Ted came trotting up wearing a backpack. "I can do a six-minute mile and I didn't have a prayer of keeping up."

He shouldered Paul out of the way and sank down in front of me. "You're alive." He pulled me to his chest and held me against him. It would have been nice if the rocks hadn't been digging into my knees and I wasn't still getting over being scared out of my ever-loving mind.

Alex came up wiping his face with a handkerchief. "Ready to hunt, Fido?"

Paul growled and snapped at him.

"Temper, temper," Alex snarled back, his fangs showing now. He turned to Ted and me and said, "We'll be back. Wait here."

They were gone in a flash of fur and flesh.

"What the hell were you thinking?" Ted's hands worked at the knots around my wrists. The ropes chafed, but I didn't make a sound. I was as steamed as he was. Where did he get off with all that righteous indignation?

"I was thinking that I would take care of this myself and no one else would get hurt." My hands came free. I swung them in front of me and hugged myself.

"Except you, of course." He came back in front of me. Swearing under his breath, he started to rub the blood flow back into my hands. He sat back on his heels and glared at me. "You were going to get yourself killed."

"I assure you, that was not my original intention." I winced as the pins-and-needles sensation flooded my wrists and hands.

He rolled his eyes. "Gee, that's a relief. So it wasn't a suicide mission. You've gladdened my heart."

"Speaking of suicide missions, do you have any idea of what you've gotten yourself into? Any idea at all?" I knew what he'd gotten himself into. He was a human—a 'Dane—showing up to rescue a Messenger in the company of a couple of 'Canes, neither of whom were supposed to be on rescue missions themselves.

He rubbed his hand across the back of his neck. "I doubt it. I'm still not sure I shouldn't drive to the closest mental hospital and ask for their first vacant padded room. It's hard to deny what I'm seeing with my own eyes, but given my family history, it wouldn't be too far of a shot to figure I'd gone bat-shit crazy. Is this real, by the way?"

I slugged him in the shoulder. Not as hard as I could, but I didn't totally pull it either.

"Ow!" He jumped up and away from me.

"You feel that?" I smiled up at him with absolutely no sincerity whatsoever.

"Yeah."

"Then it's real." I reached up my hand, and true to form, he took it and helped me to my feet even though I'd just bruised his bicep in a big way. I know how to throw a punch.

Paul sauntered out of the darkness, back in human form

and naked as the day he was born. There were three spots of blood marking where he'd been shot, but they were already healing. "Are you two done with the foreplay now? I'd like to get out of here." He held out his hand, and Ted handed him the backpack he'd been carrying. Paul rummaged through it and pulled out a pair of jeans.

Ted politely averted his eyes, but I glared at Paul. I got a snort in response. "I never figured you for a girl who liked it rough, Melina, but I swear I learn something new every day." He smiled, still looking a little too wolfish for me to be completely comfortable. I dropped my eyes.

"Who likes it rough?" Alex asked, walking up behind Paul, smoothing his hair back. Paul bristled but didn't growl. Crazy. I knew the smell of a vampire would be anathema to him, yet here the two of them were. It looked as though we were witnessing the beginning of a beautiful friendship.

"Melina. She and Boy Wonder here were slugging it out a second ago." Paul finished buttoning up his jeans and yanked on a T-shirt he'd taken from the backpack.

Alex smiled. His fangs were receding, but they were still there. "Really? How interesting. Actually, I could buy the rough stuff from Melina. Him? Not so much. Does he smell like food to you? He smells like food to me."

"Everybody smells like food to you." Paul did growl now.

Alex smiled, only a little bit of fang still visible in the moonlight. "True enough." Then the two of them bumped fists.

I'd had enough of the boy bonding. "Did you get them all? Are they all . . . gone?"

"One got away." Alex rolled the sleeves of his dress shirt back down.

Fabulous. I still had people trying to kill me on the loose. "Damn."

"It was on purpose," Paul told me. "We wanted one of them to get away to get the message back to his masters."

"Do you think that's going to be enough to get them to go away?" I brushed the dirt and gravel off my knees.

Paul and Alex exchanged glances. "I doubt it," Alex finally said. "These guys are tough. But it will make them think twice about going after you or your family. They don't know we're working on our own. My guess is, they didn't know we really existed until a few minutes ago." He shook his head. "You'd think they'd be able to extrapolate that if Chinese vampires really exist, then Western ones do, too."

Paul shrugged. "People simply aren't logical."

A wave of fatigue washed over me. The earth shifted beneath my feet. Ted slid an arm around my waist, his body warm and solid next to mine. "Let's get Melina home. We can talk strategy once we get her some food and make sure she's okay."

23

"YOU GOT HER!" NORAH LAUNCHED HERSELF AT ME FROM the doorway. She threw her arms around me and held on as though she might drown if she let go. "Don't ever do that again. We were so scared."

Sophie and Ben crowded the doorway behind her. "Is she okay?" Sophie asked.

"She's fine, but she needs to get inside and sit down. She's exhausted, and I can hear her stomach growling from over here." Ted gently detached Norah from me and shifted Sophie and Ben so we could get through.

I glanced toward my bedroom. I supposed my chances of going straight to bed were somewhere between slim and none. I sat down on the love seat in the living room, strangely content to have Ted fill up the other three-quarters of it. Alex headed directly into the kitchen. I smelled butter melting in the pan about twenty seconds later.

"Where did you go?" Norah sat down on the coffee table in front of me.

"I went to kill Henry Zhang." It had been my plan in a nutshell. I didn't feel like elaborating at the moment.

"By yourself?"

"How?"

"Where is he?"

"Why?"

Everyone was talking at once. I tucked my head into Ted's shoulder and waited for the noise to die down. All the fight had gone out of me. My big plan had failed. I had failed. I didn't have the nerve to do what needed to be done. I'd failed Mae again. Maybe I'd forget how to do a roundhouse kick next.

Alex set the grilled cheese sandwich cut in half diagonally in front of me next to a bowl of tomato soup. "Unless you go shopping, I'm not going to be able to make anything else in that piss-poor excuse of a kitchen in there. What's with all the tofu anyway?"

Norah narrowed her eyes at him, but he just smiled back. She turned back to me. "Explain why you went there alone, Melina."

"I'd endangered everyone around me enough. I thought if I took out Zhang, I'd be protecting all of you. I figured it was my problem, so I went to solve it." I took a big bite of grilled cheese. No one could expect me to say anything else while I was chewing.

Norah got up from the coffee table and flung herself in the papasan chair. "She's an idiot, isn't she?"

"But kind of a sweet one," Paul said.

I chewed.

"You know we were all frantic, don't you?" Norah asked. She pointed at Ted. "I thought that one was going to pop a blood vessel. The other two weren't much better." Then she looked at Alex. "Do you have blood vessels to pop?"

I stopped before I took another bite. "How did you find me anyway?"

"You're not as clever as you think. And no, I can't pop a

blood vessel." Alex examined his fingernails and then buffed them against his shirt. "Boy Wonder here is the one who figured out you were gone and started the ball rolling."

Ted didn't move. I wasn't sure whether it was because he didn't like his new nickname or something else, but there was a nearly imperceptible stiffening. "I stopped by to check on you and you were gone. No note. No nothing." He didn't sound happy.

"What was I supposed to write? 'Gone to kill a Triad boss. C U L8R'?" I spooned up some tomato soup and shifted away from him.

"No. You were supposed to let me help. You weren't supposed to run off by yourself and almost get killed." He was definitely still angry.

"I'm the one who got us into this whole mess. I figured I'd better be the one to get us out of it."

"Children," Alex said. "You can bicker later in private." He turned to me. "He put some kind of alert out for your car. Once someone spotted it by the Omni, it was relatively easy to figure out where you were. The tricky part was getting to you."

"He sounds all cool and collected now, but you should have heard him howling about not being able to go with us on the reconnaissance mission because it was still daylight." Paul chuckled.

"You weren't all that calm and collected yourself, Fido," Alex shot back.

"Stop calling me Fido!" Paul half rose from his chair.

"Everyone be quiet," Sophie screamed.

Surprisingly, the room fell silent, and everyone turned to look at her. "Stop fighting with each other. That isn't what needs to happen here. We need to work together. We need to come up with a plan to defeat these things."

Out of the mouths of babes.

"So does anybody know how we kill these *kiang shi* things?" Ted asked.

"You have to decapitate them and burn them," Ben said.

I turned and looked at him. He shrugged. "I can use the Internet, too, you know. I also understand about the rice and holding your breath when you fight them. The hacking-to-pieces bit seems a little mean, though."

"What would you have us do, then?" Alex asked from where he lounged against the breakfast bar. "Let them continue to maraud through our city snacking on our less fortunate brethren?"

"No. But it's really not their fault. They're under someone else's control. They're not the ones that are the problem." Ben looked as if he was going to start to sulk.

"I tried going after the Triad. It didn't work out so hot," I said.

"Only because you failed." Alex drummed his fingers on the counter.

"Hey!"

"Don't get your undies in a bunch. I'm just stating a fact. The boy has a point. We need to take out the Triad more than we need to exterminate the *kiang shi*."

"They have a tendency to dish out some pretty nasty forms of revenge on the people who try to mess with them." I shuddered. What would the repercussions of what I'd done be? Who else had I put in danger?

"Then we have to make sure that no one realizes that we're the ones that mess with them." Ted looped his arm around me.

"Who do you suggest we use as our fall guy then? Who do you really want to sic the Triad on?"

"It's too bad we can't make talismans that would make them attack the Triad instead of us," Ted said.

"What did you say?" An idea was starting to form in my head.

"I said it's too bad that we can't make talismans . . ." He started to repeat himself. Was there anything he wouldn't do for me?

I shushed him. "I heard what you said. Hold on a second."
Why couldn't we make fake talismans that wouldn't work?
Would anyone be able to tell? I'd carted the fake Kokopelli
flute around for a day and never suspected that it wasn't real.
Even Kokopelli had handled it for a while before he'd realized that it wasn't his sacred object. Would the Triad be able
to tell if the talismans were switched out? Would the priests?

I leaned forward on the couch, staring at Alex as my idea
began to firm up like a good Jell-O mold. "When you play
with fire, sometimes you get burned."

He smiled as he began to understand what I was talking
about. "Hoisted by their own petard? Live by the sword, die
by the sword?"

"Talking in clichés and platitudes until the rest of the
group smacks your heads together just for the pleasure of
hearing them crack?" Ted asked.

I turned to face him. "We get the *kiang shi* to kill the Triad."

Paul's eyes went wide as the simplicity and beauty of the
plan dawned on him as well. "Nice."

"But if there are fake talismans, the *kiang shi* will be
mindless killing machines. How do we get them to stop
before they kill us, too?" Ted asked.

"I'm pretty sure I can take care of that," Alex said. Alex
doesn't need to breathe. Vampires don't. Oxygen isn't important to them anymore. On the other hand, he does need to
make a show of breathing. It's surprising how many people
will notice when someone around them isn't breathing. He's
had to train himself to do it as naturally as he can.

Okeydokey. There was step one.

We settled down to the business of making a plan.

WE DECIDED WE WOULD PUT OUR PLAN INTO MOTION THE
following night. We figured that Henry and his gang were
still regrouping from what had happened, much as we were.

They wouldn't do anything during the day. One of the lovely things about using the *kiang shi* for us and for them was it allowed a certain degree of deniability. I didn't think they'd give that up in favor of a daytime strike against me or against the people I cared about.

Just to be on the safe side, Ted did a drive-by of my parents' house and the retirement center. Everything seemed fine. Still, it was nearly dawn when he slipped into bed with me.

Gravity alone made me roll toward him.

"Hey," he whispered into my hair.

"Hey, yourself." I wrapped myself closer around him, grateful for his warmth and the solid bulk of him next to me.

"Everything's quiet out there."

"Good."

"Are you okay?"

"Not really. How about you?"

He hesitated. "Not exactly. It feels weirdly right, though."

"You mean this?" I bumped up against him.

He kissed me, hard. "No. I mean, that feels right but not weird. I meant this other stuff. The stuff with Alex and Paul and . . . you. It feels like I've known it all along on some kind of gut level."

I laid my cheek against his chest and listened to his heartbeat. There was something different about this guy, but it wasn't supernatural. "Really?"

"Yeah. Really. You know, it's probably from growing up with a father who thinks he's about to go and address the United Nations while wearing an aluminum foil hat, but I never really felt like anybody had my back. These guys, well, when we were out searching for you, we were a team. We each had something we could do and we all counted on each other to do it." He turned onto his side and scooched down so we were nose to nose. "And as for this? Well, it feels like I've been waiting for this my whole life."

I SLEPT FOR MOST OF THE DAY. ALEX HAD BEEN RIGHT. I was exhausted, physically and emotionally. Ted left with a kiss and a whispered promise to be back at some point after work. I didn't stumble out of my room until hours later. The place was empty. For a second, I bristled. Where was everybody? What did a girl have to do around here to get a grilled cheese sandwich and some tomato soup?

I made a piece of toast and a cup of coffee. It didn't taste as good without a lecture to go with it, so I put in extra sugar. I'd need all the energy I could get tonight.

Paul and Ted showed up almost simultaneously, dressed ridiculously alike in dark jeans and black T-shirts.

"You two should really call each other before you leave the house," I said as I let them in.

I started assembling my gear: sticky rice, a dagger and a hunting knife, an amulet or two. I wasn't sure what else to put in. I sat back on my heels to think. "Where's Alex?"

Paul picked up my dagger and examined it. "He'll meet us there as soon as he can leave his bat cave."

"I thought he couldn't turn into a bat." Ted crouched down to check out my arsenal, too.

Paul shot him a look. "You are such a newbie. It's only a saying." He gave Ted a playful punch in the shoulder that would have knocked a smaller man to the ground.

Ted opened his mouth to protest, but Norah came out of her bedroom in an outfit that can only be described as Cosmopolitan Ninja. She was wrapped in black from head to toe, except the parts in between that showed her cleavage and her midriff. "I'm going with you."

"No." I started putting items into my backpack.

"Yes. I'm done being left home and lied to. I want to see what it's all about. You don't have to protect me, Melina. I'm a big girl."

I turned and looked at her. At five foot seven and about

one hundred and twenty pounds, she most decidedly was not a big girl. She was a twig that a *kiang shi* could snap and suck the marrow out of as a snack.

"No." I zipped up my pack, then checked the knife strapped to my ankle to make sure it was secure.

"How are you going to stop me?" She had her arms crossed over her chest and her hip cocked.

I turned and gave her my full attention. "You don't know what you're getting into. This isn't a game."

"And I'm not a child."

I was about to argue the point, but Paul broke in. "We don't have a lot of time. Let her come. It's her funeral if she gets in the way."

As attempts at manipulation went, it was way below even his standards. I turned to look at him, but he wouldn't meet my eyes. Damn it. He wanted her to come with us.

"Anything happens to her, it's on your head, Fido," I said and walked out the door.

I could hear Norah jumping up and down and clapping behind me and knew she looked like one of those cheesy beer commercials with girls and their hair bouncing up and down. If I thought it would have bothered Paul at all, I would have come back to the apartment just to slap him.

Sophie and Ben were waiting at the bottom of the stairs. I closed my eyes and tried to gather my strength. "Let me guess. You're coming with us."

They both nodded. Ben held up a bag of sticky rice. "We're ready."

It was like sending a kid in to take the SATs with a slide rule. They had no idea what they were getting into, and regardless of what they thought, they were woefully unprepared. I told them so.

Sophie crossed her arms over her chest. "We helped make the plan. We want to help execute it."

"Isn't it enough to be the brains?" I asked. "Trust me, being the brawn isn't all it's cracked up to be."

She pressed her lips into a hard, firm line and nodded toward Norah. "You're letting her go."

True enough. "Well, come on, then. Daylight's burning and I want to be ready."

We split up between Ted's truck and Paul's van. My car was deemed to still be too conspicuous and I didn't argue. I watched Norah and Sophie and Ben pile into the van, and then turned to Paul. "What the hell are we doing here?"

He sighed. "I'm not entirely sure myself. See you at the temple."

And we were off.

WE GATHERED BY MY FAVORITE DUMPSTER BEHIND THE Bok Kai Temple. The shadows had gone beyond long by the time Alex came inching along the edge of the building, careful to stay out of the direct sunlight. "Ready to get started?" I asked.

Alex loosened his collar and sidled over to me. "We have a little problem."

I looked at the ragtag crew assembled in the shadow of the Dumpster. "Ya think?"

He shook his head. "Bigger than that."

I sighed. "Hit me."

"I can't go in."

I chewed on that for a second. "Do I have to get George to invite you?" I didn't think George would be terribly happy to see me again. Let's face it. George was never happy to see me. There was no reason to think that this moment would be any exception. Bringing a werewolf and a vampire with you didn't make you the most welcome guest.

"Wouldn't help." He looked embarrassed. I'd never seen Alex look embarrassed. I'd never seen any vampire look embarrassed. It was a little weird. Kind of like a worried werewolf. "It's sacred ground."

I couldn't believe I hadn't thought of it myself. I bonked

myself in the forehead. "I don't suppose it matters that it's not your religion."

He shook his head. "Apparently not. I can barely stand close to the building. There's no way I'm going to be able to enter it."

"Alex, nobody else can hold their breath that long." So much for our great plan.

"You don't think I know that?" he hissed.

"What do we do now?"

Ted walked up next to us. "About what?"

"We have a problem."

"So what do you need me to do?" Ted asked.

"That depends. How long can you hold your breath?"

Ted had apparently been on the swim team in high school and started rattling off something about hypoxia and yardage and we stared at him. Finally, he said, "I can hold my breath for a really long time."

I LED MY GANG OF MERRY MEN AND WOMEN UP ONTO the Dumpster and into the office. Well, all of them except Alex. He stayed down below, crouching in the shadow of the Dumpster, ostensibly acting as our lookout.

I'd been worried that the window would be locked this time. By this point, George must have figured out how I was getting in. Yet the window remained unlocked. Methinks the gentleman doth protest too much. I don't think George had been nearly as unhappy to see me as he pretended to be.

I scrambled through first and made sure the place was empty and unoccupied. Norah came through next with a tug from me from above and a shove from below from Paul. She started to protest about the hand on her rear, but I held my finger to my lips to shush her. She scowled but kept silent.

Sophie was next in, looking a little surprised at how easily she had vaulted through. She still had almost no idea what kind of powers she was going to have. For that matter, I wasn't too sure myself. Just because I had developed a certain way didn't mean that she would. I bit my lip as I wondered if Mae would have known what was next for Sophie. Who would help her now? I could barely help myself most days.

Ben scrambled through after her, looking pale and as if he might finally be wondering what he'd gotten himself into. I didn't have much sympathy. It wasn't like he hadn't been warned.

Then came Ted, his shoulder muscles bunching as he pulled himself through the window. For a second, I thought he'd get stuck and totally flashed on Winnie the Pooh in Rabbit's window, but he gave a little twist and made it in.

After that, Paul had similar shoulder problems to Ted's, but also ended up inside without a problem.

I held out my hand and Sophie gave me the set of fake talismans that she and Ben had spent the afternoon creating. "This one has the symbols for prosperity, happiness and longevity." She pointed to the top one. "We looked them up on the Internet."

"Super. I'm sure that will make everyone feel much better," I whispered back.

I took the stack before she could start translating the rest of them and left my posse hiding in the office as I scampered down into the sanctuary to switch out the yellow talismans with the set of fakes. Sophie and Ben had done an impressive job. If I didn't know which was which and didn't have my special set of Messenger senses, I wouldn't have known which set was real and which was fake. It was exactly like Kokopelli's flute. Unless you really looked, you wouldn't be able to tell the real ones from the fake ones. I was counting on Henry Zhang's men not looking very hard or George Zhang's fellow priests either.

I was back in the office almost before my gang could start arguing.

"So is now when you're going to drop trou?" Ted asked Paul with a sigh.

"Yep." Paul started to strip down.

Ben turned and looked at me. "What the hell is he doing? Now is not the time to get naked."

"Wait for it," Ted said, checking the gun he wore in his shoulder holster and the one at his ankle.

Then Paul began to change.

There is nothing quite like seeing a werewolf change. Vampires can be subtle. There are times when I have no idea if Alex has his fangs out or not. Of course, the older a vampire gets, the better he gets at shifting in and out of his blood-sucking persona.

A werewolf change is never subtle. Paul was an impressive man in the nude, so there was that to start with. Sophie and Norah were both staring, and I certainly was starting to understand why Meredith was being so persistent. His body was thick with muscle, sturdy and hard. He wasn't wasting any time tonight, though. As he willed his change to begin, his back arched up to the ceiling, and then he swung forward, his arm already lengthening and claws forming at his fingertips.

Ben started back toward the window. I put my hand on his arm and shook my head. "It's okay," I said as quietly as I could.

It wasn't quiet enough. Paul turned his head and snarled at me even as his jaw lengthened. The growl deepened as skin stretched and bones popped. Sleek fur sprouted from his skin, running from his now very lupine head to the tail that formed at the base of his spine. When the change was finally complete, he sat down on his haunches and lifted his head.

I got right in his face and shook my head before he could howl, sitting back on my heels relieved when he didn't take my face off with his very impressive set of teeth.

I looked around. Norah's, Ben's and Sophie's faces were ashen. Even Ted looked a little sickened and he'd seen it before. I had no idea if we were going to come through this night alive if my crew was this shaken by a guy who was on our side.

24

I LED THE WAY OUT OF THE OFFICE SO WE COULD TAKE UP our positions before the *kiang shi* began to rise at sunset.

It is harder to hide five people and a transformed werewolf in a small space than it is to hide one. My "usual" hiding place in the second-floor balcony clearly could not accommodate the group of us. I managed to tuck Sophie and Ben into one nook. They looked too scared to start necking so I figured it was safe. Norah and Paul went into another, and Ted and I tucked into a third.

"Cozy," he whispered in my ear.

"Don't get any ideas," I warned him.

"It's kind of hard not to get ideas with you wiggling your butt against me like that," he observed.

The exact nature of his ideas was getting hard to hide. In fact, it was poking me. "Well, try."

"There is no try . . ." he started.

"Do not start quoting Yoda at me."

He shrugged and wrapped his arms around me. "Sorry. It was all I had."

I leaned against him, trying to ground myself against him, in his humanness and his strength, and settled in to wait.

It didn't take long.

The scene unfolded much as it had the first time I'd watched the *kiang shi* rise.

Henry arrived, and while he had the priests with him, he had fewer of his own men. Baldy was gone, as were Jimmy and Ponytail. I felt no satisfaction, although I liked our odds better.

A muffled sneeze came from Norah and Paul's alcove. Great. I thought Norah was only allergic to cats. Could she be allergic to werewolves, too? I mean, dander is dander, right?

I held my breath and watched below to see any reaction. Henry and his men were agitated enough that it didn't seem to register. I thought I spotted that little twitch in George's hand, his tell, but he didn't look around. Maybe it was my imagination. I let my breath out in a slow hiss. Behind me, Ted rested his forehead against the top of my head.

So far so good.

Then the *kiang shi* began to rise. It was party time.

The first *kiang shi* clambered out of his grave, green flesh hanging from his arms and face. The first priest started forward, took a talisman from the stack in the carved box and stuck the yellow paper to the creature's forehead. Before he was finished, the other priests were heading for their *kiang shi*. They didn't even hesitate any longer, like they had the first night I'd seen them. They looked thin and pale and it was clear even from this distance that whatever fight they had had in them was long gone.

It took a moment for them to realize that the *kiang shi* were still moving forward despite having the talismans attached to their foreheads. Henry turned to his brother. "Get them under control, George."

George rang his bell, but it did no good. He began to

shrink back against the wall as did the other priests. Henry's men, however, drew their guns and stood firm. It was go time.

I vaulted over the railing of the second-floor balcony, letting my knees bend as I hit.

One of the henchmen turned, took one look at me and squeezed off a shot. I ducked. It might have been a good idea on his part to try to take me out, but the time it took allowed the first of the *kiang shi* to grab him from behind. I didn't watch what happened next to him. His agonized screams provided more than enough information.

I heard the thump of Paul landing behind me. Henry's men began to scream and scatter. Paul herded them back toward the *kiang shi*. They were trapped between Paul's snapping teeth and the long-fingernailed grasp of the *kiang shi*. Another one went down as a snack for the Chinese vampires.

I ran to where the priests had huddled together and started scooping the sticky rice out of my bag. "Stay behind the barrier and try to hold your breath," I told them.

I turned back to where Henry's men were dying one by one at the hands of the very *kiang shi* they had used to kill and control so many others.

The priests had sunk down onto the floor into lotus position. How they could meditate in the midst of the killing chaos going on around them was more than I could understand, but each one of them had stilled. If they were breathing at all, I couldn't detect it.

Finally, Henry was the last one standing. His last man had gone down. He had no one left to hide behind. He turned to make a run for the back of the temple. I leaped in the air, spun and with a side kick to the face, thrust him back into the waiting teeth and arms of the *kiang shi* behind him.

They snapped his left arm first. He sank to the floor, disbelief clear on his face. "Help me!" he screamed.

I didn't budge.

One of the *kiang shi* grabbed his hair, pulling his head back to expose his throat. Another ripped his throat out with its teeth. Henry didn't scream anymore.

But now came the tricky part.

I turned. Ted was already standing next to me.

"I've got this part," he said. He inhaled deeply, then blew all the air out of his lungs. With talismans in both hands, he raced in.

Dear God, he was fearless. He slapped the first talisman onto the *kiang shi* that was still feasting on Henry Zhang. It froze immediately. The second went on the one that was heading for Paul. A third one was heading toward Ted. If it blindly hit him, would it attack? I had no idea. I screamed his name, and he ducked, slapping a talisman on the forehead of the monster as he did it. Within a few more seconds, he'd slapped the talismans on the foreheads of the last two *kiang shi* as they continued to rip apart Triad members.

That was it. They were all frozen. Ted stood still for a moment, then swayed and fell to his knees, gulping in huge lungfuls of air.

I ran to him. "Are you okay?"

He nodded, breathing in. "Terrific. Never better. Probably psychotic, but other than that, completely hunky dory."

Paul nudged up next to us and licked Ted's face. Bracing himself on Paul's broad shoulder, Ted heaved himself to his feet. He scratched Paul behind the ear. "Thanks, man."

I turned. The priests were standing up. George looked at me, tears streaming down his face. "Can we come out now? Is it safe?"

I nodded. "For now."

He went to his brother and cradled what was left of the broken body to him and wept. I'd have to come back and deal with the *kiang shi*. I couldn't allow them to stay here in the temple or anywhere else, for that matter. They would have to be destroyed, but not today.

George had enough grief to deal with as it was.

I made my way upstairs again, suddenly exhausted.

Sophie and Ben were leaning over the balcony. "We did it!" Sophie hugged me, and Ben high-fived me.

I found Norah crouched in the corner, shaking.

I ran my hands over her body and checked as much as I could with her curled in on herself. "Are you hurt? Did one of them . . . did you get bitten?" I wasn't sure what would happen to Norah if one of the *kiang shi* had managed to get its venom in her. It had been hard enough for me to fight off, and my immune system was probably a thousand times stronger than Norah's. I also didn't see how it could have happened. None of them got past me. I was sure of it.

She pushed my hands away. "I didn't know. I didn't know."

"Didn't know what?" Before she could answer, I turned my head and yelled for Ted. If Norah had been bitten, Alex needed to start treating her right away. We had to get her out of the temple to him.

"I didn't know what it would be like. What they would be like. How horrible it would be." She wrapped her arms around herself.

Ted came up beside us. "Is she all right?"

"I don't know. I don't see any marks on her, but I want Alex to check her. Can you get her outside to him?"

He nodded and scooped her up in his arms. She threw her arms around his neck and clung to him. I followed him down the stairs and out the temple to the alleyway where Alex was waiting.

He rushed over to us. "What's wrong?"

"You need to check her. I'm afraid she's been bitten. She's acting strange."

Ted set Norah down on the ground. Alex knelt down next to her and reached for her. She slapped his hand away. "Don't touch me. You're like them, aren't you? They're vampires. You're a vampire. I didn't know. It wasn't like in the movies or on TV."

Alex and I exchanged a glance. "We need to know that you're physically okay, first, Norah," Alex said in his soothing doctor voice.

Norah shook her head.

"Hold out your arms," he said, this time in his vampire voice.

Norah stuck out her arms, but her gaze swung toward me, wild and frightened. I rubbed her back and murmured what I hoped were comforting sounds as Alex gave her the once-over as quickly as he could. I couldn't help thinking of all the times Norah had undone me with one of her hugs, had opened her arms and heart to me in friendship asking nothing in return, not even the truth. What had I given back to her now?

Alex nodded to me. "She's okay. Some bumps and bruises, probably from shimmying in the window but no broken skin. There's no . . . no physical harm." He stood up and walked away.

I knew the moment the spell of his voice and presence had been broken because Norah collapsed against me and sobbed. I sat and stroked her hair, not knowing what else to do.

Ted crouched down next to us. "We've got to get out of here, Melina. Someone's going to have heard something and called it in." He looked at Norah. "Is she okay? Can we move her?"

"I think so." Even if I had to sling her over my shoulder and haul her to the car, we could probably go.

Norah looked up and brushed tears from her face. "You saved us. You did it. How? How did you do it?"

Ted sighed. "See, I used to be on the swim team in high school and we did this exercise where we had to hold . . ."

Norah cut him off by launching herself at him, wrapping her arms around his neck and sobbing harder. "Thank you. Thank you. Thank you."

Well, there was an interesting turn of events. So much

for her mistrust of authority figures. Apparently, once they saved your heinie, they weren't so bad.

I CAN'T IMAGINE WHAT WE LOOKED LIKE AS WE CLIMBED out of the cars and headed back to my apartment. Bloody, bedraggled and, in Norah's case, tear streaked, we shuffled down the street wordlessly. From half a block away, I could make out a dark form on my porch. Damn. What was coming after us now?

I glanced at Ted and nodded at the shape. He squinted, looked back at me and shrugged, but he shuffled Norah behind him and motioned for Alex to move forward in the group.

Whatever it was, it was 'Cane. I was totally getting the vibe. Paul walked behind Alex and me, sniffing the air. "What is it?" he asked.

"I don't know yet," I said. "But it's waiting for us."

"Then let's bring it," Alex said quietly and inched his lips back enough for me to see his fangs.

"You're itching for a fight because you got left out of the last one, aren't you?" I wanted to stop and confront him, but it was better if whatever was waiting on the porch was unaware that we were aware of it.

Paul chuckled. "Every party has a pooper . . ."

"I simply don't want someone to think our guard is down," Alex said.

"No one even knows yet. It'll be ages before anyone figures out what just happened."

Both Alex and Paul shot me looks and shook their heads. "She's so young still," Paul said.

"It's part of her charm," Alex agreed.

"Oh, bite me," I said.

"With pleasure," they said in unison.

We were almost at the porch. The thing rose, large and hump-backed. I inhaled deeply, trying to recognize the scent, but the night air was too full of us. I was surrounded by a miasma of our own pheromones, sexual and fear based, and of our own blood and sweat and tears.

"Messenger," the thing said, and I finally recognized the voice. "Where the hell's my flute?"

Alex turned to look at me as if I'd lost my mind. "What in blazes are you doing with Kokopelli's flute?"

"Returning it." I held up my hands in protest. "An imp stole it. Meredith helped me get it back."

Understanding dawned on Alex's face.

Ted and Norah came up behind us. "Everything okay here?" Ted asked in his cop voice, which almost made me want to giggle.

"Fine," Alex said. "But if I were you, I'd double-glove tonight."

I smacked him and hurt my hand. "Shut up."

Kokopelli looked back and forth between all of us. "No wonder you were confused when I said you were in love, little one. You're not in love with just one, are you? You're in love with them all."

Ben started chanting something about me sitting in a tree.

I stomped up the staircase and opened the door. "Come get your stupid flute and leave me alone."

25

I STOOD IN THE EARLY MORNING SUNLIGHT AND RUBBED
my arms against the chill of the breaking dawn. Ted put
his arm around me and pulled me close. I tucked my head
against his chest, partly for warmth and partly to hide the
tears that had started to stream down my face.

I had wanted to do this today. I had wanted to get it over
with. I wanted to put as much of what had happened behind
me as I could.

Yesterday we had held a memorial service for Mae. There
wouldn't be a funeral or a burial. Mae had left very specific
instructions, so she'd been cremated and her remains were
off to Florida to help create a new coral reef. We'd opened
the dojo and invited in the community for a celebration of
Mae's life. I'd expected our students and their parents and
other teachers in the community.

I'd underestimated the number of lives that Mae had
touched. Business owners from the rest of the strip mall
had come. People from a homeless shelter where she volun-
teered stopped in. My own parents came to pay their respects.

The hardest of all, though, was Frank Liu, still bandaged and hobbling. My first instinct when I'd seen him come in the door was to run out the back. How could I face him? I'd actually turned to look for an escape route, but Ted had been standing behind me.

"Do you want me to go with you to talk to him?" he had asked.

Feeling like a transparent fool, I'd shaken my head and walked over to Liu.

"Mr. Liu, I am so terribly sorry." I didn't know what else to say. It was terribly inadequate, but it was all I had.

"Child, why are you sorry? You saved us all."

My gaze had dropped to the bandaged stump where his hand used to be. "Not soon enough and at a rather high cost to other people."

He put his good hand on my shoulder. "You did not put the evil in those men's souls. Now let's go remember Mae. Did you know she never mastered the Snake Creeps Down position?"

I don't think I'll ever be able to remember his kindness without crying.

Yesterday had truly been about life, about Mae's life and about all she'd done and made with it.

Today, however, was about death. Today, Ted and I were disposing of the *kiang shi*. We'd taken them out into the Sierras and hacked their bodies into tiny pieces, and now we were burning them.

I figured I could say that it was the smoke from the fire making my eyes water if Ted asked. He wouldn't ask, though. He knew better. We'd known each other for less than two weeks, yet he already knew better.

Instead, he kissed the top of my head. "It's the right thing to do," he murmured against my hair.

I lifted my head to look at where the remains of the *kiang shi* were turning to dust in the fire and sunshine. "I know. It's not fair, though. They didn't have a choice. Someone else's evil made them into what they were, and someone else's evil made them into a threat now."

"I know. My dad didn't have a choice. It wasn't his fault either. That didn't change anything. He still destroyed everything in his path."

I kissed his chin. "I'm sorry."

He smoothed my hair back from my forehead. "Don't be. I am what I am because of him in some ways. I do have a choice. So do you. We're lucky."

I had thought of myself as many things over the years, lucky wasn't ever one of them until now. "You're right. I am lucky. I do get to choose. And you know what? I choose you."

He pulled me around so we were facing each other, our bodies touching. His warmth soaked into me as I held him tight. "Back atcha, sweetheart. Back atcha."

Then he lowered his head and kissed me.

Turn the page for a special look at
Eileen Rendahl's next Messenger novel

DEAD ON DELIVERY

Coming soon in mass market from Ace Books!

"DO YOU WANT TO EXPLAIN THIS?" TED DROPPED A folded copy of that morning's *Sacramento Bee* onto my kitchen counter and jabbed a finger at an article in the Our Region section.

I picked up the paper and looked at the article. Some dude in Elmville had died under suspicious circumstances. Crap. Another one had bitten the dust. Neil Bossard was the second person I'd made a delivery to in Elmville in the past two months who had ended up dead. Coincidence? Possibly. I wasn't crazy about the odds, though. Elmville was tiny. It had been weird enough to make two deliveries there within such a short time period—and both of them to 'Danes, to boot. To have both of the recipients wind up dead? Not likely to be a wacky fluke. Still, I didn't know for sure and there was no point in upsetting Ted before I knew that there was something to get upset about.

"Why do you ask?" I avoided looking up into his cornflower blue eyes. Not because I couldn't look directly into them and lie, though. I could do it. Probably. The real problem was the way my heart did that weird flip-flop thing in my chest every time I looked directly into his baby blues. The flip-flop thing made it hard to lie. I needed to focus to lie and Ted was nothing if not distracting to me.

"The case is weird, which always makes me think of you." He took a step closer and lifted my chin. A smile quirked at the corner of his lips.

Now I had no choice but to look into his eyes and there went the damn flip-flop. "Is that a nice way to talk to your girlfriend?" That gave me a shiver. I was someone's girlfriend. Who'd a thunk it was possible? It never had been before.

I am twenty-six years old, nearly twenty-seven. Ted Goodnight is my first boyfriend ever. There have been a few dalliances before but never a boyfriend. I still can't decide if it's the best good fortune that has ever befallen me or the worst mistake of my short life, and there have been some doozies, starting with the day I decided to sneak into the swimming pool behind my mother's back and drowned. That was pretty much the mother of all mistakes. It's the one that started me down the road to all the rest.

On that day, I was legally dead for three minutes. They resuscitated me and everyone said it was a miracle that no harm had been done. The doctors couldn't detect any brain damage. I would be "normal." Ha! If only they'd known. Apparently, the ability to sense supernatural creatures and see all the crazy-ass paranormal doings that go on around most people without them noticing doesn't show up on an MRI.

No other guy has been able to get past the freaky things that happen around me or my crazy schedule or what my mother refers to as my "moods." In fact, the only guy I can remember making it past two dates was David Bounds in eleventh grade and he was bipolar. Even he couldn't hang in there with me, not even with medication to help him.

I'm not saying Ted hasn't had his occasional problems

with who and what I am. The first time he saw me truly in action almost killed our relationship before it ever really started. Maybe it's because he grew up in such a crazy family (seriously clinically crazy). Maybe it's because he's amazingly accepting. Maybe he really, really likes me. I am the Sally Field of Messengers. Could be worse.

Whatever it is, it's working and while I am not the type to skip joyfully through fields of daisies, I'm feeling pretty good about the whole thing. I do try to keep most of the woo-woo things I'm up to separate from him so I don't freak him out too much, but I'm used to compartmentalizing.

The big drawback to having Ted Goodnight as a boyfriend? He's a cop.

I have always mistrusted cops. Cops mean trouble. It's not that I'm into breaking the law; it's the order part of the police department that I have issues with. Or maybe order has issues with me. My very existence is about the disorderliness of things. I don't fit neatly anywhere. Trust me, I wish I did. I think I've spent most of my life wishing that, but this beggar isn't riding and I never quite belong anywhere. All of which makes it even more interesting that I'm now dating a cop, especially one who I'm pretty sure wanted to hear that I had nothing to do with some guy running into traffic on Highway 120 and being turned into road pizza by a semi, which was exactly what had happened to Neil Bossard. According to the article, they didn't know what he was doing running onto the highway. I didn't either. I didn't like it, though.

"Looks like a traffic accident to me, Ted. What could I possibly have to do with it?" It did look like a traffic accident, but one that made me a little bit itchy and uncomfortable.

"Not every detail made it into the paper. The local cops think that maybe somebody was chasing the guy. Or, at least, he thought he was being chased. Someone saw him running down the road, screaming that something was after him, but he was all alone. Before the witness could do anything to help, the dude had run out onto the road and gotten creamed by a big rig." Ted smoothed my hair back behind my ear and I felt a little gooey inside. "They were canvassing the guy's neighborhood to see if they could figure out who might have been chasing him and somebody mentioned seeing a car that sounds an awful lot like yours. Weird plus an old Buick tends to equal you in my book, babe."

Fabulous. What more could I want than to be the solution to a funky equation? He wasn't wrong, though. I weighed my options. I could lie. Chances were that this whole thing would completely blow over and he'd never know. Of course, if it didn't and Ted found out that I'd lied to him . . . well, suffice it to say, I didn't think he'd be pleased. I could tell him the truth, as far as I knew it, which really wasn't all that far. I didn't have to mention Kurt Rawley, the other guy I'd made a delivery to who was now six feet under.

Come to think of it, his death had been weird as well. Had it been arson? I remember it had something to do with a fire.

"I made a delivery to him," I blurted. "It was days ago."

"What was it?" Ted leaned back against the counter and crossed his arms over his chest.

I shrugged. "Hell if I know."

"You don't look?" He looked incredulous.

I shook my head. It wasn't a rule, as far as I knew. Nobody had ever told me I couldn't look inside the packages that were left for me to deliver. I chose not to peek. Peeking signaled curiosity and perhaps an interest in becoming involved. I generally had neither. Or, at least, I hadn't had.

If someone handed me something, all unwrapped, then I knew what it was. If someone had taken the trouble to put it in an envelope or wrap it up in a little box, like whoever had needed me to make a delivery to Neil Bossard had, then I didn't know. I didn't care. Or, at least, I didn't want to care. With information comes responsibility and I've spent almost twenty-seven years avoiding as much of that as I can and now have more than I ever wanted.

My last experience in getting involved with a delivery hadn't gone well. I'd lost someone very dear to me and damn near gotten killed myself. It didn't make me want to change my habits now. The fact that this particular package had given off a little hum of power didn't exactly make me more interested in opening it. It did needle at me a little bit, though.

"How did you know where to take it?" He wasn't quite using his cop voice on me, but it was getting close. I liked that about as much as I liked it when my vampire buddy used his vampire voice on me, which was not much.

I smiled at him, even though I didn't totally mean it, and said, "Gee, I don't know. Maybe it was some special magical divining process. Maybe it spoke to me. Or maybe I used the address that was written on the package."

His eyebrows went up. "I don't think sarcasm is called for."

Norah, my roommate, strolled into the kitchen, hair disheveled and a pillow crease across her cheek. "She always thinks sarcasm is called for." She made straight for the coffeepot and poured herself a cup.

I attempted not to let my jaw hit the floor. Norah hadn't been herself lately and poisoning her body with the evil drug caffeine was one more hint that all was not right in the sunshine- and rainbow-strewn world of my yoga-loving BFF. "You want some cream or sugar for that?"

She shook her head. "Black is fine."

I looked at her closely. Had she been possessed by some other being? Would I find a Norah-shaped pod in the basement of our apartment building if I ever got up the guts and energy to go through it? Stranger things had happened and some of them had happened right here at our apartment. My Norah had a sweet tooth and I couldn't imagine her drinking coffee without girlying it up at least a little.

"Hey, Ted," she said, and gave him a weak smile.

No, my Norah was not herself at all. She likes cops less than I do, or she had until Ted saved her soy-bacon last summer when we were fighting off Chinese vampires as they rose out of tunnels beneath Old Sacramento.

Now? Now she not only tolerated him but often seemed happy to see him and not in an icky I'm-going-to-steal-your-boyfriend way.

"Hey, Norah." He smiled at her but then turned directly back to me. "Who gave you the delivery?"

I shrugged. "I don't know. The box was sitting on the hood of my car when I came out of the dojo one night." Which was pretty much exactly how the package for Kurt Rawley had come my way, come to think of it.

"Was there a note?"

"No. Just the box with the address marked on it."

"That was it. There was a box on your car, so you drove it all the way out to Elmville and . . ." He hesitated. "What did you do with it once you got there?"

"I left it on the doorstep." *Both times,* I added silently.

"And then hung out long enough for someone to notice your car." His eyes narrowed a bit.

"I hung out on the street for a little while and watched to make sure some guy who at least looked like he could be Neil Bossard picked it up. I don't exactly ask for ID." Again, contact with message recipients might constitute some kind of caring beyond fulfilling what was basically expected of me. Not my thing.

"Did he open the box?"

I was so done with the third degree. I threw up my hands. "How the hell should I know? And if I did know, what difference would it make? Someone needs something taken someplace, I take it there. End of story."

"Until someone ends up dead." Ted's eyes narrowed.

Norah's head shot up. "Who's dead?"

I shot Ted a nasty look. Now he had upset Norah. Who

knew how long it would take me to calm her down? "No one you know. No one I know. Some guy that I happened to deliver a box to last week got hit by a car."

She blinked at me, her eyes big and round. "That's it? No undead creatures ate him or anything?"

"Not according to the *Bee*. It was a simple case of man versus semi. The semi won. They pretty much always do." I'd seen that a few times in the Emergency Department of Sacramento City Hospital, where I work. It was never pretty.

"Well, okay then." She went back to swirling her coffee.

"It's a coincidence," I said, with way more confidence than I felt. Ted started to open his mouth, but I shook my head at him. "Not now," I mouthed at him and tipped my head at Norah.

He pressed his lips together in a tight line and headed back toward my bedroom. As he brushed past me, he whispered, "I don't believe in coincidence."

I didn't bother telling him that I didn't either.

*An Agent of death
should know when her time is up.*

FROM
CHRISTINA HENRY

BLACK
NIGHT

A BLACK WINGS NOVEL

If obstinate dead people were all that Maddy had to worry about, life would be much easier. But the best-laid plans of Agents and fallen angels often go awry. Deaths are occurring contrary to the natural order, Maddy's being stalked by foes inside and outside of her family, and her two loves—her bodyguard, Gabriel, and her doughnut-loving gargoyle, Beezle—have disappeared. But because Maddy is Lucifer's granddaughter, things are expected of her, things like delicate diplomatic missions to other realms.

penguin.com
facebook.com/ProjectParanormalBooks